Blinding White Flash
INVASION

J. Richard Wakefield

Blinding White Flash: Invasion
by J. Richard Wakefield

Signalman Publishing
www.signalmanpublishing.com
email: info@signalmanpublishing.com
Kissimmee, Florida

Cover layout by Joel Ramnaraine

ISBN:
978-1-940145-01-3 (paperback)
978-1-940145-02-0 (ebook)

Signalman
Publishing

Dedicated to my mother-in-law
Rita Dale
October 1930 – February 2013

Acknowledgments

I wish to thank the following for previewing this book.

The London Writers Group: Ruth Zavitz, Pat Brown, Clarissa Harwood, John Jeneroux, Ian Gillespie, Mitch Lenko and Carl Zvonkin. We had a great time finding each other's 'misplaced modifiers'!

To Sue Brown who patiently edited the entire manuscript. She caught those pesky typos.

To Nadine Lambert who, with great perfectionist detail, definitely made the text read better.

Finally my family: Jeremy, Charaxes, Jennifer, Brent, and most of all, my loving wife, Dorothy, for their helpful input and patience.

Table of Contents

CAST OF CHARACTERS IN ORDER OF APPEARANCE

Lynda Swift, Vancouver cop

Ken Moore, Vancouver cop

Jason & Kelly Gagnon, Vancouver

Tom, Jason's brother

Harris Jackson, Vancouver Fire Department

Archie Willis, Captain, Vancouver Fire Department

John Mills, Acting Captain, Vancouver Fire Department

Matt, Vancouver Fire Department

Don Hastings, Police Chief, Vancouver Police Department

Collin Edwards, Deputy Chief, Vancouver Police Department

Gary Hawker, Colonel, Canadian Army

Ray and Bonnie McGillis

John Revoy, Vancouver cop

Erik Stein, Professor of Geology, UBC

Sergeant Williams, Canadian Army, Hawker's aide.

Chris Staines, Captain, U.S. National Guard

William Norris-Lester, banker

Carl O'Keefe, Professor of Geology, Department Head, UBC

Susan Yang, Professor of Geology, UBC

Zhuge Wĕi Míng. Senior Colonel, Chinese Army, Military Commander, UBC

Harry Nugent, Professor of Hydrology, UBC

Guō Hào, General, Chinese Army, Supreme Commander

Andrew Jaworski, Mayor, Port Coquitlam

Anne Reeves, Mayor, Chilliwack

Trevor "Hammerhead" Hanskull, Captain, U.S. National Guard

Phil Waterford, RCMP officer

Keith Wilks, RCMP Superintendent

Al (Kappy) Kappelmann, CNR Engineer

Olivia Turnbull, Mayor, Kamloops

Kevin Popper, Regimental Sergeant Major, Rocky Mountain Rangers
John Manning, Cupric Mining Company
Roger Zucker, Kamloops Marble and Stone Company
Ron Blackcrow, RCMP Chief Superintendent, BC
Stanley Woulfe, Commissioner of Public Works, BC
James Dunlop, First Lieutenant, U.S. National Guard
Gary Kroll, Second Lieutenant, U.S. National Guard
Chuck Charbonneau, CPR Official
Gregg Milynn CNR Official
Roland "Shooter" Schuette, Second Lieutenant, U.S. National Guard
Randy Kovách, CNR Police Officer
Ross Hughes, Major General, Canadian Army, Retired
MacGregor "Mack-The-Knife" Fife, Chief Warrant Officer, Canadian
    Army
Peter Bartlet, Lt. Colonel, Royal Canadian Airforce, 4 Wing, CFB Cold
    Lake
Rita Byrde, Leftenant, Royal Canadian Airforce, Met-Tech 4 Wing, Cold
    Lake
Reginald Hamilton, Major, Canadian Army, Base Commander Edmonton
Kristina Krouse, MP, Canadian Government, Defence Critic
Michele Norman, MP, Canadian Government
Glenn Kabber, MLA, Alberta Provincial Government
William Yaegle, MLA, Alberta Provincial Government
Valerie Hartman, Petty Officer, Royal Canadian Airforce, 742
    Communication Sqn
Sally Schaffer, Corporal, Canadian Army
Gena Vanderpoel , Reporter
Jack Pokrajac, Gena's Cameraman
Harry Lipman, Chief Blaster
Dan (Danno) Stryker, Blaster
Dianne Reger, Assistant Blaster
Peter Douglas, Blaster

Vic Vickers, Fire Chief, Princeton, BC

Tina Van Der Haus, Blaster

Simon Lambert

Trevor, Simon's brother-in-law

Deb Osby, RCMP Constable

George Maillet, Genera, Canadian Army, West Coast Commander

Brent Armstrong, Major, Canadian Army

Martin Hanataris, Mayor, Merritt, BC

Ian Lanning, Leftenant Commander, Royal Canadian Navy

Ray Paulson, Leftenant Colonel, Commanding Officer of the
    Strathconas.

Ed Gosling, Major, Canadian Army

Lina Cutler, Warrant Officer, Communication System Technologist,
    Canadian Army

Ron Harrison, Major, One Combat Engineers, Canadian Army

Greg Peck, Mayor, Sicamous

Hal Hewettson, Rockey Mountain Rangers, retired

Theodore "Teddybear" Sparks, Colonel, U.S. Army

Russel Bartek, Leftenant Colonel, Second Combat Engineers, Canadian
    Army

Mitch Mitchell, Major, U.S. Army

Doug Swanell, Leftenant, Sniper Team, Canadian Army

George, Ray McGillis' friend

Ross Koenig, Sergeant, Sniper, U.S. Army

Rita Harrington, Nurse, Kamloops, BC

Unnamed Corpsman, U.S. Navy

Tracy, PSW, works for Rita

Qigang Xinming Xiaofeng, Captain, Chinese Army

Trisha, Rose's friend in Calgary

Rose, Trisha's friend in Calgary

Bob, RCMP Constable, Alberta

Sam Walsh, Major General, U.S. Army

Brad Southwick, Five Star General of the Army

Unnamed CIA Agent

Leanne Loklear, MP, Minister of Agriculture, Canadian Government

Richard Grayford, MP, Minister of War, Canadian Government

Don Ferguson, MP, Minister of Energy, Canadian Government

Admiral Sara Morgan, U.S. Navy

Admiral Reginald Kraft, U.S. Navy

Al Torres, ammo manufacturers representative

Karen Levenson, Erik Stein's student

Bill, fishing boat owner

Russ Bluebear, Canadian Aboriginal

Paul Rutherford, Police Chief, Whitehorse, Yukon

Mark Kirkland, Escapee from the U.S.

Greg Collins, Escapee from BC

Paul, Sue Barnes brother

Sue Barnes, storeowner, Manitoba

John Barnes, farmer, Sue's husband

Sandie, Tom McGillis' wife

"George", Chinese Army

CHAPTER 1

Confusion

Constable Lynda Swift emerged from the Mac's Milk at Commercial and East 10th. The pair of double-double coffees she carried sent a stream of vapor into the cold crisp spring night air. Soon as she got into the driver's side the call came.

"*Shots fired. Shots fired. TSI Container Terminal. All units respond.*"

"Gawdamnit, I won't get to finish my coffee. Another gawdamned gang fight," Ken Moore, Lynda's partner, said.

"We aren't far, let's book it."

The Vancouver docks had only three entrances into the terminal because of the railway yard. Lynda and Ken could only enter from the east off Clark Drive.

With lights and sirens they turned onto East Hastings Street towards the harbour. At Clark Street they stopped as two more cruisers barreled through from their left.

"That's a big place, wonder where we're supposed to go." Ken said.

"We'll just follow these guys."

They chased the small convoy down to the docks. At the waterfront Clark Street bridges over the railway tracks and over Stewart Street. It then curves right one hundred and eighty degrees ending at a "T" junction with Stewart. As they made the right turn on Stewart screams came over the radio.

"*We're being shot! Machine guns! Officer down! Officer down! Send backup!*"

"Our Glocks won't be much use against full autos," Ken said looking at Lynda.

"Hell, dude, your vest won't stop any automatic fire either."

Not what Ken wanted to hear.

They pass through a canyon of railway cars on their left, and factories and buildings on their right. They just turned the last bend before the main gate at the TSI facilities when the first car in their convoy exploded into a huge fireball. The cruiser in front of them slammed into the burning wreckage; forcing the two vehicles to veer left crashing into the string of railway freight cars.

Lynda hammered the brakes, fish tailing right. A rocket passed behind them exploding just as they headed towards a building.

"Jesus! Gangs now have RPGs?" Ken said.

Their cruiser slammed into a parked car, deploying the airbags.

"Get out!" Lynda shrieked.

They bolted toward the water using the back of the building. Behind them they could feel the force of their cruiser exploding. The blast ruptured the building windows showering them with shards of flying glass. Ken grabbed at the back of his neck throwing offending chunks from his collar.

Automatic fire and explosions filled the night sky. The two of them huddled in a dark corner between the building and a dumpster, pistols at the ready.

Lynda scanned the opposite side of the structure. On her left was long consist of railroad cars, with the burning wreckage of their friends.

Lynda didn't get a good look to see who were in the cruisers. Regardless, she would have known them; maybe even chatted with them a few hours before.

A great tsunami of sorrow slammed into her.

She wanted to dash across to help, however, the sinking realization she was completely helpless overcame her. Guilt also, as she was thankful it wasn't her.

Beyond the burning wrecks, in the dim distance to the container port, Lynda could see lots of figures moving around. Hundreds of them. They were lining up in military formation. But it was too dark to make much out.

Lynda looked down at her pistol quivering violently. It was her hands trembling. She realized the gun was a peashooter compared to what they must be up against. It took both of her visibly shaking hands to get the pistol into the holster.

Her portable radio was chaotic with frantic voices, people talking over each other. Headquarters was trying to get a handle on the situation. Cops screaming for help. *"Officer down!"* was common. So was' *"Send in the fucking ERT!"*

"No way they can deal with this," Lynda said to Ken.

Vancouver's Emergency Response Team, the ERT, was thirty strong at best: no match for a major invasion.

"What should we do?" Ken said.

"Retreat," Lynda said.

* * *

Jason Gagnon and Kelly, woke to gunfire. Not unusual considering the continued rioting since Black Winter. It was the automatic gunfire that caught their attention. He got up to look out the window.

Groggily Kelly said, "It's just gangs again, babe, come back to bed."

Jason's apartment in North Vancouver overlooked the harbour in the distance. He could see flashes of lights in that area. Then an explosion lit up the sky.

"Wow, did you see that?" Jason said. "Holy, something fucked up just exploded."

Now wide-awake Kelly sat up in bed. The yellow hue from the distant fireball reflected on the walls and ceiling.

Over the winter, food shipments into the harbour were occasionally attacked by gangs. However, that hadn't happened in the last couple of months since the police had regained control.

A cop car with siren and flashing lights roared toward the docks. More could be seen in the distance heading to the same location. Shooting and explosions intensified. Large balls of fire rolled into the sky lighting up the whole bay area.

"Wow, there's some serious shit happening down there," he said.

Jason's cellphone rang; he turned and asked Kelly to get it.

"Hold on, hold on, Tom, slow down," she yelled. "I can't understand you." She held out the phone to Jason, "It's Tom."

All Jason could hear was screaming. "Tom, calm the fuck down. Slow down."

"We're being invaded!!" Tom screamed. Never had Jason heard such panic in his brother before. "I'm here, down at work. They're shooting everyone. They killed everyone, man. The cops showed up. They got slaughtered."

"What are you talking about, Tom?"

"Two ships arrived an hour ago. Christ, there's hundreds of soldiers pouring out! It was supposed to be another food shipment."

"Tom, where are you?"

"Fuck, I'm not sure. We all ran when the shooting started. Near the north gate, I think. They captured it and have it..." Shooting could be heard real close through the phone.

"Tom? Tom? TOM, are you there?"

"Yeah, yeah, man. Two cops just showed up at the gate. The fuckers just hosed them down with machine guns, man. Fuck me, the car's on fire now. Oh, man, one of the cops just got out..." More gun fire. "... Oh, my God, Jason, they just shot him. Fuck man. I can't get out of here. What's this? Shit, they've unloaded tanks. They've got fucking tanks, man. They're driving this way, two of them, with big guns on the top"

There was a brief pause.

"It just blew through the gate. Forced the burning cop car off the road. What the fuck is happening, man?"

"Tom, can you get through the fence, or over it?"

"No, man. They'll see me for sure, man. Oh fuck I'm scared shitless, man. What do I do?"

"Tom, you've got to find a way through the fence. Get out of there."

"Yeah, yeah. Man, they are just pouring out that ship, man. Hundreds of them. Thousands. Eight container ships arrive today. From China. Three here. Three docked on the other side of the bay. Two are still waiting to come in."

Jason could see cop cars withdrawing.

"Jason? You still there, bro?"

"Yeah, I'm here."

"Fuck, I wish I had some of your guns, man. You guys need to get out of the city as soon as you can, bro."

"I'm not leaving my brother behind." Jason said. "You gotta get out of there. Do you want me to come and get you?"

"No, no! No Gawdamned way you are going down there," Kelly ordered.

"He's my kid brother, Kell. I can't leave him there. They'll find him and kill him."

"And you have a new son in here." Kelly held her bare protruding belly. "I won't have this baby without a father."

Back on the phone Jason said. "Tom, you gotta get out of there. It's a big place. There must be a way out. You can't stay there, there's only eight hours 'till daybreak."

"Ok, ok, ok. I gotta calm down. Christ, I'm shaking like crazy, man."

"Tom. You can do this. Maybe I can meet you part way."

"No, man. You can't get down here. You gotta get Kelly out of the city, bro. Just grab your shit, guns and all your ammo. Get the fuck out of here before they get to your building. Just go." He hung up.

"Tom? Fuck, TOM? God damn it." He hit redial. No answer. He sent Tom a text message.

He noticed there were several text messages and missed calls on his phone.

They were from his sport shooting buddies in Vancouver . He scanned quickly. This invasion was happening all over. One of his friends, a cop, texted that Chinese soldiers had stormed their station. They shot everyone. He and his partner had been heading to the scene, but turned around once they heard the fighting. They were retreating.

Another text said to get out of the city and meet at the Chilliwack rifle range east of Vancouver. That would be difficult for Jason and Kelly to get to. There is only the one bridge from North Vancouver. The Chinese would capture and close that bridge as soon as they could. His only hope was to get to the highway, just behind their building complex, and head north up the coast.

They dressed, packed a bit of food and, most important, his firearms. He got them from the safe, while Kelly got ammo and magazines. She stuffed the magazines into the hockey bag Jason kept his tactical gear in.

Jason owned more firearms than they could carry, so which to take? Logically the lightest rifles with the most ammo: the two AR15s. Including two of his handguns, a Glock 17 and a Sig Sauer P226.

As they emerged into the underground parking, a number of people were standing around asking questions. Conversations stopped. It was quite the sight: Jason with a pretty, seven-month pregnant long haired blonde, rifles over their shoulders and bags in their hands, calmly walked across the garage, got into their Audi and drove off.

They were heading north on the highway within minutes and going as fast as they could. Flashes and explosions appeared far to their left on both sides of the road where the Fraser River flowed into the Pacific. There were few cars around.

Fuel rationing over the winter contributed to the decline of traffic. Jason was a bit more lucky than most. As manager of a food distribution terminal, he received a higher allotment of fuel than most. He had filled his tank just the evening before, expecting to be busy the following week.

A safe distance out, Jason tried his brother again. It rang and rang. Finally a text message from him appeared. It read: "got out, tryg 2 mk home. If u got out kep goin. Catch up 18r."

Jason texted back, "Lefts sm guns go get."

* * *

Pumper 14's crew woke to an alarm: "*Attention, attention. All Station Two, All Station One, Engine Fourteen, Chief One. Respond to possible explosion and fire at the TSI Container docks. Dispatch time Twelve-Oh-Three.*"

In less than two minutes the crew was dressed and rolling. Soon as they turned left onto Adanac Steet they could see fireballs in the distance. "Whoee!!" yelled Harris Jackson in the back of the cab. "Look at that! Balls of fire!" Harris was only on the job two years, yet he had already lived a full career over Black Winter.

"Shut up!" Captain Archie Willis yelled at him. John Mills, Harris's partner, gave him a slap across the back of the head.

"Pumper Fourteen on route. Control, we see multiple fireballs in the distance, over." Archie was a well-seasoned firefighter. He would have been near retirement in the old economy. Now, he had to stay. He had joined Hall 14 for "quiet time" until his retirement. "Quiet time" was firefigher lingo for a slow hall—where someone goes to run out their last few years. Black Winter put a kybosh on his retirement plan. Now he was facing a real beast.

"Matt, follow this all the way to Clark, then turn right," Archie said. Archie didn't need a map, thirty-four years on the job and he knew the city like no other. Matt, on the job for ten years, had just been transferred to the hall.

"Got it," Matt said.

The radio piped up. *"Engine Two to Control. You better sound a second alarm; there's something real nasty happening at the docks."*

"Ten Four, will do," came the reply.

Situated near the docks, Fire Hall Two only needed a few minutes to get on site. *"Engine Two on the scene, what... What the fuck is that? Shit..."* The radio went silent.

"Chief One to Control, on the... Fuck! Engine Two blew..." Silence again.

"We're under attack! Ladder Two, we're being shot at! We're getting out of here!"

"Fucking gangs are shooting our trucks now?" John said. He was the most senior after Archie and the crew's Acting Captain. John was also well-seasoned, and had spent much of his time in the city core before his promotion and transfer to Hall 14 five years ago. "Arch, we should hold back."

"Maybe. We'll get in as close as we can."

Archie's engine rounded the bend to the Clark Drive Bridge, then right onto Stewart Street. Two police officers flagged them down under the overpass.

"Don't go any farther, turn around," Lynda Swift said to Archie. "We're under some kind of attack. Hundreds of soldiers are at the docks. They've killed two of our squads, and many others I've heard on the radio. Call off all your trucks."

"Yeah, we just heard that too. What the fuck's going on? Just a second," Archie said.

The radio perked up with more disparate calls. Other trucks that had been dispatched were under attack. Some had been rocketed. Others machine-gunned. Crews shot up. Everyone was falling back. Archie turned the radio down. "Get in, we'll retreat."

He turned the radio back up and called into control "Engine Fourteen we just picked up two cops. They said we're under attack. Do not send any more trucks to the docks. Repeat, do not send any trucks to the docks, over."

"*Roger. Hall Nine, Hall Six hold your position. Do not proceed until further notice.*"

All the vehicles called in confirming. One Captain could be heard asking to go in to rescue their friends.

"No way," Lynda said. "Tell 'em to stay out."

"Negative, Control," Archie said into the mic. "The cops here say do not send anyone in, over."

"*Engine Six, stay put. Do not proceed to the docks, over.*"

"*FUCK!*" was the reply.

"*Ladder Two to Control. Ladder Two to Control.*"

"*Go Ladder Two.*"

"*Fuck, they're all dead. All of them. Mother fuckers fired machine guns at us. I have two wounded including me. We're all shot up. They gawdamned fired rockets at the Chief. He's gone.*"

"*Where are you, Ladder Two? Will send paramedics.*"

"*They're here. Fuck, we're all shot the fuck up. What the hell is going on!*"

"We need to get out of here. NOW!" Lynda exclaimed to Archie. Lynda and Ken squeezed into the back of the cab and introduced themselves. Matt, pointing his finger down the road, said, "What the fuck is that?"

In the dim distance they could see a vehicle come from around a building. Its front lights illuminated the inside of their cab.

Lynda yelled, "Back up now! Go! Go! Move it!"

Matt floored the big truck backwards, trying to keep straight using just his mirrors. That is when Archie saw the flash from the approaching vehicle. Just inches in front of them everything lit up with the huge fireball.

"GO! Faster!" he pleaded. "Go, go, go, go!"

Everyone in the cab screamed to go faster. Another distant flash, another explosion; closer this time.

"Turn the lights out!" John yelled.

"Fuck, right." Matt shut everything off.

"Back into that lot and turn us around," Archie said trying to be calm.

Another near hit just as they disappeared into a chemical plant parking lot.

"Holy fuck," Matt said. "That was close."

"Matt," Archie said.

Matt looked over at Archie. "Yes, Captain."

"Matt, they're still comin'. Put it in drive and let's make like the birds and get the flock out of here."

"Right." He stepped hard on the pedal, but heavy diesel trucks don't lay rubber, they take a bit of time to get up to speed.

"Go man!" howled Harris.

Matt yelled back, "It's on the floor!"

Soon as Matt got the vehicle back on the road, Archie, looked in the mirror, yelled, "He fired again!" A huge explosion rocked the pumper making it jump into the air. Everyone was bounced around except Matt who had his seat belt on.

"We're hit, we're hit!" Harris screeched.

But they were still mobile. The shell landed in the bed of hose protecting the rest of the truck.

"Turn here!" Archie ordered.

They turned right onto Victoria Drive, over the tracks and disappeared behind a line of railway cars.

* * *

Police Chief Don Hastings barged into the Police main control room. It was utter chaos. Cars were calling in to retreat: others were screaming for backup.

"Can someone please tell me what's going on?" he demanded. Few looked his way concentrating on the phones. "Listen up, people. I need to be debriefed, right now."

The closest operator hung up. "I called you, sir."

Andy Roman proceeded to get the Chief up to speed on what they knew, it wasn't much. They were under some kind of attack, at various fronts along the docks. A number of police cars were destroyed. He figured at least a dozen police officers were dead, and at least the same number wounded. They were very short on details, but long on questions, such as who was causing all this mayhem.

When asked about division commanders, Andy could only confirm at least one was killed, and others can't get close enough to see what is going on.

"Has the ERT been dispatched?" Don asked. There was silence. "Well?"

"Yes sir, five were sent in. We've heard nothing from them since. We're trying to call in more. But its confusion big time, sir."

That this was an invading army instead of another riot was inconsiderable. Regardless that the ERT had good firepower, training and experience, Don was unaware they were out matched.

"How many people are we talking about here?" Don asked.

"Maybe thousands," someone said.

"Thousands of rioters?" Don asked.

"Not rioters, Don," Deputy Chief Collin Edwards said coming into the room. "Don't send anyone else in there, Don. Listen up, everyone. Call all cars back now. Don, you need to see this."

They entered the computer crime division squad room. There, a dozen people were hunched over keyboards.

"Where did all these people come from?" Don asked.

"Wherever we could find them; some are cleaners. But look at this." Collin pointed to a screen. "Twitter is going nuts. Over a hundred posts a minute, just from Vancouver. Thousands a minute. We're being invaded by the Chinese."

Don's face dropped. "Chine… No. Are you sure?"

"Read some of the tweets. Look this one says: 'Lots of #Chinese troops landed near Airport. I can see them.' And this one: '2 ships in English Bay unloading troops into boats. Heading my way, Im leaving.'"

"Can we confirm any of this?"

"Yeah, some have posted videos on Facebook. Some are now showing up on YouTube."

They viewed half a dozen. Amateurish highly pixilated videos showed a massing of troops at the airport, and along the docks on both sides of the bay. Exploding vehicles and buildings lit up the screen. Don was speechless.

"I tried to call the airport. But because it's been shut down since the fall, few people are there. I sent in a patrol car to check it out," Collin finally said.

"Has anyone called the Mayor?" Don asked.

"Yeah, he's on his way here," Collin said. "I tried to get the Premier, but no answer from her yet. I don't know if she is even in the Province. The Executive Council is coming too.

"Some of this on Facebook and Twitter are contradictory, and some doesn't make sense," Collin said. "Some are claiming a U.S. strike force is coming; others say the Canadian and American armies are about to counter strike. Look this one even says this is all a movie stunt."

"That's because the enemy has Twitter accounts too," a booming authoritative voice said entering the room. A well-set man stood beside Collin. He was in full combat gear, including a helmet, a leg-holstered handgun, pouches of fully loaded magazines, and a C8 carbine slung on his back, barrel down.

His apparel was immaculate, even though it was a combat uniform. His blue eyes peered from under the camouflaged Kevlar helmet.

"Who are you?" Don said looking him over with a WTF expression on his face.

"Colonel Gary Hawker from the Seaforth Armoury."

Don refused to shake his hand. Hawker continued, "You can't trust what's on Twitter; or Facebook for that matter. The Chinese are flooding both with misinformation to confuse you. The city is lost. We need to abandon Vancouver. I've already moved everything I can from the

Armoury to the Port Mann railway yard. You need to do the same. You need to evacuate the city now."

"What? No. We can contain this," Don said.

"Contain what? An invasion? Do you have any idea how many there are? It's likely thousands of them."

"There's only one option to save lives, surrender," Don said.

"Surrender? Do you have any idea…"

"Sir!" someone signaled at the door "You need to get back into operations right away, something's happening."

"Excuse me, Colonel." Don brushed by.

On the wall of the control room there was a large flat TV. Reporters were streaming live video. The view was from high up, a fourth or fifth floor of a building.

Visible were a handful of people moving towards a line of soldiers. Someone in the room said two of the people were the Premier and her Attorney General. An aide was with them with a white flag. Nothing could be heard of the meeting, only the TV reporter talking about what was going on.

Premier Gail Roland's New Democratic Provincial Government was elected just before Black Winter. The Liberals before them had been crippled due to the economic collapse. "*Working together and compromise for the good of all*" was the mantra of the NDP, Canada's most socialist party. "Compromise" to the NDP was doing things their way. However, in times of crisis people will vote for anything that promises hope of better times ahead. The NDP's propaganda was full of that during a time of unprecedented uncertainty. The people of British Columbia voted in the NDP with a huge majority.

Hawker came into the room a bit after Don. "What the fuck is that socialist doing, selling us out?" Hawker said.

Don looked at him with darts. "She's trying to save our people and make peace," Don said.

"Ha, ha, make peace? Are you people that naïve? They did not come all the way from China to make fucking peace!"

They watched as a Chinese officer and some of his subordinates walked up and greeted the Premier. There was handshaking, and a few minutes of talking. But the camera was too far back to hear anything. In fact, one cameraman who did go up with the Premier was ordered back at gunpoint by one of the subordinates.

"Can someone tell me where this is taking place? Where are they?" Deputy Chief Collin Edwards said.

"Looks like Powell and Heatley," someone said.

The operations room was quiet. Those on the radio were trying to speak as softly as possible, while eying the TV on the wall.

Minutes felt like hours. They talked, and talked. *Was there any progress?* Collin didn't think so. *Are we reaching a ceasefire?* Don wondered. Hawker was getting a bad feeling.

The air was full of anticipation; you could cut it with a knife. The bubble burst. An aide to the Chinese commander pulled out a pistol and shot the Attorney General in the head. Another grabbed the Premier dragging her off, while shots were fired at cops.

The reporter kept stammering· "Oh My God!" Over and over.

Shocked, many in the control room started crying.

"Get to work!" Collin yelled. "Everyone calm down. Be professional, people."

Slowly the chatter on the radios and phones grew.

"So much for socialist diplomacy, eh?" Hawker upbraided Don. "You can't negotiate with these people. They're here to conquer, not some gawddamned vacation."

"George was a great man and my friend!" Don shot back, anger in his eyes.

Hawker scolded, "So what are you going to do then? Whimper and cower in submission? Attack? Your people would be cut down in seconds. I'm telling you, fall back. Hell, you're too close here. You need to abandon this building."

"How the fuck do you know what they're doing?" Frustration growing in Don's voice.

"This is what I do for a living, predict military scenarios."

"We can handle this! Get out," Don said.

"Handle this? Don, what are we going to do?" Collin asked.

Don was in nowhere land, again. During the rioting Don ordered his police to stand down and stand back. He shunned all violence. His worldview was that of a typical liberal: no one is really a criminal at heart; it's society's fault if people break the law. He obtained the moniker of 'Chief Hug a Thug' from his detractors. He joined the police force to try and change policies, to be compassionate towards the criminal. He was the perfect patsy of the left, encouraged by those who would seek social engineering of Canadian politics and way of life. He was made Chief when the mostly leftist City Council voted for him to take the job.

During Black Winter, rioting on the west coast was nowhere near as bad as out east, because the weather wasn't as bad. However, rioting had been terrible enough to test Don's worldview. He still blamed the capitalist system, parroting his leftist masters in both the municipal government and especially the new NDP Provincial Government. His indecisions when making arrests and charging people with crimes, made him enemies in the police department rank and file as well as middle managers.

Don also made many in the public despise the police because of his steadfast views of gun control; that only police and the military should have "weapons" (they were always "weapons" in Don's speeches, never "firearms"). He demanded his force find the tiniest infraction to penalize citizens owning firearms.

He even ordered a parent picking up his daughter from primary school arrested. The daughter had drawn a crude picture of her father with a handgun. The school called police. Before any consultation Don had his force take their children away, strip searching the father, and holding him in a cell for hours. No attempt was made to find out if the man had any firearms. He did. An imitation plastic water gun. The father was set free, but the trauma to the entire family was devastating and costly in lawsuits against the force. However, Don got the message out: No firearms tolerated under this regime.

His disdain for private firearms ownerships was highest for those who he considered "urban warfare guerrillas". People who owned restricted firearms; pistols and semi-auto carbine style rifles for competition shooting events. Don considered those events nothing more than practice for ill-conceived goals. On more than one occasion he publicly questioned the comportment of people who only wanted to emulate their characters in *Call of Duty*.

Yet, those very people would become instrumental during the Chinese invasion.

Don's disdain intensified when he realized those with guns survived the rioting better than others who were forced to submit to home invasions, rape, and murder. He arrested many who killed armed intruders. Though such charges were always dropped by the Crown Attorneys who were flooded with criminal cases involving real crimes. This got Don pissed even more.

The police force finally gained control over the riots thanks to pressure from influential business people forcing the government's hand. This change in policy co-incidentally started when looters and home invaders started to attack the more affluent sections of the city. Collin, as Deputy Chief, was given the job to make that enforcement happen. And he did.

Collin turned a blind eye to those who used lethal force while protecting their homes. This started after a businessman blew away four thugs at his front door with a shotgun before the perps could start their rampage.

It was only after that that the city was again under some control. That was just after Christmas.

Collin repeated louder' "Don, what's our next move?"

"I don't know. I don't know! Send in the rest of the ERT."

Hawker had witnessed enough. He grabbed Don pinning him against the wall with one hand around the throat. "I've had as much as I can take of you fucking socialist retards! Look you fuckhead…" Anger was welling inside. Veins over his temples expanded. "You need to act now before it's too late. Order everyone back. NOW!"

"Let go of me. Who do you think you are?" Don croaked.

"I am taking control of this situation," Hawker said letting Don drop to the floor. "Listen up everyone," Hawker commanded. "Call everyone back. We are evacuating this building. Anyone who wants to surrender to the Chinese can take their chances. I need a map of the city."

"You don't give orders here!" Don screamed.

"Chief Hastings," Collin interrupted. "You've had your chance; we're going with the colonel."

Collin and Don didn't really get along. Collin was two years senior and felt resentful at being passed over for Chief. It had been a political decision because he didn't support the NDP.

"We'll see about that!" Don retreated from the room in a huff.

"Oh. Chief," Hawker said turning around to him. Don stopped and looked back. "You're free to go and surrender all you want. But you have no right to assume we all want to."

Don left slamming the door.

"Anyone else want to go with the Chief?" Hawker asked the room. "Before deciding, remember your chances of survival are near impossible with this enemy. And if you do survive… well, let's just say it won't be a pleasant experience."

No one left the room. "Right," Hawker said, "now about that map."

"Right here, Colonel," Collin said unfolding one on the table.

"We need a rally point, a temporary headquarters; a school, or arena, something near the highway away from here."

Collin studied the map carefully. "How about Killarney Community Centre?"

"No, on the other side of the Fraser. Something in Surrey, near the railway yard."

"Got it, North Surrey Secondary School."

"Perfect, call all units; tell them to pull back to that school. Make sure they clear all police stations of weapons, ammo and anything we need, or can be used against us."

Collin turned to one of the switchboard operators. "Get a couple of units to find a fire crew to break into these gun shops and get everything they can." He handed her a slip of Post-It note with a hand written list of stores.

One of the switchboard operators asked, "What about all the public here? You're going to just abandon them? We have a dozen hospitals with sick people. Most of them won't be able to be moved. What about them?"

"There's nothing we can do for them. We can't physically evacuate the entire city. Only able-bodied people are going to be able to try and get out on foot," Collin said to her, trying to comfort her crying.

"That's already started according to the Tweets and Facebook," someone said. "Cops are seeing all kinds of people walking on the roads already.

Social media is getting the word out."

"Fucking fuel rationing! People can't get out by car," someone else said.

"They're going to try to blitz us, aren't they, Colonel," Collin said.

"Oh, yeah. That's what I'd do. We're goin' to have to slow these pricks down somehow," Hawker said.

Hawker figured that the Chinese would move fast. They would have to move quickly to obtain supplies, especially food. Tweet reports were already pouring in that some of the enemy were hitting food stores. This would mean not only feeding themselves but also starving the residents. Once they established and consolidated their positions, they would move to take control of the bridges and railway lines.

Hawker had already moved as much as he could out of the armoury with only a handful of soldiers. He needed the rest of the militia.

The Seaforth Highlanders of Canada was a volunteer only, militia regiment; totalling only eighteen hundred from all over Vancouver and surrounding area. Calls were going out. The problem was how many could make it to the rally point.

Hawker, however, made one miscalculation. He assumed NRS Aldergrove had contacted Ottawa about the invasion. Aldergrove was the Maritime Command's primary communications relay site for the Maritime Forces Pacific; located fifty-nine kilometers east of Vancouver. Unbeknownst to Hawker this site, and the Matsqui transmitter twenty-eight kilometres northeast, had already been knocked out that same evening.

Chinese commandos had infiltrated the week before. In fact, many commando units had landed up and down the coast to prepare for the invasion. They didn't even have to be clandestine about their activities; they drove around in civilian clothes in ordinary cars.

The closest Canadian Army base was Area Support Unit Chilliwack, about one hundred kilometres up the Fraser Valley.

Hawker now had a small army of a few full-time military; of which less than three-quarters were soldiers, plus 2,000 front line cops, he figured. Then there were those armed civilians. Those "urban combat guerrillas" may come in handy after all.

"Collin, how many people own firearms here?"

"There's some twenty thousand licensed civilians; how many are still alive I'm not sure. You want to recruit them?" he said.

"I won't need to. I can bet you their firearms forum is blazing with posts. I'll bet many of them will want to join us. Get someone on their blog and post that we're meeting at the CN railway yard in Surrey."

"On to it," Collin said and then directed one of the operators what to post on the blog.

"We need to set up roadblocks to slow these fuckers down. Any thoughts?" Hawker asked.

"These four bridges will be a bottleneck for them," Collin said pointing on the map. "They can't get across the river without those bridges. We could clog the bridges with heavy equipment," Collin said.

"Outstanding. Get it done."

Collin contacted the city works departments at Surrey, Delta, and Coquitlam.

The calls went out to all units and a long convoy of police cars, fire trucks and loaded city buses made their way to Surrey across the Fraser River.

All messages were sent. The headquarters was abandoned and the last of them headed to Surrey, and not too soon. The enemy was just down the road advancing quickly towards the building.

Don did not go with them.

CHAPTER 2

Enemy at the Gates

"Ray, get your phone, it's rung four times now. Wake up, Ray."

"What, what, why are you waking me?" He looked at the clock. "It's two a.m., who the hell would be calling?"

"Maybe it's your mother."

"Hello?" Ray said into the phone. Bonnie rolled away.

"Ray, hey Ray, wake up, man. We're being invaded!"

"John, what the fuck are you calling me for? This some kind of joke, it's not funny. I have to work in the morning."

"No one is going to work in the morning, Ray. Get up, get your shit together. We're all meeting at the CN yard."

Ray sat a the side of the bed and turned the light on. Rubbing his eyes he said, "John, what the fuck are you talking about?"

"Ray, listen carefully. Chinese soldiers have landed at the harbour. We're evacuating the entire city to Surrey. Get up. Get your gear on. Get your butt to the railway yard ASAP. Both of you."

"Gear on, what gear on? John, I'm confused. What's going on? More rioting?"

"No, Ray. Just do it. Jason is already heading north up the coast. I'm trying to contact all our guys. I'm still on duty. Ray, Chinese soldiers have killed cops. We're under attack, Ray."

"What the fuck?" Ray said in a daze. "John…"

"Ray, I gotta make more calls, I'll see you at the yard." He hung up.

"Honey, what's going on?" Bonnie said.

"Weird. John said we need to pack up all our stuff and head to the railway yard."

"Which John, Honey?" Bonnie said rubbing her eyes.

"John the cop. I'll be right back."

Ray fired up his laptop in the kitchen, and logged into the firearms blog, called GunsArntEvil. "What the fuck" came through his lips several times. He couldn't believe what he was reading. He read the post by the Vancouver Police asking for anyone with firearms to rally at the rail yard.

Ray and Bonnie McGillis were in their late fifties. They had three children, one of which froze to death in Calgary during Black Winter. The other two, his sons, worked at the potash deposit mine in Saskatchewan. They talked with them just a few days earlier.

Before the economic collapse, Ray had worked as a chemical engineer in the plastics industry, which was a defunct endeavour. So he worked at the local food store.

He had several firearms, actually closer to an arsenal. He had won a couple of trophies for long distant precision shooting, commonly known as a crack shot, which was his GunsArntEvil handle. He also had other firearms, including various kinds of pistols and carbines. He fancied himself a collector too, as he had amassed some thirty World War I and World War II rifles and handguns. Like many his age, he had several family members who participated in those wars.

With no fuel, Ray and Bonnie walked the hour to the railway yard. He took with him his NEA15, and his 1911 45cal pistol (ironically made by the Chinese company Norinco), while Bonnie took his Cz858 and a 9mm Cz85. On Ray's back was his .338 Lapua Savage 111, the rifle he won his trophies with. They both carried as much ammo as they could.

Lots of people were on the streets, most of them heading in the same direction; some of them were also carrying, mostly hunting rifles or shotguns.

What stunned Ray was the eerie glow in the distance on the Port Mann Bridge. Most of the bridge looked to be ablaze.

* * *

Hawker ordered the bridges to be clogged with whatever vehicles could be obtained – snowplows, garbage trucks, school buses – and park them all on the bridges. They started piling the vehicles on top of each other with cranes on the far side first, then worked their way across the bridge. Drivers were shunted back by school bus.

The problem was the tens of thousands of people coming across on foot, carrying whatever they could, including their pets. Some did come by car or truck, which had to be abandoned before the barricades, adding to the maze the Chinese would have to get through.

It was a morass of panic and chaos. Masses of people were trying to navigate the obstacles, while crews tried to park vehicles without hitting anyone. But, of course, that was near impossible. Many were injured.

CNR crews had brought in empty freight cars as near to the bridges as they could. They were filled with refugees and taken to the freight yard.

They only managed to get a few hundred feet of wreckage at two locations when Chinese Armoured Personnel Carriers, APCs, arrived at both the Alex Fraser highway bridge and the magnificent Pattullo Bridge. People scattered as the APCs showed up. Those on the bridge's entrance ran as fast as they could to get across hampering crews parking vehicles.

Fierce firefighting commenced between police, a few militia, and some armed civilians. Shooters with their AR15s was no match against APCs with cannons.

Hawker gave the order to start burning the vehicles. This would prevent enemy soldiers from crossing. It also trapped a large number of civilians.

Realizing that the fires would burn out in a few minutes, Hawker ordered more vehicles, whatever trucks and transport rigs they could get, onto the bridge. They could pile them faster than the fire advanced into the new barricades. More than half of the lengths of the bridges were a heap of burning wreckage.

It worked. The APCs tried to barge through, but got stuck on the bridges. One even caught fire and exploded in a huge fireball; with its turret flying into the air and splashing in the river.

The Chinese tried the CNR railway overpass beside the Pattullo Bridge, but crews had already parked a long string of grain hoppers and tank cars on it. They also managed to get some vehicles on the Skyway Bridge.

If only they had some charges, Hawker thought.

* * *

Erik Stein got his call around 2 a.m. Erik was Professor of Geology at UBC. He didn't live far from campus. He rode there every day on his bike, even in winter. He was affectionately known as TheKraut on the GunsArntEvil forum. His family immigrated from Germany long ago, just before the outbreak of World War II.

Erik regretted later in life that they never found time for a family, a contention that lead to his divorce. His ex-wife, also a geologist, attempted to move back to Florida just as the economic crisis got into the depths. The last he saw her was when he escorted her to the train station. It wasn't a pleasant goodbye, more of an emotionless departure. He never heard if she arrived or not.

Though his lifelong hobby, other than geology, had been fishing, Erik got into firearms late in life. He actually despised guns as a young geology student. But something changed that transformed him, something that ran shivers down his spine. It was when the Liberal government in Canada introduced draconian firearms laws in 1998.

Erik still had relatives in Germany. His father's brother, also a university professor, lived through the 1930s rise of Nazism. Erik's uncle had no way of escaping as Erik's father did. So he was forced to endure the hardship of Germany throughout all of WWII. But the parallels of what the Liberal Government was doing, and what 1930s Germany did by disarming the public, turned his opinion. So he decided he was going to fight this violation of rights by getting his licence and buying some firearms. What surprised him was he actually had fun at the ranges. He wasn't a great shot by any means, but he thoroughly enjoyed the people he shot with.

What Erik didn't fully grasp yet, was he was now in the same environment his relatives were in.

After the call from his friend, and realizing he was likely cut off from a quick escape, he decided he had no choice but to stay behind. He understood what his uncle went through.

At over sixty he was getting too old to play sillybugger games running about. He was now an occupied person, and it did not feel good one bit. He feared for the future, worse fear than during the economic collapse.

He also feared that they would come and search his home for firearms. So he got dressed, loaded the ten rifles and pistols into the trunk of his Volkswagen, and drove the short distance to the Geology Department's warehouse where rock samples were stored. He hid them way up in the top layers of trays of drill cores.

On his way back home he could see red and orange glows towards the Fraser River. Rumblings like distant thunder could be heard coming from the downtown core.

Once at home he went back to bed. Before he drifted off, he recalled the letters from family members caught in Germany during the war. He would now be like them. Then he realized that the Chinese occupiers wouldn't be as much of a problem as neighbours who willingly become collaborators who ratted out friends and neighbours for a bit of extra food. How history repeats itself, he thought. Another chill went down his spine.

* * *

People panicked and screamed. An explosion threw a couple of railway cars into the air. One landed on fleeing civilians. An APC was on the far bank of the Fraser, across from the railway yard at Port Mann, lobbing fifty millimetre shells into the yard.

Hawker was at a loss as to what to do. He ordered everyone back from the yard. But the APC was destroying their ability to evacuate people. He, and Sergeant Williams, went to the riverbank to have a close look at what was targeting them.

Williams was the non-commissioned officer in charge of the regiment at Seaforth, responding to the armoury with Hawker that night. He did a superb job of saving weapons. Many of the cops in the firefights on the bridges were using the C7, C8s and the two C9s saved by Williams.

Through the binoculars Hawker could see the APC. The commander was exposed in the turret hatch, also looking through binoculars, obviously giving targets.

"If only we had a sniper," Hawker said.

"We have civilian sharpshooters. I saw a number of people with fancy rifles and huge scopes on them."

"Go see if one of them wants to take a shot at this guy."

Williams hurried through the civilian crowd asking if anyone was a good long-range precision shooter. Ray heard it, and popped up. "I can!"

he yelled.

Williams came over to him. "Come with me."

Ray introduced himself to Hawker at the beach. Hawker asked if he could hit a target that far. Ray replied he'd need to know the distance and get into a good firing position. There was too much underbrush on the far side. He recommended the four-story building at the south side of the yard. He would need a ladder to get up there however.

A firefighting crew helped get Hawker, Ray and Williams onto the top of the building. The sun was now starting to crest atop the mountains on their right, brightening up the area. Ray opened up the shooting matt to expose his Savage.

"Nice rifle," Hawker said.

"Oh, yeah. She's a sweetheart," Ray said with a big grin. He laid the shooting matt open on the flat gravel roof, extended the bipods on the rifle, lay prone on the matt, and adjusted his body to get comfortable. He sighted through the twenty-four power scope on his rifle, adjusting the zoom. "It's about eight hundred meters," he said, turning the elevation turret on his scope.

"You can make a shot like that?" Hawker said.

"Piece of cake. I've won trophies for shots further than this," he said putting in one of his custom loaded .338 rounds. He lined up his shot, waited and waited as the figure was moving around. It had to be the perfect time, soon as the target was still looking through his binoculars. Ray's Savage rang out loudly. There was a pause, then "I missed."

"He didn't hear it pass him, he hasn't moved. Try again." Hawker said.

"Yep, just a second, it's windage." Ray readjusted the horizontal turret setting on his scope. He loaded another round into the chamber. Taking his time sighting, Ray took a deep breath and let it all out. Holding his breath he put a tiny bit of pressure on the trigger and the Savage fired.

Two seconds later Hawker said, "Fuck me, you got him. Nice shot!"

Through his scope Ray could see a body slumped over the turret of the APC. It stopped firing, backed up, and took off down a road away from the river.

Ray figured this would not be the last time he would have to kill. He expected he would not be the first one here to have to take a life for the first time. He lay there on the roof for a few moments, head on the rifle's butt not moving even when Hawker invited him to come down.

"I'll be there in a moment. I need a few minutes."

Hawker didn't question. The two of them got down leaving Ray to contemplate the matter.

Hawker was waiting for Ray at the bottom of the ladder. "Outstanding, Ray," Hawker said patting him on the back. "You, sir, are my new best friend. You stick by my side and we're going to play beautiful music together."

Ray didn't say anything. Hawker picked up his apprehension. "Look, you did a great thing just now. You've saved hundreds of lives. You should be proud of that."

"Yeah, I guess I should, just not sure."

"It was a target. That's all. If I had a trophy for you, you'd get it right now. I'm going to keep you near me at all times. You'll come in very handy. Go get your gear and come to my office."

As Ray was walking away, Hawker called to him "Hey, you can paint a single white band around your barrel. Maybe the first of many, eh?"

Ray stopped. In a way he hoped not, but knew it would be true. He wasn't about to advertise his successes.

Then he remembered. "You guys should get my collection of firearms still at my home."

Sergeant Williams dispatched a police car to gather them up. It was a great cache, definitely appreciated. They were put in an empty create and loaded onto a boxcar full of such weapons from a number of sources. Ray asked why, and Hawker informed him that they were not making their stand here. They were evacuating to Calgary and once there the weapons would be distributed to those properly trained to use them. That made sense to Ray, but he would miss his collection.

Ray returned to Bonnie and a chorus of claps, cheers and "YEAH!" That certainly perked him up.

* * *

Hawker was on the radio trying to keep contact with Deputy Police Chief Collin Edwards, who was charged with controlling the other bridge barricades west near the coast, when a U.S. Army Captain showed up and saluted him. Hawker saluted back.

"I'm Captain Chris Staines of the National Guard, sir." They shook hands.

"Good to meet you, Captain, what brings you up here?"

"You guys have a real problem. A Chinese ship landed at Bellingham. They tried to take over the airfield where our air guard is located. But they didn't expect the resistance we gave them. We kept them at bay while we evacuated the base. But the town was overrun. There was too many of them. They cut our escape south. So we figured we'd head up this way. Get through the mountains to rejoin the rest of the American Army."

"Well, Captain, you're more than welcome to join us. How many are you?"

"About two hundred and fifty shooters. We left more than that behind. Fuck, these Commies moved fast. The problem is they're heading this way. I figure they'll need the pass through the mountains. So if you don't want to get cut off, I suggest you evacuate ASAP."

Hawker thought for a few seconds. Then a well-dressed suit showed up at his boxcar/office.

"Someone said you're in charge," the suit said looking at Staines.

"Not me," Staines said. "He is."

"Yep, I'm in charge here, what can I do for you?" Hawker said.

"William, William Norris-Lester, pleased to meet you. Hum, what's your rank?"

"Colonel, but you can call me Hawker."

Norris-Lester was a short thin man, somewhat balding with thin rim glasses. He looked like the perfect "suit", some big-shot businessman or something, Hawker thought.

"Colonel, I need your help. You see, down the tracks there's two boxcars of mine. They are very important. Vital actually. They must go first, on the next train out."

Several trains loaded with people had already headed east.

"What's so important about those cars?" Hawker asked.

"I'd rather not say."

"Sorry bud, people first. They're top priority."

"Not to this cargo."

"Well, you're going to have to convince me of that."

Norris-Lester leaned over to Hawker and whispered. "Can we talk in private?"

Hawker looked at him hard. "Fuck, OK everybody out." Once the car was cleared, "OK, hyphenated name, what's so important?"

"Those two cars are loaded with money, stock certificates and bonds. Government bonds, corporate bonds, bank bonds. They're essential to rebuilding the economy. They must get moved to safety. They cannot be allowed to fall into Chinese hands, understand?"

"No, make me understand. How the fuck did you gather all this up in only six hours?"

"Oh, no. No. No. Those cars have been there for, well, almost a year now. We moved them out of banks and warehouses during the height of the rioting. We were afraid we'd lose them all."

"How would someone steal all that from a vault?"

"Oh, I guess I'm not explaining correctly. You see it wasn't theft we were worried about. We were worried about not being able to access them again. You see, the vast majority of this money comes from out east, even as far as Montreal. It was all loaded up not to keep people from stealing it, but because we feared with cities starting to get out of control we would not be able to get back to get at the money. Back into the cities, that is.

"So early on, when the rioting started after the collapse, we decided to clear all the banks and vaults and send the money out here. Well, not initially, it kind of ended up here."

"So you hid them in boxcars."

"Oh, yeah. Hidden in plain view, you know? No one but me and two others knows this. Well, you now. So you see, it's vital we get these cars onto the train. Please?"

"Sure, what the fuck does it matter? Go see the engine crew over there," Hawker said pointing to his left. "They'll get your car first. We aren't ready for the next train to head out yet anyway."

"Thank you so much Colonel!" Norris-Lester said shaking Hawker's hand with both of his. He rushed off into the distance.

Captain Staines came back. "What was that about?"

"Something about several billions of dollars hidden in boxcars."

"Whoeee! Man!" Staines whooped.

"Sir!" The radio operator interrupted them. "The Internet has gone down. So has the phone system including cell phone service."

"Wonderful. Now we're blind," Hawker said.

"Not unexpected," Staines said.

"Captain," Hawker asked, "What can you tell me? What's going on?"

"FUBAR big time. East of the Rockies is fucked completely. Rioting has turned the cities into war zones. Soldiers abandon their posts to go home, taking their weapons with them. Command and control has collapsed. The phone system is working, well was working, along the coast, even the Internet. But east we can't get through much, if at all. The winter was real bad, especially in the northern states."

"So I've heard here too," Hawker said shaking his head. "Militarily where are we?"

"You know your fleet at Esquimalt has been sunk. That's what we heard on the radio. A number of naval ships have been sunk up and down the coast by submarines, we figure. They also stormed your facilities at Esquimalt."

"Fuck me," Hawker said shaking his head. "Do we have any air support at all?"

"None that I have heard of. The fuel shortage is brutal down our way. Fucking Saudis and Argentina has cut us off of oil. But it's people, that's the big problem."

"God help us," Hawker said. "How is it you didn't see the Chinese coming?"

"Hard to do when people abandoned their posts."

"The Chinese planned this well."

"Oh yeah. Fuck'n right about that."

"What I don't understand is why our main radio relay station at

Aldergrove didn't pick this up. I've tried to call them several times. No answers. We have people there twenty-four seven. I was thinking of sending a squad there to investigate. It's not far from here."

"I wouldn't, sir. We've had rumours of Chinese infiltration and sabotage. If that was a high priori target for them you can bet they have taken the station out. No point in sending anyone there. We need all hands on deck to get through the mountains," Staines said.

"Yeah, fuck! You're probably right. Get your men together Captain, we hit the road in thirty minutes. Do you have enough fuel to make it to Chilliwack?"

"Should have. Can we get more fuel there?"

"I sure hope so. Sergeant?"

"Yes sir," Sergeant Williams said running up.

"Pass the word to get everyone left on the bridges out. Captain Staines here will take the next train." Hawker turned to look at the captain. "I need an officer on the train to keep control of this. I'm staying for the last one, so in case I don't make it out of here, catch my drift?"

"Yes, sir, copy that," Staines said.

"Cops and soldiers are last to leave. Captain, you don't mind if I keep your guys here to hold off any advance while we load people? Then they can leave in your trucks."

"Absolutely. One of my lieutenants will take charge of them. Just make sure I get them all back."

"Colonel? Sir? You're needed on the radio, sir," someone in the boxcar said.

Hawker got in and answered. It was Deputy Chief Collin Edwards. He said a ship had arrived west of them in Boundary Bay and was unloading troops. They were heading for shore. The enemy had bypassed the bridges. Hawker ordered a complete evacuation, and to get the last of the trains rolling.

Collin was involved in a major firefight against the newly landed enemy. His forces were trying to keep Chinese from passing across the bridges over the Nicomekl River.

Collin confirmed to Hawker that they were holding them off at the bridges, but his side of the river was mostly open farmland giving them little cover. He asked for direction. Hawker asked if they could retreat back to the Serpentine River. That would reverse the exposure putting the Chinese out in the open.

Collin moved his troops back, and the Chinese followed on their heels. By this point he had lost about a quarter of his men.

Staines's men arrived at the scene to add support. That made a big difference. The National Guardsmen were armed with anti-tank weapons. Out in the open on the King George's Road enemy APCs were easy targets. All were destroyed.

It was a small thorn at best for the Chinese advancement. Hawker understood that. So he changed his mind and ordered a complete retreat. It would take Collin's crew thirty minutes by bus to get to the rally point. However, on foot it would take the Chinese three or four hours. The one advantage of the fuel rationing was there wouldn't be too many abandoned vehicles with any fuel in them. Anyone with a drivable vehicle had already left the area. The Chinese were left on foot, or had to wait for more equipment to be unloaded, which would take hours.

Collin and company arrived at the railway yard by 10 a.m. With half an hour they were well on the last train to the mountains.

Ray and Bonnie were with Hawker in his boxcar "office". Bonnie introduced herself to Hawker.

"What's that rifle you have? It looks like an Ak47. I thought those were banned?" Hawker said.

"It's not, it's a Cz858," Ray said. "It's made in the Czech Republic. Real nice rifle. Well made. I added the wood furniture and the rail on the top for the optics."

Hawker asked if he could take a look. He was impressed with the light weight, and great design. Ray turned on the Red-Dot scope attached to the top of the rail. Hawker sighted through it. "Way cool! You fucking civvies get all the great toys. I wish our guys could have weapons like this. Can I fire it?" Ray loaded a mag. Hawker fired it out the boxcar door until the breach stayed open, only five rounds. "Wow, hardly any kick. This is a great little weapon." He took the mag out. "You know you can take the pinning out of the mags, I'll allow it," he said laughing.

Canadian laws forced people to put either a rivet, or some obstacle inside magazines for semi-auto rifles, "pinning" as it was called, so that only five rounds could be loaded. The five round limit was a real joke. It was thrust upon firearms owners when the new Liberal laws came into effect decades earlier, in spite of a committee report stating that the limiting of mags to just five rounds would have no effect on crime rates or public safety. However, the Liberals at that time needed smoke and mirrors to make it appear they were getting tough on gun crime. In fact, all they succeeded in doing was restricting legal, safe, firearms owners. That was all under the bridge at this point.

Ray was handed a small drill and some tools so he could alter his mags. He figured all his shooting buddies were doing the same.

They watched through the open door as the train snaked its way towards the mountain, leaving an occupied city, and most of its residents, behind.

"I shall return," Hawker said under his breath.

Up the Coast
Without a Paddle

Jason and Kelly made it to Squamish by 2:30 a.m. The town seemed perfectly normal, and sleeping. Jason's phone rang. He looked at the screen.

"Tom, tell me you're safe, bro."

"Yeah, I'm fine. I'm at your apartment. You left the door open. Where are you, man?"

"Squamish. Thank God you're safe, dude. So what's happening there?"

"I'm on your balcony. Looking through one of your riflescopes. They have moved the two ships out and two more are coming in to dock. I can see even more out on the bay coming in. Fuck, Jason, we're being invaded big time, man."

"Have they advanced?"

"No. It looks like they're getting organized. They took the highway bridge to the City. I can see them. They've done some recons around here. No cops, man. I think they killed them all."

"You gotta get out of there, dude. Hang on a second." Jason turned to Kelly, "I need to go back and get my brother. You'll be safe here."

"What if you don't come back? What if they catch you? Or worse, kill you. Then what do I do?" Tears started to well in her eyes.

"I can't leave my little brother behind."

"Do what you have to do," she said sarcastically.

"Tom, you still there?"

"Yeah, I'm here, man."

"Take the M14, and all the ammo and mags you can. Take the 38 Smith and Wesson. Hang on, I'm going to call you back, I'm going to check Google Maps for a place we can meet."

"Get right back, bro."

"Start heading north, dude. I'll call you back."

Jason checked the map. He hit the redial. "Tom, can you walk to the bridge over the highway at Caulfield? It'll take you about an hour. Get up to the highway and follow it. I'll meet you there. I'm just going to drop Kelly off at the RCMP station."

"I'll try." He hung up.

They drove into town until they saw the police station sign. The building looked closed. The sign on the door said "Monday to Saturday 8:00AM to 4:00PM". There was a phone on the wall: "In case of Emergency".

"I think this is an emergency, what do you think Kell?"

"Just pick up the damn phone, smart ass."

Jason talked to someone at the other end. The officer said they had heard of something happening in Vancouver and they were sending some cops to help evacuate Squamish. Jason told them to bring lots of guns.

"What's going on, son?" the officer said.

"The whole fucking Chinese army, that's what."

"Well, it'll be at least two hours for us to come from Kamloops," the officer said.

The only employee at the near by 24-hour Tim Hortons was stunned to see two armed people come in the store. She looked like they were going to rob her.

"Oh, I guess we startled you," Jason said. "Sorry, I'm not here to stick you up." Jason put his rifle on a table. With a big grunt Kelly attempted squeezed her belly into a seat. "I just want to get some food for my wife."

"Why do you have guns?" the still-shaking girl said.

Jason explained the situation. He didn't think she believed him.

"You'll believe me soon enough," he said.

Jason left Kelly there and headed back to get his brother. But before he could go he had to siphon gasoline from a few vehicles parked nearby. Hopefully enough to get there and back. That took more than half an hour before he could get going. And as fast as his car could speed.

Big difference heading back: lots of cars, trucks and buses, and some cop cars, were coming up the highway towards Squamish. He was worried the congestion would hamper his attempt to get back to Kelly.

Jason had reached Sunset Beach when his phone rang.

"Jason?" Tom said, "Where are you? I'm here, man."

"Sunset Beach."

"Fuck, man. You can't come closer. The fucking Chinese just passed me in trucks. They're heading your way, man."

"Fuck," Jason pulled over. "How long ago?"

"About ten minutes."

"Hey, you got the M14?"

"Yeah, man, you know I love this rifle. I took the two ammo boxes and dumped it all into a backpack. It's fucking heavy to carry all this shit, man."

"That's almost a thousand rounds if you took the ten boxes of thirty-eights too."

"Yep, I got them with me too."

"Hang on a second." He sat there thinking how he could get to his brother. There were no other roads. But then it dawned on him. "Tom, I'll bet they're heading to the ferry. Tom? You still there?"

"Yeah, man. How do you know that?"

"I don't, logical guess. They aren't here, the road's now empty. So I'd bet that's where they're at. Hey, remember where we went shooting the last time?"

"Yeah, the hydro line."

"Exactly, it's not far. You can walk across that to near the ferry, then make it along the highway to here. No one'll see you."

"Fuck me man, that'll take hours."

"I don't see much choice. Book it, bro. Call me at various intervals on your progress. It's three a.m. now. So by sixish you should be here. Still some night left."

Jason called Kelly on her phone and updated her on the situation. She said a lot of people had shown up and moving about. Cops had also shown up.

Tom walked along the Trans Canada Highway north. He could see red and orange glow in the distance in front of him. He could hear faint rumblings. No one was on the road. He had it all to himself, except one time behind him he heard trucks and hid on the side as a few vehicles went by full of Chinese soldiers. By 3:30 a.m. he reached the hydro line clearing through the trees.

Once following the towers he was enveloped in total darkness. Stars filled the sky. If it were not for the situation it would have been a nice nightly stroll.

The distance as the crow flies was about a kilometre and a half, but on foot was almost three times the distance. It wasn't long before his feet started to ache. He had to stop and take a break several times.

He called his brother each half hour. His last call was when he was looking over Horseshoe Bay. In the early dawn hours it was a picturesque sight; except for down at the ferry. It was swarming with Chinese. Down below him on the highway they had set up a roadblock. A large number of soldiers were on guard. He would have to move through the bush a bit more before he could get down to the highway unnoticed.

He stumbled down a steep embankment to the road. The soldiers, only a few hundred metres away, shone a light in his direction. He lay down in the ditch hugging the ground not moving. The light moved across him a couple of times. Then went out. He slithered through the ditch for several hundred feet until he figured he was in the clear.

By the time he walked the rest of the three kilometres to Sunset Beach it was nearly 7:30 a.m. Jason was there to meet him. They hugged, got into his car and headed back to Squamish. Daylight was just starting to part the night sky. Jason tried to call Kelly but there was only "No Service" on the screen.

Kelly hugged and kissed Jason, and Tom, on arrival back at the Tim Hortons. The town was now fully awake and bustling with people preparing to leave.

* * *

Erik Stein woke to the 7:00 a.m. alarm. He got up, put on his robe, had his morning pee, put on the coffee, and turned on the TV. Nothing. The screen was black. Every channel he clicked through was the same. He went back into his room to the alarm clock and turned the radio on. Nothing but static on all frequencies, except a few, which had a high-pitched screeching. Jamming he figured.

He went outside the front door and looked around. No one was on the street. In the sky to the east he could see columns of black smoke, at least four distinct pillars going way up into the cloudless sky. The sun was trying to peer around one of the pillars but to no avail. Distant thunder rolled his way from that direction.

He turned on his cell phone, but it just showed "No Signal". To his surprise, the landline inside rang.

"Hello?"

"Erik?"

"Yep, is that you, Carl?" Carl O'Keefe was the department head of Earth Sciences.

"Thank God you're still alive. Erik, they arrested the President, took him right out of his house. All department heads have been ordered to get all staff to the Convocation Hall by ten-thirty this morning."

"Ordered by whom?"

"No idea, some Chinese officer I was told. Don't fuck around with these guys, Erik. Please be there. No telling what these assholes will do."

Carl knew of Erik's firearms as Erik had taken him to the range for some pistol shooting a number of times. Carl and Erik had gone on fishing trips in the Rockies for more than thirty years. They had published a number of papers together.

Erik showed up at the hall by bike. The place was like a prison. Chinese soldiers were all over the place, bayonets attached to their weapons. And they were being pointed at anyone who showed up. All they did was motion with their spikey ends to enter the hall. Erik threw them darts from his eyes.

Once inside, Susan Yang gestured for him to come and sit beside her. Susan was from Hong Kong; she left there just before the British lost control of the colony to China. She was also a geologist specializing in the tectonics of the South East Asia area.

The walls were lined with bayoneted yielding soldiers. As people came in the wallflowers screamed in broken English to shut up, sit down, and no talking. At the front on the stage were a number of Chinese officers, plus a few civilians.

"Hi Sue, where's Carl?" Erik whispered.

"All Department Heads are at the front."

"STOP TALKING!" one of the soldiers yelled pointing his rifle at Erik and Sue.

"Fuck you," Erik said under his breath.

The doors closed at exactly 10:30 a.m, and soldiers blocked the exits. One of the officers in the middle of the stage got up and signalled a civilian to come beside him. The civilian was oriental.

"Who is that?" Erik whispered.

"English Department. Shhhh."

The Officer started to talk in his language. Erik thought that strange; someone of that calibre would surely know English, so why was he using an interpreter?

The officer stopped talking. The civilian got to the mic and said, "I'm Senior Colonel Zhuge Wěi Míng. I am now running this university."

Erik noticed the wallflowers were standing at attention and looking at the stage. "Do you understand this shit?" he said to Sue.

"Very little," she whispered back.

The back and forth between the general and the interpreter the new rules were explained. This included curfew after dark. No more than three people can gather in a group at one time. The usual stuff that occupiers enforce to keep control.

The interpreter then said something that made Erik laugh out loud. "You will all resume your duties of teaching and research." The audience looked back at Erik. The interpreter stopped. That same guard pushed a bayonet to Erik's face.

"OK, OK, take a break," Erik said with his hands up.

The general continued. However, one of the flanking officers on the stage got down and hurried to the soldier who pointed the rifle at Erik's and gave a terse command. The soldier never let Erik out of his sight for the rest of the hour-long propaganda speech.

Once it was all over and the crowd was leaving the soldier again placed the bayonet into Erik's face and gestured to move to the front. Sue tried to intervene, but the soldier poked her in the arm with the bayonet, and she screamed.

"Alright. All right!" Erik said to the soldier. "Stop! I'll go. Sue, I'll be OK."

He was led off to the front of the hall. Sue watched Erik being escorted away, as blood started to seep between her fingers holding the wound.

Erik was taken into a back room, and forcefully pushed into a chair. He waited a few minutes when that same general came into the room alone.

"Who are you?" he said in perfect non-accented English.

"Erik Stein, I'm professor of Geology."

"You find it funny that we ask you to resume your work?"

"Well, Colonel, or General, or what should I call you?"

"President," the General said.

"Oh, no. You are not the President. General then. How's that?"

"As you wish."

"Well, General, you see my specialty is mineralogy of the Arctic Archipelago. You know up north of here. Way up north of here? So if you want me to resume my research you will need to provide me with aircraft, helicopters, and a small team of grad students starting in June. And, quite frankly, that would be great if you could do that because since the economic crash we haven't gotten any grants to go back there."

"Are you trying to be funny, Herr Stein?"

"Herr Stein? Oh, General, you have this wrong. I've been a Canadian all my life."

"Your name is German, no?"

"Only my ancestry. Hell, I couldn't keep a conversation going in German if my life depended on it."

"You have family still in Germany?"

"A few, why? You planning to invade Germany too? Good fucking luck with that," Erik said with a chuckle.

"So you know what it is like to be occupied then, no?" the General said with a stern look on his face.

"Everyone knows what it is like to be occupied, General. Didn't Japan occupy some of your land too? Yeah, they did, didn't they. Do you honestly think anyone in that room believed a word from your mouth?"

"Spunky aren't we, Stein. Oh, they will all obey me, and you are very aware of how we can enforce that, aren't you, professor."

"Fuck'n right I do."

"So, we have an understanding don't we, *Herr* Stein," the General said emphasizing the *Herr*.

"More than you'll ever know, fuckface."

The General looked mad, as if he was going to make a move against Erik, but then he just smiled. "We will speak again, Herr Stein." And started to walk out of the room.

"So I guess my trek to the Arctic isn't going to happen then?"

The General turned back and stared at Erik. Then looked at the soldier and nodded. The soldier gave Erik a rap on the back of the head with the butt of the rifle putting Erik on the floor. The General left the room. Erik, with blood seeping down the back of his neck, was escorted out of the building.

He went to his office. Waiting for him were his two grad students and Carl.

Carl asked him what happened ending with, "Jesus, man, I know you are one independent son of a bitch, but you can't antagonize these pricks."

Erik shrugged as he held a bit of cloth on the back of his head.

Carl ordered the two students out of the room.

"Erik, what did you do with your guns? They're searching all the homes in the area. Anyone with guns they arrest."

"Can't tell you."

"You moved them?"

"Late last night. Don't worry they'll never find them."

"Fuck, I hope not. Both our lives are at stake here. I know you, Erik. You're not going to take this lying down are you?"

"The big difference between communism and freedom is in a communist state free loving people fear for their lives, whereas in a free society communist loving people don't," Erik said. "So now we fear for our lives.

So no, I wont be taking this laying down."

"Fuck me, you are. You don't have anyone, but I still have a family that made it through this mess, you know, through that winter. You've been right, did I tell you that before? You predicted the last few winters would be bad. Those global warming fucktards over there at Climatology. They got all that grant money while we got dick all."

"Seems that's the least of our worries now. We have to be careful who we talk with. Nugent will sell us out."

Professor Harry Nugent was a vocal activist. He had regular meetings with the campus Student Communist Association in his office every Friday. His lab was one floor down from Erik's. He and Nugent had gotten into a number of heated debates and not just about geological issues. Erik wasn't overly political, paradoxically he rarely even voted. "What's the point in voting if all you do is get people who want to social engineer society?" was his excuse. A common thread in the letters he had from the 1930s Germany.

Erik's pet peeve with Nugent was when Nugent redefined words to suit his agenda. That really pissed Erik off, and he told Nugent many times. Nugent was going to be a real problem. Erik figured Nugent would be an instant collaborator and spy.

Erik looked around at the door. "Carl, close the door."

He did ever so slowly and quietly and came back inside.

"We may have to dispose of Harry," Erik said.

That stunned Carl. He never figured Erik would ever advocate the killing of anyone, not even Nugent.

"Look," Erik said. "It's just a matter of time before he gets one of us in this department if not killed, arrested. You know what he's like. Fuck, just to spite me he may make something up and squeal like some stuck pig to the Commies. It's our only logical choice."

"No, no! Absolutely not! Are you out of your fucking mind? I will not agree to murder!"

"You won't have to do anything except keep your mouth shut."

Carl got up and started to leave the lab. Quietly he said, "I don't want to know anything, got it, Stein!" Anger was clearly in his low voice.

Erik sat there alone for some time trying to figure things out. He figured it would only be a matter of time before he "disappeared" like some of his family in Germany did during the Second World War.

* * *

Chief Don Hastings watched the sunrise above the snow-capped mountains from his office. Pillars of smoke climbed in the distance. Employees who missed the evacuation had been slowly showing up at Police Headquarters; some would occasionally knock at his door announcing their arrival. He told them to either resume work, or go home. Of course, it was futile to work at anything. Why bother working on prostitution, or theft, or even murders? There wasn't any logic to it any more he figured.

He tried to make some calls, to find out where the Mayor and Councilmen were, but the lines were dead. He could call within the building, but not out. With the phones not connected to the outside world, there weren't any 911 calls coming in. His cell phone wasn't working either so he could not even call home to his wife. He was trapped.

He could see soldiers driving and moving about on the street below. He knew it would just be a matter of time before they came to visit him. His flat screen TV on the wall was black as no stations were broadcasting. No one replied to repeated calls on the radio.

Finally at noon the visit he dreaded happened. Three Chinese officers and four armed soldiers burst into his office.

In perfect English the middle officer said, "I'm General Guō Hào. I am Deputy Commander of the Western Sea Board Inv…." He paused for a bit "…liberation force. Are you Don Hastings?"

"I am."

"Am I going to have a problem with you?"

"No sir. Gentlemen, please sit down."

Only the General sat, but not in the chair across from the desk. He moved around, slid some papers out of the way and parked his butt on the end of the desk, towering over Don. One of the armed soldiers moved in behind Don.

The general laid out the rules, and what was expected of Don's men. Those police officers that did not "defect", in the words of the General, can remain on the job. But because of the loss of so many, they were to work twelve hour shifts to keep the street safe. They were to surrender all guns; no one was to carry any kind of weapon. Martial law now existed in the Vancouver area; the police were only there to help maintain that law. He informed Don of the curfew, indicating it would not be tolerated to disobey that, or any order. Those who disobeyed, the General said, "Would be dealt with… *swiftly*." Emphasizing that last word.

He asked Don what happened to the rest of his men.

Don spilled the beans. He told the General a number of his men who had left, including his deputy. He informed the General about the Colonel who displaced him.

"So that is who I'm up against," the General said turning and looking out the window. "You see that smoke in the distance there?" The General got up and walked to the glass. "That's your Colonel's handy work. It slowed us down a little, but it will not stop us."

Returning his butt on Don's desk, he asked about where they were heading, and what their arms complement was. Don wasn't sure of either. The General let that go, for the time being.

The General was very clear; he would not tolerate anyone who didn't play by the new rules. He also expected Don to let him know directly of anyone who didn't. He could reach by calling the Mayor's office. He got off the desk, and moved back around the front and sat in the chair. He asked if Don had any questions, which he did.

"Where's Premier, the Mayor and City Council?" Don asked.

"They are all safe. You need not concern yourself about them. They have given me excellent cooperation. Since they are no longer in charge, they won't be coming back to work," the General said.

"I'd like to go home and see my wife."

"No, but I will have your wife brought here. You are to live here, at this Headquarters. I am going to keep you, how do you say it? On a short leash? Yes, that's it."

The General left, along with the entourage. Don turned his seat around to face the window. He was shaking, and had pissed his pants.

Chapter 4

Vedder Canal

The GunsArntEvil web-group rallied at the baseball diamond and soccer field just south of the railway line in Chilliwack. Lots of people were there, mostly police from various locations, and many were RCMP from the local detachment in Chilliwack. Canadian Forces personnel rallied in the parking lot next door where Staines had gathered them.

Ray and Bonnie were the last to show up in the final train from Surrey. He saw many familiar faces from his precision shooting group. He was pleased many of them made it. They numbered thirty-three, less than half the numbers who had attended some of their events in the past. They were armed with their high-powered large scoped precision rifles in a wide array of types. Some were hardly military in appearance with chromed barrels and red or blue stocks. Some had wrapped their rifles in green cloth.

Ray asked if anyone had seen his friend, Erik Stein. Ray and Erik were often paired up at shooting events. They were close in age, older than most in the little clique, and had formed a good bond over the years. Someone said he didn't get out. "The Chinese will have their hands full with him," Ray said to Bonnie. But he also feared for his friend's safety.

Another civilian assembly, of about one hundred from the Service Rifle group, were all together chatting and preparing. They were all decked out in camouflaged clothes with webbing gear, loaded with magazines, and pistols in leg holsters. Each had some kind of carbine rifle, mostly AR15s, but there were some M14s, a few Cz858 or Vz858s and even fewer Swiss Arms SG751. One had a Tavor.

Most of them were still getting the pinning out of their magazines to allow for full capacity; others were cleaning their rifles or pistols. The age range was as diverse as the firearms, from twenty all the way to sixty. There were even ten women in the group, all decked out and at the ready like their male counterparts. Their former range officer, a retired Canadian

Forces Warrant Officer with experience in Afghanistan, assumed the role of leader for the time being. He was the go-between between them and the military.

Constable John Revoy, who had called all his GunsArntEvil companions, rallied with the cops but made several trips to his civilian friends taking an inventory of who had what.

Constable Lynda Swift was there too, with her partner Ken Moore. Lynda was telling some of the others of their ordeal. And how Archie had taken them both back to Hall 14, and gave them his vehicle to get out of the city. And since Archie's place was near one of the bridges, he told the two cops to get his wife out, and to take whatever firearms Archie had with them. Archie was an avid hunter, though all he had were a few sport rifles. Lynda took his shotgun while Ken took his Remington 700. The two had successfully got Archie's wife on a train, which was well on its way east. Lynda worried about what was going to happen to Archie and his crew because they decided to not abandon the people of Vancouver.

The third group of civilians were the collectors, mostly of vintage firearms. A couple hundred of them were on the field with their Lee Enfields, Garands, Mosin Nagants and K98 Mausers. Some even had automatic World War II machine guns, legal as long as one had the proper licence, which was meaningless in the current situation. One of the old timers had a working MG42, recalibrated in 7.62mm. He had ten belts of 200 rounds each for it.

Another old-timer from town showed up with five unopened spam cans of 303Brit ammo from WWII . They still had all of the labelling on them, stamped 1944. They each contained 300 rounds of ammo on stripper clips, in bandoliers. He cried as the cans were opened and the ammo distributed. "From one war to another," he said.

Colonel Gary Hawker couldn't rely much on that group because they weren't frequent shooters, and most of them were of late retirement age. But they were eager to help where they could.

The last, and largest, group of armed civilians were hunters, those who didn't participate in shooting sports, but hunted only a few times a year. All they carried were their hunting rifles, some just had shotguns. Hawker was unsure how much they could help with so little shooting experience. Many were eager to do their part, something.

Hawker had set a meeting of all senior people at the AFC Chilliwack base for 3:00 p.m. The mayors from all the local towns and cities east of the Fraser, and some from east of Vancouver that made it across the river at Mission, attended including Captain Staines, and Deputy Chief Collin Edwards.

Staines's men, coming by M35 trucks, had not yet arrived, almost an hour overdue.

Andrew Jaworski, Mayor of Port Coquitlam, was there. He was a black man with a Polish name. When asked, he would say his grandmother was a coloured English woman serving as a nurse in London during the Blitz, who married a Polish RAF pilot who was shot down and under her care. After the war they came to Canada and their only child, his father, married a black woman from Quebec.

Andrew was explaining to the others his day's events. He had gotten a call from Al Knight, the Mayor of Surrey, along with the other mayors, and had organized some evacuations using police and city bus workers to wake people up. He organized a number of trainloads of refugees at the CPR yard in town—including using five of the double-decker commuter trains they could get running from Mission. They were still sending trains out while the fighting at the Pattullo Bridge was going on. Train crews ran out of locomotives, however, so a large mass of people were left having to get over the railway bridge and the Pitt Bridge on foot.

Those people also had to navigate the mass of vehicles used as a barricade. Many did not make it when two APCs full of Chinese soldiers showed up and a small short firefight with police and civilians took place on the bridge. They won that battle, in no small part because of the civilians with scoped hunting rifles, killing all the Chinese and essentially captured the APCs. Not being able to take the vehicles across the river, they just burned them, later erupting in explosions as the cannon ammo let loose.

CPR crews also left a long train on their bridge, though some of the Chinese attempted to cross. They were easily cut down with sniper fire, mostly by civilians.

Hawker had to cut the conversations off to get down to business. The meeting was about options. The mayors all wanted to evacuate everyone they could to Alberta. The problem was there weren't enough locomotives to move all the cars available to them. There just wasn't enough capacity to move everyone out.

It was decided that tractor-trailers would be used to move as many people out as possible in a huge convoy east. However, that was limited too due to lack of fuel. Whatever vehicles they could utilize started immediately to evacuate women and children first. Older men and younger men not married volunteered to stay behind. So too did a number of women, mostly older.

By 5:00 p.m., most of the town and surrounding area was well underway to being evacuated. Staines's crew showed up part way through the retreat. They brought bad news with them. Everyone was in serious trouble. Captain Trevor "Hammerhead" Hanskull informed Staines that they stopped at the Aldergrove facilities to check it out as they were going right past it anyway. He said they dispatched about a dozen Chinese who had wrecked the facilities and killed all the employees.

But that wasn't their problem. On the way there, Hammerhead decided to send a Humvee to the border crossing at Sumas. If the Chinese had moved out of Bellingham, assuming they got transportation, that's where they would be seen moving north.

They were right. The Humvee was only fifteen minutes behind them balls to the walls to get back as they had indeed sighted the enemy. They radioed ahead that the enemy were crossing the border in strength, mostly using commandeered busses from Bellingham. The worst was they would be in Chilliwack in some thirty minutes.

Hawker was stunned at the news. So was everyone else as chatter erupted.

"OK, listen up people, pipe down!" he yelled above the commotion. "We still have people trying to get out of town. We're going to have to hold the Chinese off as long as we can to evacuate as many people as possible." He turned to the senior CNR employee. "You keep one train back, for our escape, you got that?"

"Yes sir, I'll leave our most experienced engineer for you." he replied and left the building.

"Collin," Hawker said. "Can I count on you to do the back door logistics? We need that hospital running, there's going to be casualties. We're also going to need food delivered."

"I'm on it," Collin said. "There's a number of EMS around here with their ambulances. I'll keep them nearby."

"Outstanding. Now," Hawker continued. "We need a defensive position somewhere. I'm open to suggestions."

Sergeant Williams piped up. "Way ahead of you, sir. I've already scouted for that possibility. Come and look at the map."

Hawker, Staines, Collin and Williams went over to a table where a map of the area was laid out. Williams pointed to the Vedder Canal. "Look here, there's only two road bridges, the highway here, and the road we're on here. The only other place is the two rail bridges, the CN bridge here up by the Fraser and this bridge south of us here."

"Outstanding, perfect bottleneck. How deep is the canal?" Hawker said.

Chilliwack's Mayor, Anne Reeves, overheard and said, "This time of year with mountain snows melting, the canal water is at the top of the sidewall dikes. It'll be near impossible to ford the canal. The only place wide and shallow is the river bend at the south here. People can wade there, it's chest deep at most."

"That seems a long line to defend but I see no choice," Hawker said. "This is where we make our stand. Sergeant, do you have a count of how many shooters we can get?"

"It's four kilometres from end to end, but we only have to concentrate at the four bridges. Theoretically not too many guns."

"Right. If we only had some demolition," Hawker said.

"We do," Staines said. "We have some C4, not much, but maybe enough to take out those two railway bridges. We really shouldn't leave them intact for the Commies."

"Get it done, Captain. So, Sergeant, how many shooters do we have?"

"Let's see, sir, we have two hundred and fifty of Captain Staines's men, about two hundred police officers, one hundred reg-forces from here, and over five hundred armed civilians with various weapons."

"And some are damn good shots," Hawker said.

"Ah, yes, sir for sure, sir. Maybe better than our own guys."

"What about weapons? We should have enough in that boxcar?"

"Oh, sorry, sir. That train wasn't here when we arrived; it's likely halfway to Calgary by now."

"Fuck," Hawker said frustrated.

"Every civilian shooter has a weapon."

"What about ammo?" Hawker asked.

"The bin rat had lots of that, stockpiled during the rioting in case it was needed. There's a quarter million rounds, seven-six-two, five-five-six and nine mill."

"But no boats."

"Sorry, sir, no armoured vehicles."

"Get it to the front, Sergeant. You organize the defence. Get it done. See if you can muster up some more people too. You'll need as many beebee-stackers as shooters."

"Roger that." The Sergeant left.

Staines added, "That's maybe a thousand shooters we have, but how many are we looking at coming at us? Thousands were coming off the ship at Bellingham."

"How many more were coming on your six?" Hawker said.

"Likely thousands, tens of thousands. But they'll have to keep some behind. They can't have them all come here. There won't be enough transportation for them for one. So, we can take an educated guess," Staines said. "Hammerhead said the Humvee crews saw twenty to thirty busses. So, at thirty soldiers per bus, times thirty busses, is…"

"Nine hundred," Hawker said.

"…right, nine hundred, maybe a grand. So we have them outnumbered."

"Barely."

"And we have the advantage of both surprise and defensive position," Staines said with a smile.

"Theoretically, yes."

"And, we have field grade weather working in our favour."

"At least one thing on our side. Captain, after you blow those bridges, I want you to take control of the defence at the highway bridge here. I'm going to the bridge down the road here."

"Affirm on that," Staines said as he started to leave.

"Oh, Captain."

"Yes, sir."

"We can't afford to let them get through. A lot of people's lives are at stake here."

"Fully understand. They won't get through me, sir." He left.

Not long after Sergeant Williams had left that he returned in an unhappy mood. "Colonel, we have a problem, sir. A fight broke out between the civvies."

"A fight?"

"Well, sir, more of a shoving and shouting match."

"What ever the problem is, get it solved, Sergeant."

"I tried, sir, so did some of the cops there. They broke it up. But, there are a group of civvies who refuse to be with some of the others. They want to speak to you."

"God fucking damnit. I don't have time for this. Where are they?"

"Down at the parking lot, sir."

Hawker, with Williams, faced a group of about forty angry civilians.

"We don't want to be associated with those Chuck Norris wannabes," one said pointing to the civilians in military gear. The comment was joined with cheers and jeers from their group, along with boos from the Service Rifle group who were the brunt of the objection.

"I don't care about your rivalry. I need you to work together…"

"Never!" "You got guys there with holstered pistols with no qualifications." "They are too – too, inept, lax in their safety!" Amongst other objections screamed out.

Hawker let them speak for a few seconds. Then cut them off. "Enough! I can assign you gentlemen to different and separate duties."

"Not good enough," one said who appeared to be the ringleader. "We heard you want to set up a defensive position to stop the Chinese. We didn't sign up for that."

"You didn't sign up for anything. You are free to leave," Sergeant Williams said.

"In what?" the man said. "All the vehicles are gone. We're trapped. We're not murderers, not like *them* over there."

Boos followed from the Service Rifle group.

"There's no distinction today," Hawker said. "I'd hope that all of you would have some patriotic duty to protect your country, your families…"

"Our families are out east by now!" one yelled.

"Mine are still in Vancouver!"

There was much grumbling which Hawker had to stop. "And my family is on Vancouver Island!" he said firmly.

The crowd went quiet. Hawker thought for a bit then said, "I'm not going to force anyone to do anything they deem against their personal views. I'll leave it up to you to make up your minds. But if you're not going to be part of the solution, then I'll demand that you not be part of the problem. Those of you who do not want to help with the defences are to leave this area and find somewhere else. I will ask the cops here to make sure you do that. We're done here."

Hawker left, with some dozen cops escorting most of the crowd out of the parking lot.

Keith Wilson Road went due west out of town, then made a forty-five degree left turn over the canal. The bridge was steel spans with concrete pillars. It was some two hundred meters end to end, and some fifteen meters above the canal. After the bridge the road turned another forty-five degrees left, then straight about a kilometre into a small village where the road made a tee junction. With the land so flat, all farm country, and few trees, they had a perfect long view of the roads leading to the bridges. There were few buildings, mostly farms, scattered on both sides of the canal.

A dirt lane paralleled both sides of the canal. It meant a nice embankment for their side to fire from and it also meant exposure on the other side.

The Trans-Canada Highway, at the north end of the canal, was a four-lane freeway. It came from the west to the canal at a forty-five degree angle, turned right to go over the bridge. The bridge was two spans of two hundred meters long, and twenty meters above the water.

South of the highway, on their side, was a golf course. This offered a clear unobstructed view for two kilometres up the highway. The sand pits closest to the canal would make good machine gun positions. The only structures there were the golf club buildings, which had a five hundred meter clear line of fire including down the highway bridge. Staines took that as his command post.

On the north side of the highway's turn, west of the canal, was a wooded hill. Too much cover for Staines's liking, so he set up the MG42 and a few M240's in the farmhouse on the north side of the highway, which overlooked the canal.

Hawker made his way to the Wilson Bridge to oversee the preparations. Sergeant Williams had done a lot in the short time, and short time is all they had. Less than fifteen minutes remained when the enemy could show up.

Williams gave Hawker an overview of their defensive positions, pointing to each of them as he named them off from north to south.

"We have about a thousand shooters, so I set up sixteen squads with sixty each. Each squad has fifteen Nationals, five or six regs, a dozen militia, fifteen or sixteen cops and twenty-five civvies. The best-equipped shooters are first on the line.

"The units are from the golf course south: Golf Charley One through Four, then on their left flank along the canal is Hotel One through Three. Then here at this bridge we have on the right Whiskey Two, and on the left Whiskey Three. Whiskey One a bit further over there. Between them and the river bend is Kilo One through Three along the canal, and finally at the bend Romeo Bravo One through Three.

"Now those guys may have to cross the river because there's too much underbrush on the far side obscuring the road there. Lieutenant Hammerhead is in charge."

"That's fine, move them," Hawker agreed. "Where have you stationed our snipes?"

"Four groups along the canal. Up by the highway is more difficult because of the golf course, so I have them interspersed with Hotel and Kilo squads. Thirty-three snipes.

"We also have M60s, six of them, which I deployed two at each Romeo, Kilo, and Golf. M240 crews, and some of our C9 guys, about a dozen, we have stationed at a number of places around the two bridges. We have about a dozen LAWS rockets, split evenly between the two bridges. I suspect we'll hit the hostiles with those first."

"That's affirm," Hawker said.

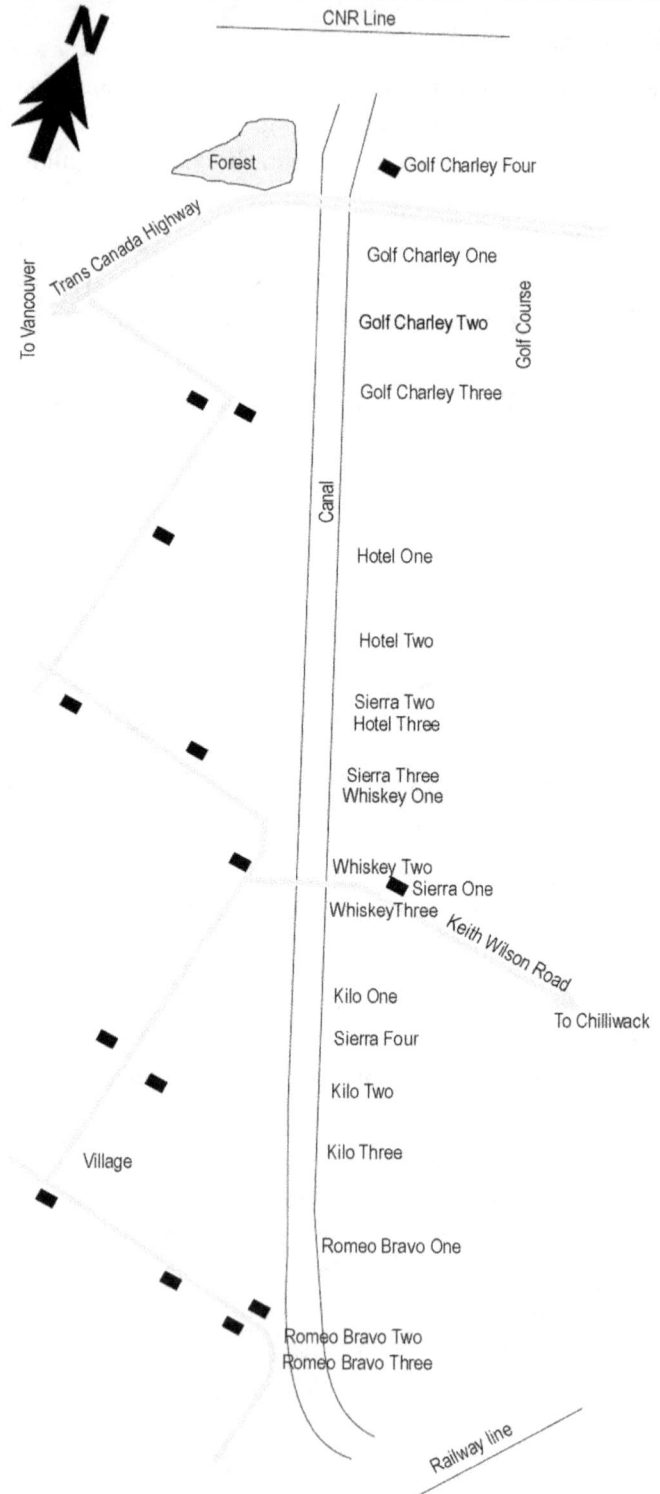

"Oh, and…" Williams started to laugh. "Get this, Captain Staines put an MG42 in the house at the top end of the canal overlooking the forest."

"A what? Who the fuck had an MG42?" Hawker said chuckling.

"Some old guy had it. He said it's time it got used to help our side for a change. It's seven-six-two. It has about ten belts of two hundred rounds each. He said it was hidden in his basement."

Hawker just shook his head in disbelief. "So an illegal. Well, that'll sure cut up the Chinese PDQ."

"Oh, that it will, sir," Williams said. "There's a few others with antique full autos; a Bren, but he doesn't have much ammo for it, a couple of Thompsons, a few Stens, an MP40, from that same old guy. Get this, he even has an Stg44, but rather useless with out any ammo. I'm hoping our uninvited guests won't get close enough to use any of those weapons."

"Amen to that," Hawker said.

"I had the Humvee's ma deuce taken off and deployed on a tripod at the highway bridge, nice line of fire. That about sums it up, sir. Chief Edwards has a number of EMS deployed well back at both locations. So, I think we're as ready as we can be."

"Outstanding job, Sergeant, well done," Hawker said.

"Thank you, sir. Would not have been able to do it without a lot of help."

"Morale is high?"

"Oh, yeah. The civvies are nervous, but even the cops are ready for some payback, sir."

"Outstanding," Hawker said patting Williams on the back.

Staines radioed all was ready. Hammerhead radioed all was ready.

The only problem area Hawker could see was the line of farm buildings on the far side between the two bridges. They would make good cover for the enemy. Hawker assigned two rifle squads from Hotel Two and Three to keep a close eye on those buildings and keep him informed of any movement.

One thing Hawker had forgotten was to check if anyone was still in homes down range. It was too late for that.

Hawker asked Williams where Ray was set up.

"He's Sierra One, up in that farm house there behind us," Williams said.

Ray had picked the best spot of all. A farmhouse, looking right down the bridge. Ray was in a small boy's bedroom that had a clear view over the canal and surrounding farmland. The room had posters of trains, of all kinds, on the walls. Toy trains were on the dresser, and under the bed was a small set up of Thomas The Tank trains. From the second floor bedroom window he had a clear line of fire in all directions. Bonnie was there as his sighter and loader.

When Hawker got there, the bed had been removed, the dresser cleared and put in lengthwise to the window but back several feet. Ray's Savage was prepped on the dresser, with the end of the barrel well inside the room. The sheer drapes were closed.

Bonnie was in the adjacent room, decorated for a young girl, as Ray's spotter. The problem was there wasn't enough room for the two of them at one window, and Ray needed instant communication with Bonnie, so he kicked in the wallboard between the two rooms to make an opening so they could see each other as well as walk through. Bonnie had a dresser parallel to Ray's on the opposite side of the opening. She had Ray's spotter scope on a tripod, as well as boxes of ammo at the ready.

Hawker brought him 500 rounds, from the local gun store in Chilliwack., of 338 Lupo ammo, factory made not custom loaded, but that gave Ray nearly 800 rounds for his Savage to feed from.

"Nice spot you have here," Hawker said. "How far do you recon?"

"It's four hundred meters to the end of the bridge, give or take. Along the road I can see to the village, which is shy of two kilometres. I'll have to wait for them to get to those trees there at that first farmhouse, that's eight hundred meters.

"This high up is perfect, no heat distortion from the ground, especially on a sunny day like this. I have a clear view."

"Outstanding. I see you have ear protection," Hawker said.

"338 ammo fired through a muzzle break, in a small confinement, oh yeah. Remember how loud it was on that roof?"

"Deafening."

"So imagine in this closed small room."

"Roger that, I see your point." Hawker started to leave turning to

Bonnie. "Did you take the pinning out of your CZ mags?"

"Yes," Bonnie said. "All ten are full to thirty rounds each. I hope I don't have to use it though."

"Amen to that," Hawker said. "Ray, I may give you the first shot. If you think I haven't and shooting starts…"

"Not a problem, Colonel."

"You're sure you can do this, right? It's going to get messy. Real messy."

"I'm as ready as I can be."

The radio cracked and hissed as Hawker was about to go down the stairs. "Kilo Three, Uniform coming on the road, repeat Uniform on road heading this way."

Hawker went back into the room with Ray and looked through the binoculars towards the village. Ray sighted with his Savage.

Some of the U.S. soldiers got on the end of the bridge with a couple of LAWS rockets on the ready.

"It's a school bus," Ray said. Through the much higher magnification on his Savage he could make out a woman driver and children in the back. "It's got kids in it."

"Stand down! Stand Down!" Hawker yelled into the radio. "Friendlies! Let them pass the bridge, and get them out of town, fast."

Soon as the bus cleared the bridge, the radio kicked in again "Command, this is Romeo Bravo One, we see six, maybe seven Tango's heading to the village, over."

The three Romeo Bravo crews at the river bend south of the bridge could see down the far road, more than several kilometres, before it turned north towards the bridge.

"Here they come, I'm heading to my command post. Good hunting, Ray. Both of you. Give'em hell."

"You bet," Bonnie said. Ray gave a thumbs-up.

Hawker 's command was a farmhouse on Blackburn Road, with a view of the killing zone.

On his way to his command post, along with Williams, they heard an explosion to the south. "The rail bridge," Williams said.

"And the other…" An explosion to the north cut Hawker off.

"You were saying, sir?" Williams laughed.

The radio clicked as they got in the door. "Command, this is Golf Charley Three, eyes on ten, maybe more Dink Tango's on the highway. Range three klicks, over."

"Command, Romeo Bravo One, seven Tango's turning onto road, in village, over."

"Command, Hotel One, eyes on Tango's, range two klicks, over."

"Command to all units, hold fire until convoy is on bridge, over," Hawker said.

"Romeo Bravo One, seven Tango's rounded turn, five more on the road behind them, over."

"Kilo Two, Tango's now one klick, *Ai-ee-yah* we are about to engage, over."

"Command to all units, wait until the first vehicle reaches within one hundred meters of the bridge. Whiskey One, you take out lead vehicle with LAWS, over."

"Whisky One, copy that."

"Command to Highway Control, over," Hawker said into the mic.

"Highway Command, go."

"Captain, hit them on the bridge, over."

"Roger that. Out."

The wait was painful. It seemed forever to Ray for the first vehicle to make the right turn to the bridge. His heart was racing the whole time. One bus headed right for him as he sighted the crosshairs on the driver. The bus started to cross the river when his view through the scope went all yellow. He backed away from the rifle as the concussion from the explosion blew the drapes back. The bus went up in a ball of flames.

The radio was a chatter of calls, "Whiskey Two, engaging hostiles. They're piling up at the doorways, *hooweeyah*!", "Kilo Three, get the last vehicles too." "Tracers setting vehicles on fire, burn you Dink suckas!"

Machine gun fire from their side, two M60s and five C9s, opened up spraying the buses. It was perfect, the front and side doors, the exits from the busses, were on their side. Bodies dropped, or exploded in droves as fire crews targeted the doors. Red appeared on the windows and walls around both exits. The enemy kicked out windows and started to fire towards them. However, at some 500 meters it was a tad far for the medium sized 7.62 ammo the Chinese were using. They weren't hitting anything but the ground or the water in the canal.

The third bus back from the bridge pulled over to pass the wrecks in an attempt to get across the bridge. "Kilo One to Whiskey Two, bus coming onto bridge, LAWS them, over."

"Whiskey Two, wilco."

One of the American National Guards corporals crept up to the left end of the bridge with a LAWS rocket. He waited for the bus to get past the first burning wreck then fired. The rocket exploded on the left side of the bus over the wheel making it jump into the air and swerve to its left. It then tipped over onto its right side and screeched down the road roof first until it got wedged between the sides of the bridge and stopped.

Flames started in the engine area. Some Chinese tried to get out of windows but were cut down before any could escape, bodies draped over the window frames. The same Corporal fired another rocket at the centre of the roof of the bus, which exploded tearing the bus in two, flying some bodies in the air, which splashed into the canal. More of the bus quickly turned into flames with a thick black smoke cloud rolling above the vehicle.

Ray finally had some targets. At twenty-four power and eight hundred meters, a person is quite clear, as if only forty meters away. Ray could see facial features, it was almost too personal. He picked one in a window of a bus, anyone would do. His heart was still racing, his palms were sweating and itchy. His rifle's composite stock felt tacky to the touch. He rubbed his palms on his shirt, and took a deep breath and let it out. He sighted again on the target. He was about to squeeze off a round when the body disappeared with holes showed up under the window.

There was another target at the next window. That's what he had to call them, targets, to get around what he was doing. He took a deep breath, let it out, and held it. He put a bit of pressure on the trigger and his Savage fired. The recoil took the rifle out of view, so he wasn't sure if it hit. Except for when Bonnie said, "Oh, my God." and backed up from the spotter scope. "That was gross. His head exploded. I don't know if I can do this."

Ray went over to Bonnie, "You don't. I'll find my own targets, but I have to do this, people are expecting me to do my job. You just look for anyone trying to escape so I can take them out. Do you think you can do that?"

She looked at him with tears welling in her eyes.

"Baby, can you do this my love?"

She nodded her head.

"Ok, take your time," Ray said. He hugged her.

He went back to scoping targets. "Oh, and remember to keep my magazines loaded."

Of the seven buses on the road, only the last two weren't burning. Tracer rounds had started the upholstery and diesel fuel on fire. The first five busses were fully involved in fire within a few minutes of the start of the firefight. Soldiers were bailing out also in flames. Some of them were shot down, others were left to burn alive.

Through his scope Ray could see one running from the back of a bus while on fire. Flames ran up his back as his hands waved about trying to get the fire out, but he fell. Ray watched. He could not take his scope off the wriggling burning body. He finally realized what he was seeing and fired a shot.

The last two busses tried to back up, but the M60 crew at Romeo Bravo One, at the top end of the curve in the river, fired at them at 1000 meters.

The five busses still in the village continued straight on the road once the firefight started. That road, called the No. 3 Road, came down through the village to the river bend, then turned to the south away from the canal.

At the bend, trees and scrub brush lined both sides of the river. Romeo Bravo Two and Three crews could not fire across the river, as their line of sight was blocked. Most of them waded across the shallow parts and hid themselves in that bush. They had a close clear line of fire right down the road. The rest of the squad, all civilians, stayed back to guard the river.

They waited for the busses to get to about the two hundred meter mark when Hammerhead ordered them to open fire directly into the front of the vehicles with their M60 and three M240s. It was like shooting fish in a barrel. A couple dozen of the enemy tried to make a dash to the house and farm buildings to the left. However, crews with M4s, C8s and a few civilian shooters with M14s cut most of them down. A few of the enemy made it to the house and barn, especially those from the last bus. About twenty of the foe used the smoke from the busses as cover as they ran for the barn and house on the right.

Another dozen went into the ditch and crawled their way up to another house on the north side of the road.

The sixty or more Chinese enemy who escaped the flames and bullets through the busses outnumbered a total of fifty friendly soldiers, ten of Hammerhead's National Guard, plus a dozen cops, the rest civilian shooters.

One of the cops was John Revoy, the cop who had called his shooting friends to escape from Vancouver. John was matched up with five of his friends who were all excellent shooters, and quite apt at using their own semi-auto carbines and battle rifles. Two of them, including John, had Chinese made M14's, three had AR15s, and one had a Vz58. John's group was assigned to help an M60 crew.

Their adversaries occupied the two homes on either side of the road. They opened fire, including with RPGs, from windows on that M60 crew killing three Americans and two civilians. John was beside the men who were killed. The concussion from the rockets threw him back away from the blast, stunning him for a few seconds.

Hammerhead ordered two people to take control of the machine gun, which John did by crawling back to the weapon. He concentrated fire on the two homes.

"Just fire through the walls," Hammerhead yelled.

The two of them with M14s, which had close quarters scopes on their rifles, sniped any heads that peered out of windows. The M240 crews, along with the rest of the cops and civilians, covered the entrances in case some of the enemy tried to bail, which some did and were cut down.

A few Chinese tried to throw grenades but the distance was just too far to the tree line. They exploded harmlessly in front of John's crew.

At the same time on the Trans-Canada Highway Bridge, Captain Staines waited for the convoy, all school buses, to get onto the two spans. Five on the left, and six on the right by the time they got half way across. It was the perfect confinement channels.

Staines ordered the two LAWS crews, one for each span, to fire. The crews got up out of the ditch, calmly walked to the middle of the road at the start of the bridge, kneeled with their rocket tubes on their shoulders and fired.

The right rocket hit the front of the bus in a huge explosion driving the engine into the asphalt. The bus slowly stopped against the left side of the lane. On the left span, the rocket went through the passenger's side window and exploded in the back of the bus near the wheel area. It careened to its right through the bridge walls, leapt into the air and landed upside down in the canal with the back of the bus bursting into flames. It slowly sank disappearing in a hiss of steam.

The two M60 crews along with a pair of M240 shooters, and a dozen small arms riflemen got onto each of the lanes at the entrance of the bridges. They laid on the road, and opened fire. Behind them M16 crews with grenade launchers lobbed some shells onto the busses blowing roof shards into the air.

The 50 cal machine gun opened fire at the busses still on the road that had not made it onto the bridge. One of the busses there turned off the road, drove down the embankment towards the canal, and plunged into the water. Chinese soldiers poured out of the back of that bus, but fire crews of Golf Charley Two rained lead onto them.

On the bridge spans the enemy tried to bail from the last busses, out the back doors, but the hail of fire was too much, and they had nowhere to hide on the bridge. Some tried to fire back, but none of their bullets found a target, snapping over the heads of Golf Charley One.

One of the busses in the westbound lane drove off the road into the forest on the north of the highway coming to a stop when it slammed into a tree.

One bus at the very back in the eastbound lane tried to back up, but Golf Charley Two's C9 crews fired on it. The bus swerved around and lost balance landing on its side screeching to a stop. Chinese tried to escape through the top windows. Fire crews targeted them. Some did manage to get away.

Another bus managed to back around that carnage, even running over their own men, until it got out of range where it stopped and their cargo exited. Some thirty enemy headed down No. 1 Road towards the canal, running to a number of homes and farm buildings.

At the forest, Chinese soldiers made it to the bank of the canal and attempted to wade across. The MG42 and two M240 crews of Golf

Charley Four opened up. Spikes of water filled the far bank, which turned red. Spray and chunks of bodies flung into the air splashing down stream. All, except a few who managed to get back into the forest, were nothing but body parts floating towards the Fraser when the firing stopped. A light red mist hung over the far bank.

One of the busses that the 50 cal targeted exploded into a huge fireball spewing gasoline all over the asphalt, which also caught fire producing a thick black column of smoke.

Crews targeted the fuel tank of the flipped bus until it too exploded into a ball of fire as the burning gasoline overran those trying to escape the flames.

Meanwhile, Ray was still targeting any head or body part he could see. Bonnie wasn't getting used to the gruesome scene in her spotting scope. She was using a crayon to mark on the wall every kill Ray was getting. He was up to twenty-five.

Ray knew that AK type assault rifles couldn't fire accurately beyond five hundred meters, so they were well beyond range. Besides, he figured the enemy had no clue where his shots were coming from. He was one of thirty-three snipers taking a toll up and down the canal. Every one of them was getting high scores picking off targets other fire crews couldn't see.

Bonnie noticed a few of the enemy had managed to make it to the farm buildings on the right of the bridge. Some of the shooters of Hotel Three and Whiskey One had already started to engage them, but it was difficult. So Ray diverted his attention to those buildings.

He scanned the three barns and house side-to-side looking for a target. There was one. He was leaning out of one of the doors on a barn. He would come out, shoot, then go back. Ray counted the seconds. One, two, three, he would appear, fire, then dart back. One, two, three, he came out again, fired and disappeared. One, two, Ray fired.

Repositioning his scope at the location he could see the body flopped dead at the door. "Whoa, now that was a lucky shot," he said.

Ray picked off three more which fire crews would not have been able to see without high-powered scopes.

Shooting started to quiet down as the buses were now fully involved in flame. Black smoke towering up to the blue sky, then anviled about a half a kilometre up where it took a ninety degree turn east and tracked above them.

Firefights could still be heard to the north on the highway bridge, where larger columns of smoke rose into the sky straight up and also bent ninety degrees making a long tail east.

Staines radioed Hawker that they had engaged some dozen bus loads and had success in dispatching the enemy. Shooting was quieting down. Squads were reporting in that they had stopped engagement, all except Romeo Bravo Two and Three.

Hawker came out of his command post with Williams to check things out. Shooting could still be heard in the distance south.

"Command to Romeo Bravo Three sit rep, over," Hawker said into the radio but there was no reply.

Things were far from over at the river bend. The best they could do was to hold the enemy in the homes. Hammerhead heard the radio. "Romeo Bravo Two come in, this is Command, over."

He replied back, "Romeo Bravo Two, we're still engaging. Hostiles have occupied two houses, over."

One of the National Guardsmen crawled up to Hammerhead through the bushes. "We could throw a phosphorus grenade into each home and burn them out."

The radio came back on. "Command to Romeo Bravo One, move in and help, over."

"Roger that."

Hammerhead thought about it. "You'd have to get right up to a window."

"Copy that. Give us cover fire. Give me a lane."

"We have no choice. Get ready."

After a few minutes to get repositioned, two National Guardsmen were ready to dash to the homes, one each. "Suppressing fire! Suppressing Fire!" Hammerhead yelled.

It was a deafening sound of automatic and single fire aimed at both houses. The two National Guardsmen ran up to the homes, one each, with the shooters giving them a narrow corridor. Bullets couldn't have passed them more than a meter or two on each side.

They reached the homes at about the same time. One dove under a blown out window and lobbed in a grenade, it exploded in a bright white flash. The other soldier stood beside the open widow and threw in his grenade, with another white flash. Both dashed the two hundred meters into the woods. It wasn't long before both houses were burning, first with smoke billowing out windows, then flames. Chinese tried to get out, but were gunned down. John took two out with his M14 as they tried to run.

By the time Romeo Bravo One showed up the houses were fully involved. Hammerhead radioed in "Romeo Bravo Two, we have secured the buildings, hostiles down."

Hawker stood at the edge of the bridge with Williams. "Roger that. Outstanding job, Two," he said as Captain Staines showed up in a golf cart.

"Sir, there'll be many we missed, especially from those two busses way back there. That's at least sixty hostiles on the loose," he said.

"Hotel Two said they saw some of them go into those farm buildings," Williams said.

"They're probably watching us right now," Staines said. "We aren't going to be able to get across the canal to flush them out."

"Roger that," Hawker said. "Sergeant, get down to the river bend and get those crews back from the other side. Captain, do you have any claymores?"

"Absolutely, about a dozen or so."

"Let's get them lined up along the river bank down at the bend," Hawker said.

"I'll see to it personally," Staines said and started to leave.

"Ok, Williams, stay here. Captain, do that and get those crews back on our side."

Staines gave a thumbs-up as he headed south in the cart.

"Sergeant, instead let's get everyone to the train and get out of here. We've bought the time we need."

"What of the remaining hostiles? What if they take the offensive?" Williams said.

"They won't attack. We'll retreat slowly. There's less than thirty of light left, so let's get to it."

"Roger that," Williams said and left.

Hawker stood at the bank of the canal looking around at the carnage he caused. Smoke billowed into the air and settled over Chilliwack. Bodies were all over the far side, with wreckage burning on the bridges. And all in just under an hour from start to finish. At least the mess made it difficult to cross the bridges, Hawker thought. He ordered the Whiskey teams to get whatever farm vehicles they could and load up the bridge with them, then burn the lot.

It was dusk by the time they boarded the last train. Those who volunteered to stay behind watched. Williams informed Hawker that they lost only five men, all at the fight at the river bend. There were no wounded.

Staines informed Hawker that they set up the mines, one row over the river triggered by motion detectors, and three rows in the bush on trip wires. He said on his way back he heard some of them go off.

Ray and Bonnie were walking past to get into a boxcar when Hawker asked how many he got.

"Thirty-one." Ray said with some pride on his face.

"Outstanding. You really need to put rings on your barrel, eh?" Hawker said.

Hammerhead passed by them saying, "Rough day, at least it went our way."

"Gawdamnit, this is just the beginning," Hawker said. "Now you've put a hex on the whole damn thing."

CHAPTER 5

It has to be done

Erik Stein spent several hours in his lab after Carl left, marking papers and thinking. His thoughts were directing him in one direction and one direction only. There was no way they could form a French-like resistance movement. The French Resistance in WWII was largely supported from England. With British Columbia being on the coast there was no close-by support for them there. They were completely alone with the mountains cutting them off on one side and the ocean on the other – completely cut off from the rest of the world. Whatever they did next to resist the occupation, they would have to be very creative and resourceful. Above all, Erik had to figure out how he would even organize an effective resistance. Who could he trust? People like Nugent would be a serious problem.

Nugents are always a problem in war. Nothing pissed Erik off more than people who would give up their principles to save their own butts. Nugent was just one of many people in the past, and now present, who would sell themselves out to the enemy. Human history is full of such people. Not this time, Erik thought. This time is going to be different. All occupations throughout history have eventually failed, he thought to himself. It was just a matter of time.

Erik knew he needed to make the first move, and soon. Nugent had to be killed. Likely the first of many to come.

He didn't know where Nugent lived, but knew it couldn't be far because he walked to campus every day. Erik went to the department's administration office. No one was there. The secretary hadn't shown up since the occupation started. She lived in North Vancouver, which was now cut off and no one was allowed across any bridges. So he helped himself to the personnel records. There Nugent was, and not far indeed.

Mid afternoon Erik went to the drill-core library and climbed up to get his Smith & Wesson 44 Magnum revolver. He had won a few pistol competition shoots with this gun; it was his favourite. He loaded it, and put it in the bottom of his backpack. He rode out of campus through a route he knew he would not get stopped and checked. Roadblocks had been set up at the campus entrances.

After a dinner of potatoes and cream corn from a can, he went downstairs to his shop and got his gun out. He needed a way to keep the noise from the shot down. 44 Magnums were very loud. He had already figured out how to deal with that at the lab. Before going home, he went into the men's washroom at his building and purchased a condom from the machine.

He put the condom over the end of the barrel and taped it tight with duct tape. Next, he filled a water bottle to near the top, then carefully suspended the pistol's barrel into the neck of the bottle into the water. He sealed the neck of the bottle to the barrel with silicone calking and let it sit hanging from a chemistry rack. A homemade silencer.

At midnight, he checked everything on the gun and it appeared to have worked; nothing leaked. He washed the rest of the gun down with isopropyl alcohol and a bit of acetone, including the cartridges, to remove any prints. He got his ski mask on, put on the darkest clothes he had, and headed out the back door. He had already picked the route from a city map. It was four kilometres to Nugent's home, he figured. Almost all of it he could do through the forested area that separated the city from campus. Hugging the homes he crossed the main road and into the golf course. Keeping in the trees he made his way south.

He had to wait at the road to the park entrance and campus, the same road he rode into work on, as several military vehicles were slowly driving by. It was the same ones that passed his place not an hour before he set out. Adrenaline was rushing his system, his heart was racing, and at the same time he was drenched in a cold sweat.

He waited until they disappeared into the dark on his right, and then checked left for anything else. It was quiet; only the occasional dog could be heard barking in the clear calm night. He dashed across the road into the trees beyond.

Through the woods he followed West 16th Avenue. He had to duck down a couple times as those same vehicles came back from behind him and disappeared in front. He continued along this route until he came to Imperial Drive, which was a small road through the forest heading south.

He only needed to follow this road until he cleared the soccer and track field at the corner.

Keeping to the woods he flanked the field until reaching Camosun Street. More dogs started to bark. Erik was getting nervous now the closer he got to Nugent's house. The dog barks worried him the most, as it might alert anyone.

As he followed that road through the woods, a rustling sound right in front scared the wits out of him. Seems he wasn't the only one scared. Three racoons scurried from the bushes and scampered across the road to the homes. He knelt there for a few minutes regaining control.

That damn patrol car came up the road from around the far corner just as he was about to progress. As it turned, the lights shone right on him. He didn't move. Movement is easily caught by the human eye, he remembered. He made himself part of the forest – stiff and unmoving. The vehicle slowly passed him by, turning to the right behind him.

He gave a great sigh of relief. His hands were trembling, but making fists several times wouldn't stop it.

He continued past the turn in the road and followed a hydro cut through the trees. Then he trekked diagonally to the forest through an open area ending up at the road Nugent's house was on.

Homes there had a service road at the back for their garages. Nugent's house was just down the lane. He scurried across the road and down the lane, keeping against the fencing. Another dog started to bark on his right. He counted the houses as he made his way down the lane, until he came to Nugent's.

It crossed his mind: was this the right house? He had to be sure. Sure enough, house numbers were on the fences at the back as well as the front. He was at the right spot. Putting surgical gloves on first, he got his weapon from his pack. None of the water got out of the bottle. The condom was doing its job. He looked at his watch: almost 2:00 a.m.

The gate into Nugent's yard wasn't locked, so he crept in with the gun in his right hand. The back door to the house was locked. It was solid wood with a small window up high. He was either going to have to force it, which would wake Nugent up, or abort the attempt. If he aborted the job it was only a matter of time before Nugent ratted him out to the general, if he already hadn't. He had no choice.

He stood at the door trying to muster the courage. "Fuck it," he said and gave the door a boot. It flung open. Erik figured there was no point in going in too far into the kitchen since he didn't know the layout of the house, nor which room Nugent was in. He didn't have to wait too long. A light came on down the hall, then footsteps. Nugent turned on the hall light. Erik could see Nugent's shadow extending in front of him. His heart raced like it had never before. His hands were shaking. Then there he was.

The only words out of Nugent's mouth were "What the fu…" as Erik fired, right in the face point blank not ten feet away. Nugent went down. Blood, chunks of bone and brains were splattered on the wall behind where Nugent was standing. Erik looked down. The back half of Nugent's head was missing, with shards of flesh, brains, bone and hair thrown around it. Blood pooled in the cavity, then overflowed down the side of his head.

The silencer worked. The sound wasn't a normal blast of a large calibre pistol, but more of a muffled *whomp*. The bottle was gone from the end of the pistol and water had splashed all over, dripping on Erik from the ceiling.

Then the chill he was not expecting. A woman screamed. Nugent was not married, but was known to have some of his female students stay overnight.

It was time to leave. Erik booked it as fast as he could out the back yard and into the lane. The woman screamed even louder. Some lights were coming on in the homes next door. He made his way hugging the fence line to the road, then dashed into the forest beyond.

He buried the pistol, wrapped inside a Ziploc bag, under a fallen tree near the soccer field, and made his way home. It was nearly 5:00 a.m. by the time he got in the door. He was shaking uncontrollably. Sweating profusely, his under garments soaked like he walked in a torrential downpour. His chest was pounding so hard he thought he was going to have a heart attack. He showered to calm himself down, afterwards putting his clothes in a garbage bag. He couldn't sleep. So he sat in the dark staring at nothing, as the sun filled the sky with light.

In the morning he took a different route to the Geology building passing through the Medical buildings. There were always a number of dumpsters there. Without being seen he threw the garbage bag into a dumpster and headed to his morning class.

Mid afternoon he was in his office at the lab marking papers when that familiar voice said, "Herr Stein."

Holy fuck, he thought, he had been caught. But how? How so fast? No way anyone saw him. He didn't look up, but said, "I'm busy marking papers, General, what do you want?"

The General came in and parked himself in a chair beside Erik. An armed soldier waited at the door.

"Did you hear about Professor Nugent?"

"Hear what?"

"He's dead. Someone shot him in the head last night. Do you know anything about that, Herr Stein?"

"You're fucking with me. Nugent killed?" Erik looked up at the general.

The General nodded just a little.

"So someone finally put him out of his misery, eh?" Erik said.

"Why would someone want to do that, I wonder. Do you?"

"Oh, that's easy, General. The shit was, well, not liked by many, and not just in this department."

"Why is that I wonder?"

"Nuge was as well known womanizer. He probably fucked the wrong woman and someone put an end to it."

"No, he wasn't seeing anyone according to his friends. We feel it was politically motivated. What do you think, Herr Stein?"

"Oh, come on, General. I'd wager a bet that he got on his knees in front of you the minute you took control didn't he."

The General looked surprised at the comment.

"You can't fool me, General. We both know who he was. He was a commie sympathizer. He's probably already given you names of people. And I'm likely on the top of that list. That's why you are here isn't it – General."

"Where were you last night, Stein?"

"Home sleeping, alone. But you already know that."

"Where are your weapons, Herr Stein? We know about your guns."

"I hope they're being used against your men right now."

The General looked confused.

"Someone came to my door the night of your invasion and I gladly handed them all to them. So if you want my guns you are going to have to go find them. They're probably half way to Calgary by now, so if you hurry you might catch up to them."

"Where are the weapons you kept, Herr Stein, we want them."

"Sure, General, I kept my PAC75, FLAK88 and my Tiger Tank. I drive the Tiger around campus every Sunday, ask anyone."

"You don't like us do you ,Stein?" The General said with a glaring stare.

Erik laughed. "What a stupid question. Are you really that dumb, or are you just trying to play games with me? I'm a lot smarter than you, General, you can't fool me."

The General got up, towering over Erik and pushed him in his chair against the wall and screamed, "You are a conquered people!"

Erik stood up. The guard pointed his rifle at Erik.

"That's number two," Erik said calmly.

The General looked confused. "Two what?"

Erik put his nose right up to the General's. "That's twice you've assaulted me. I don't suffer fools very well, General Ching Clang Bang, or whatever the fuck your name is. You are pushing your fucking luck."

"I could have you shot, Professor!"

"Oh, no you won't because you're afraid."

"Afraid of what?" the General said, backing up, opening his personal space.

"Occupations never last. One day we'll be free again. Then you would be hunted down and found guilty of war crimes like all your predecessors before you. And you know that, don't you, General."

The General moved back, his anger changed to a smile. "We will get this person who killed Professor Nugent; you will see."

The General started to leave the room, and Erik returned to his desk and papers. "General, why are you here?"

The General stopped and turned back around. "To find the killer."

"No, I don't mean that," Erik said and looked up at the General. "I mean, why have you invaded our country?" Of course, Erik already knew the answer to the question. For years, almost a decade, Erik had been writing and doing some lecturing on peak oil and peak natural gas. He was fully aware of what China was doing worldwide, such as hording oil fields, buying huge swaths of land in Africa for food, and so on before the economic crash. Erik figured China played no small part in precipitating that crash by dumping hundreds of billions of American bonds on the market. But he wanted to play mind games with the General.

The General returned to the same seat. "We want your resources, but you already know that don't you, professor. Being a geologist and all. You understand our plight back home, being as smart as you claim, right, Professor Stein?"

Erik smiled at the General. "You won't succeed."

"Really, Herr Stein, do you think your weak people can stop our army? We are unloading thousands of troops every day. We are already half way through the mountains. We will be at your oil sands before June."

Erik knew that was a lie; there wasn't enough time for them to get that far so fast. The General was now playing with him.

"Well, General, you have forgotten two critical things."

"And what is that, Professor?" the General said, leaning back in the chair and folding his arms.

"The resilience of the Canadian people. You do know your military history, well, you are supposed to right? Being a General and all." The insult evaporated the smile on the General's face.

Erik continued, "So then, you know that Canadian soldiers were the most feared by the Germans in both world wars."

"I do not fear your soldiers. Your army is, how do you Germans say it, kaput? They are puny, under equipped, and devastated by the collapse because of your capitalist society. This is why we have a foothold in the United States. California is almost all ours; we have defeated the once mighty U.S. Military. And you think your puny little army is going to stop us?"

"General, you don't get it do you. You are not fighting just our army now; you are fighting all Canadians. We are, for the first time in two hundred years, defending our own lands from invaders. You have no clue how our people will react to that. But you'll see, to your peril I predict."

"*Red Dawn* was just a movie. Your people wont stop us."

"Ah, but General, we have the biggest weapon at our disposal, one you cannot win against."

"You have no nuclear weapons."

"I'm not talking about nukes. I'm talking about winters. I, and a number of other scientists, have been predicting winters here in Canada will get a lot worse. Sun cycle twenty-four will bring more snow than in the past, and much colder. There will be more winters like the one we just had, just like they've had in Europe since 2012."

"We will have occupied your country long before then. Your scientists claim the planet is getting warmer."

Erik laughed. "It doesn't surprise me, General, that you would still believe socialist crap from socialist scientists. Believe what you want, General; it's your army to lose. And our future to win."

"These last winters were anomalous because of Mexico's Popocatepetl volcano in full eruption. These bad winters will end," the General said.

"Boy, you really have no clue do you. Tsunis published a paper years ago about the causes of climate shifts. Popocatepetl has been erupting for four years now. It will just push us faster into a cooler phase."

"This conversation is pointless." The General got up and moved to the door. Right at that time a student came into the lab.

"Professor, I need some help with my project? Are you busy or should I come back?"

Erik got up and put his face into the General's again. "No, John, the General was just leaving."

With that, the General stormed out of the lab.

"Come in, John, what can I do for you?"

"What was that about?" John asked.

"Oh, just some mental chess gaming. Oh, yes, you're doing a paper on the Grenville Supergroup in Ontario aren't you?"

"Yes, you remembered."

"Getting old, John, but not senile, not yet," Erik said looking at the open door to the hallway.

At 5:00 p.m. Erik was heading out of his lab with his bike when Carl came in behind him.

"Was that you, Erik? Did you really kill Nugent last night?" he said anxiously.

"You don't want to know, so why are you asking?"

"Fuck me you did," Carl said with his hands to his face. "Holy fuck, man. You've brought the whole Chinese army down on us!"

"Let's not talk in the hallway, Carl." Erik opened the door to the lab across from his.

Carl closed the door while looking both ways to make sure no one saw them. "Fuck, Stein, you're gonna get us all killed! They're talking to everyone. They're going to everyone's homes, even yours. Are they going to find anything there?"

Erik shook his head.

"So where, gawdammit, have you hidden your guns? That is what you used wasn't it?" Carl was starting to panic.

"Carl. Calm down. They won't find anything. My firearms are in a safe and secure place."

Carl walked around the room saying "fuck me" over and over. Then stopped and stared at Erik. "You do realize half the faculty is liberal, more than half. And a lot of them are bordering communist. Hell last night they held a rally cheering the Chinese liberating them! Are you planning to kill them all?"

Erik had thought about that very problem, but he did not know they held a rally.

"Fucking useful idiots. Who was there?"

"Who was there? Who was there? Fuck me, you want a fucking list now? You want a fucking hit list? I don't know. I wasn't invited. Fuck me."

"Can you find out who the ring leaders were?"

"What? What? Are you fucking mad? Of all the years you have told me of what it was like in Germany being oppressed, how awful it must have been for your family, and now you're resorting to murder? I can't be part of this. I won't be part of this." Carl went to open the door. Erik shut it.

"Carl, we have known each other for more than thirty years. Are you going to rat me out, or not?"

Carl was silent.

"I need you to trust me," Erik said with his hand on Carl's left shoulder.

Tears welled in Carl's eyes. "Ok," he said in a soft voice. "I'll be quiet. I just hope they don't torture me. I won't do well with pain, you know."

Erik laughed, "Oh, yeah I remember when you got stabbed with your own fishhook. You squealed like a stuck pig."

Carl smiled, "Yeah, that was funny. It fucking hurt, you know."

"Carl, I promise I won't let you down. I will keep you out of this as much as I can. You have been a great friend, Carl, especially since Alice left. I don't know how I could have gotten through those months if it were not for you and Wendy."

Carl smiled again and Erik let him open the door. "Don't do anything stupid," Carl said heading out the door.

"I already have," Erik said.

* * *

Tom, Jason and Kelly arrived in Kamloops at nearly 3:00 p.m. They didn't get out of Squamish until just after 10:00 a.m. because of the confusion and the long convoy of evacuees. Kelly needed to sleep and eat. Jason pulled into the first place they came to, the Comfort Inn off the main highway. They had no problem getting a room as everyone had already left. While Jason got Kelly settled, Tom went into town to get them something to eat.

The first thing he did was to stop at the Esso service station at the corner to get some fuel. The limit was ten litres, at twelve dollars a litre. Luckily he had enough between the three of them, but that was it, only a few bucks for food remained.

He couldn't get too far; the roads were jammed full of vehicles, mostly busses and transport trucks, all loaded with people, coming along the Trans Canada from Chilliwack and the towns between. So he ended up getting some dinner at a near by restaurant, though the pickings were slim since people all over town, and coming through town, had either eaten everything or had stocked up before their departure.

Once Kelly had eaten and was sleeping, Tom and Jason went into town to see what was going on and to find out what was planned.

They had to turn left on 3rd Avenue to get downtown. The main hospital was on the north side of the road. As they passed by, they could see city and school busses stacked in front of the main lobby and emergency entrance. They were loading patients for evacuation.

The brothers were able to drive most of the way into downtown, but the gridlock of vehicles forced them to park in a lot on 3rd Avenue and Battle Street. They walked down 3rd to the CPR yard, as that is where they were told to go. Virtually everyone was heading that way anyway. At the intersection of 3rd and Victoria they could see why the jamb of vehicles; three cars were tangled and abandoned. All along Victoria, which was the road south of the railway yard, was a mass of cars all over, many of them collided, doors left open. Some people were trying to siphon gas out of many of them.

The centre of Kamloops, down at the CPR station, was masses of people and chaos. CNR Trains, which had arrived from Chilliwack, were being brought in over the Thompson River from the CNR yard north of town. They were being switched to the CPR line before heading west to Calgary, the shortest route through the mountains. It was one train after another with barely a minute between each. People were everywhere waiting their turn to get a ride.

The shortage of locomotives forced the Kamloops Heritage Railway people to fire up their steam locomotive, Ex CN 2141.

Jason asked an RCMP officer when he could get his wife out. The officer said it would be hours, especially by train. The cop said if they wanted to get out by road they could try, but the roads were full of traffic.

The cop had to leave when a fight erupted nearby between a CPR official and several owners of businesses and factories. They were arguing about getting equipment the companies had loaded into freight cars onto trains ahead of people. The CPR official stood his ground that people were first. The official called the cop over that Jason was talking to when one of the company owners tried to bribe the official with a big wad of money.

The RCMP officer arrested the man, handcuffing him to a post, and told the others to get lost or he would arrest them all.

One of the men pulled out a handgun and pointed it at the officer. Jason got his AR15 off his shoulder, cocked it and walked up behind. He poked the armed man in the back with the barrel and said, "Put it away if you want to live."

The RCMP officer disarmed the man, and put him into handcuffs thanking Jason. Jason safetied the rifle and put it back on his shoulder, leaving a round in the chamber. He figured things may start to get out of hand if panic set in.

Walking back up 3rd to the car showed them how badly things were deteriorating. With cops occupied around the railway yard and arena, people were looting stores along Victoria Street, breaking windows, mostly at food stores.

Two civilians at each of the two banks at opposite corners pointed shotguns at the brothers as they walked past. As the pair moved across Victoria, three looters coming out from the pharmacy with handfuls of booty. They gave Jason and Tom a wide berth when they saw the two were armed, especially when Jason figured he better load a mag into his Sig and cock it. Tom followed suit by loading the Cz75 Kelly had given him before going into town.

On the opposite side of 3rd, people had broken into the McDonalds and were carrying out boxes of frozen food and bags of buns. They took no notice of Jason and Tom as they scurried off.

What was weird to Jason was someone was walking up and down the road photographing the looters. Likely some reporter, Jason figured. Anything to get the story, he thought. She even took several photos of the two of them, rifles over their shoulders and loaded pistols in their leg holsters.

Both were relieved that their car was still in the lot, but so too were many others, likely with no fuel, so useless to steal. They managed to weave their way back to the hotel.

On their way back up Columbia Street they saw a fight, almost a riot, at the Husky fuel station. Cars poured out onto the street in line for some drop of juice. The sign on the road said: SEVENTY DOLLARS PER LITRE. It never got to that during the worst depths of the economic collapse and subsequent oil decline. Rationing by the government put an end to gouging. But now, with nothing to enforce any regulations, it was a free-for-all. And drivers didn't like it one bit.

The Esso station across the road from the Husky had a big sign on the drive: NO GAS. But the worst was when they drove past two food stores on opposite sides of Columbia just past the fuel stations. People were pouring out of the doors, while others were trying to get through. Some with cartloads were being ambushed by armed looters taking their cache of food.

The brothers were hoping to stop in and get something, and had planned to on the way back. It wasn't like this on the way into town just a few short hours earlier, so something had triggered the stampede. Jason poured on the gas to get out as fast as he could.

As they turned the corner to the hotel the same Esso, where Tom got some fuel just a few hours before, now had a big sign: NO GAS. Jason was getting worried.

They returned to the vacant lot at the hotel, and debated their options before getting to their room. Kelly was still asleep and Jason didn't want to wake her. Tom said they needed to get out now. But Jason was forceful that she needed her sleep, doctors orders.

Black Winter was a huge worry for Kelly. They didn't want to get pregnant, but of course accidents happen, as it is commonly called. Ironically they had tried to get pregnant for years before and couldn't. Kelly was not going to abort something they tried for so long to have, regardless of the economic and societal uncertainty. It was the only time in their years together they had a serious disagreement, and Jason lost.

They decided to let Kelly sleep a couple more hours, then head out east by car before midnight when it was dark. He had half a tank of fuel left, which he figured might get him to Calgary. Not one fuel station in Kamloops had anything left, Jason figured.

No one was in the lobby behind the desk when they came through to leave. So they left the key on the desk and went out the front door into the night. Their car was gone.

Tom cursed up and down. Jason stood where the car was, keys in his hands, looking around. Kelly walked back into the lobby.

"Did you leave anything in the car?" Tom asked.

"No, I brought everything in. I wasn't going to leave our guns in the car."

"Well, at least you were smart enough to remember that!" Tom said sarcastically.

"What the fuck does that mean, Tom? How was I to know someone would steal our car? Maybe you should have stayed in it, eh?"

Tom shrugged. "So what do we do now, bro?"

Jason walked back into the lobby. Kelly was just shaking her head.

"We'll get out of here Kell. Don't worry."

"Yeah, right…" she muttered.

Jason looked around the ground floor of the hotel. No one was there. It had been abandoned. He sat back down beside Kelly; Tom was also there.

"So now what, dude?" Tom asked looking annoyed.

"We could walk to the train station; we may be able to get a ride on one of the trains."

"And how far is that, Jason?" Kelly asked.

"About six maybe seven kilometres."

"It's four in the morning. No fucking way I'm going to be able to walk for hours eight months pregnant, Jason."

"She's right, bro." Tom said.

Jason sat there unable to come up with a solution. There was no traffic on the highway that they could see. Then it occurred to Kelly. "Think the phone is working?"

"Yeah, call nine-one-one, man." Tom said.

Jason went behind the desk and called. An RCMP officer answered the phone. Jason explained the situation. The officer said that the last train had arrived in town, and to stay put. He would come and get them.

The officer was taken aback when he saw the three of them fully armed, rifles and pistols, including a very pregnant woman. It just looked out of place.

On route, Jason asked the cop, Phil Waterford, what he knew of what was happening. Phil said that the guys coming off the train had encountered the Chinese in a big battle in Chilliwack, and won. But as to what was going on in Vancouver, he said, there was nothing. The phones were cut, the Internet was down. All they had were a few people broadcasting from their homes, but they quickly stopped within an hour or so. Vancouver was completely occupied.

Jason asked when the army was coming from the east. Phil said that they heard that the Canadian Army was preparing in Calgary, along with some American troops, including aircraft and tanks. But none of that was confirmed, only rumour. The goal at the moment, Phil explained, was to get everyone they could east.

CHAPTER 6

Buying Time

Hawker, Collin and Staines got into the cab of the locomotive. It started its trek out of Chilliwack towards Kamloops, the front lights making a bright narrow corridor parting the black of the night.

"Soon as we get to Kamloops... When will that be?" Hawker queried.

"Three hours," Keith Wilks, the RCMP Superintendent in charge of the South East District Command, replied. He got into town just before dusk, driven down from Kamloops after taking one of the trains out of Chilliwack to rally people along the route to evacuate.

"That's just after 3 a.m. then," Hawker said. "Soon as we get into town I want a meeting right way, so Keith wake everyone up."

"Not to worry about that, they're already woken up. I'll call ahead and get that meeting together. Who should be there?" Keith said.

Hawker rhymed off a quick list: The RCMP Chief Superintendent for the province, Kamloops Mayor, someone from the Roads Commission, someone from one or more of the mining companies, one of Staines's officers as Staines was going to go ahead to Calgary, and lastly two railway officials. Keith got the message sent ahead by the still working railway radio system.

What wasn't working was the landline system. Hawker tried to call Ottawa from AFC Chilliwack but got no answer. He had no idea if Ottawa was aware of the invasion; he hoped by now they would be. He hoped that the powers-that-be were getting ready to repel the invaders.

"Why the mining people?" Keith asked.

"We need to blow bridges," Hawker explained. "To buy us some time; otherwise the enemy will be in Calgary by the end of tomorrow."

"But won't they just walk around that?" Keith said.

"No, it has to do with logistics."

Keith looked confused.

"Here's why," Hawker continued. "A foot soldier can only carry about three days of food. So after three days he has to stop and get more food. Problem is the supply of food also has to go by foot, so the supply person has to not only carry the soldier's next three days of food, but he also has to carry his own food for three days, there and back. So in total a supply person has to carry nine days of food to supply a soldier for three days. Unless the supply person walks with the soldier, the soldier has to wait three days with no food to get his supply. So the supply people need to go with the soldiers, that cuts your fighting force in half. It also means the supply people are in harm's way.

"And so on. The further the soldiers get from the supply depot the more impossible it becomes, pretty quick, understand? Many advancing armies have ground to a halt because of this problem.

"So once those bridges get destroyed the Chinese will have no choice but to repair them. That will take weeks. It is vital we nail every possible route through the mountains."

Hawker went over to the engineer of the locomotive and leaned on the back of his chair. "Which bridges would you recommend we destroy?" he asked the engineer.

"Did you blow up the CPR line like you did mine?"

Hawker had to think. The engineer then asked, "You know, the one on the north side of the Fraser?"

"Shit, no I don't think so."

"Well, if you want to stop them like you said, you'll need to. They'll have two routes out of the city. North through Whistler and up the route we're taking."

"Fuck," Hawker sighed. "So what would you recommend?"

"Five miles south of Lytton both the CN and the CP lines cross the Fraser. I'd recommend you blow those bridges. There's tunnels too. What I suggest is you get some freight cars, like LPG tanks, and blow them inside the tunnels. It'll burn for days and leave a hulk of molten metal on the roadbed, as well as bringing the tunnel roof down. Hence destroying the tunnels and making the entire rail line useless to an army."

"Outstanding, thanks a lot, eh?"

"My pleasure, anything I can do to help," the old engineer said.

The train come across the river in Kamloops at just past 3:30 a.m. stopping at the old CPR station. Mayor Olivia Turnbull, and the Regimental Sergeant Major of the Rocky Mountain Rangers, Kevin Popper, met them on the platform. The mayor had arranged for them to meet in the hockey arena next door. In fact, she had arranged for everyone on the train to eat, with people serving meals on the rink. She also arranged for everyone to be housed in either the railway station, homes behind the station, or the two hotels not far from the tracks so the warriors could get some sleep. They were going to need it.

Hawker waited last in line for his food. But because of the meeting they had to go to, the Mayor said she would have food delivered to the meeting room. The first thing Hawker did before going into the meeting room was to get Captain Staines on his way to Calgary to find out what was going on. Staines grabbed some sandwiches and a Pepsi, then headed out without delay on the next train out.

Hawker came into the small conference room, put his C8 against the wall behind him, and sat at the head of the table. Some dozen others, those he wanted, plus others, were around the table. Hawker also asked that someone be present from the civilian shooters and designated Ray to be that go-between.

"OK, people, if I can have your attention, please," Hawker interrupted the chatter. "I'm Colonel Hawker. I'm taking control of the defence in this region…"

A knock at the door stopped him. "Come in," he said. A couple of women came in with plates of food and drinks, placing them in front of people with hands up. Once they were out the door, Hawker continued.

"Everyone knows what's going on. The purpose of this meeting is straightforward. We're the only line of defence between the Chinese Army and the freedom of the rest of Canada. Who's here from the mining industry?"

Two men at his left put their hands up, John Manning from Cupric Mining Company and Roger Zucker from Kamloops Marble and Stone Company.

"How much explosives do you two have between you?"

John explained they had several tonnes, at several locations, which he listed. Then he asked, looking a bit perplexed, "Why do we have to blow these bridges, won't the air force do that? I mean, we can expect an air strike soon, right?"

"I'm not counting on it," Hawker answered. "The Canadian Forces is not prepared. Even if, or when they strike, it could be days. The Chinese could be in Calgary by nightfall today. And that's assuming Ottawa knows of the invasion. I can't get through to them."

"They must know," Roger said. "Surely they must know."

"We can't assume that. It's only been twenty-four hours since the invasion started. So I'm not assuming anything at this point. It's up to us. Get all the explosives you can and meet up at the mall near the highway. By sunrise you'll move out."

John objected, "This is impossible for two men to do."

"Then just do your best," Hawker said. "That's all I expect."

Both men left the room.

"RSM Popper, how many of your Rangers do you have?"

"Fifty, maybe sixty here, all reservist. Everyone else is scattered around the province. With the budget cuts of the last few years we're stretched thin, anorexic actually. Our Commander and his Deputy are in Victoria."

"They won't be getting out. That makes you in charge," Hawker said.

"Roger that, sir."

"Any working vehicles? A LAV would be nice."

"None of the LAVs are working. We have about a dozen trucks of various types."

"My suggestion then is to go to Calgary and join up with forces there. Tell them what's going on."

"With respect, sir, we'd like to be in the fight."

"Oh, you will be. But not this fight. Your time'll come. Get prepared first. Pick up as many of your guys along the way as you can."

"Roger that, I'll head out now."

Hawker then turned to the RCMP Chief Superintendent, Ron Blackcrow. Keith was beside him. "Fill me in on what's happening."

Ron explained, "We have called in every officer, and civilians on the force to help with the evacuation as well as trying to keep the peace. That, is proving to be difficult."

"Ok, how many shooters can I get from you?" Hawker asked.

"None," Ron retorted. "They're just too busy. You know, it doesn't take long for three thousand officers to be used up. Hell, twenty of them were guarding foodstores after the riots broke out. A dozen are guarding the food store behind us, otherwise you would not be eating now."

"Well, you're just going to have to do some reassignments," Hawker almost ordered. "I want at least five hundred officers who are comfortable with firearms."

Clearly, Ron's expression was uncomfortable at being dictated to. "The problem," he explained, "is we didn't even have that many rifles and shotguns combined."

Hawker turned to one of the railway officials and asked, "What happened to the train with all the firearms?"

He was disappointed, again, when he was told those cars were now in Revelstoke where they were unloaded so people could be move instead.

Hawker then asked Ron, "How many civilian gun owners are likely still in town, and is it possible to get their firearms?"

"I would suspect most have left, taking their weapons with them, and some guns had been confiscated."

Hawker asked him, "Can you get the addresses of all licenced gun owners, break into their homes, and get whatever guns remained, please." The please was hard to get out. Hawker was getting the feeling he was being given a run around.

"I'll get some officers to check the local gun and sports shop," Ron conceded. "I know they had a few of your military style weapons." Ron then called someone on the phone to get that started as local phones were working. After the call, Ron said, "It looks like some gun owners had stayed behind, less than a few hundred. They're in the arena."

Hawker then turned his attention to the Mayor. He asked her to make sure the town could support their people. He would be using Kamloops as a staging area. He wanted the hospital ready for any wounded. He asked her to also find out how many body bags were in town. He then also asked that she get a vacant lot ready for graves.

The room was quiet after that comment. Hawker looked the crowd over. They were all looking at him in disgust, except Ray and Sergeant Williams. Hawker matter-of-factly stated, "Get used to this. It's our new normal."

Susan got on the phone to arrange things.

Hawker turned his attention back to the RCMP Chief Superintendent. "Why can't we get a call out to Ottawa?" he said. "How come we can make local calls, but not long distant calls, like Calgary or even Ottawa?"

"Someone took out the switching station here in town last night," Ron said. "They completely blew the place up. The entire trunk system from the west coast came through that building."

"Fucking Chinese infiltrators, did you get them?"

"No."

That surpised Hawker tremendously. "So they could be in town right now spying on us?"

"Probably."

"Fucking great. Fucking great."

"If the system is down how could the enemy communicate?" Ray asked.

Sergeant Williams leaned over, swallowed his food and said, "Satellite radios."

Ray nodded his head.

"OK, well, this changes everything," Hawker continued. "Our next moves must not get out. I'm going to ask you, Chief Superintendent, to do something you are not going to like. I want you to round up every oriental person your officers see. No exceptions."

"And what am I supposed to do with them, shoot them all?"

"No, do your job and figure out who they are."

"You do realize there are hundreds of Chinese people living in town."

"Yeah, so?"

"I won't do it," Ron retorted. "We did this to the Japanese in World War Two. Doing this, putting them in concentration camps based on race, is, so, so grossly un-Canadian. I won't do it."

"Ron Blackcrow, you're First Nations aren't you? You look it. So I can see your apprehension at wanting to do this. If we do not keep a lid on this meeting, and our plans that I will lay out soon, then you are condemning millions of people to slavery and occupation. You want that on your hands?"

"I won't detain people because of how they look, I don't care how many lives are at stake."

"Unfucking believable," Hawker hissed. "This is war, don't you get that? If I could fire you I would. We don't have time for this liberal political correctness…"

Ron interrupted, "If you do this on your own, not only will I order my men to not help you with anything, but I will arrest you."

Hawker sat in silence for a few seconds pondering his options. "Ok, what do *you* recommend then?"

"Tighten up your security for anyone. You don't even know if the people who destroyed those facilities were oriental. They could be caucasian for all you know."

That did have merit, Hawker thought. "Sergeant Willams."

"Yes, sir."

"Post guards around this facility. Check everyone who comes in or leaves. Use Captain Staines's men if you have to. Put his officers in charge of locking this place down."

"Roger that." He left, finishing off his meal on the run.

"That better, Chief?"

"That will do," Ron said.

"Who here is with the Works department?" Hawker asked.

"I'm Commissioner of Public Works," someone said at the far end of the table. "I'm Stanley Woulfe."

"You, sir, are my new best friend. I need maps of every road between here and Vancouver. I need to know where we can blow bridges or bring down rock cuts. We need to keep them from getting past this area."

"You want them now?"

"Right now."

"I can get a basic road map from the store just around the corner," Keith said. "Plus, I know just about every road."

"Get one."

Keith got up to leave the room.

"Keith, send someone else," Hawker interjected. "I don't want any spies following you."

"Right." He left.

Hawker paused to finally eat something. Someone knocked at the door, again. Sergeant Williams came in to let Hawker know Staines's men finally arrived by truck. Hawker asked him to make sure the men got food and a place to sleep.

Keith came back in. "I got one of the civilians to get your map."

After a few minutes, Hawker started a mild chat to pass the time. "You know, I really did't see this coming. Who would have thought we would be invaded? I figured if we were going to get into a world war it would be between radical Muslims and the rest of us infidels. An escallation of Afghanistan. But not this. Not here on our own soil."

Chief Superintendent Blackcrow got up, walked behind Hawker to the door. As he was leaving he said, "You're a bigotted asshole."

Hawker turned to the door. "Chief Blackcrow."

The Chief stopped, holding the door open, turned to look at Hawker.

"You find those spies and bring them to me for interrogation."

Ron just slammed the door without saying anything.

"I'll get it done, Colonel," Keith said.

 He started to leave as well, when Hawker asked him to stay, he would be needed to help with the demolition of the roads. So Keith made a call from the phone instead. Hawker continued to finish his meal. He looked at his watch, 4:10 a.m.

"One hell of a day, eh Colonel?" Ray said.

Hawker just snickered and shook his head finishing his drink of Coke.

* * *

Phil Waterford, the RCMP cop, got Tom, Jason and Kelly as close as he could to the ice rink down to were all the activity was unfolding. He told them they could get some food and a place to bed down if they needed it.

Jason saw familiar faces when they entered the arena. Tables were set around the boards of the rink, people behind the tables were setting up food for hundreds of soldiers. Cops and armed civilians were milling about, some eating, some waiting in line for food, others describing recent events. BBQ's were outside cooking burgers, steaks and chicken.

The familiar faces he saw lining up for food were some of his shooting buddies. They were glad he and Kelly got out of Vancouver. Kelly, bulging with child, didn't have to wait in line for food. They parted the way and let her right up to the front. Jason and Tom waited in the queue with Jason's friends. Besides, Jason wanted to hear their combat experiences down in Chilliwack.

Kelly sat on one of the team benches at ice level to eat. Jason and Tom joined in with a large pile of food on paper plates. Kelly said she needed more sleep, and was getting uncomfortable sitting. Jason asked one of the people behind the table where she could bed down and was told to ask one of the RCMP officers outside.

Jason came back to Kelly with a female officer, who escorted her to a condominium complex behind the railway station. The cop ordered some soldiers in one of the units to vacate for a pregnant woman. She also got an ambulance crew standing near the arena to go and check her out.

The two female EMS told her she was getting close to delivery, a week or two, less than a month at best. Likely advanced because of the stress. She was to get some sleep, and if need be they would take her up to the hospital. The two paramedics would stay with her.

Jason and Tom went back to the arena to see what was up, and what was planned.

At the parking lot they witnessed two groups of soldiers preparing to leave. They seemed excited, and their officer was yelling orders. One group boarded a train, which had a number of tank cars at one end of the locomotives, while on the other end the soldiers were boarding into two boxcars.

Other soldiers left on two trucks, which headed out of town.

* * *

Hawker got up to answer another knock at the door. The railway engineer that brought them up from Chilliwack came into the room.

"I've got your train made up, sir," he said.

"My train, what train?" Hawker asked.

"To blow the tunnels, eh. Remember I suggested we put cars into the tunnels and blow them? Well, I've got one train with a dozen cars on the CP line ready to go. The other is up at Lillooet. I have to get up there by car, but I've confirmed there is at least one locomotive in the yard there. I figured I'd use cars loaded with lumber and logs from the lumber mill to burn in the tunnel. We just need the explosives."

Hawker laughed. "I completely forgot about that suggestion. That was fast."

"It had to be done, sir. Those Commies could already be coming up the lines, so we need to move fast, eh."

"Not yet," Keith said. "I have officers still in Squamish, Whistler, Chilliwack, and none of them have called in any movements."

"You're assuming phones are still working," Hawker said. "What's your name engineer?"

"Al Kappelmann, but everyone calls me Kappy."

"We have to wait for the explosives to show up, that could be hours," Hawker said.

"Hours is too long, they could be rolling into town by then. We should do this now," Kappy replied.

"What about LAWS rockets?" Ray piped up. "Would they blow up a rail car? I mean, all you need is to start one burning, right?"

"Good idea," Kappy agreed. "Yes that will definitely get LPG cars rolling. However, that won't start the log cars ablaze. But we could leave the locomotive in the tunnel, I suppose, and rocket it. Full of diesel fuel and all, that would burn pretty good."

"Outstanding," Hawker said. "You'll need a fire crew for protection. I'll get Williams on that right away and you can get your trains rolling. I hope we can get this done in time. What's the drive, two hours?"

Kappy nodded. "Two and a half. I'll need another engineer for the train here. I should get the engine at Lillooet."

"I can operate a locomotive, I used to be an engineer," the CP railway official said.

Kappy, Hawker and the official got up to go out the door. Hawker ordered Williams to find two of Staines's officers, make up a squad of a hundred men for each train, and get on the move ASAP.

Keith got off the phone when Hawker sat back down. "I'm in contact with Squamish, and Hope, but not Chilliwack. I've sent the Staff Sergeant at Hope to see what's happening down there."

"Sounds good," Hawker said. "I hope they get those tunnels blown in time. It's 4 a.m. now, two hours to get there, too damn close for me."

"I'll get notified as soon as they see anything."

"As long as they can keep in touch—soon as the enemy cuts the rest of the phone system we're screwed."

"We can use the railway system," the other railway official piped up.

"What's that?" Hawker asked.

"We have our own radio relay system. It's still working even right into Vancouver. I talked with the Yardmaster there just a few hours ago. The Chinese haven't figured that out, I guess."

"Outstanding! Why didn't you bring this up earlier?"

"I wanted too, but you were too busy."

"So you can tell me what's going on?" Hawker asked.

"For CN yes, not CP. He just left with that engineer. But I'm sure someone around here will know. But I can tell you, no trains have come through Dentville. Company police are there. We'll get word if any trains or vehicles head our way."

"And by daylight you can bet they'll be, right through there. So can you find out if they're making up any trains?"

"I'll be right back," the official said and left the room.

"Where the fuck is my map, it's been an hour," Hawker said, pacing up and down the room when the door knocked. Williams came in, "Here's your map, sir. The guy had to check a number of stores to find one."

"Thanks, Sergeant. Ok Stanley, let's see what we have here. What I'm looking for are places we can blow bridges and or bring down rock faces onto the road," Hawker said.

"Lots of potential for that," Stanley said. "I would imagine you want to keep near here as possible. I mean, it would take too long and you don't want to get too close to Vancouver, so."

"Maybe, let's see."

They looked at the map. There were four routes from Vancouver to Kamloops. They went through them systematically one at a time. Highway 99 was the north route through Squamish, Whistler and Seton Lake, the same route as one of the rail lines. This route was important, as there were no restrictions to stop any advance up the road. At least the four bridges south from Vancouver, which they barricaded, would buy them some time. Not so for Highway 99.

"So where are good places to stop them?" Hawker asked.

"My suggestion would be at the east end of Seton Lake, here. There is a railway tunnel here…" Stanley circled with a black fine-point marker "..which I presume is the one you're going to blow, that would stop them in their tracks, pardon the pun, so.

"The road there offers several good places where you can ambush them forcing them to abandon vehicles. The bridge, here,…" he drew another circle, "where the lake empties into a canal, is one lane and not the best of bridges. Wood floor truss bridge, so. It would be easy to blow, you know? But if you want to inflict some damage as well, I mean, there are two horseshoe curves you can nail them at." He circled those two places, not far from the bridge.

"Now eventually they'll get through that. Where else can we hold them off?" Hawker asked.

"There are only two routes from Lillooet to here, so. The shortest is through Pavilion, along Duffy Lake Road, which runs north here. It's a valley all the way with a couple lakes."

"Is there anywhere we can bottleneck them?"

"Not really. I mean, there's farms at the west end, to the east likely there's something we can use. So, this location here I'll label as 'A'. The lake is on the south side of the road, while the north side is a kilometre of rock face at one location here, so. But there are a few other cuts back up here. We can blow much of that down onto the road, so.

"Problem is it will take hours to drill the rock and fire off the charges, you know? Then make sure enough is on the road, then drill again and more charges. It could take all day to do each cut, know what I mean?"

"Well, then we better hope the Seton ambush works," Hawker said, pointing to that location on the map. "That should give us a few days before they can replace the bridge, maybe longer. The advantage is they'll commit to the shortest route, then once they see it's a dead end they'll have to back track and pick another route. That's the best we can hope for. Once they realize they can't get through it will take them days, maybe weeks to get heavy equipment in and clear the roads."

"Or they send scouts to check the roads," Williams interjected.

"Sure let them," Hawker replied. "That means they have to wait for the scouts to return. Works out the same for us regardless."

"We're cutting people's escape route too, you know," Stanley said.

"Can't be helped," Hawker said. "Now what about other locations on that road, are there more cuts we can bring down?"

Stanley marked a letter 'B' on the map saying, "This is much farther along. The land is not rugged enough between the two, unfortunately, so. B is good because the canyon narrows with high sides. The problem with it is there isn't any rock we can bring down on the road. So."

Stanley marked a 'C' as the next one. "This spot is also narrow, not as good as B, but suffers from the same problem, no rock to bring down on it. So."

"And last is 'D' here," he said as he marked the last location, quite near to Kamloops.

"Getting a little close isn't it?" Hawker said.

"Yeah, I mean, but it has potential. The road drops down and there are three cuts where we can drop the rock face onto the road. It's actually a good spot to ambush them if we had to, so."

"Ok," Hawker said, "so we blow at A first. If we need to we'll blow D."

"I'm not so sure, now I think about this, Colonel," Stanley confessed. "I mean, it's, it's...

"Spit it out, man. I need to know all the issues."

"Well, Colonel, it's the time and equipment. Not to mention the explosives. Now I think about this, I mean, there just isn't the time and manpower to do all this. So."

"What do you recommend then?"

"That's my problem, sir. I just don't know what to recommend. I mean… Hell I don't know what I mean."

"What I'm hearing then," Hawker sighed, "is we are pinning all out hopes on Seton Lake."

"You're the military tactician, sir. I mean, that's your call isn't it?"

Hawker didn't say anything for a few seconds as he looked at the northern route. He sighed again. Then said, "This bottom route. What's there?"

"Where are you referring?" Stanley said.

"Here, this road south of Lillooet. It joins the highway at Lytton," Hawker said.

"Oh, that's Highway 12. We don't have to worry about that. I mean, if you hit the railway bridges south of Lytton, and we hit the highway north of Lytton. Somewhere along here…" he said pointing to the map, "We should also take out the rail and road bridge over the Fraser in Lytton. So.

"Now, twelve kilometres or so north of Lytton is a long section of highway where it is hugging a cliff. We can completely close that by blowing the rock cut. But that should be last resort, so we need to take out sections of the road south of Lytton. But we're back to time and manpower again."

"So, again, we are putting all our eggs in the bridges and tunnels," Hawker said, nodding. "What about this road?"

"So," Stanley continued, "that's Highway 5 out of Hope. As you can see it runs up to here too, so. You can see there are a number of routes they can take to get around anything we set for them. So we need to concentrate south of Merritt."

"I don't see any bridges or tunnels," Hawker said.

"Yeah, you're right. Besides Highway 5 and Coldwater Road, there's also the old Kettle Valley rail line that goes up that route, it's a trail but passable, so. There is a small bridge that goes over the Coldwater River here.

"There is also Brockmere Road, here. It follows the same valley and will be a problem. There are two bridges over the Coldwater River that could be blown, I guess. The valley is rugged, so would pose a real problem to get off the road. For the Chinese that is. The Kettle Valley rail bed has a bridge there too, so. And at that location up on Highway 5 each lane is at different levels with a high cliff on the west side, which could be brought down. Having the equipment, so.

"There's one bridge the highway goes over, a double span. It's blowable, I would think. But that's thirty kilometers from Merritt, so."

"What about this road going east from Hope?" Hawker asked.

"Yeah, Highway 3, Crowsnest highway. If we have to hit that road we should do it west of Manning. It's not a valley, though there are a few bridges. Not big bridges mind you. They all have short spans. That's two hundred kilometers from Vancouver, so we might have time to take one out before the Chinese arrive.

"So that should be it. We can start at those locations. It might buy us some weeks, I don't know. You're better at this than I am, so."

"So let me see if I have this straight. Two hours to get to the Trans Canada highway locations, and three hours to the Crowsnest road locations. So if we leave now we should get the roads blocked by midday," Hawker said.

"We can hope. I mean, if we have the crews. But I have to worry. I mean, what happens if the Chinese show up while we're drilling?"

Hawker thought for a bit. "You'll have fire crews, but that may not be good enough. What if we were to put vehicles on the roads before the demolition crews and burn them? That would prevent enemy vehicles from attacking your men making it easier to defend. Same at Pavilion at those road cuts, and the Seton Lake hair pin turn."

"So, that's at least six separate demolition crews, so. I hope we have the people and equipment to do that," Stanley said.

"Not to mention explosives," Hawker said. "Ray, do you think some of your long range shooters would be of value at any of these?"

Ray got up and looked at the map. "I have already been thinking along those lines. Maybe at Seton Lake we should be able to pick them off as they come down the road, but without actually being there to see the landscape, well, it would be iffy to speculate. The others, I have no idea. There's likely places we can snipe from, but you'll have to go there to figure that out."

"So what I'm hearing is in your opinion you really can't do much. If that is the case, then there is no point in sending any of your people as seats will be limited. I suggest your shooters just hang around here and help with logistics," Hawker said.

"Makes sense to me." Ray left.

"Now, Stanley, get your road crews ready. The mining guy should be back soon, I hope."

* * *

Kappy and crew arrived in Lillooet in two M35 trucks just after 8:30 a.m. Lieutenant Gary Kroll was in charge of the fifty men, all but six of which were National Guardsmen, the rest Canadian Forces Reservists. Kappy was the only civilian.

He checked in with Hawker by radio. However, time was running out. Hawker told him the CN Police at Squamish said a train had passed through town at high speed. It contained flat cars loaded with APCs, and thousands of Chinese soldiers on board. They would be at Lillooet by 10 a.m. Kappy had to move fast.

He fired up BC Rail's locomotives GE 4642 and SD40 750, which were stored at the yard, shunted some boxcars and one tank car loaded with toluene. He then added a gondola car onto the opposite side of the locomotives. He would use one of the locomotives to get back from the tunnel. The soldiers were loaded into the gondola car.

Kappy took the train down to the lumber mill and grabbed a dozen cars loaded with logs and sawdust. He pushed the lot down around the bend to where the line hugs the side of the mountain against Seton Lake for thirty kilometres. The track turned and curved following the contours of the shoreline against the foot of the mountain.

Seton Lake Tunnel was at the west end of the lake; it would take an hour to get there. The tunnel did a fishhook turn at the east end where there was a power generation spillway.

He pulled the train into the tunnel, leaving 4642 just inside the east portal. The soldiers got out of the gondola car and set up a defensive line. Kappy uncoupled 750 and pulled a few hundred yards back up the line.

There was no time to lose. Some of the soldiers fired their rifles into 4642's fuel tank letting diesel fuel run along the tracks. Others opened the bottom valve of the toluene tank car, spilling its contents.

They waited a few minutes for the fluids to migrate before one of the National Guards sergeants fired off two LAWS rockets into the locomotive. The first one went into the cab blowing the roof open like a tin can. The second one went into the side hitting the fuel tank, erupting into a huge ball of fire that rolled along the tunnel ceiling, out the opening and up the rock face. The fire then seemed to die down. It took a few minutes for it to get rolling and fully involved, sending up a long column of churning black smoke.

Then a huge crash could be heard deep inside the tunnel, with the cars at their end lurching from the entrance, pushing the burning 4642 completely out of the portal.

"What the hell happened?" Kroll said.

"Shit, I'll bet you the train coming up the line just smashed into the back of those cars inside the tunnel. Coming around the corner at speed they wouldn't have seen it until it was too late." Kappy said.

The fire had engulfed the locomotive, and smoke started to curl out of the tunnel, not from the fire at their end, but from the carnage deep inside.

"Get everyone onto the train. We better get out of here fast," Kappy hinted.

They loaded on and started back up the tracks to Lillooet. They stopped at a curve with a clear line of sight to the tunnel entrance, two kilometres across a bay. The fire at their end was quite rolling, sending a pillar of black smoke into the sky. But they could also see a smaller column of smoke coming from the far end of the hill above the west entrance to the tunnel.

Suddenly the toluene car BLEVEed sending most of the tank directly into the tunnel right through the boxcars, leaving a huge fireball trail which went rolling into the sky. The end cap could be seen careening down the track after clearing the top of the burning locomotive.

Kappy got onto the radio in the cab of 750, "Tunnel secured. But I think their train collided into the back inside the tunnel. There will be survivors."

"Roger that. They'll regroup at Seton Portage," Hawker said.

Hawker told him to take the train to the east end of the lake and get the

National Guardsmen to hold the bridge. To do that, they had to stop at the dam and canal entrance.

Two bridges would have to be held, the main road bridge into Lillooet and the small single lane road bridge over the dam.

On the northeast end of the valley there was a tall thumb of mountain that stuck out. At 250 meters high, the view Kroll had from the summit of this thumb of mountain was spectacular. He could see the only road that came through a separate valley on the south side of the lake. It snaked its way down from that valley to the floor below. He had several kilometres of clear view of anything coming their way.

They were all set up except for one thing. No explosives. That had yet to arrive. Kroll worried his men may have to engage a huge force before the charges turned up.

* * *

CP Official, turned engineer, Chuck Charbonneau, and his crew of fifty soldiers commanded by First Lieutenant James Dunlop, arrived at the CP tunnel south of Lytton just before 9:00 a.m. As with the Lillooet train, the LPG cars were being pushed, with two boxcars trailing behind the locomotive with the soldiers in them.

The tunnel on the west side of the Fraser Canyon ends when the track goes east onto the bridge over the Fraser River. The line then swings north after the bridge and goes under the CN line, which itself then goes across the canyon to the west side. Thus the two railways switch sides of the river at this location.

The tunnel was only a few hundred yards long, and straight through with a two-kilometre view down the winding line hugging the sides of the canyon on the north, with a steep cliff down to the river below on the south.

Chuck pushed all the cars into the tunnel. Through the far portal Chuck could see another train was heading towards them, just coming into view from around a bend some three kilometres away, he had to move fast.

"Can you send cars down to roll into the front of them?" James inquired.

"No, it's a slight up grade, it will just roll back down to us. We'll blow the cars now," Chuck said.

"But when they get here, can't they hook up the cars and pull them out of the tunnel?"

"Burning?" Chuck said.

"Why not? Can they do it and just dump the cars over the cliff into the canyon?" James asked.

Chuck thought about it for a minute. The brakeman perked up and said, "Why don't we derail the last cars? They won't be able to pull the cars out if they are jammed into the sides of the tunnel."

The brakeman took the rerailer off the locomotive, while Chuck pulled the train back across the bridge until the last car was the only car in the tunnel. The brakeman placed the rerailer on the track under the wheel, and radioed to move the train forward.

They had to move fast as the brakeman said the train coming towards them was halfway along the canyon and moving fast. Chuck gave the engine a quick shot forward. The tankcar jumped off the rail and onto the track bed. Chuck then gave the engine full throttle forcing the cars into the tunnel. The derailed car made a high pitched screeching contact with the walls of the tunnel. With more force, another car jumped the tracks squealing against the side of the tunnel. He managed to force the last car in. At least half of them derailed and were jammed into the sides of the tunnel, the brakeman said.

They could hear brakes being applied from the oncoming train.

He ordered the brakeman to uncouple the cars from the locomotive and took the engine and soldiers to the east end of the bridge. James and a few men stayed behind to fire LAWS rocket into the first tank car. The first shot ripped open the front end of a tankcar sending liquefied gas down the side of the cliff below the bridge; the flames followed it down like a waterfall of fire. The car completely emptied down into the river below, where the Fraser carried the burning liquid downstream until it either burned off or evaporated.

They had to wait for the smoke to clear when they realized just few flames stayed in the tunnel. James had another LAWS fired. It exploded ripping open the back end of the same car, but failed to ignite the car behind it. James was starting to get frustrated and angry. They couldn't get into the tunnel. So he took the last rocket they had from the corporal who fired the previous two. He moved to within a hundred feet of the entrance to the tunnel and fired the rocket into the side of the second car.

That did it. He hit the top portion of the tank. It ripped open like a sardine can. Flames roared out of the gash against the roof of the tunnel, curling up the top face of the cliff. James had to run for his life to get away from the searing heat.

When they got back to the engine Chuck said, "It'll have to do. We need to get out of the line of fire." Chuck took the short train of one locomotive and two boxcars up the track to where the CN line bridges over the top. They stopped and watched the fire grow.

"It won't take long," Chuck said.

"Long for what?" James said.

"A BLEVE," he said.

"A what?"

"Boiling Liquid Expanding Vapour Explosion. When the flames heat a contained tankcar, it starts to boil and fails the tank, releasing a tremendous explosion. Your military weapons pale in comparison to a BLEVE blast. I think it won't be long now, listen to the sound."

The canyon walls echoed what sounded like a huge jet engine. They didn't have to wait much longer as one of the cars indeed BLEVEd. A huge explosion and fireball emerged from their side of the tunnel with a brightness that exceeded that of the sun. The sound was deafening, even at that distance.

Something appeared to hit the ground on their side of the canyon, sending up a large dust cloud. It rolled down the cliff and into the Fraser giving off an enormous ball of screeching steam.

"Holy fuck! That was amazing!" James howled. "Un-fucking believable! I still have it seared into my eyes, like looking into the sun. Man that was bright, and loud." James, who was used to gunfire, had ringing in his ears after the sound died down.

More fireballs erupted further jetting out the portal like a dragon breathing a line of fire out of its mouth. But they could also see a large fireball rising from the far side of the mountain the tunnel went through.

"Yepper, that's a BLEVE. I've only seen one before, years ago, when I was a kid living in Mississauga. A big train derailment there had a BLEVE.

It is so powerful that ton-sized parts of the tank can be thrown hundreds of meters away. That's likely what we saw thrown out."

Another huge explosion jettisoned out their side of the tunnel. Chuck swore he saw rocks jump on the top of the hill the tunnel went through. Another piece of tankcar, it looked like one of the wheel trucks, was thrown out of the tunnel, bouncing a couple times along the top of the bridge before falling into the river below with a high pitched screech of steam.

"I sure hope one of those cars flew into their train," James laughed.

"Oh, fuck, that would be great if it did. But I'll bet you they backed up pretty fucking fast," Chuck said laughing.

Chuck radioed back to Hawker the mission was a success, tunnel destroyed. As Chuck was talking, another car BLEVEd.

CHAPTER 7

So Much for Retirement

Retired Major General Ross Hughes was just about to sit down to a small lunch with his family when a knock at the door interrupted them. Hughes retired just before the economic collapse, four years previously. When Black Winter hit, he had his two sons and their families, six grandchildren in all, moved to CFB Edmonton, as several other senior officers had done. Hughes' family occupied a number of units in a wing at the barracks. The move was more for protection than convenience. Protection not only from the elements of the winter, but also protection from roaming gangs in Edmonton, which had created a war zone.

The base's Chief Warrant Officer, MacGregor "Mack-The-Knife" Fife, was at the door. He sported the classic handlebar moustache, in bright red.

"Chief Fife," Hughes said. "Come in out of the cold. What can I do for you?"

"Thanks, sir. Bloody nippy out there. Sorry about the snow on my boots."

"Don't worry about it. Looks like the snow has let up."

"Aye, sir, but another front is expected tonight or tomorrow. But we have something far more serious happening. It appears we're being invaded, sir. In Vancouver, in fact all along the west coast."

"Invaded? By whom?"

"Before the internet went down, there were Tweets and Facebook postings that it's Chinese. Thousands of them. They arrived some time last night."

Hughes went back into the kitchen area where his family was seated. They offered Chief Fife some coffee, which he gladly took.

There was a lively discussion on the news brought to them.

"Sir, can we talk in private?" Chief Fife said in a low voice.

"Sure, come with me." They headed out a door to a communal hallway between units.

"Sir, we need you to take command of the situation."

"Me? I'm retired. Where's General Maillet? He's the senior ranking officer on base."

"He's off to Calgary, sir. He's already getting crews prepared to defend against this invasion. He specifically asked for you to take charge. He wants you to call a meeting as soon as possible and hammer out some kind of strategy."

"Has Ottawa been contacted yet?"

"Well, hum, sir, that's the problem. Everything's down, again. And we can't find any techs to fix it. Landlines are dead. Cell phones aren't working. We're kinda cut off. Hell, I don't even think they know what's goin' on."

"Civilian radios are working, right? We were just listening to a local station this morning."

"Aye sir, about half of them are back on the air."

"So broadcast on all of them…" Hughes paused for a bit. "Take a note of these names, got a pen?"

Fife pulled out a pen and pad.

"OK, so who's the RCAF commander on base? Go see him first. We've got some CF18's on base, right?"

"Aye sir, four of them, but we have no fuel for them."

"Damn. How about Cold Lake?"

"They likely have fuel, sir."

"OK, go see the base commander…" Hughes stopped to think. "Who's in charge there now? Isn't it General Jon Babineaux?"

"It was, sir. Except the government of Quebec ordered all Quebec officers to return to their 'homeland' to defend their own people from the rioting."

"Right. That was in December."

"November actually, sir."

"I never thought Jon would heed that call. Shows how long I've been out of the loop. So who's in charge then?"

"Lt. Colonel Peter Bartlet, sir."

"Oh, I know Pete. Great guy. Met him once at a Christmas dinner several years ago. Seems like another life now. He was a Major then. Good for him. See if you can contact him to get some planes in the air and get up here for that meeting.

"Then get on the radio and get the following people here. All senior officers, the Premier of the Province…"

"She's in Calgary."

"Well get her up here. Damn, we have no MP's in government here. That damned leftist coalition. OK, we need a couple of MP's. The Defence Critic, that new guy they just elected. Get his name and get him to the meeting. Someone from communications. Got it?"

"Aye, sir. That 'guy' is a lass, sir."

"Which guy?"

"The defence critic for the Conservatives, sir. It's a woman."

"Bloody hell, I have been out of the loop."

"That's OK, sir, you've had other things to worry about."

"You have a family, Chief?"

"Aye, sir, mostly back in Scotland. My wife went back to look after her parents. My son is here on base with me."

"Good, good. Ok…"

"Where do you want the meeting, sir?"

"You know the base better than I do, but whatever you pick, make sure it is heated first."

"What time, sir?"

Hughes looked at his watch. "Twelve twenty. Let's give them all four hours to get here, so O-Sixteen."

"The snow could be bad by then, I suggest we give them more time."

"If they come late they come late. We have no time to waste. The Commies could be in Edmonton by then."

"Aye, aye, sir, I'm on it."

Hughes went back into the kitchen. His family were waiting for more news.

"Johnny," Hughes said to one of his grandchildren. "You still have that Ham radio working?"

"Yes, Gramps. It's in my room. I just haven't set up the antenna."

"Roger, help your son set up the largest antenna you can. Run it across the parade square if you have to. I want John to hear the whole world."

"Right, Dad. Johnny, let's get at it." They left the room.

Hughes sat beside his wife, Barbara, at the table.

"What are we going to do Ross?" she said.

"Here I thought I'd get through my career in the army without getting into a war. Looks like my wish isn't going to come true."

She hugged her soldier.

* * *

Hughes showed up at the base lecture room around 3:00 p.m. There were already a number of people waiting, including the Royal Canadian Airforce Deputy Commander. Hughes brought his fourteen-year-old Ham Radio operator grandson with him. In all eleven people were in the room.

They all stood and saluted when Hughes came in. "At ease, everyone as you were."

The tables in the room were arranged into conference style. Hughes sat at the head of the table, the head being with the white board behind him.

Chief Fife wasn't there; someone said he was out trying to get more people to show up.

"This will have to do," Hughes said. "Starting on my right around the table please tell us who you are."

"Leftenant Colonel Peter Bartlet, Deputy Commanding Officer, RCAF, 4 Wing, Cold Lake."

"Colonel, how many operational aircraft can you deploy tonight?" Hughes inquired.

"Four, maybe six. They should be in the air by 8 p.m., 9 p.m. the latest. The runway has to be cleared, the planes prepped. They haven't flown in over a year. So they needed a complete check-up," Bartlet said.

"It will have to do. Communications," Hughes said pointing to the person beside Bartlet.

"Petty Officer Valerie Hartman, on loan to 742 Communication Squadron."

"You're the senior officer?" Hughes said.

"I'm afraid so, sir. We lost a few people over the winter. Everyone else is out east, in Ottawa. I'm the highest ranking person in that division out here. I'm very good at what I do, sir."

"OK, then what's the sit-rep on communications?" Hughes asked.

"I wish I could give you good news, sir," Hartman confessed. "We have no communication with Ottawa. Not even land lines. Our system at Aldergrove went down earlier yesterday. We're completely blind over the Pacific. I have a very small team working on it now. But I think it's at their end not ours. However, as backup we're looking at short-wave radio. But, of course, someone has to be on the other end on the same frequency. So far only civilians."

"Wonderful. Blind as a bat. Next, who are you?"

"I'm Lieutenant Rita Byrde, Met-Tech, 4 Wing, Cold Lake."

"Excellent. So what's the forecast for the weather?" Hughes said.

"There's a cold front moving in. They'll get rain in Vancouver, but more snow further north. We expect a half a meter of snow overnight in Prince George. Half that here tonight. The next few days after that a high pressure system will settle over us, so it will be cold, below freezing for the high."

"In May, unbelievable. This has been going on for four years now, when will it let up?"

"We can't predict that. We were totally wrong on global warming. Winter temps have been steadily getting worse for the past four years, this year being the worst. The volcanic eruption in Mexico hasn't helped. They got it even harder out east. Record lows were reached in Ontario, Quebec and northern States. It's been bad."

"Hard to imagine it was worse than here. And you are?"

"William Yaegle. Provincial MLA."

"Any word on your federal counterparts?" Hughes asked.

"Not sure. Another MLA should be here shortly."

"Major, for the benefit of the others here," Hughes said.

"Major Reginald Hamilton. I'm acting Base Commander here."

"Yes, and we remember your commanding officer who was killed off base by muggers. Senseless killings everywhere. Our thoughts go to his family. This is my grandson, John Hughes. He's here because his hobby is short-wave radio and he has a report on what he's heard. We need a secretary to take notes. Who is available? Hamilton?"

"Yes, sir, I'll get someone." He left.

"So everyone's clear on what's happening?"

They all acknowledged.

Hamilton came back in with a private, note pad and pen in hand. "She's never taken notes at a meeting, so go easy on her."

"Best we can do, thank you for doing this important job, private."

"I'll do my best, sir," she said.

"OK, let's get started. First, for the record, let's recap what we do know. Chinese soldiers arrived along the coast some time after midnight. Vancouver, Prince Rupert, and along the U.S. coast. We can only assume they are taking advantage of the chaos here and the U.S. So anyone want to hazard a guess as to why? And why they are not marching through the streets of Edmonton right now? It's only, what, an eight-hour drive through the mountains. They've been here now…" Hughes looked at his watch, "…eighteen hours."

"Sir, I might be able to answer the second question if I may," Byrde interjected.

"Please speak," Hughes said.

"Thank you, sir. Snow in the mountains from Prince Rupert is at least a meter or more. Avalanches have wiped out the highway in the western section to the coast. They picked the wrong time of the year to land. I don't think they expected this much snow here."

"I find that hard to believe," Bartlet retorted.

"Explain, Colonel," Huges said.

"They would have had intel before they got here. So they would have known the snow situation."

"So how to you square that circle, Colonel?" Hughes said.

"I can't, sir. They must have some plan. You don't come across the Pacific to pick a fight with us only to get bogged down in snow they would have known existed. I suspect they are using the snow, which is to our disadvantage without equipment to clear it, people trapped, in their favour. I would not underestimate their ability to deal with the snow. That's just my opinion, sir."

"And a good one at that. I agree," Hughes said.

"Explain from Vancouver then," Hamilton said. "I came through there a week ago by train, from Surrey, and there was snow, yes some, but not that much. So how come they're not knocking at the Calgary door right now?"

"We've had a lot of rain in the south of the province," Byrde continued. "That's cleared out much of the snow. Why they are not knocking at that door right now, sir, I can't explain."

"Well, something's holding them back," Hughes said.

"Logistics maybe," Hamilton said.

"You don't plan a major invasion, travel thousands of miles across the Pacific only to get bogged down on your first day because of logistics," Bartlet said.

"I agree," Hughes said. "They know the best offence is a fast Blitzkrieg, take by speed and surprise. That hasn't happened. Let's hope your aircraft will tell us as soon as they get into the air."

"That's another question," Bartlet said. "Where's their aircraft?"

"Maybe your recon will tell us that too," Hughes said.

A knock came at the door as four new people, civilians, came in and sat down. Chief Fife was with them.

"Sorry we're late. I'm Kristina Krouse. Defence Critic for the Federal Conservatives. And this is my aide."

"And I'm Glenn Kabber, Provincial MLA."

"Michele Norman, MP for Edmonton Centre," the last person said.

"Ms. Krouse, can you tell us if the government is aware of what's going on?" Hughes said.

"I'm not in communications with Ottawa. Last time I talked with our leader was two days ago."

Hughes shook his head. "Ok, the Liberal/NDP coalition government is going to flip handsprings, but we're going to act regardless."

"You will have my support on that," Krouse said.

"I talked with our Premier an hour ago, she will take responsibility for whatever we need to do," Kabber said.

"Ok, so let's get everyone up to speed on what's going on in the world as this is not just our fight. Now, John, don't be shy. Just tell them what you know. What you have heard on your radio."

"Sure grandpa." John was shaking and having a hard time focusing with other's eyes on him. He didn't say anything.

"John is better on the radio than in public," Hughes said to the group. He turned back to his grandson and said "Johnny, just tell us who you talked with, and what they told you."

"Ok, grandpa. Well, hum, I talked with this guy in England. I wasn't sure what he was talking about. But, hum, I mean, he said that Muslims have taken control. I talked with someone in the Middle East, Egypt I think he said. He said people were fighting in Israel. There was a lot of talk, speaking that I couldn't understand."

"That's fine son. I'll take it from here. Good job," Hughes said patting the youngster on the head. "I talked with some of these people on John's radio, so here's what I figure is happening. Muslims have taken control of many European countries—France, Holland, Germany, Spain, and the UK. And by control I mean forcefully at gunpoint storming governments. Rioting continues in the EU, and in the US, especially on the east coast.

"Someone, who we could barely hear in India, said something about fighting breaking out in Tibet with the Chinese moving west. So whatever is going on, it's world wide, but not just with China. The guy in Egypt, which we had trouble hearing, claimed the Royal Family in Saudi Arabia has been overthrown by radical Islamists. But his English was bad, and his reception was broken up."

"Sir, if I may add to that," Hartman said.

"Sure, absolutely, Petty Officer."

"Your grandson is correct. We've been on short-wave as well, not just communicating with people around the world, but listening in on others. It's really bad, everywhere. As you said, governments in Europe have collapsed. We heard from a couple of ships in the Atlantic heading to North America with refugees…"

The phone on the desk beside Hughes rang. Everyone looked in surprise.

"Hello, General Hughes here." He put it on speaker.

"Sir, this is Corporal Sally Schaffer downstairs. We have a phone call from Ottawa, I think it's the Minister of Defence."

"Can you connect us through?"

"Yes, sir, one moment…"

The line clicked a few times. Then, "Hello?"

"Yes, Minister, this is Retired General Ross Hughes."

"Hughes, where's General Maillet?"

"He's not here. He asked me to take command in his absence. Are you aware of what is going on? Do you know we're being invaded?"

"This is not an invasion, General. We just completed a meeting with the Chinese ambassador and he has assured us that this is humanitarian aid. They have arrived with a major shipment of food. No different than the last ones all winter."

The panel in the room looked in amazement.

"Minister, we have reports they have arrived with troops," Hughes argued. "We don't know what's happening. But you don't bring in food with armed soldiers."

"Those soldiers are there to help us stop the rioting and to fairly distribute the food to our residents."

Hughes was getting frustrated. "With all due respect ma'am, the Chinese have invaded the west coast of the U.S. This is no humanitarian aid drop."

"General, listen to me very carefully. We have been assured by the Chinese this is not an aggressive act. We have no reason to dispute that. You aren't planning any retaliation are you? You are ordered to not respond to this in any way. We will handle this diplomatically. We will take it from here."

Hughes knew exactly what that meant, and wasn't going to relinquish his view. "I was planning to send a couple recon planes to see what's going on."

"No, absolutely not. You are ordered to not send any aircraft anywhere, do you understand?"

Everyone's frustration grew stronger. Bartlet bellowed, "With all due respect, Minister, daily operations are my responsibility. I do not need your approval for any flights off my base."

"Who is that?" the Minister said.

"That was Colonel Bartlet of CFB Cold Lake, Minister. And he is right. We're proceeding with the flights. We're blind. If this is indeed a humanitarian aid drop as you claim, our recon will show us that."

"No flights! That's an order! You will all stand down. We will handle this situation. I will get back to you with orders. In the meantime, your soldiers are to be utilized to help keep the peace. You will hand over all your soldiers to the local police. End of conversation." She hung up.

"Could that be the case?" Michele Norman said confused.

"No way," Bartlet said firmly.

"We'll find out soon enough," Hughes said. "Colonel, get those planes in the air."

"Yes, sir." He got up and left.

"What about General Maillet?" Hamilton said. "He's already down in Calgary getting a response force ready."

"Are we in contact with the General?" Hughes said.

"No, sir."

"Then, Major, we can't implement the Minister's order can we?"

"No, sir," Hamilton chuckled.

"Good, then we proceed as planned. Miss Krouse, I'll leave it to you to deal with the Minister."

"She's a real bit of work," Krouse said sarcastically. "Trust the Liberals to assign defence to an NDP. And you people though the cuts to the forces the last four years was brutal. The NDP would have gutted everything."

"This will certainly test their world view then," Hughes said.

"That it will," Krause said.

"Next item," Hughes said. "Since the phones are working I want mobilization of all units we can…" He looked around the room, "…do we have an org chart here?"

"Yes, sir, right here." Fife went over to a cabinet and pulled out a chart from one of the drawers.

"Perfect, thank you, Chief. Ok, let's see." He started to circle the units on the organizational chart. Even as far east as Manitoba, and the Lake Superior Scottish Regiment in Thunder Bay, Ontario. "Arrange for them to come here by train, Chief," Hughes said. "Once they're on their way, arrange for the Eastern Area Land Forces to mobilize."

"We'll have to contact Major General Black, and he's in Ottawa. He would have gotten his non-marching orders from the Minister," Krause said.

"I know Blacky. Get me in contact with him and he'll do the right thing," Hughes said. "OK, next on my list. Volunteers. How do we get the message out to get civilian volunteers? We're going to need a drive for boots the likes of which we have not seen since World War Two. We're going to need training camps…"

"Training? We don't have time to train anyone. The Chinese could be in Alberta before summer. We don't have months of training volunteers will need," Hamilton interjected. "Sorry, sir."

"No, you're quite correct, Major. We don't have months. So you give them a bare bones two or three weeks training. We'll intersperse those who show clear readiness now in with the regular forces. The rest we give training. I suggest we set up camps in Manitoba and Saskatchewan along railway lines. That's how these people from across Canada will get here. Major, get people on that right away."

"Yes, sir. They'll need weapons."

"I suspect many will have their own. There's at least seven million guns in civilian hands."

"Sure, old Enfields," Hamilton said chuckling.

"Well, do we have anything in storage?" Hughes asked.

"About four thousand FN's from the seventies, about half that are stored right here on base."

"I thought they were all destroyed?" Hughes said.

"They were supposed to be. Forty years ago the base commander refused to ship them all for destruction. He packed them all up and they've been in storage ever since."

"Then I suggest, Major, you get someone to unstore them and get them ready for battle."

"On it, sir." Hamilton was about to leave the room when he turned back to Hughes. "Except, …we have a major problem."

"How so, Major?"

"Ammo. We're likely to get two hundred thousand volunteers, eventually. If they practice with only one hundred rounds, I can shoot four times that in a day, that's twenty million rounds of seven-six-two. Just for the training."

A blank stare came over Hughes.

"Sir?" Hamilton said.

"How much ammo do we have stored?" Hughes said in a low voice.

"We'd be lucky if we have a million in store, across the whole country."

"Damn it," Hughes said as he put his head in his hands. "Well, Major, then I suggest you find a way of getting several hundred million rounds of ammo, and fast."

Hamilton left the room.

"What are we supposed to shoot the Chinese with, spit wads?" Glenn Kabber said.

"This is going to be bad, isn't it," Michele Norman mumbled. "They are going to defeat us and occupy our land."

"As Oddball used to say, 'Enough with the negative waves'," Hughes said.

"Who's Oddball?" Petty Officer Hartman said.

"Never mind, before your time. Ok, that's enough for tonight. I want another meeting first thing in the morning. Everyone be here with updates by seven a.m. Dismissed."

* * *

The night's snowfall was not as bad as predicted, but had lasted longer than expected, resulting in more snow over a longer period. Ross Hughes made his way through the powder to the building for the morning briefing. Lt. Colonel Peter Bartlet met him outside the door on their way in. "I could use a cigarette. Man, I miss my smokes," Bartlet said.

"Your health will be the better for it, Colonel."

"But not my craving. Very interesting news from last night's flight, sir."

"Ok, leave it for everyone to hear," Hughes said.

The same group were present, including Chief Fife. They all stood up when Hughes entered.

"Please sit. The Colonel here has some news. Go ahead Pete."

"Thank you, sir," Bartlet said, looking at his notes. "We sent six CF 18's, four over Vancouver, and two over Prince Rupert. The Defence Minister is very very wrong. Two of our planes were shot at with SAM missiles. The Chinese have landed in force. As you can see from these photos..." He handed out a number of aerial photos. "...you can see fires burning at the docks where they landed. We suspect local police tried to stop them. But the interesting part of those photos are the bridges over the Fraser. Notice here, and here, and here, they're burning. Our best guess is that people loaded the bridges with vehicles to prevent the Chinese from getting across."

"Whoa, stop right there, Colonel," Hughes interrupted. "Are you saying there is an organized resistance already started?"

"Ah, yes, sir. And there's more. Look at these photos." He handed out three more. "This is Chilliwack, specifically the canal just to the west. A major battle took place there late yesterday while we had our meeting. Looks like a defensive last stand."

"Unbelievable. Someone must be coordinating this, any ideas?" Hughes said.

"No, sir," Bartlet said.

"Maybe the police," Hamilton suggested.

"No way. No disrespect to our fine police, but cops could never organize this. It's someone military. Who's out there? Major?" Hughes said.

"I have no idea who we have out there, sorry, sir," Hamilton said.

"Well, it is someone who has their head on straight. The Minister is going to be real pissed."

"If that's the case, sir," Bartlet said, "we need to help them out."

"That's what Maillet can do. Any news from him?"

"Yes, sir," Fife said. "We got contact from him by phone. Seems the system is on more than it is off now. He said he is just about completed organizing and collecting equipment. They are readying a train in Cochrane as we speak."

"Get this information to him ASAP," Hughes said.

"Roger that, sir," Fife said and left taking the photos with him.

"Petty Officer... Hartman, right?"

"Yes, sir."

"How's the communications going?"

"Well, sir. The trans-Canada phone lines went down again last night. So Ottawa can't contact us at the moment."

"That can be considered good news," Hughes said as the room laughed.

Hartman continued, "We have contacted radio stations all across the country by relaying one to another. They're already broadcasting calls for help. But how are people going to know where to go or how to get here?"

"Good point. Is the short-wave still on line?"

"Yes sir."

"Can you contact bases around the country that way?"

"I don't see why not."

"Good, then send out a broadcast by short wave and tell all military bases in the country to set up staging areas to get people here by train. They'll know what to do locally. But we gotta get communications working better than this."

"It's improving sir, slowly. It's being worked on 'round the clock."

The phone rang to everyone's surprise. Hughes picked it up looking at Hartman. She just shrugged.

"Probably our Defence Minister again," Michele Norman said.

Hughes put it on speaker phone. "Hello, this is General Hughes."

"General, this is U.S. Army Major General Bradley calling you from the Pentagon. I understand you are in charge of your western defences."

"Wow, this is unexpected," Hamilton said.

"Maybe not," Hughes said. "General, we have you on speaker phone with a number of people. We have not planned any specific defence, but we're trying to get our act together. Have you contacted our government?"

"Don't worry about your government. They are now out of the loop. I'm sending you a number of officers who are going to take control of your situation."

"With all due respect, General, we're quite capable of…"

"General, this is not meant to step on your toes. The situation is far more precarious than you know. Once our men get there they'll fill you in. I cannot tell you anything over the landline, it has ears."

"When can we expect them?"

"They are already in the air, and should be landing at your location before noon. So please have your runway cleared. I can see from the photos you don't. That is all." He hung up.

"What the fuck is this? They're taking over?" Glenn Kabber snarled.

"I don't know. But he was right. They may know something we don't," Hughes said. "Get the runway cleared, Major."

"Roger that, sir." Hamilton left the room.

"I don't like all this uncertainty," Krouse said. "Major battles outside of Vancouver by who we don't know. An American General giving orders, even telling our government to stay out. Not that it's a bad thing with this group of idiots in Ottawa, I just don't like the loss of autonomy."

"I don't like it any more than you do," Hughes agreed. "But I suspect our future will be filled with reacting instead of planning. Colonel Bartlet, what's happening at Prince Rupert?"

"Right, sir. Yes. They're just sitting there. The Chinese that is. The passes got a lot of snow last night. That's probably holding them back."

"For now," Hughes said. "Do we have contact with the Rocky Mountain Rangers?"

"Only at Prince George. Kamloops is dead. No contact with them, sir," Hartman said.

"Ok, tell them to get ready for evacuation. Get everyone they can east through the mountains."

"Yes, sir." The Petty Officer left the room.

"Sir, if I may," Hamilton interjected. "I have been going over some maps of routes through the mountains. We have a major hole."

"Continue Major."

"Well, you can see from my arrows here…" Hamilton slid the map to Hughes, "… are the only places through the eastern Rockies. We should have no problems getting defensive positions set up. But it's this northern route, Highway 97. One hundred and fifty kilometres through tough terrain. May I suggest we get the Canadian Rangers down and fill in that gap."

"They're armed with seventy-year-old Enfields! Spit wads to the Chinese," Bartlet retorted.

"How would you get five thousand men scattered over a thousand kilometres of Arctic to there?" Hughes asked.

"I have no idea how, Colonel. But we must get a call out to them and see how many…" Hamiliton looked at Bartlet, "…with their Enfields, we can get. I would suspect the north is still supplied by air, are they not? How else are they getting food?"

"Shooting seals and polar bears with their Enfields," Bartlet said chuckling.

"Please, Colonel, this is serious," Hamilton continued. "General, we can fly them into Chetwynd, there is an airfield there…"

"Fly them, from all over the Arctic? It would take weeks, maybe months," Bartlet interjected.

"Ok, that's enough," Hughes ordered. "We need every shooter we can get our hands on. That pass is a straight line to the oil sands. If that's a short route, you can bet they'll take it. Is that a bridge there?"

"What does the oil sands have to do with this?" Michele Norman inquired.

"Yes, sir." Hamilton said at the same time.

Hughes replied to Norman, "We can take an educated military guess that the oil sands is their primary objective."

"And then some," Bartlet agreed.

Hughes continued, "We need to take all these bridges out. Colonel, when can you arm your CF18s with bombs and get them in the air?"

"I've already got crews working on that. We have some bombs, but with the recent cutbacks, and the mood of this government, most of them were sent to Ottawa for storage."

"See what you can do, Colonel."

"I better head back to Cold Lake, with your permission, sir," Bartlet said.

"Granted, but keep in touch."

"Yes, sir." And Bartlet left the room.

"I'll head out too, sir, to get the Rangers mobilized," Hamilton said.

That left Hughes alone with the politicians. They sat in silence for a few moments. Hughes played with a pen as he thought. Finally he broke his silence. "Ok, do we have things under control in the cities?"

"I wish," Glenn Kabber said. "It's a mess. And it will get worse if you take cops away from us."

"Well, I suggest you get some volunteers to help the cops. I would also suggest you stop with the kid gloves. You may have to resort to lethal force to squash these riots."

The politicians looked at each other. "Lethal force?" Kristina Krouse said. "Those are ordinary people trying to get food and keep their families from freezing. No one is going to use lethal force on them."

"Let me clarify," Hughes said. "You're still having problems with gangs, correct?"

"Yes, General. They're a real problem," William Yaegle admitted.

"Then I suggest you do something about them first. The rest should fall into place. Is the public aware of the invasion?"

"Yes, radio stations have been broadcasting for volunteers," Kabber said.

"Good," Hughes nodded. "That means people now have a collective reason to put their differences aside. That'll work in our favour. Put the word out that we'll no longer tolerate gangs in the city. Tell them it's open season on them."

"It's worse than that, General," Krouse said. "Jails were opened over the winter. It wasn't made public. So we have murderers and such roaming the streets."

"Leave that with me," Kabber said. "I've been wanting to deal with them for a while. I have just the solution."

"What's that?" Hughes asked.

"You don't want to know," Kabber said and left the room.

"Well, there's not much we can do now. We'll reconvene after the American General gets here, so say around 2 p.m."

* * *

The meeting was delayed until after 3 p.m. as the plane carrying U.S. Lieutenant General C.G. Grover and his aides was late due to weather. Hughes and company were waiting in the board room for the general when a call came in. It was Corporal Schaffer with an email message from General Maillet.

"Email? The web's up?" Hughes asked.

"Just locally, sir. We're able to work with providers over night and got email up."

"Fine work. Ok, read it," Hughes said.

"It reads: 'Preparations all done, heading to Kamloops within the hour. Great news, Colonel Gary Hawker has battled the enemy in Chilliwack. He's demolished tunnels and bridges in the mountains. Will meet up with him in Kamloops. Keep planning going.' That's it, sir."

Hamilton's eyes opened wide with a big surprised smile.

"Well that explains a lot," Hughes laughed as General Grover came in the room.

They shook hands and introduced each other. "Just a minute, General, I need to get a message out," Hughes said. "Corporal Schaffer, you still on the line?"

"Yes, sir."

"OK. I want you to send Maillet an email and attach the last meeting minutes with it."

"Roger that."

Hughes hung up the phone. "The floor's all yours, General," he said.

"First, I want you to know I'm not here to take control of your forces. But I am here to tell you what we're going to do. We cannot let the oil deposit, your oil sands, fall into Chinese hands. We're convinced that's what they're after. All efforts will be to stop them from getting anywhere near it, but we have to face reality. Our military is a shambles. A small shell of its former self. We're doing our best to get our people back, but that takes time. And we're not sure all will return. AWAL was wide spread, everywhere. Plus, not all our soldiers have survived the rioting.

"So our ability to take on a force is highly compromised. We're down, but not out. We're going to get into this fight. We're getting as many soldiers as we can up here to help you stop the enemy. I have ordered an air strike against bridges in the mountains, not just in Canada, but all along the cordillera. Those strikes should happen tonight or at the latest tomorrow morning."

Hughes got on the phone. "One moment, General."

"Yes, sir," Schaffer said.

"Get a message out to General Maillet immediately, notifying him of air strikes on bridges…"

"We're only going to strike on the western-most structures first," Groves said. "Our plan is to hold them within the mountains. So bridges east of Kamloops won't, yet, be hit. They'll be if we deem it necessary to."

"Did you get that, Corporal?"

"Roger that." She hung up

"Sorry, General Grover," Hughes said.

"No, that's fine. You need to inform your subordinates in the area. Now who can we trust to take command of the defence of the oil sands?"

Hughes thought for a moment. "I got him. Colonel Gary Hawker. He's going to need a break from his activities. Soon as I get in contact with him I'll send him up there to prepare.

"We do have a serious problem – ammo…" Hughes started to explain.

"Don't worry about that," Grover said quickly, anticipating the question. "We'll need billions of rounds. We're working on that now. But it's not easy. Brass is a problem. We're going to have to mine abandoned homes and buildings for anything copper. Most of the new ammo will be steel cased, however.

"General Hughes, I'm going to set up a command post in Calgary immediately to coordinate efforts here. Then I have to head back to the Pentagon. I want you to go down there once it's set up to control your efforts. I'll leave it up to you to defend that oil sands."

"I'm only temporary. I'm supposed to be retired."

"So was I. No such thing today," Grover complained.

CHAPTER 8

Getting the Scoop

Colonel Gary Hawker went over to the CN yard north of Kamloops where the relay radio station office was located. CN Official Gregg Milynn was on the radio with someone in Vancouver.

"We just got cut off," Gregg said. "Guess the Chinese are on to us. The last message I got was they had made up two trains."

The radio piped up. It was the CN police officer in Squamish. He said a train had rolled through town heading up the line out of Vancouver towards Seton Lake. The train consisted of two locomotives, a number of flat cars with military vehicles, including what looked like tanks and APCs, plus a large number of cars loaded with soldiers. It was at least one hundred cars long, the officer said.

Kappy also came on the radio to say they had arrived at Lillooet. Hawker got onto the mic and told him the situation and to hurry blowing the tunnel.

After the radio went quiet, with time to kill, Hawker rubbed his eyes with his fingers, yawned and dropped his head.

"When was the last time you got some sleep, Colonel?" Gregg said.

"Fucked if I can remember. I got a bit on the train, but nothing for two nights really."

"You've got to get some sleep. You can't keep going like this."

"I'll rest when I'm sure we have blocked these fuckers from getting through."

"That could be hours, maybe days."

"So be it. I need a gawdammned shave too," Hawker said as he rubbed his prickly chin with his hands. "Damn itches when it gets this long." He bowed his head back down and closed his eyes.

Thirty minutes later, CN Official turned engineer, Chuck Charbonneau,

133

radioed they had arrived. Hawker informed him there was a train heading his way. Chuck said they could see it coming. He said he would radio back when the job was done. Hawker put his feet up on the desk, leaned back into the chair, folded his arms on his chest and dropped his head again.

Stan showed up and came into the room just after 9:40 a.m.

"No fucking rest," Hawker mumbled, putting his feet back on the floor.

"The explosives guys arrived. They're looking for you. We've got several tonnes of explosives. It's up at the mall near the highway like you asked," Stan said. "They've got some diamond drill rigs on trucks, plus some crews to operate it."

"Great, not too soon. You need to move fast. Send a crew to Lillooet. That bridge needs to be blown now. Kappy is there to blow the tunnel and a train load of Commies is heading right at him."

"Already ahead of you on that. I called Roger to hightail a crew to Lillooet. It won't take much to blow those two bridges."

"Two, I thought there was only one," Hawker said.

"There's another small bridge over the canal and dam. They both need to be blown. I sent the crew up there about an hour ago, they should get there by ten a.m."

"Outstanding," Hawker yawned. "What about the other locations?"

"I haven't briefed Roger on the other locations yet, but I did show him our identified list of targets. I guess we need to prioritize, we really didn't do that much. Roger said he doesn't have too many people, stretched a bit thin. If need be I could second a few civilians and train them on the job."

"Call Roger and get him up here. That way we can keep in contact," Hawker said.

Stan called Roger to get him to come, and bring the maps to the CN yard north of Kamloops. The BC Interior Defence Command was hence moved from the arena to the CN railway yard.

Roger Zucker, Senior Operations Officer of the Kamloops Marble and Stone Company, arrived stating that a train had arrived from Calgary, mostly with empty cars to evacuate more people, but a number of media people had arrived and were scouring for who was in charge. Roger brushed them off hoping to keep Hawker out of the limelight.

"Gawdfuckingdamn media," Hawker said. "We need to contain them before they blast our plans all over the air. Stan, you and Gregg sort out the priorities and send crews out now. Get a hold of Sergeant Williams and make him keep the fucking media away from our people."

"You're not coming?" Roger said.

"I can't. I need to keep on the radio. I want to know the minute they've blown the tunnels. I also want you to use the railway crew's radio to keep me informed of your activities."

"Oh, almost forgot," Roger stopped and turned back into the room. "That police chief, Collin something…"

"Collin Edwards," Hawker returned.

"Yeah, him. He said he was going on the train to Calgary . He said to tell you that he saw no reason to stay, something about being a tit on a bull."

Hawker laughed. "That's fine, tell him he deserves to get out of this hell hole."

On the drive back, Stan and Roger decided they would send one crew to blow two locations on the Trans Canada Highway, north of Lytton. A rock cut first, then on the way back a bridge.

Another crew was heading to Highway 5, while a third crew would work on Highway 3. That location was the most dangerous because of its proximity to any Chinese advance. The problem was the interior highlands of BC, which Highway 3 went through, held few places where roads could be blocked.

Roger said that he only had three drilling rigs, and less than twenty people trained to do the jobs. He would need more men. They would have to not only boost the manpower needed to do the work, which they could get some of the armed civilians to do, but they would also need a large force of soldiers to protect them, at least several dozen people per location. Of course, they would also need the transportation. The National Guards crew had eight trucks and a humvee, Roger's crew had six trucks. Stan's road crew had five pickups. They would need more.

Sergeant Williams greeted them on the bridge into town, away from the reporters.

* * *

Gena Vanderpoel and her cameraman Jack Pokrajac arrived on the train from Calgary. They were in a group of some twenty reporters and media looking to get a front line story, the story of the century.

The other reporters didn't waste time interviewing people who came from Chilliwack. There was going to be enough of that coverage, Gena figured, even if it was the first military combat on Canadian soil in more than two hundred years. Instead, Gena wanted to get the scoop. She was good at that. During the economic collapse she hounded bank CEO's, even at their homes. It was a huge story of these "scum," as she called the bankers, making the decisions to throw people out onto the street in the depths of Black Winter. A few concerned bank employees told her stories of deliberate acts to take homes from people who could not pay their mortgages due to lost jobs, particularly in the government sector of the economy. Austerity measures forced on governments because of the economic collapse required large layoffs and closures of programs not deemed essential. This started in the EU first, then spread like wildfire to the US when their government was denied loans and couldn't make their own payroll.

Gena's coverage was exemplary; no one could touch her because of her contacts she had made over the previous dozen years. She also made many enemies. Most notably because of her "harassment" of political figures who made stupid mistakes. She would cut them no slack, regardless of the political persuasion of the politician.

This time would be no different. She was going to get the scoop, one way or another.

Her tactic was simple. Jack's presence with a camera would always make potential "victims" of her interrogations run for cover. So she would leave Jack hidden and call him in by radio when she was ready.

She wandered up to the arena as it was clear much activity was taking place there. It was guarded by RMCP officers and military people in full gear with loaded weapons. She tried several times, but none of them would let her in. She watched as someone drove up in a pickup truck with "Kamloops Marble and Stone Co." on the sides of the door. She watched him go in, then she went over to the vehicle to have a look inside. On the floor of the passenger side was a wooden box labelled "DANGER BLASTING CAPS" with the WHMIS explosive icon in the corner.

"Can I help you?" someone said behind her. She turned to see the driver of the vehicle.

"Oh, no," Gena smiled that pretty smile that often got her the story she wanted. "Planning on blowing something up?"

Roger was not amused. He realized he should have covered the boxes with a blanket. He got in the driver's side and just smiled back as he backed out of the driveway onto Lorne Street and headed eastward.

Gena waved Jack to come over and follow him with his camera. Roger could be seen turning left onto the bridge over the Thompson River.

They went down the lane in front of the arena where a number of U.S. military vehicles could be seen. But they didn't get far when a U.S. Staff Sergeant blocked them from proceeding. He wouldn't take any questions.

"We need a vehicle," Gena said.

"Fat chance of that," Jack replied.

As they walked back to the road Gena said, "This has got to be the centre of whatever's happening."

"The whole Chinese army arrives on our shores and nothing's happening here," Jack said disappointed.

"Oh, something is happening, I can feel it. Someone here knows what's going on," Gena said.

Just then an obvious civilian, long hair hanging below his cap, came out of the arena and headed east along the road away from them. He was all decked out with military gear loaded with magazines of ammo, a holstered pistol, and a rifle over his shoulder.

Gena ran down with Jack following until she caught up to the person as he was going through the door of the condominium units just down the road from the arena. There was an ambulance parked on the road in front of the building. They followed him up the stairs to a unit on the second floor.

At the door Jason said to Gena, "Can I help you?"

"I'm Gena Vanderpoel and this is my cameraman Jack Pokrajac. I'd like to ask you some questions."

"You're one of those reporters that came in on that train, aren't you."

"Yes, can you tell me what's happening?"

"I don't know. My wife's in here. She's pregnant."

"It will only take a few minutes, please."

Jason thought about it for a second. Maybe he shouldn't, but what could it hurt? "No camera, only you. It's a small place."

They went in. Jason took off his tactical vest and put it with his rifle on the floor near the door. The EMS women were at the kitchen island drinking some tea. "She's still asleep, so please keep it down," one said.

"Tom's coming in a minute to bring her some food. I just wanted to check to make sure it's all OK."

"She hasn't woken once since we got here."

Jason and Gena went into the small living room. "I like your tee-shirt, 'Canadian Infidel'," Gena said.

"Yeah, my father bought me this, and all my tactical gear, from OpsGear years ago. He died in Toronto over the winter."

"Oh, I'm sorry to hear that."

"Yeah, he was a firefighter there. It was pretty bad from what he told me."

"We had too many deaths over the winter. So, this is your place?" she said.

"No, I have no idea who's home this is. I guess they've already been evacuated. So what do you want to know?"

"Well, first off, who are you?"

Jason gave her a quick bio, his age, twenty-four, his occupation, simple stuff.

Then Gena asked, "You're wearing military gear and packing, are you some kind of militia?"

"No, I belong to a gun club. We do military style shooting events. At least we did before all this started."

"You're good with that weapon?"

"Fair enough, I guess. Others beat my score all the time."

"Have you used it to kill any Chinese yet?"

"No. And truth be known, I hope I don't have to. But I will protect my family however I must."

"So you weren't at the battle that took place in Chilliwack?"

"No, I wasn't there."

"Shit. Fuck. I was hoping you were. I really want to get that story. Someone else will beat me to it now. So how did you get here?"

"We got out of North Vancouver," Jason said. He then explained his ordeal. Gena wrote it all down. Tom came in a few minutes later.

"This is all the food that's left, bro. There's nothing in that food store across the tracks. Cleaned out, man."

"There's no food in town?" Gena said.

"Nah, it's all gone. Zippo, nodda. People raped the other stores in town. There ain't nothing left to eat, man," Tom said.

"They'll come up with something, dude, don't worry," Jason said.

Gena asked Tom what he saw at the docks. His story intrigued her as she asked for details about the Chinese, most of which Tom couldn't answer.

She asked if they knew what the American soldiers were doing there, and if more were coming. Jason said he had no clue other than they came up from Chilliwack. Tom knew a bit more as he wasn't spending time with Kelly like Jason was. He had mingled more with the crowd at the arena getting stories. He told her what he knew of the battle from those who were there.

After she was done with them, and obviously eager to get out the door to poke around some more, Jason asked her some questions.

"What's happening out east?"

"Chaos," Gena said.

She told them that many trains had arrived from Vancouver at Calgary. It was a big mess of what to do with all the people, tens of thousands of them. With resources as scarce as they were after Black Winter, hordes of people from the coast made matters much worse.

"I've heard word that Ottawa knows what the situation is," she continued. "But apparently they're at a loss as to what to do about it. Some have claimed that government cutbacks to the military is having a major impact on their ability to get any force together. Though I did see some army being formed in Cochrane. But whether they're going to arrive any time soon is anyone's guess."

She also said the roads through the mountains were a mass of vehicles and people walking from towns and cities east of Kamloops.

She did ask one more question. "Do you know who's in charge?"

"I think it's some Canadian Army Colonel," Jason said. "Not the RCMP."

"You wouldn't happen to know where I can find him?"

Jason shook his head, so did Tom.

She left, thanking them very much, and wished them safe passage east. She told them the train was heading back to Calgary some time in the afternoon and Jason should get his wife on that train.

As Gena and Jack came out the door, that same pickup went past them and turned into the arena. This time with one other person in the cab, and a Canadian soldier in the back. Jack filmed the three of them disembark the vehicle and go into the arena. The American soldiers at the parking lot entrance would not let them pass.

"Jason said the RCMP was not in charge. I'll bet they are pissed about that. Where's their office?" she asked Jack.

Looking at his notes Jack said, "560 Battle Street. We can walk from here. Couple blocks."

Several RCMP cars cut in front of them as they passed the rear parking entrance to the RCMP detachment building. Gena and Jack stopped to watch. The cops pulled eight people, all oriental and all handcuffed, out from the back of their cruisers and shuffled them into the basement of the building. Jack filmed it.

Gena and Jack then went into the front of the building. There were a number of reporters waiting there. Chief Superintendent Ron Blackcrow was going to give a media briefing in a few minutes, they were told.

He showed up in full dress uniform in front of the podium set up in the lobby. He gave a speech, mostly about people being evacuated. The train that arrived will be loaded with retired people and those in critical care in the hospital, he said. He mentioned little about the Chinese, and even less about the military presence in town.

Then the questions started. Ron dodged the questions about the invasion, and any questions about the military. Someone asked why the phone system was out. He replied there were technical difficulties and crews were working on restoring communications. Someone else alluded to the rumour that Chinese spies were in town and had sabotaged the phone system. Ron said those allegations were unfounded.

Gena put two and two together. She asked, "Chief, isn't it true you just arrested eight Chinese spies and they are in detention, here, right now?"

"We're arresting people all over the city, mostly for looting."

Gena was sure that wasn't anywhere near the truth.

Someone else asked who was in charge. Ron emphatically said he is in charge, including the military who were there only to help keep the peace in town, as well as aiding the evacuation. He wouldn't explain why US National Guardsmen would be brought in to help evacuate a Canadian city.

Someone asked what would happen here if the Chinese come through the mountains. His response was surprising to Gena. He said there was no indication the Chinese will be moving further west. Then someone else asked about the battle at Chilliwack. Ron replied that there was some "interaction" between Chinese solders and the American soldiers there. He then suddenly said no more questions, and left the room with a barrage of people asking over top of each other.

"Fucking liar," Gena said aloud. "We won't get anything here. The action is back at that arena, I can smell it," she whispered to Jack.

They made their way back down to the CP rail yard. "Let's stop into the radio station we passed earlier and see if they know something," Gena said.

Radio 610 AM was at the corner of 6th and Lansdowne. It also housed FM stations. Gena went in and asked to speak to a producer. They said the radio system was down for the most part. The FM country station was playing music. They were under orders to stand by in case announcements had to be made. None of the staff at the station knew much more than anyone else. They only heard that some of the coastal stations had gone off the air completely.

Gena and Jack decided to go into the Tim Hortons on the other side of the street for some coffee, but it was closed and locked. Gena walked the few meters to the railway yard and looked around. The yard was empty but for one train, with its locomotive idling.

People were being loaded into boxcars, mostly elderly and EMS crews helping patients from the hospital. Gena walked towards the east end of the train towards the engine. No one was in the cab, but the radio was on. She heard the back end of a message that surprised her.

"…tunnel blown. But another train rammed into the back of our cars in the tunnel, over."

"Outstanding, Kappy. So the tunnel is unusable, please confirm, over."

"Oh, yeah, there's no way any train is going to come through that mess. It will take them months to clean it up, over."

"What about the road bridge? The Chinese from that train will try to come across that bridge. Demolition crews should show up momentarily. Can you hold on, over?"

"I guess we have no choice. How's the other tunnel going, over?"

"Chuck said they destroyed that tunnel too. He said a train was on the way up the line, they stopped it. I've dispatched a demo crew to blow highway rock cuts. They should be leaving soon, over."

"What do you want me to do, over?"

"See if you can get back here, we could use another engineer. Train arrived to evacuate more people. See me at the CN yard, over."

"Will do, Kappy out."

"Holy fuck," Gena said to Jack. "That's who's in charge. Where's this CN yard?"

"On the other side of the river," Jack said looking at a map.

"We need to get up there."

"It's too far to walk. But I'll betcha that pickup truck with the blasting caps you saw was one of those demolition crews that guy was talking about."

"Yeah, good idea. Let's go."

The train blocked the road, so they had to go across the yard to Lorne Street. They went through a fresh cut in the fence that separated the tracks from the road.

They arrived back at the east driveway entrance to the arena. The pickup was still there, but what was different were the soldiers and armed civilians being loaded into military trucks in the back parking lot. The driver of the pickup came out and got into his vehicle, started it up and headed to the exit Gena was standing in the middle of. She would not move. The driver stopped short of her being a new hood ornament.

"Excuse me," Roger said. "Can I get past please," he said in an angry tone. Jack stood in front of the truck while Gena went to the driver's door.

"You're going to blow some bridges aren't you. To prevent the Chinese army from coming through. Am I right or am I wrong?"

"What do you want?" Roger said obviously annoyed.

"I want to go with you and video what you're going to do."

"I can't do that."

"Oh, come on now. We won't get in the way. It would make a great news story."

"I guess the whole lot of you will want to go, won't you," Roger said.

"Nope, this is an exclusive, just Jack there and little o' me."

"I'll regret this, I know it. Get in."

Gena went around the front, winked at Jack and opened the passenger door. On the floor was the box of blasting caps. "Just get in, it's safe to put your feet on. Besides, that box may make you regret coming along," Roger said.

* * *

Ray and Bonnie McGillis made their way through the mass of people in the arena to get something to eat before they packed it in for some sleep. Many familiar faces greeted him. The military like civvies tended to huddle together, exchanging stories; even a few exaggerations got added. In spite of the issue at hand, most of them were jovial. The winning of a great battle, the first in Canada in more than two hundred years, played a big part.

Some of the military, especially the National Guardsmen were wandering around, and quite impressed with the civilians, especially their equipment and gear. In many cases they could not tell the civvies apart from the Canadian Forces personnel.

One person in particular, who made the rounds, was US Lieutenant

Roland "Shooter" Schuette. He asked Bonnie about her Cz858, thinking at first it was an Ak47. He was very impressed with not only the carbine, but that Bonnie was proficient in its use.

Shooter talked with a number of civilians asking about their firearms and equipment. About a dozen of them, all with M14's, were showing off their stuff. Shooter gravitated to them.

"Hey, fellas," he said. They all introduced each other. Tom, Jason's brother, was there with his M14.

"I gotta say, guys," Shooter said, "I love the fact that you got to use the last great battle rifle in a real firefight. The M14 hasn't seen this much action since Vietnam."

"You know these aren't Springfields, they're Norincos," Simon Lambert said. "So is this 1911." Simon pulled his 45cal pistol out.

"Yes, I'm aware of that. We couldn't get those imported into the States. But they're just as good as the Real McCoy, from what I've heard anyway. It's poetic justice that a Chinese weapon is being used against them."

"Yes," Simon said, "with a little work and TLC. Not counting today at the bridge, I've put some four thousand rounds through mine over the years. Never failed me. It's a damn good rifle. I can see you like them since you have that Real McCoy."

"Actually, this is an M21. I converted it from an M14 I bought new about ten years ago. As you can see I have modified it at tad, tweaked it to be more precise. I've hunted Taliban with this rifle."

There was some oohing and ahhing as he took the rifle off his shoulders to show it off. It hardly looked like an M14. Besides the flash eliminator replaced by a muzzle brake, the wood stock had been replaced with a specialized aluminium fore stock with rails fitted with equipment, specifically a large scope made by Leatherwood. The rifle had a pistol grip, and the back stock looked like it came from an M4.

"How many have you killed with that?" Tom asked.

"I lost count in Afghanistan. During the last few years I used it more than once to put down someone trying to get into our house. I even used it a couple times when we were called in to put down rioting. We were being shot at, I had no choice. They had shot and killed a couple cops and a few of our men. Someone aimed a shotgun at me, but I was able to fire first.

"But I can safely say, you guys are real good. I'll have any of you watch my back any time." Shooter moved off to talk with others.

"Tom, I see your M14 is stock," Simon said.

"Yeah, it's my brother's," Tom said and then explained his escape from North Vancouver.

Simon said he normally lived in Victoria, but was out of work and spent most of his time with his girl friend, Trevor's sister, when the invasion took place. He admitted that he too didn't get to use his rifle at Chilliwack as he was on the train out of Coquitlam which didn't stop in Chilliwack, so he missed the battle. Both Trevor and him decided to stay and help out, sending Simon's sister east.

Tom loaded up a plate with a bit of food and a carton of milk, and excused himself as he had to go and feed his pregnant sister-in-law.

Shooter noticed one fellow sitting in one of the team benches with his M14 and walked over to him. The fellow had simple web gear with about a dozen magazines in his pouches ammo side up. He was wearing a green shirt, blue jeans and a Vancouver Canadians baseball cap covering his partly balding head. Shooter figured he was over forty. His rifle had a small powered scope over the breach. The man was cutting thin strips of masking tape and wrapping them around the barrel of his rifle. He'd done seven so far and was working on an eighth.

"Are those kill stripes?" Shooter asked.

"Damn straight, I got nine of them at Vedder as they poured out of the busses."

"Don't you think that's a tad much? I mean, I've killed many more than that and I would never think of advertising it."

"The Germans did this not only to mark their scores, but also as a fear factor. When a Sherman came up against a Tiger with thirty or forty stripes, you can bet the crews'assholes puckered. That's my goal. Should these commies kill me they're going to see how many of them I got first."

Shooter couldn't argue with that logic.

* * *

Kelly came out of the bedroom rubbing her eyes, her protruding belly preceding her. "Hey babe, what's for lunch, I'm hungry?" she said.

"Tom's got you a sandwich and a quart of milk," Jason said.

"Oh, man, great, I could eat a horse."

The EMS crew got a radio message to go to the hospital and help bring patients to the train. One of the women said that Kelly needed to be on that train and Jason should not leave her side. The two EMS women left the apartment.

"I want to stay and help," Tom said.

"Stay? Why would you stay, dude?" Jason said.

"Look, bro. You have a new family. I don't have anyone. They need help, they're going through everyone asking who can shoot. They need to protect crews going down to destroy the roads. I want to help, man."

"Jason, don't you even think about joining your brother," Kelly ordered between bites.

"She's right, bro. You two need to get as far east as you can, man. Manitoba, or even Ontario. Anywhere but here."

"Ok, then you're going to get all of Kelly's tactical gear, and her Cz. Take her Ar15 too," Jason said.

"Won't you need both rifles?"

"She's going to be carrying a baby, so she can't carry a rifle too. We should be fine with two pistols and one rifle."

Tom and Jason hugged hard. "You look after yourself, little brother. When this is all over, you come and find us. I'll try to leave you a trail," Jason choked with tears in his eyes.

"Don't cry my big brother. You keep your family alive, bro. Hey, if it's a boy name him after me, eh?"

Kelly started to cry and hugged Tom hard. "You and your dad's name, for sure."

They left the apartment, walked the short distance to the front entrance of the arena. Soldiers and armed civilians were being loaded into military trucks in the back lot. Tom hugged them both one last time. Then they parted. Tom went to join his new family. Jason and Kelly headed to a boxcar with an open door. The RCMP officer had no problem allowing the two of them into a car. He told them the train would be leaving for

Calgary within the hour.

There were no steps for Kelly to climb to get into the open boxcar door. Deputy Chief Collin Edwards was in the car and held both her hands, while Jason pushed her up by her butt and into the door. It wasn't easy and took a couple tries. Collin then helped Jason climb aboard.

Once in the car, Jason looked back to his brother. Tom was standing in line to get on a truck. He looked over to his brother in the boxcar doorway and waved. Then disappeared into the back of the military vehicle.

Jason couldn't hold his choking and tears back any more. He figured that was the last time he would ever see his little brother again. Kelly held Jason tight with her head on Jason's shoulder, and one hand on her belly.

CHAPTER 9

Walking into the
Valley of Death

K appy stopped the train at the small road crossing near the dam and canal at the east end of Seton Lake. The soldiers had gotten out and set up defensive positions at the dam and the bridge where Duffy Lake Road, a.k.a. Highway 99, went over the canal. The bridge was single laned, steel trussed with a wooden floor.

The soldiers were waiting for a team of blasters who were coming up from Kamloops.

Kappy stayed in the locomotive so he could keep in contact with Colonel Hawker at the CN yard office north of Kamloops. The fifty National Guardsmen and Canadian Reservists guarding the bridges had their own radios. A Canadian soldier was with Kappy so he could relay messages between Hawker, Kappy and the soldiers. The officer in charge, Lieutenant Gary Kroll, was 250 meters above the valley floor atop a protruding thumb from the mountain. He had a clear unobstructed view of the entire valley, the lake and mountains beyond.

Through his binoculars he could see an SUV coming out from between the mountains on the main road south of the lake. The vehicle was travelling at high speed heading towards the bridge. It fishtailed around the S curve and raced down the hill.

Kroll radioed it was a CN Police cruiser, and to not fire. The car bounced across the bridge screeching to a halt on their side.

CN Police Officer Randy Kovách rolled down the window and told the soldiers who came up to him that the Chinese on the train were gathering in Seton Portage looking for vehicles. He also suspected more were coming up highway 99 in vehicles from North Vancouver. He did say the train wreck was wonderful.

The Staff Sergeant down at the bridge radioed the message to Kroll. Another message came through that the demolition crew had arrived in Lillooet and was coming up to the bridge. Kroll told them to make sure they gave him a timeline on how long it would take to set up their charges.

Kroll could see them gather at the bridge, some of the half dozen demo crewmen were looking the bridges over. After some fifteen minutes they started to unload some crates and the Staff Sergeant got back on the radio.

"They need at least an hour, two would be better," the Staff Sergeant said. "Just a sec, the foreman wants to speak with you."

"Hello, who is this?"

"Lieutenant Gary Kroll, so what's the scoop on these bridges, over?"

"Well, the road bridge isn't a problem. Hell, it's crying to be blown. Basically, it's the dam bridge. It's five short spans of about six meters each. They have doors, gates I guess, to regulate the flow of water down the canal. Now I'm not a bridge demo guy, I blast rock faces. But basically I can't see this bridge blowing without drilling into the top. That's going to take hours. Basically, the problem is we didn't bring a drill with us, we'd have to bring one up from Kamloops."

"Roger that. No time, over." Kroll said.

"All bridges have expansion or rolling joints, we might be able to exploit one of those."

"Roger that, see what you can do. I'm sure you're aware we don't have hours, over," Kroll said.

They could be jumped on by then, Kroll thought. They were going to have to slow the Chinese down should they arrive before they were invited. He looked the map over and radioed back.

"Staff, I want you to set up an ambush on the hair pin turn back into the valley. Take a dozen men. How many LAWS do we have left, over," Kroll said.

"We have three, sir, but we'll need a vehicle or two, over."

"Use the CN cop and the demo crew vehicles if need be, but get a fucking crew up there ASAP, out."

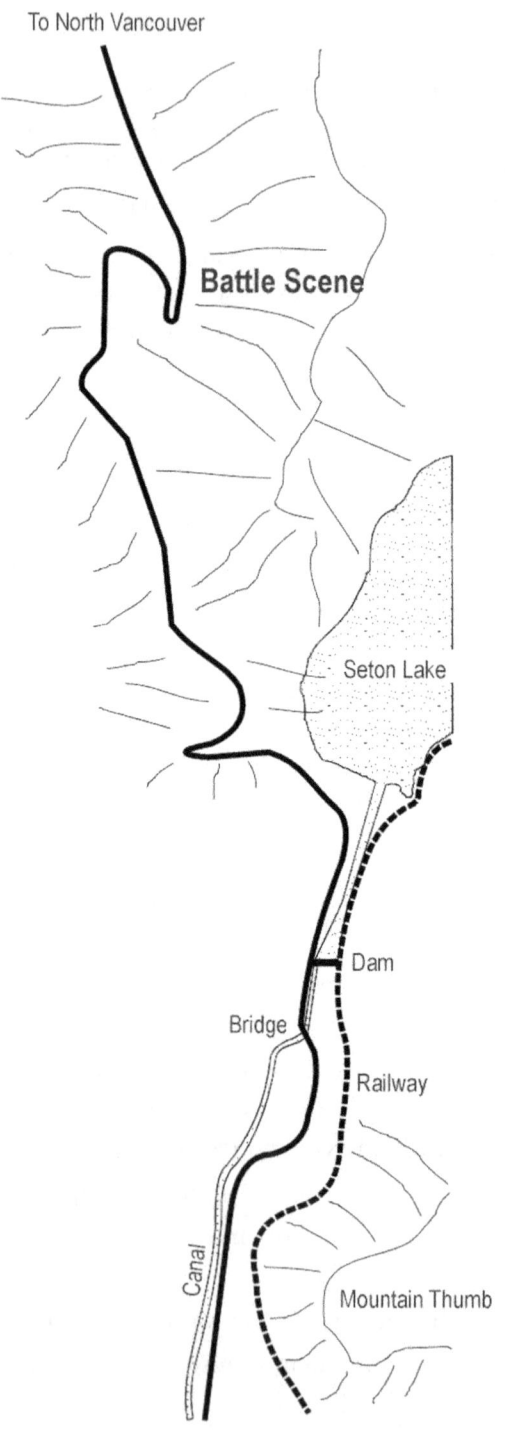

Five kilometres up Highway 99 from the bridge is a tight hairpin turn. It's a perfect ambush location. The road comes eastward down a shallow grade. On the north side along the entire length it hugs a steep angled wall of unconsolidated sand and gravel dotted with a few short evergreens. The crest of the wall is thick with tall evergreen trees and scrub brush. The south side drops off in a steep slope to a thick forested bottom of the canyon.

Most of the south side of the road was lined with a short height concrete barrier to prevent vehicles from going off and down the steep slope. At the beginning of the curve, the wall of gravel was some twenty meters to the top tree line on the north side. But as the road curved the tight 180-degree turn, the wall in front was level to the ground thick with forest beyond. The road swung south in a steep grade some fifteen meters below the upper portion of the road, before turning east again, in a tight S curve, down into the canyon.

The Staff Sergeant took ten men in two vehicles up to that location. Eight of the men got out at the turn, and set up three fire lines in the bush. One squad with the only M60 was on the level ground right at the cusp of the curve with a clear straight line of sight of more than a kilometre up the road. The other two squads took up positions on the top of the gravel wall on the north side. There was one LAWS rocket for each location. Their only two M240s were set up on the ridge to fire down. The rest of the men had their regular issue M4s. They concealed themselves well within the brush.

Two drivers took the vehicles back around the bend out of sight giving the fire crews a short three hundred meter dash through the bush to escape.

The Chief Blaster had his crews set the charges in the centre of the trusses of the road bridge. It would split the span in two dropping the ends into the canal, so they hoped. They used as little charge as they thought they could get away with, the rest allocated for the dam bridge. The bridge charges only took a few minutes to place with the wire running back about two hundred meters to the plunger on the side of the road.

The dam bridge was another matter. The bridge was supported by four short concrete piers each supporting short narrow, barely car width, spans made of concrete. Gates to regulate the flow of water was between each pier with hand wheels to raise and lower the gates. The Chief Blaster and his assistant debated long as they inspected every inch of the bridge, especially underneath where the piers supported the spans.

After minutes of deliberation, the Chief Blaster made the decision they would place charges on either side of the middle pier right under the floor of the bridge. His hope was the combined pressure from each side would throw the centre span up, then down into the canal. They only had one shot.

The Staff Sergeant up at the hairpin turn radioed to Kroll that they could see a column of vehicles coming down the road, one thousand meters away. Mostly trucks of various kinds, some cube vans, some dump trucks, some pickups, and one APC, with a cannon turret on top, which was at the front. As the convoy came down the road he counted thirty-three vehicles in total.

Kroll told them to hold off until they were on top of them, fire what they could quickly, stopping them by blocking the road, and to get out of there fast.

Soon as the APC was within one hundred meters of the turn, three LAWS rockets, two from atop the wall, and one from the front hit the APC making it turn to its right, jumping the concrete barrier, and careened down the slope stopping upside-down on the road below. It rested across the road with its wheels sticking into the air like some dead animal, smoke pouring out of the orifices, its engine still screaming.

The machine guns fired on the lead vehicles. The first one, a dump truck loaded with the enemy slid down the road, its front window all shot up, tires blown, until it came to the end of the curve. It went up the bit of hill at the turn and into the tree line where the one M60 crews was stationed. The M60 continued to fire on it the whole time. A number of Chinese bailed out, but cut down by M4 crews. The ground squad threw a couple of grenades into the vehicle turning it into a ball of flame and smoke.

The second vehicle, a cube van, they fired on swerved to its left when the front tires were blown. It traveled up the gravel wall and fell onto its side on the road dumping its cargo of soldiers. The M240's on the hill cut them all down.

The third vehicle, another but smaller dump truck loaded with men, slammed into the second vehicle crushing and running over a number of Chinese soldiers while dumping its cargo over the road. More mincemeat for the M240's and M60.

The fourth vehicle, another cub van, swerved to its right to avoid the third vehicle, but caught the barrier, and flipped onto its side making a nice jumble of vehicles coming into the hairpin turn. More grenades were tossed from above blowing the vehicles and throwing a few bodies into the air. The other trucks stopped, and Chinese soldiers bailed out scattering in all directions.

The Staff Sergeant ordered his men out. They were able to make it through the bush, down the slope, and to their vehicles. The CN cop's SUV was first, the blast crew's Dodge Ram pickup was second.

Once they were all loaded, one of the M240 shooters said the Chinese were coming on the road behind them. The Chinese fired first, one round bouncing off the M240 shooter's Kevlar helmet, another hitting one of their men in the arm. The drivers floored it down the road as the crews in the back opened up leaving the enemy in a cloud of dust.

Kroll watched them come around the S curve then down the hill to the bridge. He radioed that he could see Chinese soldiers coming down the road behind them on foot.

The vehicles came across the bridge, and were waved through to where the plunger was located. As soon as they past the Chief Blaster, he turned the plunger dial setting off two small explosions, one on either side at road level, with hardly any flash or even smoke. Just two small puffs which moved east along the road. It looked as if the bridge was still in tact. But slowly it started to sag in the middle, and in slow motion it split in two and fell into the canal. It's top truss steel beams bent and contorted.

The Chief Blaster grabbed the other plunger, and turned its dial setting off the dam bridge explosives, which was a much larger bang. The concussion from it was felt by the National Guardsmen on the road several hundred meters away. A large white and grey cloud went vertical into the sky. When the dust cleared two of the spans opposite each other at a pier, were down into the canal. The Chief Blaster and his helper gave themselves a high five.

Kroll radioed that it looked like the Chinese were coming down the road on foot, they were already near the S curve. He ordered them get their asses out of there and meet at the railway yard in town. The CN Police officer hightailed it to Lillooet in front of the demolition crew who were loaded up ready to go. The National Guardsmen went over to the train where Kappy was waiting for them, and they too headed back to Lillooet. Kroll watched the retreat from the top of the hill, once they were well back from the front, he made his way down into town.

As Kappy moved his train around the bend into Lillooet, he radioed to Hawker, "Mission accomplished."

* * *

Stan Woulfe gathered the main players of the three demo crews together soon as they all arrived at the mall up on the Trans Canada Highway. John Manning would take one crew to Lytton, Roger Zucker would take a crew to Highway 5, while Stan would take the last crew to Highway 3. Keith Wilks, the RCMP Superintendent, would go with Stan in hopes of meeting up with the constable coming in from Hope.

The soldiers and armed civilians would be unevenly split. Stan was assured by Hawker that the Trans Canada road north of Lytton would not be a conflict area, there was no way the Chinese could make it there before the crews arrived. So a truckload of just armed civvies would take that route with John's crew, just in case.

A small group of National Guardsmen, Canadian Forces and a few experienced civilians was to take Highway 5. The bulk of the soldiers, commanded by Captain Trevor "Hammerhead" Hanskull, was going to Highway 3 since any chance of the Chinese being at any location first was there because of the proximity to Chilliwack.

Each of the three teams would also have a blaster, a blaster helper, and drillers from the mining companies, plus civilians who volunteered to help with the drilling and moving equipment.

Gena Vanderpoel, and her camera man Jack Pokrajac, were wandering around looking at the equipment. There were two tracked mobile drilling rigs on trailers behind dump trucks, they look like a crane with the drill bit positioned on an extending boom. Four pickup trucks had a pair of small portable drilling machines in their backs. A van, with explosives icons on the front and back, was being unloaded with boxes and loaded onto the back of the pickups with the drill rigs.

After about half-an-hour of organizing, the vehicles started to head out.

* * *

John Manning stopped his vehicle on the north end of Spences Bridge, forcing the other vehicles to stop behind him. It was just coming up to 12:30PM. This was the only place where the Trans Canada Highway went over the Fraser River. The span from end to end was almost 400 meters, first going over the CPR railway line, then over the river into the small hamlet of Spences Bridge.

John surveyed the area contemplating options. His Chief Blaster Harry Lipman got out of his pickup and walked over to John.

"What's up?" Harry said.

"It makes no sense that we blast the sides of a road cut. It would take hours of drilling and lots of explosives. This bridge will be far easier and faster to blow, don't you think?"

"I mean, yeah. I would think so, let's have a look, eh."

They went to the edge of the bridge and looked down. Each span was supported by only three concrete pillars, which made up each bent. "Oh, yeah," Harry said. "We can get right down there and drill two bents and bring this sucka down onto the tracks and river."

"Do it," John said. "Then when this one is done you'll have to blow that truss bridge up stream there," he said pointing north up the canyon. The Bridgeway Street deck truss bridge was about a kilometre up stream spanning the Fraser.

Harry looked at it with his binoculars. "Yeah, I mean, that's going to be a bit different. Someone' s going to have to be lowered to the middle of the lower support beams and blow them. Then the whole middle span will come down."

"Can you do both at once?"

"Think so, no drilling needed. I'll send a crew over there."

They reversed their vehicles and went back up to the first intersection at Bridgeway Road. One vehicle continued on that road over the bridge, while John took Murray Creek Road, which followed the CPR line under the Trans Canada Highway. John's crew got to work unloading two portable drilling machines, and started to drill the pillars.

The concrete was easy drilling, and the pillars were quickly punctured.

One of John's blasters carefully inserted the explosives into each of the four holes, in each of the six pillars making up two bents. He filled them to the ends, then added a primer to each one. He ran three hundred meters of cable back up the road and attached the firing box.

John got onto the radio to Harry to ask about his progress on the Bridgeway bridge. Harry replied that they had installed the explosives, and wiring. It all had to be done by suspending people over the sides of the bridge. The work was difficult dangling over the river. He would radio back when he was ready.

But then he radioed back right away. "Hey, John. Isn't there a train of ours down the line? Didn't someone say they went to blow a tunnel?"

"I think so, yeah, why?"

"Have they come back yet?"

"I don't understand, arnt they on the rail line on the other side of the river?"

"Are you sure which railway line they're on, John?"

"I have no idea. Guess we better call and find out."

"And how are we going to do that?" Harry said.

"I have no fucking clue."

John didn't see any train on their way to Spenses Bridge, and indeed he was aware of the train crew hitting the tunnel, but where they were was a big mystery to him. If he blew the highway bridge and blocked the rail line, he would trap them there, if, that is, they were on the CPR line. He had no idea what to do, and no way to call Hawker.

Harry went to the far end of the bridge to the small CN yard that was on the south side of the river in hopes of finding a cabin or communications building, but there was nothing.

John looked around the CP property, but there was no building there either. He thought for a bit looking at his map. Lytton was only thirty minutes down the road, if the train was near the tunnel, they would know for sure by driving down. So John got two civilians to use his pickup to go and check. That would give him about an hour of pause time before he could blow the bridge.

John radioed Harry to blow his bridge when ready. John drove back up Murray Creek to get a good view of that event. He could see Harry's vehicle drive back to his side of the river and stop. About fifteen minutes went by when Harry radioed "Three, two, one." Four blasts took out two joins of cross braces at the bottom of each side of the truss. The bridge immediately collapsed into the river, first on an angle, but then the ends gave way on one of the blown sections and the entire length fell into the river.

All that remained where the bridge once stood was a cloud of white and grey smoke that slowly drifted to the far side, up the embankment in a long tail.

John waited the full hour when he saw his pickup return, and in the distance, beyond the Highway Bridge, the railway signal light came on red. He drove back to the detonator. In the distance across the bend in the river he could see the train heading his way. It appeared to be backing up, two boxcars first, then the locomotive. The two civilians returned to his location with his truck and told him they found the train in Lytton waiting for them to arrive. Obviously some miscommunication.

The train pulled up and stopped beside John. Several soldiers where in the open boxcar doors. Chuck Charbonneau yelled out of the cab that he was glad to see them.

John walked up to the locomotive and asked Chuck if he was in contact with Kamloops, which he said he was. Chuck called into Hawker informing him of the change in plans, that they were at Spences Bridge and that the truss bridge was already blown...

John made a throat cutting gesture with his right hand several times.

"Hold on a sec, Colonel," Chuck said. "What is it?" he said to John.

"Tell him we've already blew the highway bridge," John said. "I'm going to blow this bridge and then ask for forgiveness after."

"What? Why?" Chuck wondered.

"Because he wanted the road near Lytton done, not this bridge. He might not like it and demand we not blow the bridge, so tell him we already did."

"Ah, Colonel, sorry, got interrupted. Ahum, ah, we also blew the highway bridge here, over," Chuck said on the radio.

Hawker was pissed. He went on and on, up one side of them and down the other about not contacting him about the change. Disobeying orders, etc. Chuck used his right hand to pretend to be a talking hand while shaking his head. John just laughed. Harry showed up just as Hawker finished his rant.

"He's obviously tired. He hasn't slept in two days," John said.

John got up into the cab of the locomotive with Chuck and got on the radio. "This is John, we already blew this bridge, it's all done. It's collapsed into the river. I made a judgement call that this location that it was easier to blow these bridges than rock cuts further south. I haven't even used half our explosives."

Hawker yelled, "FUCK!" Then there was a pause. "Ok, but this had better fucking work! When you're done head over to Highway Three, they'll need the help and the rest of your explosives. Tell NG guys on the train to go with you. They'll need the defence, out."

John got down from the locomotive, went to the detonator. "Guess we better do what we have already said we've done, eh? Three, two, one." And twenty-four charges exploded blowing large chunks from each pillar into every direction. The bridge didn't move.

Once the dust cleared, they could see each pillar were still holding the bridge up. They were nothing more than thin spines of concrete, with spaghetti like exposed rebar.

"Fuck me," John moaned.

"Holly shit, you could breath on that and it'll go down," Harry said.

"So boys, now what?" Chuck laughed from the locomotive cab.

"This is not funny!" John howled.

"Actually, I think it is rather comical, John," Harry said with a smile on his face. "When was the last time one of your blasts didn't work?"

"Don't bring that up again. I've been the brunt of blasting jokes ever since."

"I'll do it," Harry said.

"Go in there? Fuck, no fuck'n way, too damn dangerous," John said. "You start drilling and the whole thing could come crashing down on your baldhead. Not that I would care, just we need someone of your experience."

"Funny, oh, funny, eh. I see no choice, someone's going to have to do it."

Harry called over one of the drillers and told him to get a machine ready.

Harry and the driller carefully drilled one hole in each of the pillars. John was sure the bridge would collapse with him under it, just from the vibration alone. In fact, two of the pillars did crack right up the full length to the deck above with a loud snap. It made Harry and the driller jump and run for their lives. The bridge collapsed.

One section fell onto the rail line, the middle section between the two blown bents dropped down pancaking on the ground below in a cloud of dust, while the third and longest section dropped into the river with a huge splash creating a small tidal wave which propagated out into the river.

Harry emerged coughing from the grey cloud, alone. He was covered from head to toe with the fine concrete dust. He turned to look behind him. No one was there.

He called to the young man. There was no reply.

The dust settled enough for Harry and a few others to look around the rubble. There was nothing.

"He was right behind me," Harry pleaded. Tears cleaned streaks from his cheeks. "I got thrown free. Must have been the air rushing out from under the falling slab." He paused. "He's gone, isn't he?"

The others looked around some more, but they found no evidence of the young man.

"He's gone, Harry," John said in a low voice.

"I should have listened to you. I got him killed. He was a nice young man. What a horrible way to die," Harry cried.

All but Harry walked back to the train. He just stood there hoping the boy would emerge somehow.

Chuck got onto the radio and told Hawker they were heading back. He didn't say anything about the accident. Hawker told them to head to Princeton, there was serious trouble there that required more people.

* * *

Most of the road along Highway 5 south to Hope had few bridges. Where there were some, but they were over small creeks, with short spans made of concrete. On top of that the old CPR's Kettle Valley right of way snaked through the same area beside the highway. So even with taking those small bridges out any enemy would be able to use the right-of-way to bypass the obstruction.

There were no rock cuts either, so it seemed Roger Zucker's team had few options.

Roger decided the only viable bridge with any potential of causing real harm would be the arch bridge over a dry gulch only 40 kilometres north of Hope. They got there just before 1:00PM.

Roger was told by the Blaster, Dan "Danno" Stryker, that the arch bridge was impossible to blow. It was too well designed and too sturdy. The only hope they had was to take out the large beams that held the bridge to the arch. But because there was no way anyone could just walk under the bridge, and they had no equipment to hang from it, it was an impossible task.

The two of them climbed down at one end into the bowels of the overpass. "Look at those steel beams running parallel to the roadway. I don't have metal bits to drill those. They're far too thick for our explosives to do much more than take a bit of paint off," Danno said.

"What about those support columns?" Roger asked.

"Sure, it might be possible to blow the joins to the arch, but would you go out there and plant the charges?" Danno asked sarcastically.

Roger just looked at the bridge.

"Yeah, exactly, no one would be able to do that. Well above my pay grade to risk my life going out there," Danno said.

"Fuck," Roger moaned. As they made their way back to the road he said, "There has to be a way."

"Sure, just call in an air strike. A couple thousand pound bombs will do the job," Danno said.

"Right, funny guy. Maybe we can't take the bridge out, but how about taking out sections of the roadway?"

"Maybe. It's asphalt on concrete. I'd have to drill it and see."

"Get started."

"That'll take hours, if not the whole day to prepare. We're only forty kilometres from Hope. We could be attacked any time."

Roger thought. Then he asked, "How easy it would be to take out some of the snow shed, enough to buy us some time?"

Ten kilometers south of the arch bridge on Highway 5 was a concrete snow shed. The structure was to prevent snow slides from taking the road out. It was almost three hundred meters long. At its entrances on each end were images of bears cast into the concrete. The inside support wall between the road lanes was a series of columns two by four foot.

Danno knew the snow shed, and said it would be simple to take enough of it down to give them lots of time. Roger took a pickup and the Assistant Blaster with one drill machine. One pickup had the drillers, the other had the drill machine. The three M35 military trucks, with all the soldiers to guard them while they worked, went with them. Trailing was Phil Waterford in his RCMP cruiser. The small convoy headed south.

Danno got the tracked drill machine off the trailer, and prepared to drill a portion of the road in the middle of the arch bridge.

Roger was driving with the Assistant Blaster, Dianne Reger, as his passenger. They were driving south along the highway with a high wall rock cut on their right, and a clear view of the valley to their left. In front of them was Markhor Peak, which the highway curved to the right in front of.

As they came up a crest in the road, Dianne said pointing to the front of them, "Who are those guys?"

Coming around the curve in the opposite direction was three SUVs. The vehicles stopped and some men in uniform poured out onto the road. Some jumped over the median concrete barrier that separated the lanes.

Roger hammered on the breaks as bullets pierced the window and front of the radiator. He put the vehicle in reverse and backed up, peddle to the floor, past the M35 trucks in his convoy. They too stopped and their soldiers bailed out. Phil and the other pickup backed up half a kilometre to get out of the way.

There was no cover for either side, save for their own vehicles.

The National Guardsman in charge was Lieutenant Roland "Shooter" Schuette, a stockbroker in his former life, but he was a sharp shooter who had served in Afghanistan with Hammerhead. He was an excellent marksman with his M21, he had sniped Taliban from five hundred meters, and beyond, on more than one occasion with his rifle.

Shooter placed some of his men over the far barrier of the highway, thinking the Chinese will try to outflank him on his left. The canyon drops off, quite steeply, three hundred meters to the creek below, but there was a narrow buffer of land between the concrete barrier and the drop off. He also figured they would try to out flank him on the right side atop the rock cut, so he sent an M240 crew up there.

On the ground, crawling under one of the trucks, Shooter dropped the bipods on his M21, opened the lens covers of his Leatherwood HiLux M1000 scope, and sighted down range. Using the mil-dot reticle and zooming in to frame one of the enemy vehicles between the cross hairs dots, he figured the distance was just over four hundred meters. Which was good for him because Ak47's are not accurate at that distance. But child's play for his M21. He started to pick off targets, specifically those lying on the ground in front of him.

The M60 crew on his left jumped over the median barrier into the northbound lane and opened fire onto the vehicles, one of which went up in smoke. An RPG was fired from behind another vehicle, but it bounced off the road in front of them, blowing up against the median barrier.

Shooter noticed a number of the enemy getting up and running to the rock cut on his right, he took two down on the move before they could get there, but half a dozen or so made it.

The crest of the rock cut was very rugged and thick with small coniferous bush. The M240 crew, six soldiers in all, had made it along the top to half way between the two fire lines. At a slight drop in the rock cut, they had a clear line of fire to the enemy and opened up on those using the vehicles as cover. They got the message over the radio from Shooter that half a dozen where heading their way.

They didn't wait long. The Chinese moving along the top had gotten close enough to open fire on the M240 crew killing two of their men and wounding one. The corporal on the M240 opened fire back while another soldier radioed that they needed backup.

Shooter sent six more men to re-enforce the M240 crew. Not long after he sent the men, shooting stopped from down the road. Shooter didn't have any moving targets left, neither did the M60 crew. All three of the SUV's where burning. Occasional gunfire could be heard from the top of the rock cut.

"Are they all down?" one of the Canadian soldiers near Shooter said.

"I don't know. They maybe trying to position themselves."

Shooting started from behind the concrete barrier on the left side against the drop off as some of the Chinese had tried to advance there. The firefight claimed one of their soldiers, a National Guard Corporal, and wounding two more before the Chinese had been dispatched.

The M240 crew atop the road cut radioed that the re-enforcements worked and they had killed the Chinese, though two had run back to the road.

Shooter ordered the M240 to make their way along the top to the Chinese vehicles, and ordered the crew on the ledge to his left to make their way up unseen to the vehicles.

"There's one!" someone yelled. Shooter sighted his M21 on the hood of a truck at a man dashing across the road to the right. It took two shots, but he downed the runner.

After a long period of quiet both teams made it to the burning wreckage radioing, "All clear."

Shooter boarded a truck, with a few soldiers, telling the rest to wait. When he got to the burning enemy vehicles a Sergeant said he counted seventeen bodies including the four on the top of the rock cut and the five that tried to make it along the ledge. The M240 Corporal swore two got away.

"So, what do you think, sir? A scouting party?" the sergeant said.

"Afrim on that." Shooter ordered the rest of the convoy to come up, and the crews to move the bodies off the road.

Phil Waterford, the RCMP Constable, at the rear of the convoy, and well back of the firefight, had already radioed to Hawker of what had happened. The RCMP vehicle was the only method of communication to HQ, and Phil had volunteered to go.

Once all boarded, Shooter ordered the military vehicles go first, and let Phil and Roger come after. Roger's Dodge Ram was steaming from the hood. Not only the windshield had multiple holes, but so did the grill. Roger assured him the pickup would make it to the snow shed, just around the bend in the road, but not likely drivable back. Shooter told him he was damn lucky he didn't get blown to smithereens since the explosives were in the bed of the pickup.

Shooter kept six men at that location to look around for the two enemy who might be missing, they would be picked up on the way back. So would the bodies of their fallen soldiers.

The soldiers set up a defensive position at the south entrance of the snow shed, while the demo crew started to drill columns in the centre. Two portable machines worked for two hours with Dianne putting the charges in each hole once it was bored half way through. She ran lines back three hundred meters from the north entrance. Once ready, Shooter called all his men to join them. Soon as the area was clear, Dianne fired off the explosives. The sound was muffled. A combination of smoke and grey dust churned out of the entrance. Nothing else could be seen.

"Did it blow?" Roger asked.

"Soon as the dust settles we'll know," Dianne said.

They waited for about fifteen minutes until they could see inside. Then Roger, Dianne and Shooter went in to have a look. Sure enough, the centre of the show shed had come down onto the road, completely covering it with fallen slabs of concrete. The road in both directions was completely blocked.

"This may be a better stoppage than the arch bridge," Roger said.

"It couldn't hurt. Let's get back," Shooter said.

Roger left the pickup as it had overheated. They had to load the portable drilling machines into one of the M35's making the seating a tad compacted for those who had to ride in the back. Roger and Dianne got a ride with Phil who radioed to Hawker they succeeded in blowing the snow shed.

They picked up the crew left where the firefight was, who reported they could not find anyone alive. They had checked the wood thoroughly.

"If they're out there, they won't last long without food. Leave them," Shooter said.

The crew had retrieved the bodies of their dead and had them on the road covered with ponchos. The seriously wounded were loaded into the trucks first.

Shooter stood over the bodies. "What a fucking waste," he said. "I hate war."

Roger and Phil were beside him. "A soldier who hates war?" Roger said.

"Only a deluded fool would not hate war. It's so destructive," Shooter said. "Just because I understand that there are people out there who want to destroy us, and I want to do my part to protect my country doesn't mean I have to love war.

"The difference between me and people like those fuckers over there…" Shooter pointed up the road to the still burning Chinese vehicles, "…is they are doing it for a cause they believe in and willing to die for. I do it because of the situation that is forced on me. I take no pride in picking off – killing people – with my rifle. For every one of them I kill, I save the lives of how many of our own people?

"Humans are still savages. Deep down we're still barbaric. We haven't evolved beyond our basic instincts. I saw it in Afghanistan. I saw it in my own country during the rioting. I had to kill in both places."

"A philosophical soldier," Phil said.

"Death is always a waste," Roger agreed.

"They are with Jesus now," Phil said.

Shooter just looked at him for a moment then moved away saying, "No, preacher boy, they do not exist any more. They aren't with anyone. Their memories, their experiences, everything they were has been erased. Sergeant!" Shooter yelled.

"Yes, sir," the Sergeant said running over.

"Are we ready to go?"

"Yes, sir, just these bodies to load. But we have no room."

"Move the demo crew's equipment out of their pickup and double the men up in an M35."

"Yes, sir."

They got back to the arch bridge to find the northbound lane had large square holes through to the outside world. Three sections had been drilled and blown opening voids in the road three meters wide and five meters long. They were drilling the last square to make it even.

The southbound lane was untouched. Once at the north end of the bridge the portable drilling machines were unloaded and crews started to drill the southbound lane.

Danno explained that they could not bring a whole section of the road down, the steel girders were too thick. He figured if a long enough section of the bridge was left gaping, no vehicles could cross. People maybe, but not vehicles.

They worked for the rest of the afternoon. Eventually they had opened three large sections of the road on each lane, six voids in all.

It was well after 6:00PM when Phil Waterford radioed to Hawker their job was done and they were heading back to Kamloops. Hawker asked if they had any explosives left. To which Danno said no. Hawker told them the demo crew at Highway 3 were in serious trouble and needed more drilling equipment ASAP.

* * *

RCMP Superintendent Keith Wilks was pulling into Princeton, just after 1:00PM, at the tail end of his convoy when he got a disturbing radio message. Constable Deb Osby was racing up Highway 3 from Hope. She said a convoy; some one hundred or more vehicles had pulled into Hope. She said she watched three of them head up Highway 5, while some stayed in Hope, with fifty or more were coming up Highway 3 behind her. She had just passed through Manning Park.

The other shock that Kieth got was Princeton wasn't evacuated. In fact, it was a normal afternoon from appearance.

Keith raced past the military and mining vehicles to get to Stan's pickup, and waved him over. The convoy stopped, Hammerhead got out and joined Keith at Stan's truck. Kieth told them about Deb's call. She would be here within the hour, and the Chinese not long after that. The three of them discussed options over a map laid out in the hood of Stan's GM pickup.

The Blaster for their group was Tina Van Der Haus, she came up to the meeting to see what was going on.

"What's up fellas?" she said.

"The Chinese are already past our objectives. We're looking for alternatives," Stan replied.

She looked at the map. "Well, how about the bridge right there. I used to work at the copper mine right beside it. You can see it's a tight curve. I know the area well, did a lot of my PhD work at UBC on the geology of the area."

"Let's move like we have a purpose," Stan said.

"I'm going to stay here," Keith said. "Pass Constable Osby through when you see her. I'm going to ask around 'cauz I don't think anyone here knows what's going on."

The convoy left. Keith went over to the Esso station on the main road. The lone employee said they had heard nothing about any evacuation, and the phone system was down. He asked the kid where the firehall was. He said it was just over on Penryn Street, Keith couldn't miss it.

Keith parked in front of the doors of the firehall and got out. A large pot bellied man came outside to great him.

"I'm Vic Vickers, Fire Chief, what can I do for you?" he said.

Keith asked if he had heard about the invasion. Vic was completely floored at the news. He said the phone system was out, but that had been normal for the past few years, especially over the winter when he said the town had been cut off for months. He told Keith the winter was especially brutal, snow was several meters deep. His men had to dig tunnels to get to people's homes. He said it did not surprise him that he had heard nothing, he had the feeling the province had abandoned small towns like his. They decided with the immediate peril heading their way, they had better try to evacuate as many as can be loaded onto the few vehicles they could fuel up. So much for the imposed rationing at the gas stations. The task of organizing an evacuation was going to take most of the day.

Keith informed Vic of what the plan was.

"You'll never blow that bridge," Vic said. "I used to work, in my youthful days, at the copper mine up there."

"Too late to stop them now, they're on the move."

"David!" Vic yelled.

A young man came out from the firehall. "Yes, Dad?" he said.

"Take the chief car and head up lickidy-split to the mine and tell the people there to forget the bridge. Radio back when you get there. Now move it along."

"Sure, Dad."

"Now," Vic turned back to Keith, "your best bet would be to take out the two truss bridges here in town. Now Highway 3 bridge, that's a bitch. You will never blow that. Let me think…" Vic stood there pensive, rubbing his chin. "Oh, I have an idea."

"Share it please," Keith said.

"On the other side of the river are hundreds of concrete barriers. They've been there for years, when they were working on the highway. We could move all of them onto the bridge. There's a concrete Ready-Mix plant just up the road. We mix up a truckload and pour it between the barriers. That would make a solid mass of concrete. They'd never get through that."

"Sounds like a great idea. But we're going to need some help."

"That's no problem, the logger here in town is my brother. He can get half a dozen of his log trucks to move the barriers. I know the guy at Ready-Mix too, he lives on the other side of the river. I'll get right on it." Vic got into one of the engine pumpers and drove off.

* * *

The blast crew started to unload their tracked driller off the trailer at the curved bridge just north of the abandoned copper mine. The road makes a tight 180 degree turn inside of the valley. The hills on either side towered over the bridge to the south and north. Eastward, the valley widened and fell some 300 meters to a river below. A small tributary fed the river from under the bridge.

Gena Vanderpoel and her camera man Jack were there. They got out of Stanley Woulfe's pickup and immediately started to tape the activities, with Gena making comments.

Crews unloaded the tracked driller, while Tina looked the surface over. "Start here," she said to the drill operator.

Gena went over and asked Tina the reason for her choice. Jack taped the conversation.

"In the old days in South Africa," Tina said, "when they were terrified of terrorist acts, my father-in-law, a retired Colonel, was put in charge of security and anti-terrorist measures to make sure the military could get around in the event of a revolt.

"He made all the bridge engineers and maintenance crews go in and pump foam or something equivalent into the voids at the rolling or expansions joints. That way it was a lot harder to casually insert a stick of dynamite into the Achilles heel of the bridge.

"We're going to exploit the weakest part of the bridge, the expansion joints. The only problem is time. We need the time to drill enough holes to place the charges we need. It's going to be up to the military guys to make sure we get the time."

Hammerhead looked around checking for places to set up a defensive position. But he needed to get a visual on the road to give them a heads up. Tina said the road was straight from the mine south where they could get a good view. Hammerhead took a pickup and three men up to the mine. They didn't get far from the bridge when an RCMP truck raced down the highway towards them. The vehicles stopped side by side with driver's windows open.

"You the army?" Constable Deb Osby asked Hammerhead.

"Yep, along with about seventy of us."

"That won't be enough. The whole fucking Chinese army is heading right this way. They could be here within the hour."

"Fuck me," Hammerhead muttered. "Go tell the rest that at the bridge. I doubt they'll be able to blow a bridge in an hour."

Deb floored it down the road. Hammerhead continued up to the mine. Just past the mine entrance on the highway, the road was elevated above the valley as it made a long left turn south. Hammerhead drove up that part to a rockcut where the elevated road ended. He figured he could get a crew to blow both sides of the cut, which would buy them some time.

He noticed that the tailings from the mine made a huge hill on the east side of the road. He turned around, and drove back along the road to the mine entrance. He pulled into the mine road and followed an S curve climbing the tailings. He then drove along the top of the tailings to the thumb that protruded high above the road. He had a clear line of sight for just over a kilometre down the highway.

He told one of the men to take the pickup back to the bridge and get a crew to bring the rock cut down.

Twenty minutes later three trucks showed up at the rock cut and got their equipment out. Gena and Jack were with them. The crew got to work using portable drills on either side of the top of the cut the road went through. Hammerhead's men returned to his location with the pickup.

They had been drilling for about fifteen minutes when Hammerhead saw the first of the enemy vehicles down the highway. Through his binoculars there were at least three APC's with gun turrets, and a few other vehicles behind them. He radioed to the rock cut team to blow the cut now. He looked back again at the long continuous stream of vehicles heading their way.

He got into the pickup and drove off the tailings back to the highway. When he got to the entrance to the mine, a large explosion occurred to his left. He could see a plume of grey smoke follow the road north, then over the valley. The vehicles raced back to his position, then they all returned to the bridge.

Peter Douglas and Tina were directing drilling in the centre of the bridge at the expansion joints. Hammerhead told them they were out of time, they had to blow what they could. Peter said they would need at least an hour if not more.

"The rock cut won't hold them that long," Hammerhead argued. "If they come through here with their APCs they'll blast the shit out of all of us."

"You gotta hold them off somehow," Peter said. "We could side drill into that rock face there up the road. It's about a kilometre and around a bit of a bend. They wouldn't be able to see us." He ordered the crew who blew the other cut to head back up the road. Hammerhead sent some thirty men with them and set up a defensive position.

He looked up at the steep slope on the north of the bridge. There were few trees along the crest. He remembered there was a logging road just before the bridge.

He took the rest of his men and drove up the steep narrow logging road. At the top he had a great view down to the bridge and up the road where the Chinese would come down. He couldn't see where the crew was going to blast another rock face, however. It was beyond the curve in the highway.

He set up two M60s, and three M240s aiming to the highway beyond the bridge. The rest of his shooters lie on the crest at the ready. They had a clear view of the road at just under 400 meters.

The busy ants below were drilling as fast as they could. But to Hammerhead they weren't getting ahead. He heard an explosion, but it was too far and in the wrong direction for the rock cut crew. The Chinese were clearing their previous roadblock.

"Fuck me," he said as he saw a plume of smoke emerge over the hill to the south.

Not long after that, another explosion occurred in front of him. The crew blew the rock face. Their vehicles came down the road to the bridge in a hurry. There was a lot of scampering at the bridge. The crews from the rock face helped by drilling more holes. They weren't going to make it, Hammerhead thought.

He was right. Through his binoculars he could see green uniformed troops, hundreds of them, coming down the road. He screamed into the radio to abandon the attempt and to get the hell out of there.

Hammerhead ordered the M60 machinegun crews to open fire. He could see tracer rounds arch down to the road. The impacts of the 7.62mm bullets ejected dust and sand into the air, as well as chunks of asphalt. Through his binoculars, he could see bodies falling. However, return fire started to impact around them. The Chinese had set up their heavy machine guns, known as Type 88s, behind a concrete barricade on the side of the road.

Hammerhead tried to get his crews to fire on them, but they couldn't hit it. Then mortar fire started to land on the side of the slope in front of them. The impacts slowly crept up the hill.

Hammerhead look down at the road, some of the vehicles had left, but others were still loading up the portable equipment. Chinese were sending fire down on them as well. Hammerhead ordered his shooters to target the Chinese solders aiming at the bridge crew. They got some, but not all. Once the last vehicle left the bridge mortars started impacting around them on the ridge. Hammerhead ordered his men to get out.

He took one last look down at the bridge, not only did they leave the tracked drilling rigs behind, but at least a half dozen bodies lay in the middle of the road amongst growing pools of blood.

CHAPTER 10

Between a Rock
and a Hard Place

Captain Chris Staines arrived at Cochrane by train from Kamloops just after 3 p.m. They stopped in town beside another train, which was on the north passing siding. It was facing to go into the mountains with a long string of boxcars. A third train was on a siding south of the main tracks. It consisted mostly of VIA coaches and flatcars loaded with military equipment including 7000-MV trucks, half a dozen M777 howitzers, a dozen LAVs and three Leopard II tanks.

Thousands of troops huddled around hundreds of 45-gallon drums of fire at the Esso transfer field on Railway Street south of the tracks, as well as in the abandoned Ford dealership parking lot just down the road. There were no new automobiles on the lot, and the building was empty, as it had been for a number of years since the economic collapse. Smoke from the fires hung low over the area.

Staines figured this was the response force getting ready to head into the mountains. So he disembarked the train to seek out who was in command.

It was cold, below freezing, and the ground was a foot thick of a crusted layer of snow. Small snow pellets were falling from the dark grey sky.

He went into the showroom of the Ford dealership, which had a number of tables set up, with lots of people, mostly Canadian Armed Forces officers, pouring over maps and issuing orders. Against the windows more 45-gallon stoves were burning with makeshift flues protruding through the walls to the outside.

He was greeted by a Leftenant. Staines told him where he came from and asked to see the commanding officer. The leftenant asked him to wait. While the officer was gone, Staines looked around. Many of the curious officers greeted him, considering he was the only American officer in the

172

room. He helped himself to some food on a table, and some hot coffee.

The leftenant came back and asked Staines to follow him. They went into what was obviously the dealership owner's office. Three senior officers, including a Brigadier General, were in the room. They introduced each other.

"So, Captain, I understand you came from Kamloops," General George Maillet said in a thick French-Canadian accent.

"Yeah, Colonel Hawker..."

"Gary Hawker?" one of the other officers interrupted.

"Yeah, why?"

They all looked at each other and smiled. "Oh, I know Gary well," Maillet said. "We served together when he was a Leftenant in Bosnia. He spent t'ree tours in Afghanistan where he got his major. I should have know t'at was 'im at Chilliwack. Major Armstrong, make a note t'at we give Hawker a medal."

"Yes, sir," Armstrong laughed.

"Can someone let me in on the joke?" Staines said.

"Gary Hawker is one of our best commanders. He's the type of officer who never asks to do something, just does it, then asks for forgiveness after," Armstrong said.

"Hell, I've never 'eard Hawker ask for forgiveness after anyt'ing," Maillet laughed.

"Affirm that, sir," Armstrong chuckled.

"If he runnin' the show he goin' to give t'ose fuckers a shellack'n. I should have figured it was 'im to just unilaterally blow tunnel and bridge," Maillet said.

Captain Staines looked confused. Maillet caught it. "We just 'eard t'at t'RCAF sent in four CF18 to check out what going on. The Chinese fired SAMS at 'em, almost lost 'em both. But we got a good look at what going on. So we ' ave seen the blown tunnel and the bridge. What Hawker doesn't know is the Chinese are amassing in Hope, preparing to move east to Revelstoke. That's where we're heading just as soon as we get our act together. We're waiting for some supply to arrive."

"Great," Staines said. "They need lots of ammo and food too."

Someone opened the door and said, "General, the Internet is up and running. We're in email contact with HQ."

"Wonderful, 'bout bloody time. Send t'em an email and update t'em wit' what we're doing."

"Yes sir."

"Oh, and Corporal, tell HQ we now know who was responsible for the fights inland. It's Colonel Hawker."

"Roger that, sir." He left closing the door.

"We're working on the food with local beef farmers," Armstrong said returning back to Staines' query. "Ammo we have lots of, well kind of. What's the makeup of the men? How many of you Yanks are there?"

"I had two hundred and fifty, about that many of you Kanucks, and at least two thousand armed civvies, and I mean armed. Some of these guys are better equipped than my men." Staines laughed.

"Sir," the same Corporal said coming into the room. "We're ready to go, supplies have arrived."

"About time, excuse me gentlemen." Maillet got up from behind the large modern desk and left the room.

Armstrong continued, "We're getting radio messages out across the country for volunteers. We're setting up training camps to get them up to speed. You know they've landed in Prince Rupert as well. Half a dozen container ships showed up and thousands of soldiers poured out of them. Thousands of them. They're going to try to make their way east from there. But the weather isn't good. They got a lot of snow there this winter, and none of it has melted. A big storm is heading in tonight; it's expected to dump six inches or more. I guess you know that the Chinese have also landed in the U.S.?"

"Tell me about it, I was there. In Washington when they arrived on our coast. So yeah, I know what's happening."

"So what do you want to do, head back to the States?"

"No I want to get back to my men first. Then I want to get them back into the States. No insult to you guys, but we have to defend our own land."

"We should be able to get them off the line. This is going to be our staging area. Revelstoke will be our FOB. Once the civilians are trained we'll assign them here. You do know some of you Yanks are coming here, that's the rumour anyway. We could really use your help. But the choice is yours."

Maillet came back in. "Pack up Gentlemen, we're leavin'." He picked up his helmet, C8 and left the room followed by the others.

The showroom was empty, including the tables, no one was there. Outside, while heading to the train, Staines saw that the train he came in was gone, so was the one with all the equipment on the passing siding. Men where filing into the boxcars of the train on the north tracks. Another one had just arrived with a number of freight cars. Armstrong said it was the supplies they were waiting for. The train had food, ammo and other provisions for the front. Armstrong invited Staines into the cab of that train. Then two trains headed west.

* * *

Colonel Hawker moved his HQ from the CN railway yard north of Kamloops to the RCMP building in town. They had no more trains out. Kappy's crew returned, and Chuck Charbonneau got his short train of one engine and two boxcars full of soldiers into the CPR yard.

Hawker needed to be in contact with the crews taking out the bridges, and the only radios were those in RCMP cruisers who went to Highway 5 and Highway 3.

Chuck had radioed in that they successfully blew the two bridges at Spences Bridge, which Hawker was not happy about. The map showed that the Chinese could bypass the gap in the road by taking another road to Merritt. From Merritt the Chinese had clear sailing to Revelstoke. He wanted a rock cut further south on Highway 1 blown to prevent that from happening. He hoped the Chinese wouldn't be too quick, or they could be in serious trouble.

He got a sinking feeling that their luck was about to change. Things had gone their way for too long. The other shoe was about to drop, he thought. He worried Spences Bridge would be the first of many mistakes to come.

Before Chuck and John Manning's crew left the bridge, Hawker ordered them to help at Princeton. RCMP Superintendent Keith Wilks had radioed in an hour before that they were unsuccessful in blowing a bridge south of Princeton, and had engaged the enemy. They were retreating back to Princeton.

Hawker realized their only hope at stopping the Chinese was at the three bridges in Princeton. If they made it over the north bridge on the road to Kamloops they could be seeing Chinese in the streets that day. If the enemy proceeded along Highway 3 the Chinese could be in Revelstoke, most of the way through the mountains, by the end of the next day.

Their only hope, short of the cavalry riding in from the east, at stopping the Chinese from taking control of Alberta and the booty that awaited them, was to stop them in Princeton. So he had no choice but to commit everything they had to there.

Before Hawker could send reinforcements to Princeton he had to wait for Kappy and Lieutenant Gary Kroll to arrive from Seton Lake as they had the only remaining running vehicles. So the combination of Kroll's men and the soldiers on the CP train couldn't be sent to Princeton until after 7 p.m. That was Hawker's major mistake. He didn't call for Kappy to return until after dusk, after he got the call of the retreat at Princeton. He was frustrated at the mistake as Kappy's crew was sitting idle for hours babysitting a bridge they had blown at noon. He invented a few new swear words, and brooded about it for hours. He worried his mistake of miscalculating the enemy would cost lives.

Adding to Hawker's problems was his move into the RCMP building in Kamloops. Chief Superintendent Ron Blackcrow wasn't pleased and they had a heated argument of jurisdiction over Ron's people. They compromised that Ron would deal with the transmissions from his people in the field as long as he and Hawker didn't leave the control room.

Then the tension upped another notch when one of the officers came into the control room and said that the prisoners weren't talking. Hawker was stunned.

"You captured the saboteurs and didn't tell me?" he howled with a stern stare, and his ears turning red.

"People we arrest are my responsibility, not yours," Ron retorted with his head raised a bit looking down with his eyes narrowing. "In fact, Colonel, you have no jurisdiction here at all. I would be within my rights to arrest you here and now."

"On what grounds?" Hawker was getting even angrier.

"Lots, destruction of property, namely bridges and tunnels. Hell, I can even arrest you for weapons violations, walking around everywhere with a loaded gun." Ron's black eyebrows looked knotted, his head still bent back looking down at Hawker.

"You're a fucking idiot." Hawker left the room. He could be away from the radio for a bit as everyone would take time to get to their destinations. Besides, he needed to talk to the prisoners.

He wasn't in the basement jail very long, about to start his interrogation of the prisoners, when Ron came in with two RCMP officers, pistols drawn. Ron ordered his men to disarm the Colonel, and put him in a cell, and made it clear to lock the door.

Pistols pointed at him, Hawker capitulated and was placed in a cell.

* * *

John Manning and the crew that took out Spences Bridge, before returning to Kamloops, was ordered by Hawker to help the effort at Princeton. They turned on to Highland Valley Road, also known as Highway 97C, from Highway 1, in Ashcroft. On the way they past John's company's copper mine complex. They stopped and picked up some more explosives, and in the dusk headed to the junction with Highway 5. They turned south towards Merritt, the first town before coming to Princeton.

It was dark when they neared Merritt from the north. Highway 5 went under a bridge at Voght Road, just coming into town. John's vehicle was first, lighting the road ahead. He saw a yellow flash from the bridge, with a long fiery tail heading towards him. Then his truck exploded in the engine sending it into the cab. The truck turned upside down and slid under the bridge wrapped in flame.

Another RPG hit the next truck, loaded with civilians, turning on its side and dumping the men along the highway. Bullets from both sides of the road riddled the third vehicle, which careened into the second.

Chief Blaster Harry Lipman was in his pickup at the end of the convoy. He hammered on his brakes, turned out his lights, did a quick U turn on the highway, and peddle to the floor raced back up the road with bullets piercing the back of the pickup's bed. He was the only vehicle to escape.

* * *

RCMP Superintendent Keith Wilks was watching Vic and his crew laying concrete barriers lengthwise on Highway 3 bridge in Princeton. They had to work from the east side as that is where all the barriers were stacked. One logging truck moved the barriers into place, neatly lining them up. In the lane beside him, a cement truck was laying down a layer of concrete about a foot thick. Another logging truck was picking up the barriers and bringing them to the bridge. A third truck on the town side of the river was placing a load of logs between the barriers, setting the bottom ones into the wet concrete, for as far as he could reach.

Keith was beside Vic who was in a fire truck. A hose line was laid out to the bridge and someone there was spraying the barriers with water to make them wet enough to adhere the new concrete to the asphalt.

Vic called Keith over.

"Major problem, lad. My son just radioed in that they're under attack up at the mine. They're retreating. They'll be here any moment."

Keith ordered the west side effort to block Highway 3 bridge to stop; they would have to cross on the Highway 5 truss bridge north of them. The main problem was that the town wasn't fully evacuated. The barricade crew left a single walking lane along each side of the bridge. This allowed people to walk across, which they were doing en masse carrying whatever they could, some with infants in their arms or in tow.

Keith got in his vehicle and headed up the highway to the south entrance into town to meet the retreating convoy. When he got to the top of the road where the town's welcome sign was, he could see vehicles coming towards him. The first one was Constable Deb Osby in her RCMP vehicle, a Ford Bronco. She said they didn't blow the bridges. They were attacked before they could finish the drilling. She told him some people were killed in the firefight, but she didn't know how many. Keith told her to help with the rest of the evacuation and to meet him on the other side of the Highway 5 bridge north of town.

The other vehicles passed Keith, some screaming they were attacked. The last vehicles to pass were Hammerhead's crew. They stopped beside Keith. Hammerhead got his crew out and told some of them, with two M60s, to make an ambush at the Welcome sign. It was a good spot, with a clear view up the road, their cover being the big rocks that adorned the base of the sign. He told the crew to put a vehicle behind them for escape, in the home with a carport. Hammerhead also told Keith he had better get on the radio to Hawker and ask for help. They would need it.

They all met at the north side just out of town. Keith was the last to cross the truss bridge where Highway 5 went over the Tulameen River. There were no more pedestrians. Hammerhead had already set up a defensive position along the bank of the river and a knoll facing down the road where it made a bit of an eastward turn.

There was a problem, however. Vic was on the road kneeling with Tina, the assistant blaster. She had blood on her clothes. She was in a fetal position in the middle of the road, crying.

Gena, the reporter, was sitting on the barrier at the side of the road near them, Jack's camera at her feet. She was also crying. Keith stopped and got out beside Vic.

"She's in a real state," Vic said of Tina as he held her. "I can't get anything out of her."

Hammerhead came over and said, "We're missing some people. That road commissioner, Stan, Douglas, the Chief Blaster, a few of my men, a couple civvies too, and that reporter's cameraman. Thirteen in total were killed. Times two wounded, most not bad."

Keith knelt down at Tina, she did not look at him. She stared into space, her body shaking. "Get her out of here. Get her back to Kamloops," he said.

David, Vic's son, helped him get Tina into the cab of the Fire Chief's car and the three of them headed up the road north.

Keith went over to Gena. She had stopped crying and looked at Keith and said, "His body just exploded in front of me. He's gone, he's dead," her voice cracked. Tears welled in her eyes.

"But you managed to save his camera," Hammerhead barked in discuss.

"So what do we do now?" Keith asked.

"We blow the bridges," Hammerhead said.

"You know how?"

"Not a problem." Hammerhead got some of his crew together and divided up the explosives they managed to bring back with them. It was dark by the time they got both the truss bridges and the new pedestrian bridge set to blow. He called in his crew at the town Welcome sign, who radioed no one had yet arrived, but they could see lights in the distance heading their way.

Once that last of those vehicles was over the main bridge, Hammerhead fired the charges. The explosions filled the sky with light like a lightning strike, the smoke disappearing into the darkness when the flash died off. The bridges collapsed into the river with the middle down, but the ends still on each side at road level.

Keith got on the radio, but Hawker wasn't at the other end. It was his boss, Ron Blackcrow. Ron informed him that Hawker had been arrested, and he was now in charge. Keith called Hammerhead over to listen. Ron ordered them all to leave immediately and return to Kamloops. He ordered them to not engage the enemy. He didn't want any one else killed or wounded.

Hammerhead got on the radio and asked, "Are the other crews coming as expected?"

"I'm not in contact with the crews ordered to Princeton. And if you meet up with them tell them their orders have been countermanded. They are to head back to Kamloops immediately," Ron ordered.

"We aren't going anywhere," Hammerhead argued. "We leave, and the Chinese will come across the river. We have a good spot here to take them on."

Keith interrupted, "You mean like at the mine?"

"No, better. We can take them on here."

"They have tanks," Keith pleaded.

"APCs, they won't be able to cross..."

"I have to obey the command of my boss," Keith retorted. "My responsibility is to the safety of all the civilians heading up that road. I'm leaving."

"Not with my soldiers you don't. Nor any civvies who want to stay. I'm waiting here for the rest of our men to arrive," Hammerhead said forcefully.

"Please yourself, Lieutenant." Keith then yelled out, "We leave now! Everyone."

Vic came up to Hammerhead. "Sorry, man. But with everyone walking, it will take a day to get to Merritt let alone Kamloops. And that's the closest town."

"Are you staying or leaving?"

"These are my people, I have to be with them. We have a few vehicles to get the old and young out."

"Good luck," Hammerhead said and shook Vic's hand. "Oh, and great job on that bridge with the barriers. Good idea."

"Thanks, and good luck to you, eh?"

Vic drove off into the dark with his fire pumper loaded with people.

Gena got into the last vehicle, Constable Deb Osby's cruiser. Hammerhead asked as they started to pass him, "You're not staying to record this next battle?"

"I'm no war correspondent. Only a fool would stay behind." She left the camera on the road, and they drove off.

Fool? Hammerhead thought. "Just may be. Only history can judge that," he mumbled.

* * *

RCMP Phil Waterford got the message from Hawker to help at Princeton. Assistant Blaster, Dianne Reger, suggested they don't take the road to Merritt then back down as Princeton was due east of them. No point in going north just to go south, she said. She knew the area well, and suggested they take the back roads through the mountain. Though it was getting dark, she said she had taken the route a number of times doing geological work, and said it was quite passable.

Though the road twisted and turned through narrow valleys, logging trucks used it all the time, even in winter. She would have to guide them in the lead vehicle because of all the dead end logging roads all along the route. It would be easy to get lost.

The junction to Tulameen River Road was just two kilometres north of the arch bridge. They turned off Highway 5 and proceeded along the dirt road in the dark. Dan "Danno" Stryker was driving the first vehicle while Dianne navigated.

After about five kilometres in the total dark, only their lights giving them a path, they came to a fork in the road. They stopped.

"I think it's straight through," Dianne said.

"You think? I thought you said you knew this road."

"I do. I'm pretty sure it's straight."

Danno shook his head, "I sure as fuck hope so!"

He was just about to pull away when she said, "No, wait. Stop. Go right. I just remembered."

"Fuck, woman, you're going to get us all lost."

"No, I remember now. It's been a while since I came through this way. Last time I was on this road I came from Princeton. I'll know for sure when we hit a hairpin turn."

Danno mumbled under his breath, and turned on the road to the right. The road often opened into cleared areas where logging had taken place, and then into dense forest and so on several times.

"Wow, that's a lot of logging since I was here last. Yeah, this is correct, we're on the north face of the mountain," Dianne said.

Danno just turned and looked at her briefly, his right eyebrow raised.

"Hey, it's dark. I can't see any landmarks. Just keep going. We'll know in a moment if the road turns south," she said.

Indeed they did a long right turn around a mountain one hundred and eighty degrees, then a sharp left turn, and down in elevation, over a small single lane bridge to a tee junction on the other side.

Danno stopped. "Left or right?" he asked.

"Left," she said.

"Are you sure this time?"

She turned to him and gave him the raised eyebrow back.

"Left it is then," he said.

The road hugged the north side of a mountain which was laid bare on either side, even way up on the right steep slope. In the dark they could see the clear cutting as it allowed more of the night sky to illuminate the road.

After two kilometres they came to another tee junction.

"Déjà vu," Danno nagged.

"Jesus H. Christ," Dianne muttered.

"You don't know which way do you."

Dianne got out, walked to the right and disappeared into the dark. After a few minutes she returned and got in. "Go left."

"You're sure?"

"Yeah, there's a sharp hairpin turn over there. I know where I am now. Go left."

Not even one hundred meters on the road and they came to a fork. Danno stopped.

"Don't stop, go to the right."

"How can you be so sure?"

"The road is more open and well used to the right, besides, it goes down not up."

"Ok, better be right."

They came down the grade to a sharp right hairpin turn. "Stop," Dianne said.

Danno stomped on the breaks sliding down the road to a stop digging a shallow trench in the gravel. "We're lost aren't we?"

"No, turn left."

"Left? That's a small road, are you sure?"

"Yep, Tulameen is at the end of that road."

They started to proceed along the narrow dirt road. It was a steep drop off on their right and a rock face on their left. Danno only did forty kilometres an hour.

When they came to a narrow concrete bridge, Dianne said, "Yep, we're on the right road. I did some sampling up that valley several summers ago. It's going to get tight and curving for the next little while."

Indeed it was. Danno did barely twenty kilometres an hour. "We might actually get to Princeton by daybreak," Danno said sarcastically.

Not long, after the road straightened up, they came into Tulameen. "See told yeah, smooth sailing from here on," Dianne said gleefully.

"Lucky guess. I wouldn't be surprised we've lost everyone."

As they came out of town Danno said, "What the fuck was that, shoes in a tree?"

"Yeah, that's the famous shoe tree. Wait until we get into Coalmont."

"What's in Coalmont?"

"It's like the town hasn't changed since the 1800s. It used to be a railway town."

When they came into Coalmont Dianne said. "There's a sign in at the far end warning people, salesmen, that their safety can't be guaranteed. It also warns women there's lots of bachelors in town. I've stayed at the hotel here many times when doing my PhD thesis. They are a great bunch of people. Too bad it's dark."

No lights were on in any buildings as they passed through town, same as Tulameen. They had only ten kilometres left to get to Princeton.

They came to a very narrow, one lane wide, with a road cut on their left side as they climbed up and onto a flat plain at the top. As they made a right turn emerging from the forest, they could see the lights of Princeton in front and below them. It was almost 1:20a.m.

* * *

RCMP Chief Superintendent Ron Blackcrow was asked to come up from the basement cells to the control room. He was told that a disturbing message came over the radio.

As he entered the dispatch room the sole radio operator said that the crew that Hawker dispatched to Princeton, one of their officers who went along to keep contact was on the radio.

"Corporal, repeat your message, over," the operator said.

"We encountered a truck coming up the road. He said they were attacked and everyone was killed but him, over."

"Attacked where, over."

"Merritt, over."

"The Chinese must be in Merritt," Ron said. "Tell them to return at once."

"Command orders you to return at once, over."

There was silence. "Sir," the operator said to Ron. "Superintendent Wilks is bringing people, mostly by foot, but some by vehicle north to Merritt from Princeton."

"So?"

"So, sir, they'll get ambushed too."

"Contact them immediately and have them stop." Ron said.

"Control to Superintendent Wilks, over."

"Wilks here, we received the other message. We're in the middle of nowhere, and it's starting to rain. We have hundreds of people here with no shelter, over."

"Jesus," Ron muttered.

Wilks came back on. "We're near Sunflower Estates. We'll take refuge there, out."

"Surrounded, what are we going to do, sir?" the operator said.

"I don't know," Ron said confused.

The radio clicked back on. "Hello, who's there, over?"

"RCMP command, over."

"Where is Colonel Hawker, over?"

Ron grabbed the mic. "Your Colonel has been arrested. I'm now in charge."

"Like fuck you are, put the Colonel on the radio, over."

"Who is this?"

"This is Lieutenant Gary Kroll of the U.S. National Guard, and I only take orders from a military commander, and that's Colonel Hawker. So put him on the radio, over."

Ron stood there anger building on his face. "I order all of you to return at once!" he said into the mic.

"That's a negative, will not comply."

Repeated requests by Ron to make contact only returned static.

* * *

Captain Chris Staines, Major Armstrong, and General George Maillet arrived at the CPR yard in Kamloops just before 9 p.m, with some three thousand troops and armed civilians, along with much military equipment. Maillet ordered the equipment to be unloaded immediately.

Staines asked someone at the arena where Hawker was, and was directed to the RCMP building a few blocks away. Maillet went with him leaving Armstrong to direct the unloading, specifically the food into the arena. There were more than enough people to assist in that task.

Staines and Maillet were escorted to the control room, where Ron Blackcrow and the radio operator were. They introduced each other congenially. Maillet asked where Colonel Hawker was. He fumed at the reply that Hawker was in jail. The General ordered Ron to stand down, that martial law was now in control in all of Canada by order of the House of Commons. "And if you do not stand down, Chief Superintendent, I will march my men in here and arrest you myself," Maillet ordered with his right hand on his pistol in its leg holster.

Ron looked hard at Maillet, the two stared at each other for seconds. Maillet flinched his pistol hand on his Beretta. Ron backed down. "He's in our jail in the basement. The officer will show you the way." Ron sat down in a chair and turned his back to Maillet.

Staines whispered at the General, "Martial law?"

The General winked and left. Staines stayed in the control room trying to hide his grin.

Hawker and Maillet returned to the control room with Hawker saying to the General, "At least I got a bit of sleep."

Ron got up and left not making eye contact with anyone. "Chief Superintendent," Hawker said. Ron stopped at the door, but did not turn around. "This isn't personal. This is war. We need to be in command. I suggest you help continue to take charge of the evacuations." Ron just left the room.

Staines got Hawker and Maillet up to speed on who was where, and going where.

"Your orders, General," Hawker asked.

"Oh, no. T'is is your show Gary, please continue. But I do have a warning. We're planning a surgical air strike tonight, some time around one a.m. T'U.S. is sending in a number of A10 Warthogs. T'ey are targeting t'bridge you missed. I suggest you get into contact wit' your people at

Princeton, it's going to be carpet bombed. And I want you to evacuate Kamloops as soon as t'rest of t' trains arrive and your people get back here."

"About time. A10s, I'd love to see that."

"I have," Staines said. "They are one impressive sight. They'll make mincemeat out of the Chinese."

"So we finally have air superiority," Hawker said.

"I fear t'is is a one-time event," Maillet said. "T'U.S. is getting hammered all along t'west coast, and I fear aviation fuel is in short supply."

Hawker shook his head with his eyes closed.

"General," Hawker said, "We need to dispatch the Chinese at Merritt so I can get my people out, sir."

"Colonel, take whatever equipment and people you need to extract everyone, including civilian."

"I'm personally going."

"So am I," Staines said.

"Well, I guess t'at mean I'm in charge here. See you two when you return, eh?" Maillet said.

* * *

Hammerhead in Princeton engaged the enemy just before 10 p.m. It was raining. The battle started with flares launched from the hostile side over the river parting the night into daylight. Hammerhead ordered all to stay down and hold fire.

The front line was mostly military shooters, but the battle at the mine thinned his ranks too much. Some of the lightly wounded stayed behind. Those police officers in their troop who were good shooters filled in the gaps, so did a number of civvies. Tom, Simon and Trevor were back on the top of the ridge that overlooked the collapsed bridge.

The ordeal at the mine stunned the three of them. It was their first combat experience. Earlier they had been on top of the ridge at the highway bridge when the firefight at the mine started. Tom fired a few rounds from his M14, but didn't think he hit anyone. Once the mortars started, the three of them crawled back into the forest.

Now they wondered what would happen next. They knew they were trapped with the enemy in Merritt behind them, and the ever-increasing mass of enemy in front of them.

The only reinforcements they were expecting from Highway 5 were very late, had not yet arrived, and were out of communication.

The first wave of attack started near 11 p.m. with flairs opening the darkness as the Chinese tried to ford the shallow river. Hammerhead ordered to open fire. The problem was their flashes from their own weapons pinpointed where they were, and Chinese on the far bank targeted the bursts. The first wave failed, but the cost was more killed and wounded on the friendly side. They were grossly outnumbered. Hammerhead ordered a retreat.

They caught up to the stationary evacuees at Sunflower Estates. Hammerhead set up a defensive position on the road. He fully expected it would not be long before he was between a rock and a hard place.

* * *

As Danno's convoy descended down Tulameen road into Princeton, what they thought were the lights of the town were in fact large explosions. They stopped where the road made a forty-five degree north turn. They had a clear elevated view of the town. Balls of flame rose into the air from several locations. Everyone stood in the rain and watched the spectacle. Several jets screamed overhead in a high-pitched whine. Then more explosions in the valley.

"It's a goddamned air strike, *yahoo!*" Shooter yelled with his fist in the air. "Those are our A10s. I'd recognize that sound anywhere. Nail those Commie suckers!"

RCMP Constable Phil Waterford got on the radio, finally making contact with Kamloops, but it was General Maillet who replied. He told them to hold out until the strike was over and to rendezvous with those at Sunflower Estates north of town.

They didn't wait more than fifteen minutes when the strike stopped, leaving the town in a blaze of fire with subsequent secondary explosions.

They drove into the north part of town then up Highway 5. They met up with the rest of the evacuees with a chorus of high fives. Maillet got back on the radio and told them to stay put; they would be rescued in the morning.

CHAPTER **11**

Final Farewell

Colonel Gary Hawker planned the attack against the enemy who took out an entire crew at Merritt. The problem Hawker had was he had no idea how many Chinese were in the town. So he planned a three-pronged attack to take back Merritt. One route, which Captain Staines would command, would attack from the west from Mamit Lake Road, which they could get to from Highway 5 via Meadow Creek Road through the town of Logan Lake. Staines would take three LAVs and ten trucks of men.

Another route would be where First Lieutenant James Dunlop and Second Lieutenant Gary Kroll had met up with Harry Lipman, the only survivor of the massacre at Merritt. They were hiding the night out on a logging road about ten kilometres north of town.

The third prong of the attack would be commanded by Hawker. With an eleven truck convoy, they would come in from the east along Highway 5A through Stump Lake, which comes to the bridge where the attack took place. But Hawker checked on a map and found a small road that comes in south of the airport in Merritt right next to that bridge.

Hawker got the crews into position to wait the night out. Staines camped on a logging road behind a small hill just two kilometres north of Lower Nicola, minutes from Merritt, while Hawker took the most time to get to the field behind the airport. Dunlop and Kroll got their crews to within two kilometres of the bridge where they stopped, concealed by the mountain on their right. They took their crews up the mountain and positioned themselves on a protrusion overlooking the bridge some 700 meters away and 200 meters above. Some of that crew got down closer, to within 300 meters of the bridge. With their high vantage point they would be able to see what was on the bridge once daylight broke.

The attack would coordinate at the same time at daybreak.

The rain had let up, but the ground was wet. Hawker was soaked through to the skin since they had to march more than two kilometres over wet ground in the rain. They had to because it was too dark for vehicles, and he didn't want the sound of trucks to alert the enemy. They hid in the WalMart, located between the airport and the bridge, by breaking down a back loading door. Through the glass front Hawker could see clearly right to the bridge.

About an hour before daybreak, Hawker got a radio call from Shooter down at Sunflower Estate. He said he could bring his small band up from the south and give the enemy a real pincher. Hawker told him it wasn't necessary, but Shooter insisted he not be left out of a good payback.

As the sun started to make the ground below discernible, Kroll radioed to Hawker at the WalMart that they could see some thirty soldiers on the bridge. The enemy had set up two machine guns facing up the highway, and a number of men could be seen along both sides of the road. Three burned vehicles littered near the bridge along with a large number of bodies scattered around them. Smoke and steam still welled from two of the vehicles, one under the bridge, and the other just in front of the bridge.

In town they couldn't see any other movement or enemy, as it was too far, and the air was still grey with mist from the night's rain.

There is always the unexpected. Gunfire started at the bridge. Hawker radioed asking who was shooting, as he had not given the go-ahead. Everyone reported it wasn't them. Kroll, from his vantage point, could see the enemy turn their guns around and fire into the direction of town. On the southwest corner of the bridge intersection was a Canadian Tire. There were people on the embankment that led up to Voght Street, the road that went over Highway 5. They were firing at the Chinese on the bridge with nothing more than hunting rifles. Directly below Kroll, at the dead end of DeWolf Way, he noticed about thirty people had crawled up to the edge of the rise above the bridge. Most of them had bolt action scoped hunting rifles. They too opened fire on the Chinese.

Kroll radioed to Hawker what was going on. Hawker ordered a full-on assault to help the civvies.

Kroll noticed some of the Chinese down at the highway level were moving towards the civvies on DeWolf. He moved his men closer and fired down on the advancing enemy. He also sent one of his men to the civvies so they would know their back was covered with friendlies.

Hawker moved his men up the WalMart parking lot, onto Voght Street and opened fire at less than 200 meters. The Chinese were surrounded by fire on three sides.

The firefight lasted about fifteen minutes when the last of the enemy laid down their weapons and stood up, hands in the air, surrendering.

Kroll went down to meet the civvies below him. Hawker moved onto the bridge to seize the prisoners. The civvies were very pleased with the arrival of the military. Civilians from the Canadian Tire came up to the bridge, one of them with a canister of large zip ties, which were used to handcuff the prisoners.

Hawker radioed to bring their vehicles up, and with them came Shooter's crew. The officers met at the bridge, while crews lined up the prisoners on their knees. Shooter came up to Hawker and said, "Hey, you guys started without me!"

"It wasn't us who dispatched the enemy, it was the townsfolk. We hardly fired a shot," Hawker said.

The radio piped up, it was Staines, "Alpha One, this is Jerico One, over."

"Go ahead, over," Hawker said.

"Colonel, we're in town at the lumber mill, you ain't going to believe this. The town captured some sixty Tangos. We never fired a shot. The mayor is heading up your way, over."

"Roger that, out." Hawker said. "Lieutenant Kroll!"

Kroll ran up from the far end of the line of prisoners. "Yes, sir."

"Send a crew to the Canadian Tire and get all the shovels they have, and make a burial detail out of these prisoners."

"Roger that, sir."

Some civvies volunteered to get the tools. Kroll looked for a suitable burial site near the bridge. Hawker told Kroll to make a cemetery in the island of land behind the town's welcome sign inside the cloverleaf of the intersection. It would become a permanent reminder of the fallen.

The mayor arrived in a GM pickup. He stopped beside Hawker and ran the window down, sticking his hand out. "Hello, I'm Mayor Martin Hanataris. Praise the Lord! Am I happy to see you guys."

"I'm Colonel Hawker, pleasure to meet you too. What the hell happened here?"

Hanataris explained that the Chinese had arrived, some two hundred of them he figured, just before midnight. They immediately set up roadblocks. Right after the Chinese ambushed the men coming down Highway 5, the town decided they had to do something. So they gathered all the armed men they could, almost a three hundred of them, mostly hunters, but a few members of the Rocky Mountain Rangers, and decided they could take the Chinese on before they killed more.

In town, Hanataris explained, was the easiest, as the Chinese were mostly along the main drag. First thing the enemy did in town was to raid the local food stores, and when some people protested, they were shot on the spot.

"We were not going to take this from atheist heathens!" He said "atheist heathens" more than a few times. However, the Chinese made a major mistake, he said. They thinned themselves out too much, strung along the main road in town. When the signal was given, the townspeople tasked to take out the enemy only had to open fire and throw Molotov Cocktails. He said being so outnumbered, what was left of the "atheist heathens", about half of those who were killed or wounded, surrendered. Hanataris said they are all tied up in the parking lot of the lumber yard.

"So what do we do with them?" he said to Hawker.

"We'll transport them to Kamloops."

"Not before you pick up my people at Sunflower Estates. We have hundreds of civilians on foot," Shooter said.

"Right," Hawker said thinking. "Mayor, do you have any working buses?"

"School buses," he said. "Maybe twenty or so. God willing, we might be able to scrounge up enough fuel. But will more of these Agents of Satan show up any time soon?"

"There was an air strike last night. I suspect it took out enough bridges to hold them off for a while."

"Thank Jesus for that," the Mayor praised.

Hanataris organized a detail to go get the people at Sunflower Estates and shuttle them to the trains waiting in Kamloops. Between those people and the rest of Merritt's population, it was an all-day job.

Hammerhead handed Gena her camera, which he rescued from the road. "Here, use this to tape what's happening here," he said to her. "This is what you need to show the world. How we fought back with pride. Go interview some of the townspeople involved." She agreed.

Staines marched the prisoners the three and a half kilometers from downtown to the bridge, who were ordered to finish the burial detail. Hawker watched from the bridge. Hanataris came up to him. "They are with God now." He promised they would make a proper memorial for the fallen when the war was over. Hawker thanked him.

The burial of their dead wasn't an easy task, many were entombed in the burned vehicles. The local fire department rescue van was required to pry open some of the trucks to get what they could of the bodies out.

The Chinese bodies were loaded into dumpsters brought over from the WalMart and Canadian Tire. They were piled up just south of the bridge in an open field that had been cleared for new homes that never got built. A couple of truckloads of logs were brought in and dumped amongst the bodies. The lot was set on fire.

Shooter walked around the mass of wrecked vehicles and bodies being moved from under the bridge. He went first to a car south of the bridge. It was completely burned. He could make out the outline of some lettering on the passenger side door: Princeton Fire Chief. Three charred bodies were inside.

He went to the carnage on the north side of the bridge and looked around. He spotted something he recognized. An M14 lay beside a mutilated body. The barrel of the rifle had nine rings of thin masking tape on it. Shooter knelt, picked up the undamaged weapon and said to the dead body, "I will make sure someone gets this and avenges your death. Rest in peace my brave friend."

He took the eight loaded magazines from the man's pouches, two he couldn't because a bullet pierced right through them. Several of the mags were covered in blood, which Shooter washed off from his water bottle.

By the end of the day, with heavy overcast and some light snow falling, the town was evacuated. All that remained were the soldiers. They lined themselves in front of the graves. All the officers were there: Hawker, Staines, Hammerhead, Shooter, Kroll, and Dunlop. Gena videotaped.

Seven soldiers lined up at one side, raised their rifles into the air. Shooter was one of them with the banded M14. He insisted the entire line be M14s; a long traditional twenty-one gun salute rifle. Upon the salute order from Hawker, Shooter yelled "ATENNSHUN! Ready, Aim, FIRE!" First volley. "Ready, Aim, FIRE!" Second volley. "Ready, Aim, FIRE!" Third volley. "Present Arms!"

They stood silent for three minutes. A tear welled in Shooter's left eye and ran down his cheek.

CHAPTER 12

Trouble at Sicamous

Sergeant Williams was leaving the arena into the darkness of the parking lot; every light in Kamloops was out with the blackout in effect. Another Sergeant came up to him and asked, "What's this I hear we're to load all the equipment back onto the trains?"

"That's affirm. We're bugging out."

"Fuck me, we haven't been here twenty-four hours. Most of this stuff never moved out of the parking lot."

"We can't make our stand here, too difficult to defend. We're moving further east to a small town, Sicamous I think it's called. So get started, they want it all out of here by daylight."

The first train headed east around midnight, arriving at its stop in Sicamous before 1:00 a.m. The town was selected as the defensive position to stop the next advancement of the Chinese army. It was only a matter of time before they fixed the bridges, couple weeks, a month if the defenders were lucky.

Sicamous had the advantage of being the doorway into the Rockies eastward. It was the only valley. Plus, where Shuswap Lake to the north, joined Mara Lake to the south, there was a deep narrows, with the only way into town over a long two-lane bridge. There were two high peaks, one north of town, and one south of town, which gave good vantage view of the approach to the bridge. A third peak overlooked the town from the west side of Mara Lake.

Sergeant Williams was in charge of the unloading of equipment on the siding in Sicamous. The problem was crews could only unload the railway cars at the only two road crossings at each end of town. They were not even a quarter way unloading the first train, when the second train arrived and occupied the only other track on the main line, with a third waiting on the bridge west of town.

"This is unacceptable, you people are taking too long!" he yelled at crews, some of which yelled back they were working as fast as they could. Kappy, who engineered the second train, was standing idly by watching the chaos unfolding.

From a distance he said, "Ten kilometres up the line there are more sidings and more places to unload."

"What?" Sergeant Williams yelled as a vehicle driving past him drowned out Kappy's voice. The two walked away from the noise to talk.

"I said we can unload the trains about ten kilometres up the line. There are more sidings and more room to put all your equipment."

"OK, work it out with the rest of your crews, but we're running out of time, it will be daylight soon."

Hawker and Maillet arrived on the last train from Kamloops. It was well in the afternoon by the time they got off at Sicamous. Williams got them up to speed.

"Gary," General Maillet said, "I'm going back to Calgary to secure more equipment and plan a better defence, but I want you to stay 'ere and draw a line in the sand. You'll be our first defence. This is a perfect place to stop them. Get the job done as fast as you can."

"Consider it done, sir."

Hawker needed a command post and a rally point for the troops. He picked the Finlayson Park Arena, right in the middle of town, a stone's throw from the bridge over the river, with a large park area for a military tent city.

Few people were still in town, most had moved out east. However, a continuous stream of refugees crossed the bridge, as well as coming up from south of town. A few were in vehicles, many on horseback or horse-drawn carriages, and even some by bike, though most were on foot towing their children and a few belongings behind them.

Hawker needed to keep the flow going as long as possible. But the congestion greatly slowed the disembarking and organizing of equipment.

Hawker also needed locals to help with logistics. They were hard to convince, though the local volunteer firefighters, RCMP and other first responders agreed.

He ordered Parkview Elementary School next door to be set up as a field hospital. Two doctors who lived in town volunteered to stay.

His next order of business was to set up the defensive position. Both the highway bridge and railway swing bridge would need to be set up to be blown, but only at the last minute.

Next was the defensive set-up, so he called a meeting at the recreation centre.

Twenty-six officers attended the meeting, including the U.S. National Guardsmen. Hawker stopped Shooter as he and his men came in.

"You guys are staying?"

"Until we get orders from Captain Staines, I see no reason to do anything else."

"So I guess that means you haven't heard from him since he went back to Calgary."

"Well, sir, you know what the communications are like…"

Hawker nodded.

"…but I suspect he's making arrangements to get us home. We have our own battle, you know. No disrespect, of course."

"Oh, none taken," Hawker said. "I'd want to get home if I were you too. Your help here has been greatly appreciated. I'd be lying if I said I didn't want you and your men to stay."

"So with your permission, we'll sit in."

"Absolutely, pick a seat."

The room was full of chatter. "Ok, pipe down everyone. Let's get down to business. For you new people, welcome to the edge of hell. I'm Colonel Gary Hawker, commanding officer of this fucked-up mess. No need to do intros, you can do that later. Right now I'm going to spit out what needs to be done, and if you are the specialist then speak up. First, food and ammo. So who can do logistics?"

No one spoke up.

"Give me a fucking break, no one here is from CANOSCOM? Anyone from 38 or 39 Service Battalion?"

People looked around at each other. One officer in a Royal Canadian Navy uniform slowly put up his hand barely above his head.

"Speak up man, what have you got for me?"

"Well, I'm, I mean, I was for a time in Eastern Command. I did a bit of logistics on HMCS Preserver. So I have some knowledge on how to do logistics, just under these circumstances I'm not sure how to implement and get what we need."

"What the fuck are you even doing here?" Hawker asked.

"Well, with the navy down. I mean, with the cutbacks and lack of fuel, you know. There was nothing for me to do, so I came home two years ago. My parents are in Revelstoke. They're quite old and needed my help. I saw all this equipment coming here, so I hitched a ride thinking I might be able to help."

"You're now our logistics... What's your name?"

"Leftenant Commander Ian Lanning, sir."

"Well, Ian, you're now our logistics officer. Get out of that navy uniform and into fatigues, get a weapon from someone, and get on the blower, ASAP. We need food, and we need lots of ammo. Oh, and get us some gawddamned razors, I can't stand not being shaven. And a barber too, I'm not the only one here who needs a hair cut."

The room chuckled.

"Colonel," someone said. "That's being organized in Cochrane. I was in the General's office. I can get Ian in contact at the other end."

"Outstanding, get it done."

"Now sir?" Lanning said.

"Who are you?" Hawker asked the second officer.

"Major Gosling. Ed Gosling, sir. I really have no command, no soldiers. Like the commander, I'm a bit of an orphan."

"Ok, then neither of you need to be here for the rest of the meeting. But before you go, who here is from 38 or 39 Signal Regiment?"

A woman stood up. "I am, sir, Warrant Officer Eugene Cutler, Communication System Technologist. I have been assigned to your command to set up communications, which is ongoing as we speak. My crew arrived about an hour ago. They're unloading our equipment. We just need to know where you want us to set up."

"Outstanding. Pick a room in this building. I'll need local communications as well as a link to FOB. You better stay for the rest of the meeting so you know what to set up. So Commander, hook up with Miss Cutler."

"Roger that, sir."

"Next, artillery and heavy equipment." Hawker checkmarked his list.

"That would be me, sir. Leftenant Colonel Ethan Paulson. Commanding Officer of the Strathconas. We have three leopard tanks, one of which is serviceable. The other two broke down."

"One tank, wonderful. Can you get the other two working?"

"Maybe, crews are working on one of them now. We had to pull them both off the flatcar with the working tank. They're at the information centre up on the highway."

"Get them on the highway facing the bridge. I want them to have a clear line of sight to take out anything on the bridge."

"Roger that, sir. More tanks are coming, from Manitoba. No idea when they'll get here."

Hawker just shook his head looking down. Then said, "Any LAVs?"

"Yes sir, we have eight here now, and a dozen more waiting to be moved out of Cochrane."

Looking at his shopping list, Hawker said, "And artillery?"

"Well, sir, at the moment that would be me again," Paulson said. "We have six M triple sevens, and a number of mortar teams from Edmonton. As with the tanks, more artillery is coming from out east. Or so I was told."

"Can you get them up to the top of the two mountains, three on each side? I want a clear view for them to fire on the other side of the narrows."

"Yes, sir, we can use the LAVs to get them up there. I would imagine there's logging roads we can use."

"And shells? You have enough?"

"Well, sir, as with all ammo, there's never enough."

"And more is on its way," Hawker said sarcastically. "Right. We all prey the ammo arrives before the Chinese. Get at it, Colonel."

"Roger that, sir."

"Next, demolition. Who here's from One Combat Engineers?"

"That would be me, sir. Major Lewis Harrison. We have a mix of crews, including reservists from Calgary. If it's bridges you want blown, we can do the job."

"Major, I want you to identify and prepare for demolition every bridge, road and rail, from here to Revelstoke. Including any tunnels. We may need to blow them at a minute's notice. Also identify any rock cuts you think you can bring down on the roads. Particularly south of town."

"Roger that, sir."

"And tell me you have enough explosives."

"We should sir, but as with the rest, more is coming."

"Ok, that leaves the army." Hawker check marked his list. "The rest of you officers get your men stationed along this side of the narrows. No one is to be on the west bank. I'll need one volunteer to scout the route from here to Revelstoke for defensive positions. Possible fallback should we have to retreat."

"Retreat, sir? Isn't that a tad pessimistic?" someone interrupted.

"Glad you volunteered for that mission..." The room laughed. "No, not pessimistic, realistic. You got forty-eight hours to complete your task."

With a very reluctant tone the officer muttered, "Roger that, sir."

"Finally, snipers," Hawker continued. "Shooter, I want you to take charge of the sharp shooter civvies. Which reminds me, you new officers, you'll have a large contingency of armed civilians. They have proven themselves in battle. You will, and this is a direct order, you *will* give them the respect they deserve. Intermix them with your own men.

"Now, Lieutenant. Can you take command of the civvy snipers? Set them up where you think they can do the best shooting."

"Well, sir, I've been meaning to talk to you about this. I've talked with some of them, particularly Ray. I understand you know him. In their opinion, there's no point in utilizing them across the narrows. I concur. The south road is more exposed. There's little to stop the enemy from getting into town. Just south of here the highway hugs a cliff against the lake for several kilometres. It's a perfect bottleneck.

"I recommend we take some of the demo guys to blow rock cuts, and move logs onto the road. There's a large field of logs piled up not far from here. We can set up snipers there to take the enemy out as they try to clear the road."

"Outstanding, get it done." Hawker scribbled a checkmark on his list.

"Sir, there's a lot of people still coming up that road, from Armstrong, and such. Most of them on foot," someone said.

"Yeah, he's right, sir," Shooter said. "I was down there reckoning the road earlier, and it is loaded with people still streaming through."

"So set it up, but don't blow the cliffs until you have no choice, keep me informed," Hawker said.

"Roger that, sir."

"I guess that's all we can do for now, we'll meet again first thing in the morning. I'll have a status board set up by then. Dismissed."

"Sir, before you go, where do you want us medics?" someone said.

"Right, of course. The school next door. Which reminds me, has anyone seen the mayor of this town?"

Everyone shook their heads.

"Ok, I guess they've all evacuated."

"No, sir," Hammerhead said. "I've been watching that. Not everyone has evacuated. Some are griping about leaving and want to stay."

"Can you handle that, Lieutenant?"

"Yes sir, we'll round up the rest of the town."

* * *

Hawker was pouring over a map of the area when a knock came to the door. Two men entered and stood opposite the table from Hawker.

"Good morning, Colonel," the short darker haired man with a moustache said. "I'm Greg Peck, mayor of our little part of the mountains. This is Hal Hewettson of the Rocky Mountain Rangers."

Hal appeared past middle age, grey dominated his brownish hair. They shook hands.

"Gregory Peck, like the actor?" Hawker said as he sat back down in the chair behind the table.

"Yeah, my parents were fans of him, but I don't have his debonair looks I'm afraid."

"What can I do for you gents?" Hawker sat back crossing his arms.

"Well, Colonel, ah, hum, I don't want to cause a fuss. but..." Peck looked at Hewettson.

"I don't have all day, please out with it."

"Well, Colonel," Hewettson continued. "It looks to us like you're going to take on the Chinese right here, in our town, am I, I mean, are we right? I mean, more of you and your equipment keep pouring in every day for the past two weeks now."

"And the townsfolk, well, all of us don't want our town destroyed, 'cause that's what's gonna happen, isn't it?" Peck said.

Hawker shook his head and looked confused. "I was under the impression you had been evacuated, why are you still here?"

"We did evacuate, but most of us have returned to save our town," Peck said.

"Look, Colonel, I don't have the political tact the mayor has, so I will be forthright. We want you all out of our town, now." Hewettson pointed his finger into the table with a thud.

"Unfucking believable," Hawker said under his breath. He leaned forward in his chair. "And exactly what would you have me do, just let the Commies walk right through?"

"That's not our concern, Colonel," Peck said. "Our town is."

Hawker sat back into the chair, pausing to think. "What's your rank, Ranger?" Hawker said.

"I'm retired, but I was a Captain in the reg forces. When I moved here, I joined the Rangers."

"Well, Captain, just what do you think we should do? I will ask again, let the Commies right through the mountains?"

"At least they won't destroy our town," Hewettson retorted.

"Look, Colonel, we have endured floods, wild fires, mudslides and this damned depression, I think we can survive a Chinese occupation," Peck added.

"So you think you can endure the Chinese," Hawker snickered. "Rather naive in my opinion."

"Better than you destroying our town," Hewettson argued.

"Colonel, the town had a meeting last night," Peck said. "In Malakwa, where we stopped. And we voted…"

Hewettson interrupted, "We voted to take back our town. We're prepared to forcibly remove you, all of you, if we have to." His stare at the Colonel held no lie.

Hawker got up and moved to the door, opened it and said loudly, "Sergeant Williams!"

A few seconds later Williams came to the door.

"Sergeant, I want you to place armed guards on both sides of the main bridge. I also want you to post armed guards at all the major intersections. Then I want you to make a detail of as many men as you can and round up the entire town. Make sure everyone's on the next train out of here. You are authorized to use force if necessary."

"Roger that, sir."

Hawker came back into the room. "You have my answer, good day, gentlemen."

The mayor stomped out with a humph, while Hewettson stood fast with a stern stare. "Colonel, I have seen what war does. I was in Bosnia. It wasn't a pretty sight…"

"So was I. I saw the destruction," Hawker interrupted.

"So then you know what you have planned for this town, don't you. It will be rubble before you're through. And for what? Why is it you people must destroy everything?"

"You used to be one of 'you people', but now you're not? Why are you still a Ranger?"

"I joined the Rangers to help the town in times of crisis."

"And this does not qualify as a crisis?"

"By crisis I mean a threat to the town. You are now that threat. Maybe if you experienced the horrors I did, you too would be a former war loving soldier…"

"Excuse me, I'm not a 'war lover'," Hawker hissed. "I do not start wars, but I'm sure as hell going to finish this one."

Hewettson shook his head, "There's no point in discussing this with you. You're clearly going to do what you do regardless of the carnage you will leave behind." He walked out the door slamming it shut.

Hawker sat back into the chair and lowered his head. Hewettson was right, of course, he thought. If he takes on the Chinese, the town would be destroyed.

A light knock at the door stirred him from his thoughts.

"Enter!" he said. "Goddamned interruptions."

It was Sergeant Williams. "Sir, sorry to disturb you, but those guys looked pissed, and lock down the town? What gives?"

Hawker filled him in, then asked him to get the general on the radio, as they could be in for trouble and wanted some direction.

This was a first for Williams, he was witnessing his commander at a loss as to how to command.

"Don't looked confused, Sergeant. If I had my way, I'd arrest the entire lot. I want to know if we have other options, that's all. Go to it."

"Roger that, sir."

Later that evening, Hawker was going over his plans. He knew he was forgetting something, but it just would not come forward. A knock came to his door.

"Enter!" he said. "Goddamned more interruptions."

A Corporal came into the room. "Sorry to disturb you, sir, but Sergeant Williams said it was OK to come and ask you."

"Oh, he did did he."

"Yes, sir. We're going to show movies tonight, in the school gym. We found a large flat screen and a BlueRay player. We got this list of DVDs from the library. We thought you'd pick what you want to watch. Sergeant Williams said you needed a break."

"Nice of him to presume that. No I have too much to do, but thank you." He paused for a bit as the corporal was just about to leave the room. "No, wait. Let me see the list."

The corporal passed him a small folder. He looked through the pages. "Lets see if I can find something inspirational."

"Inspirational, sir? I didn't know you were religious."

Hawker looked at the young solder sideways. Back to the list, he said, "Here it is. I want you to show *Zulu* first, and…"

"*Zulu*, sir? I've never heard of it."

"Long before your time, son. But I guarantee you it is very fitting to us right now. The second one I want to see, after that, is *Last of the Mohicans*. Another classic. Will also inspire our men."

"Yes sir. We'll have the flicks ready by 8 p.m. Is that enough time for you, sir?"

Hawker looked at his watch. "Gawdfuckingdamnit. It's seven-thirty already. Yeah, that's fine, Corporal."

Hawker made it to the school gym on time, his men had a seat for him in the front row. A number of the Guardsmen officers were also present flanking the seat. The room was full of noise of people yacking, as well as the odd paper airplane floating around. "Where's the goddamned popcorn?" someone asked.

The films were a success; the room was quiet through both. As *Last of the Mohicans* finished and the credits started, everyone got up to leave. Someone was about to turn off the player when Hawker said, "Wait, leave it on, I want to hear the music."

He sat in the chair, eyes closed, moving his right hand to the composition. He listened to the very end. When he got up, a few people were still in the room, also listening.

"Hey, the skipper has a soft spot after all," someone said.

Hawker rubbed the tear from his eye, and said, "Fuck off," and left the room.

The next morning the message on paper that came back from the General was clear, "Remove all civilians from the town. Town essential to stop Chinese advance." That's all it said.

The problem was, in the hours before the message arrived by courier, not on the radio, the townspeople had occupied the bridge over the river. The armed soldiers could not stop them, save firing on their own people. None of the soldiers would do that.

Hawker tried to negotiate with the mayor and Hewettson, but they just went around in circles, getting nowhere. Hawker gave up. He figured once the Chinese showed up the town would come to their senses and leave.

Hawker came into the duty room early in the morning with his sparse breakfast of bread and peanut butter and thin coffee. He first checked the status board on the wall.

"Eighteen days, and still no Chinese. Town still occupying the bridge," he mumbled. "Artillery in place out of sight in the mountains, sniper crews report ready. Food in storage is holding up. More ammo arrived in the night. Very good, very good. But no tanks or artillery arrived. Any messages from FOB Corporal?"

"No, sir, the radio has been quiet all night."

"I don't like it, the proverbial quiet before the storm. I'll be at the bridge. See if I can talk some sense into those people."

He spent the day at the bridge, talked to a few townsfolk, but left after noon with no hope of moving the crowd, which had more than tripled since the first day, numbering some five hundred, including their children. Tents were erected all along the length of the bridge and on the banks of both sides of the river. Small fires for cooking dotted along the bridge. It was quite the picturesque sight at night. Children played games on the pavement. It was clear they were not going anywhere.

It even prevented escapees from crossing from the west side who did want to evacuate. Several fights broke out, which Hawker left to the RCMP to sort out.

Hawker did plant an officer in the middle of the bridge with a radio to keep him informed as to what the townspeople were up to.

* * *

Ray and Bonnie came into the school auditorium for the dinner call. Not much was being served, mostly pork, beef and chicken. There were no vegetables of any kind. The meat came from the local farms who were moving their livestock out from pastures to the south of town, then loaded on trains eastward. However, some were slaughtered locally for the consumption of the thousands of troops and civvies pouring in.

The room was packed, mostly with those newly recruited civilians. The majority of the military personnel were eating outside on the soccer field where a large fire was lighting up the area. The room wasn't quiet either.

The two sat at a table with a small number of people they knew.

"Hey, Ray and Bonnie!" John Revoy cried out. "This is Lynda Swift, Ken Moore and Phil Waterford." They shook hands.

"Hey, those look like new duds, dude." John said.

"Yes they are," Ray said "A shipment of clean new clothes came in this afternoon. The big tent at the far end of the baseball diamond. It sure feels nice to shower, shave and have on fresh clothes."

"Oh, man, soon as we eat. I gotta get out of these rags." John said.

"Please, before you get too ripe, John," Lynda agreed.

"Hey, woman, you're no bed of roses yourself," John said laughing.

"All cops I guess, eh?" Ray said.

"Yepper!" Ken said. "So you're one of John's shooting buddies, eh?"

"Yeah, we've fired off a few rounds together," Ray said.

"A few rounds? Ray here beats me every time. I still can't fathom how you get those moving targets. I can't hit shit!" John said laughing.

"Well, John, I keep tell you to get rid of that Remington and get a Savage," Ray joked.

"Moving targets?" Lynda asked.

"Yeah," John said. "We have to hit moving targets at three hundred yards. You don't know which direction they're going to move, and you have only six seconds to get the shoot off. It's fucking brutal."

"I wish we had good training like that in the force," Lynda pouted. "I've been lucky to get to the range twice a year. I don't feel comfortable firing my pistol, let alone a rifle. That's why they had me guarding the train in Chilliwack while you guys did the fighting." Lynda pointed to the Cz858 beside Bonnie. "And I'll bet you know how to fire that, right?"

Bonnie smiled a tiny bit. "Yes, Ray has had me out at the range a few times."

"See," Lynda sighed with her hands going into the air. "You civilians are so lucky…"

"Hey, it's Sergeant Williams. Hey Sarg, any news?" John said.

"Hi, guys." Williams came over to their table. "You know you're to be on the train tonight, right?"

"So it's a done deal?" Phil asked.

"What deal?" Ray said.

"There's more than enough people coming, they don't need us on the line," John said. "Because so many are coming they need us to police in Revelstoke."

"Hell, I've been running the beat here. Rowdies and drunks. I guess they've raided the homes for the booze," Phil said.

"Yes, it's all done," Williams said. "All the cops are going, except you Phil. The colonel wants you to stay and watch the people on the bridge."

"I guess. If I have to."

"Good, so if you will excuse me, I have to get the Colonel his dinner."

"Any news on the Chinese?" John asked.

"Nothing. We have scouts all the way to Kamloops, no sign of them yet. Gotta get back fellas, have a safe trip."

"So we'll be on the train together then…" Ray tried to finish, but their conversation was interrupted at the far end of the room were there was rumblings of loud voices.

"I think we should leave," one said to a chorus of "yeah!"

"I didn't sign on to be killed," another said to claps.

"Let the Rambos do all the fighting, they like killing people anyway," another said pointing across the room from Ray where civvies dressed in military gear were quietly trying to eat. One of them held another back who wanted to turn around. Two others picked up their trays of food and walked out.

"Yeah, that's right," the man yelled again standing up, "just leave Rambo. Can't take the heat, eh?"

It was obvious to Ray that the man had been drinking.

Someone grabbed the man and put him back into his chair. "I don't give a fuck what they think," he said stumbling to get back up.

Others in the room told the man to shut up, or leave.

Another in their group stood up. "Look, the Chinese are coming and this Hawker thinks he can hold them off. It's hopeless. Even the town people know that. They had a meeting with His Majesty, and want him, and all of us, to leave. Now. I say we go."

"You're free to leave any time," Ray said.

Bonnie whispered into his ear, "Stay out of this."

"Yeah, what do you know about this, nothin'" the drunk said.

"I do know you can't reason with a drunk," Ray replied.

The drunk made a move to Ray, but stumbled and fell on the floor cursing. His friends picked him up. Phil got up and forcefully suggested they get their friend sobered up. They left the room with the drunk rambling on.

"None too soon," one of the civvies in military gear said.

"I don't blame them, to be honest," Ray said. "My wife here thinks we should leave too. I'm wondering if I've had enough of this already. I killed at least thirty at Vedder. I'm not sure I want to kill more. I think we'll leave on the train tonight."

"Well, you go and be in a nice comfortable bed, bud. Every now and then just give us here a thought, will yea, eh?"

"I said I'm not sure. But what I am sure of is the fight eventually will come to me regardless where I am. I want to see my wife safely out of here, a long way out of here, before that happens. Now if you don't mind, we would like to finish our dinner in peace."

"So you're leaving too?" John said. "I thought you were part of the sniper team south of town, with that Yank, Shooter, wasn't it?"

"I was. Most are going to stay. But Bonnie wants out. So…"

Tom, Simon and Trevor came in at that point and sat at the table beside Ray and Bonnie. They all introduced each other.

"We saw you two at Kamloops," Simon said. "You were with a bunch of snipers. Did you see any action? I heard you guys did well at Vedder."

Ray looked up from his burger, "Yes, I was there. We were just talking about it."

"Well, I was at the fight south of Princeton. We got our asses kicked, big time. I don't want to go through that again," Trevor said.

"Me neither, man," Tom said.

"We asked to go to Revelstoke and help with logistics. That we can handle, eh guys?" Simon said.

They nodded in agreement.

"More dropouts," the same civvie in military gear groaned. "At this rate we'll lose our entire army. It will just be us, eh boys!" he said turning back to his friends at the table. They gave him high fives.

"Don't mind them," Ray said.

Shooter came into the room with his full gear and M14. "Man, I'm starved, what's for supper?"

"Chicken, pork, or burgers, take your pick," someone said.

"What, no spuds?" Shooter said disappointed. "I love mashed spuds, with lots of butter. Man, it's been a long time since I saw butter. And beer. Wash it all down with a Bud."

"Beer, tits and pussy, that's what we need," one of the civvies in military gear said. His friend gave him a slap across the back of the head. "Shut the fuck up, dude, there's women here."

"Sorry," he pleaded to the ladies in the room.

"Hey, no buns for the burgs?" Shooter said looking over the layout of food on the table.

"No, sir, sorry," the girl serving replied. "Not even condiments."

"Fucking great," Shooter complained. He picked an empty table beside Simon. He put his M14 on top, then took off his tactical vest and lay it out beside the rifle.

"Hey, is that loaded?" someone from the drunk's group said.

"And you should not be bringing any ammo into the room," another said.

"Maybe your rules, but not mine," Shooter said calmly. "No the rifle is not loaded, the mag is full, but the chamber is empty." He went over to the line to get his chow.

"Fucking yanks," someone said aloud.

"I'll pretend I didn't hear that," Shooter hinted. He returned to his table with a plate load of chow. Between bites he field stripped the rifle and got his cleaning kit out.

Simon went over to have a look. "Do you mind?" he said.

"Not at all, have a seat."

"That's one cool rifle. I always liked the M14. Your gear is neat too. That's a Springfield M14 right, not one of those Norc knockoffs."

"Yep, I bought it all. I have three Saw pouches here on the belt..." Shooter spread his tactical vest and webbing out. "I can carry three hundred rounds in them. Then I have M14 pouches here on the chest and belt for ten mags, that's two hundred rounds. So I can carry five hundred. This pouch here has my camo covering in it." He opened the zipper. "It's a camoed scarf that I cut up, and can tie around the rifle and scope to 'blend in'.

"In here I have four grenade pouches..."

Simon reached.

"No, hands off please, those are live grenades," Shooter said.

"He even has live grenades in the room, idiot!" the previous complainer said.

Shooter ignored him. "Here's two flashbangs, and this bag contains some tools. I have a Beretta in the leg holster here," pointing to his right leg. "And six more nine mill mags in these pouches. Plus the camel back water pack on the back."

"That must be heavy," Simon said.

"A bit, but you get used to it pretty quick. I don't even notice it any more."

"Why are your pistol mags upside down in those chest pouches?"

"So I can grab them in the correct orientation and slap them into the pistol fast. I can do it with my eyes closed."

"You've been doing this a while."

"Oh, yeah, goin' on twenty years now."

"So you were at the canal fight?"

"Yep, and on the highway where we blew a tunnel. Though I missed the fight at Merritt. I got there too late."

"So you've killed," Tom said.

"Yes, only bad guys."

"I was at Princeton. I fired off some shots, but I didn't hit squat," Tom said in a low voice as if embarrassed.

"Well, no one's expecting you to be experts at this this early in the game," Shooter said.

"What's your plans?" Simon asked.

"Well, I'm waiting for our Captain to show up. He should be here any minute, then we'll have our orders."

Captain Staines came into the room with Hammerhead. They sat together at Shooter's table. Simon excused himself.

"Well, I have good news," Staines said. "A battalion of our boys are coming here, including crack sniper teams. So we should have enough to hold the commies off."

"That's the good news, Skipper?" Shooter said.

"Part of it. The rest is the Army here has agreed to take the National Guard into their control. Or…" he said with one figure up, "Or, you can all go home. On the next train. Transfer at Golden, just east of here, an' another train to the States."

"Wonderful!" Shooter said with glee. "We can leave now?"

"Soon, my friend. The train leaves after dark. You should be State-side by the morning."

"You coming, Trev?" Shooter said to Hammerhead.

"I'm all packed, and so are our boys. They're saying their goodbyes to our Canuck friends now."

"So, you boys have a good trip and good hunting," Staines said.

"You're not coming, Skipper?" Shooter said.

"No, I've been asked to stay and help coordinate the effort. There are thousands of civvies coming who need training and equipment. I'm going to help out behind the lines. I don't have anyone in the States waiting for me. Anyway, I got to meet with Hawker, so finish your chow and head to the railway line when you're ready." He got up and left the room.

Hammerhead and Shooter discussed things, happy to be heading back home.

* * *

Hawker was sitting at the desk in the principal's office when Sergeant Williams came in with his food.

"Where's the bun for my burger?" Hawker said.

"Sacrifices, sir, sacrifices."

"Gawddammit. I'm so hungry I could eat a dead horse."

"That just may be, sir."

Hawker stopped, the morsel just about to touch his tongue, as if Williams pushed a pause button. His eyes slowly drifted to Williams, who had a smile on his face.

"Smart aleck," Hawker snarled. "Ok, so what's going on?" as he took a bite.

"They're trying to connect you with General Maillet, and here she is now."

A Corporal came into the room. "The phones should work, sir. I tapped into the school's system. Just dial zero and the general should be on the line, sir."

"Outstanding, Corporal. I'll put in a medal for you," Hawker said, picking up the receiver and pressing the zero.

The phone rang five times, Hawker looked at the corporal. Then someone picked up.

"General Maillet, please." There was a pause for a few seconds. The corporal left.

"Hello, Hawker, Gary, is t'at you?" came from the other end of the phone.

"Yes, General, isn't modern technology wonderful?"

"Yeah, when it works," Maillet said. "First and foremost. T'town. You are to stay put, that an order. Arrest the mayor if you 'ave to, but get t'ose civilians out of t'ere"

"That's not going to be easy, sir."

"T'at why it your job, Colonel. Get it done. OK, 'ere's what's going on. Ammo and food is on it way…"

"Food we have sir, lots of it. Local meat. We should have enough for the time being. But ammo, yeah."

"OK, we'll leave t'food here t'en. You may be 'ere before long anyway," Maillet said.

"You have news of the Chinese, sir?"

"No, but we 'ave no more air support of any kind. I can't get an answer why. But it is zilch, but promised to have it soon. I'll believe t'at when I see it. But t'good news is an entire battalion of American soldier 'ave arrived in Cochrane. T'ey should be up your way wit'in a few days. T'is the army, not reserves. Plus, we 'ave more of our boys arriving every day. So we should have a good force to hold back any sized Chinese advance."

"As long as we get the ammo."

"Yes, the ammo. I'm told t'ey are working on it."

"General, you know the yanks are heading home tonight. I've asked them to leave their ammo behind. It was a hard sell."

"Yes, t'ey're being replaced by t'e regular army, so you'll 'ave the gaps filled. OK, Colonel, I leave t'is in your 'ands."

"Wilco, good night, General."

"So now what do we do, sir?" Williams asked.

"Don't ask."

Hawker went to the railway line to bid farewell to the U.S. Guardsmen. They were huddled around a campfire. Some sitting on crates, others on logs, some just squatting on the ground. Some Canadians were with them listening to the stories.

"Hey, Colonel," Hammerhead gestured, "Come and join us. Shooter was just about to tell us what happened to him in Afghanistan."

Hawker stood over the group. Shooter continued.

"Well, as I was saying. I was on the fifty turret on a Humvee. We were coming into a town in a convoy. Out of the corner of my eye I caught a vehicle heading towards us down an alley. From our nine. It was a taxi. I thought it was a suicide bomber going to crash into us. I didn't have time to swing the gun around, so I pulled out my forty-five. The last thing I remember was the taxi veering away with bullet holes in the windshield and my pistol was empty. I had racked it and fired all my rounds before I knew it.

"I can tell you I was scared shitless. Getting shot doesn't bother me, but getting blown up, your insides turning into mush, well, that scares me more than anything."

"Both ways you're dead, dude," Knoll laughed.

"Yeah, but a bullet... I don't know, it's the thought of getting blown up, just gets to me. Not a way I want to die."

"How about you, Colonel?" Hammerhead said to Hawker. "You must have some story you can share with us."

"Not really."

"Oh, come on, Gary, you must have some whopper of a lie you can tell us," Shooter said.

"Well, there is one thing. Kinda funny, not then it wasn't. It was when we were at the range in Connaught. That's near Ottawa. It was during my first year as a cadet at RMC. Well, we were supposed to be running one hundred meters to the next position when your target appeared down range. All morning we were running from the three hundred line to the two hundred, kneel, or go prone, and fire on our targets.

"Then we did that from the four hundred; run down to three hundred. And so on. But when we were at the five hundred we weren't supposed to run. We were supposed to just drop prone when the target appeared and shoot. But for some reason, I was clueless. So as soon as the target appeared I started to run down range.

"I get about twenty yards and the range officer is screaming 'Stop, Stop, Stop'. I don't know how many times. I didn't hear it at first. So I stopped and turned to look back. Everyone but me was prone on the line. I was standing all alone in the middle of nowhere.

"Man, I can tell you I've never been so embarrassed. When I got back to the fire line, the warrant officer went up one side of me and down the other with a royal shellacking."

The group laughed.

"You must have gotten razzed by your mates big time," Shooter said.

"Oh, to this day. To this day I get reminded of it when I run into those guys. They still call me the Swiper."

"Swiper?" Hammerhead asked.

"Yeah. Because as I went back I forgot that my weapon was cocked with a round up the pipe. It was facing everyone up range as I ran back to the line. I swiped everyone, so the name stuck."

"Oh, shit!" someone said.

"It was on safe, of course. But still. It's funny to think about it now, but I never lived it down the whole time I was at RMC."

Kappy came running past everyone. "All aboard, all aboard!" He stopped at Hawker, "The line's finally clear. We can leave now." He went back up the line towards the locomotive.

"Ok, boys, this is it. Have a safe trip home and good luck and good hunting," Hawker said. "And finally, thank you for all your work here."

"Our pleasure," Hammerhead said.

They shook hands as each American climbed into a boxcar. Hawker watched them leave.

"Happy hunting indeed, my good friends," he said to himself.

* * *

Day twenty-one had a different status board when Hawker came in at 5:00 a.m. The Chinese had been spotted; they would be at the bridge by noon. And it was not just a small force, they had arrived en masse, in the tens of thousands.

There was no warning from the scouts. In fact there was no more contact with any of the scouts west of Sicamous.

"And the town is still occupying the bridge," Hawker muttered. "Are we still in radio contact with the bridge?" he said aloud, looking at the status board.

"Yes, sir," the radio operator said.

"I want to talk with them now."

"Bridge One go, Waterford here."

"Get me the mayor, I assume he is still there."

"I'll get him, sir."

"Peck here," the next voice said.

"I assume, Mayor, that you are aware that the whole Chinese army is about to arrive," Hawker said.

"Quite aware, Colonel, their scouts arrived in the night. Hal is negotiating with them now as we speak. They intend us no harm, and guarantee they will not damage our town. They're even promising food."

"I'm on my way to you." Hawker handed the mic back to the corporal. "If he believes that, I have swamp land in Florida for him to retire to. If anyone is looking for me I'll be at the bridge."

"Yes, sir."

Hawker met a large group of people at the bridge, the mayor had gone back to the west side to meet Hewittson. Phil Waterford, in charge of the bridge, came over to Hawker with a radio. "From the north peak, sir, they see some new development on the other side."

"Hawker here, go."

"Sir, we see a large number of Tangos at the far side of the bridge. A number of vehicles have arrived, mostly civilian. One is a large white limo. It looks to be their commanding officer. I can see him talking with some people, over."

Phil handed Hawker a pair of binoculars. Peering through to the other side, he could see Hewittson and the mayor talking with a delegation of Chinese officers. They spent a good ten to fifteen minutes in discussion, at the end of which Hewittson shook the hand of what appeared to be the commanding officer. After which the three of them made their way across the bridge navigating through the camped out occupiers.

Hawker started across from his end, followed by Phil. "Maybe they're going to surrender," Phil said with a snicker.

They met at about the halfway mark on the bridge, a large number of townspeople gathered around to listen.

Hewittson started first. "Colonel Hawker, this is Major General Ho Mei Chen, he's the comm..."

"Commander of the invasion force," Hawker interrupted.

"We are not an invasion force, Colonel." General Chen extended his hand for a shake, but Hawker just folded his arms. The General's smile evaporated.

"You don't need to be rude, Colonel," Hewittson said angrily.

"General, I don't have the facilities to accept your surrender, I suggest you just pack up your men and go back to China, or we'll be forced to kill most of your army."

Chen's smile returned. In perfect English he said, "Colonel, we do not wish to harm anyone. I have personally guaranteed the safety of everyone in this town, should you and your men surrender, of course. Should you wish to take us on, well, blood will be on your hands, not mine."

"And you believe this guy, Hal?" Hawker said.

"I have no reason to doubt his sincerity," Peck replied.

"We have no choice!" someone in the crowd said followed by "Yeah!" and clapping hands.

"You see, Colonel, we have your own people on our side. Hearts and minds, and all that, right, Colonel?" Chen said.

There was a pause for a few seconds, then the General said. "Look, Colonel, all I have to do is to march my troops across this bridge through this crowd. You can't blow the bridge; you can't even take a shot at us, without killing your own people. You don't want that on your conscience now do you? Hmmm?"

There was more silence. He continued, "Colonel, I'm a fair man, I will give you and your brave men twenty-four hours to decide. Tomorrow we meet here again, no? After that we march across, surrender or no. I have you, how do you say it, 'over a barrel'?"

"Tomorrow, General." Hawker turned and walked back to the east end of the bridge.

"Colonel?" the General yelled after a few steps away, "Was that you at the canal?"

Hawker stopped, turned to face the General. A proud look quickly formed on his face.

"I will not underestimate you again, Colonel." The General, the mayor and Hewittson returned to the west side of the bridge.

As Hawker and Phil made their way back across to the east side, Phil said, "And now what do we do? He does have us over a barrel."

"I'll let him think he does, but no he does not. I do not succumb to over-the-barrel disease."

He paused for a bit, then turned back around saying, "What I decide, the choice I make right now, could change the course of what will come next to a major degree. Surrender and they could take over all the west coast and enslave our people for generations. Not surrender and at least we have some chance to stop them. This is a General Patton moment for me."

"Patton?" Phil asked.

"Patton wanted to rearm the Germans and push the Soviets back to Russia. Had he been able to do that there would not have been a USSR, no cold war and millions would not have died from communist oppression. This is one of those moments. A decision I make right now that determines the course of history."

"You're quite the philosopher, aren't you sir."

Hawker looked at Phil with a raised right eyebrow. "No, just a realist."

"Your orders, Colonel?"

Hawker started his trek back to the east side of the river. "Our artillery is behind the peaks out of their view right?"

"Yes, sir, as per your orders."

"And most of our heavy vehicles are back about ten kilometres, right?"

"Yes, sir, save the three tanks, back at that railway yard waiting for your orders."

"Ok, this is what we're going to do. We're going to move everything back further into the canyon. We'll keep this town safe, we'll take the defence back beyond the town. I need this done tonight, get started."

"Roger that, sir," Phil said with a big smile.

Hawker looked Phil over. "I just realized you don't carry a weapon? I think you should at least have a pistol."

"Never again," Phil said in a low voice, the smile instantly vanished.

"Care to elaborate? Or is it a soft spot?"

"No. Well, yes it is. It was long ago. I had only been on the job a few years. I came across a bad accident, not far from here actually. Several vehicles all smashed up because of dense fog. Some of the cars were burning. I could hear people calling me when I arrived. A young girl, Jasmine was here name. I'll never forget that. She kept saying she was only sixteen. She was trapped in the passenger side of the car. Her mother was dead beside her.

"Both the girl's legs were pinned and crushed. The car was burning in the engine. Three of us tried to free her, but the flames were too fast. We had to back off. One guy still tried, and got badly burned on the face." Phil paused a bit holding back his chocking.

"It was horrible, just awful. The poor girl was screaming franticly to get free. But there was no hope." Phil stopped to regain some composure. "I pulled my gun out and shot her in the head." A tear slid down his right cheek.

"I was in psychiatric treatment for a year after that. I've never worn a gun since. All I ever wanted to be was an RCMP cop. All my life I dreamed of being one. But after that, I never want to have to shoot anyone ever again.

"And to top it off the government wanted to charge me with second degree. I got a good lawyer, pro bono. She worked her butt off for me. I owe her my life. Every time she argued they dropped to a lower charge. Eventually we went to court with involuntary manslaughter. But the community rallied behind me, testified on my behalf. One of the witnesses, the guy who got badly burned, he has a permanently disfigured face now, testified for me. It was a highly emotional testimony. The judge acquitted me.

"Then the RCMP wanted to fire me. But the father of the young girl was an influential businessman who knew some politicians. They lobbied on my behalf. So I ended up spending the last of my thirty years on what they call 'Reasoned Accommodation'. That's just a fancy term for them keeping me from active duty.

"I still have nightmares over that day. I wake up with the girl screaming in my ears." Phil stopped unable to get more words out.

They stood silent for a few moments as Phil wiped a tear from his eye.

"Life certainly throws horrible curves at us," Hawker lamented. "But I can't imagine what that must have been like. I saw some pretty nasty things in Bosnia. Boy, some of those people are just gross barbarians. I was just a young leftenant at the time. My squad came across five Serbs after they had raped and murdered three young women on the side of the road. We zip tied them, but their leader was just smirking at me. I couldn't understand what he was saying, but 'U.N.' was in there a number of times. I guess he figured we couldn't do anything to them because we were with the U.N. He was right, of course. If we handed them over to the U.N. authorities, they would likely just been released. He must have known that. I was not going to let them get away.

"So we put them in the back of the truck along with the bodies wrapped in tarps. We drove them into a Croatian town about sixty klicks away. We carefully put the bodies on the road in the town square, then unloaded the men beside them, all zipped together. By that time a crowd had gathered. That fucker was scared stiff, I tell yeah. I put my nose to his and said, 'No U.N. here.' As I walked back to the truck all I could hear him say was 'U.N. Geneva Convention' over and over. We just left them there.

"That's the first time I told anyone about that. We kept it to our selves. The whole time I was there, that was the only time I was pleased with our job. That we ever did the right thing. Only that day was justice served."

"I wonder how much of this kind of stuff we'll have to go through this time," Phil sighed cleaning his cheek.

"It never ends," Hawker snarled.

* * *

The next morning a radio message from the bridge asked for a meeting with the Chinese. It would take place half way across the overpass at 10:00am. Hawker radioed back he would be there.

Through his binoculars, Hawker could see Hewettson, the mayor and the General arrive on time at the designated place. Phil went to meet them. Even though Phil was given a message that Hawker was busy and would be a few minutes late, Hawker could see that Hewettson was not pleased. But he planned to be much more than a few minutes late. He would deliberately make the General wait a long time.

After thirty minutes the radio piped up. Phil was asking when the colonel would arrive. "Tell them a few more minutes, something's come up," Hawker said to the corporal on the radio. She smiled as she passed on the message. Hawker watched through the binoculars. He wanted to wait until the General was about to give up.

That took more than an hour, with several more messages, and several more lies from Hawker. Just as the general threw his hands up and started to walk away, Hawker told the corporal he was on his way.

Hawker took his time walking across the span of the bridge, navigating through the residents who occupied the pavement. Eyes glared at him as he made his way across. The anticipation was as thick as cold molasses. He could feel the emotions. Was he going to surrender? Was he going to start a fight?

"Sorry, General, things to do. Command decisions and all that, you understand eh?"

"I don't like being left waiting. Have you made up your mind?"

"General, we have the means to stop you. Air support will be back, you can count on that."

"No, Colonel, I guess you have not heard. You won't have much air support. We have already seen to that."

"Explain," Hawker said.

"Colonel, you have mass defections, you have rioting in the U.S. taking troops from the front. You have Muslims trying to take control of your cities. Gangs running free to rape and murder your people. Not only do you need more men, you don't have the fuel to feed a military machine, especially aircraft. We have eliminated every oil refinery on the continent. You have been bombed back into the Stone Age. Haven't you noticed there have been no planes to bomb our advancement?"

Hawker didn't say anything, he had not heard of any attacks on their infrastructure, but then again communications was still a major problem.

Hewettson broke the silence with, "So you will surrender, right, Colonel?"

Hawker looked hard at Hewettson. "You do realize you are now a collaborator with the enemy. That makes you a traitor of your country."

"Colonel, the country I once knew called Canada no longer exists, hasn't since before these people arrived. We're in new territory now. You have no country to fight for, please give up. It's the right choice for everyone."

That was the answer Hawker needed to confirm his choice.

"There will be no surrender." Hawker turned and walked back to his side of the bridge without waiting for any comments to his decision. All he heard was the General saying with a loud voice, "And so it begins!"

CHAPTER 13

Battle of Eagle Pass

General George Maillet was woken up from a nice dream, sitting on a beach with his wife, enjoying sips of margaritas. "General, sir, we have important news," his wife said. "General, can you hear me? Wake up sir."

Groggy, he said with his eyes closed, "What time is it?"

"Four a.m., sir."

He said a few choice swear words in French as he moaned and sat up at the end of his bed. "Okay, Corporal, what is it?"

"Colonel Hawker has moved out of Sicamous into Eagles Pass, sir."

"What?!" Now fully awake, "I told 'im to stand ground. Goddammit, where is my robe? Turn on the fuckin' light."

"Yes sir," the aide said turning the light on, almost blinding the general. "Four fuckin' a.m.... Goddammit."

"Here sir, your robe."

"Ok, let go down stair and see what 'e's up to. And get me some goddamned coffee!"

In the command room, Maillet looked at the tactical map, sipping on his coffee.

"Damn good coffee," he said. "Just what I needed at four in t'morning. Make sure you t'ank our American friends for t'java."

"Already have sir," the Corporal said.

"OK, so where Hawker at."

"Here, sir. He has set up a defensive position on the east side of Perry River, fifteen kilometers from Sicamous."

"God damn 'im disobeying order. We need 'im to stall t'e enemy. What t'status of our defence in t'at valley."

"WC1 is almost complete..."

"WC?"

"Oh, yes sir. Colonel Bartek named each. He thought it fitting that we call them the Walls of China. Ironic since the Chinese built the Great Wall to keep invading hordes out."

"I see. Continue."

"Well, sir, as I was going to say, WC1 is almost completed. They have laid two kilometers of logs four meters high, and five meters thick. Shooting platforms at the top the full length. The only section not filled in is the road so Hawker and his men can get through. But we need him to hold the line for at least three maybe four days to complete it."

"And t'e ot'ers?"

"WC2 here is underway. Soon as the men are free from WC1, they will be used for the other four. WC2 is very narrow, only two hundred meters wide. This entire valley between the two has been cleared, or should be by the time we have to defend WC1.

"WC3 to 5 haven't started yet. The site has been selected, also very narrow. WC3 is not even two hundred meters wide in the valley. More than a kilometre of clear killing zone. We just have to get the rest of the trees cleared. That's happening for the lumber."

"This should 'old t'em."

"It will buy us time sir."

"And t'manpower?"

"Lots are showing up daily, the yanks who came in last night have artillery.

Some are heading to Hawker's position, the rest we'll position along the road behind each wall. They also have a dozen Abrams, four of them went to help Hawker."

"So it's up to Gary now to 'old the line so we can finish t'ose walls."

* * *

Through his binoculars, Colonel Gary Hawker watched as the sun behind him lit up the vale in front. He was on a logging road some four hundred feet above the valley floor. He had a clear view of the two kilometers before him as it turned to the south. He was some fifteen kilometers east of Sicamous.

The mountain he was on towered into a tall spike at the east end of the valley, which made a southward curve behind him.

Directly below, the Eagle River came in from his left, hugging the south side of the basin disappearing into the distance. The Perry River transacted the vale right in front of him, from the north side to the south, going under the highway and railway line, then feeding into the Eagle River. Both rivers were running fast and deep from the spring runoff.

The valley was narrow, no more than half a kilometre wide, filled mostly with bush and thick trees. It was not a good firing zone. Directly below him, crews on the west side of the Perry River were clearing a three hundred meter killing zone, including bulldozing down a few homes and the Esso fuel station located at the end of the bridge.

Below him along their bank of the river, he could see crews rolling out barbed wire, which had arrived during the night along with three thousand more troops. Some of these were regular American Army commanded by full-bird Colonel Theodore "Teddybear" Sparks. They brought with them four Abrams tanks, a dozen M117 105mm field howitzers, and a dozen Stryker light armoured vehicles.

The plan was to hit the Chinese as soon as they came into the open with the tanks and artillery. Mortar crews were lined up to take the enemy out should they get to the one thousand meter line, clearly marked by a trailer park. They would also be used to light up the night sky with flares.

The dense bush and trees along the steep slopes of the valley on both sides should, Hawker figured, keep any advancing army in the killing zone. He was confident they could keep them at bay.

His confidence was given a bit of a hit when Maillet radioed two hours before, scolding him for disobeying orders. Hawker's reply was typical, "You want me to do the job right, then you'll have to trust my instincts. They've done us well so far."

Maillet could not disagree, and it's not like Hawker could return to town. Maillet told him he must hold the ground for at least three days. Rear guard defences were incomplete.

Scouts on the peaks around Sicamous had radioed early in the morning that the Chinese had removed the townsfolk off the bridge by force and were preparing in town for their next advance.

Sergeant Williams showed up with Sparks, a rather large African American, made more robust because of his tactical gear. He took off his helmet to reveal a well-worn pudgy face covered on top with densely curled short black hair. The "Teddy bear" moniker fit the man perfectly.

"Good mawin t'yah ,Colonel Hawker," he said in a deep southern drawl. They shook hands, "Y'all can call me Ted. It's Gary right?"

"Yes, good morning. Boy am I glad to see you guys."

"Well, we ain't gonna miss out on a good fight."

"Have you eaten, Colonel? I'm sure we can find you something. I haven't even had breakfast myself yet," Hawker complained looking at Williams.

"Kitchen is being set up at the back of the line, sir, they should have food served by ten a.m.," Williams said unapologetically.

"They gonna serve grits?" Ted said.

Williams laughed, "Not likely, sir, we'll be lucky to have bread."

"Well, I could eat the ass out of a dead possum, I'm so famished."

"Maybe a raccoon road kill, sir, but no possums, sorry, sir."

"Y'all don't need to worry, I'll inhale whatever grub you gents serve."

"Colonel..." Hawker started to say.

"Please, it's Ted."

"Sure, Ted. Where have you set up your battery? It's a nice view from here, you're welcome to place them beside ours."

"No disrespect, Gary, but I'd rather my artillery be down yonder. Two kilometres is mighty short to throw shells. You're too exposed up here fer return fire."

"We have no indication of them having artillery. I have spotters in the mountains. They can see the Chinese advancing. No heavy equipment. They have seconded civilian vehicles so far, which means to me they have not repaired the main bridges yet."

"Y'all can bet they will."

"That I have no doubt. Would be nice if we can get some gawddammed air support."

"Reckon you haven't heard."

"Heard what?"

"The Chinese nuked our refineries, all of them."

"What?" Hawker paused, shaking his head. "The General was right." He lowered his head. He understood not only the ramifications to them, but the strategic advantage for the enemy. He rose his bead back up and sighed. "Of course, that makes sense. Destroy the key underlying source of energy. Tell me you guys returned a measured response."

"I wish that were so. But last I heard it didn't happen. Not only our lack of manpower, but there seems to be a snafu with our computer systems."

"But you guys have nuke subs. They didn't launch?"

"Well, all I can tell y'all is that we have lost contact with our subs. So it does't look like they fired, but they could have fer all I know. Even our satellite systems have been affected. There's talk they used anti-satellite satellites."

"High tech warfare in the push button age."

"Y'all got that right."

"Hey, don't you guys have a stockpile of aviation fuel?"

"No, we ner 'ave. The strategic receives of erl, unprocessed crude that is, was exhausted a couple year ago. Hell, they even nuked our marine strategic erl field. That's the erl we used just to run our ships. They've nuked us back into the dark ages, I reckon. So no planes. maybe later, but not now."

"Did they nuke Canada's refineries? We have a few big ones too."

"I haven't heard, but I would suspect they would not take ours out just to leave yours in place."

"Yeah, makes sense. Jesus fucking Christ, that changes everything. But you have diesel fuel, or you wouldn't be here."

"A bit for a while, as it lasts. We've been tapping whatever we can find juice in. It won't last long."

A Sergeant came up to them. "Sirs, food is served."

"Whooyehaa! Let's go eat, Gary."

After breakfast, which wasn't much, except the unexpected coffee the yanks brought with them, Hawker and Ted took a tour of the fortifications.

The highway bridge had several concrete barriers preventing any traffic from coming across, not that there was much. What occasional vehicles did pass, including by horse and cart, had to navigate the barrier, then came face to face with an Abrams and a Leopard tank.

"I see you've set the bobwar nicely yonder," Ted said.

"Bobwar? Oh, you mean the barbed wire, yes. A trainload showed up last night. As you can see we have it ten feet high on the far bank of the river over there; in front of that we have it set two foot high in a horizontal grid pattern. That should slow them down."

"Well y'all look squared away. Except, no mines? You need to mine the far bank."

"No, unfortunately Canada has not endorsed the use of landmines."

"Well, it'll be hard to hold them off without mines, especially at night. I'll see if I can procure some, but I reckon they won't get here in time."

"Well if you do get some, I won't see you plant them."

"Gotcha. I've concerns about ur M177s yonder on the mountain. I understand y'all think they have a good line of sight, but they're sitting ducks for enemy artillery."

"If that happens I'll have them moved. Yours are where, in that open field here?"

"That's affirm, y'all want to come and see 'em?"

Hawker toured the howitzers lined up in a row in a clearing back from the front, on the north side of the valley. Two Abrams were in the miniature land theme park, which overlooked the Perry River, their barrels sticking through the trees. Hawker was impressed, and talked with the U.S. crews. Spirits were high.

"We'll sure miss your National Guardsmen," Hawker said as the two of them strolled to the command tent well behind their lines. "They're great fighters. We would have been in serious trouble if it weren't for them."

"I saw them at Golden on their way back home."

"Why did you come here, Colonel? I would have thought you would want to be back home defending your own people. Not that I'm ungrateful."

"Unlike my National Guard brothers in arms, I have to follow orders from the Pentagon. They ordered me here. No disrespect to you and your country, but I would rather be back home. But hell, it's the same enemy.

I'd rather fight them than my own people."

"Your own people?"

"We had a lot of rioting in Louisiana, where I come from. That's a whole 'nother story. Eventually we had to be called in to help police and the National Guard. There were so few of them to hold back the crowd. Hell, some of the people in the crowd were cops and guardsmen.

"Then I was up in New York for a Muslim uprising. They were trying to take control of New Jersey. Gawdam, they're fierce fighters. They a'scared me shitless. Gawdam suicide bombers attacked us. It's darn hard to fight an aarqeunaamaaei who doesn't care if they die. Hell, wants to die for their cause. That's the most dangerous kind of enemy."

Hawker had no idea what an 'aarqeunaamaaei' was. It sounded like a contorted 'arch enemy'. He guessed from the context it wasn't a complement. "I wonder, do you think our Chinese friends over there will be like that?" Hawker questioned.

"Well, they were in Korea. Here I have no idea. We can only hope not. We can hope they'll be reasonable enemy."

"Sounds just a tad oxymoronic. You're joking right?"

"No, just trying to reassure myself."

"So did you win that fight?"

"With the Muslims?"

"Yeah."

"Hell no. That'll be a never-ending battle, I reckon. It's happening all over the U.S. – Chicago, Miami, Atlanta. But not in Texas, I tell yah, they tried but ordinary people stopped the Muslim coup. Everyone's packin' in Texas yah know. I reckon the Muslims from Texas went to Jersey there were so many there. I was ordered to come here, but that fight's still goin' on."

"I can just imagine what's going on in Europe with that bunch of religious fanatics. They're already prophesizing they would take over various countries, and started during the economic upheaval."

"I haven't heard anything from Europe. The Pentagon isn't telling us what they know, except this war," Ted said as they entered the command tent.

Music was playing on the radio.

"Excuse me a minute, Ted. Where is that coming from?" Hawker said to the warrant officer in charge of communications.

"It's CIFM in Kamloops, they went on air about three hours ago."

"Kamloops? Gawdammed Chinese have them up and running. Anything other than music?"

"No, sir."

The song ended and a woman's voice came over the air. "That was Sarah McLachlan's *Building a Mystery*. This is Melissa Stiller on 98.3 CIFM in Kamloops. It's a bright morning, sunny all day, with showers expected tomorrow. The high today will be a chilly five-Celsius, with a chance of freezing tonight.

"I want to say hello to all the Canadians hunkered down in Eagles Pass. Specifically, we want to say hello to Canadian forces Colonel Gary Hawker. I want to ensure you that your family is alive and well in Victoria. Our new friends, who are here to fix our problems, ensure your family is well. They ask for you and want you to come home. So please, come home to your family as soon as you can. Do it now.

"And as for you Americans who just arrived to help your Canadian friends, you are wasting your time. Why do you fight for people who do not like you? You know Canadians hate Americans. So why are you here? You should go home and bring law and order to your own country first."

"Turn it off, Warrant," Hawker said. "Sorry, Ted, we don't hate you. Well, only the socialists here do. But not us good guys."

"Of course, they'll lie. How do they know your name, Gary," Ted said.

Hawker didn't say anything at first. He wondered about his wife, he wondered about his grown children. He felt sick to his stomach. He was furious at himself for leaving the day before the invasion. The armoury had a break-in, one of many, and he had to go deal with the situation. He promised his wife he would be home within two days. Then the invasion happened.

"I met their commander a couple days ago in Sicamous," he finally said to a repeat of the question. "They wanted us to surrender. I told him to fuck himself. This is just communist propaganda. It won't work on me. Warrant, make sure no one tunes into that station, that's an order."

"Yes, sir."

That night was clear, with no clouds. Indeed it was cold, below freezing, the long winter refused to give in.

A call came in from one of the scouts. "Eagle Nest, this is Charley Victor Three, over."

"Eagle Nest, go, over," the warrant officer in the command tent said. Hawker came over from his desk to listen.

"Eagle Nest, we have movement on the road, two klicks. Tangos on foot as well, over," the voice on the radio said."

"Here we go," Hawker said.

"Let's lasso this steer!" Ted roared to Hawker.

"Let's get into your hummer and head up to the logging road and have a look."

It was way too dark to see, Hawker and Ted shared night vision goggles. They could see a number of vehicles coming down the road. Lots of bright green figures were moving to fill the valley.

Ted called on the radio to his howitzers, "Captain, when they get to fifteen hundred meters, let 'em have it."

They didn't have to wait too long. The light artillery opened up. Hawker watched through his binoculars. Bright explosions, six at a time, lit up the valley within the advancing soldiers. It was too little to have an effect. Hawker ordered their tanks and their M177s to also engage.

Mortar fire rained down soon as the advancing enemy was within range. Explosions were far more frequent, and started to have an effect. Vehicles burned on the road. Trees were on fire. The few buildings in the valley, especially the trailer park, were in flames.

Once the foot bound figures made it to the three hundred meter line, in the cleared killing zone, flares went up, and machine guns opened fire.

Tracers sent streaks arching horizontally into the darkness, with a few ricocheting up as they bounced off the ground.

Flares lit up the whole valley. There was no darkness to hide in. Hawker had set up his sharp shooters in strategic positions. They were engaging any movement they could see.

After two hours, Hawker looked the valley over. There was no more forward movement. He ordered a cease-fire.

"I'd keep the flares yonder, at least a few of them to make sure." Ted suggested.

The two of them stayed atop the mountain for the rest of the night.

Fires in the distance had long burned themselves out when morning broke. Sergeant Williams showed up.

"Sir, remember the prisoners at Kamloops, the ones you asked me to find out about? Well, I got a reply. Nothing from them at all."

"Did they try any persuasive measures?"

"They didn't say, sorry sir."

"They should have been left with me, I would have gotten something out of them."

"That's not the bad news, sir." Williams handed Hawker a sheet of paper. Hawker's heart dropped in his chest as he read it. Shaking his head he passed the paper to Ted.

"Let's see... Chakos, we used a quarter of our artillery rounds, a third of our mortar rounds, almost all of our flares, and a quarter of our small arms ammo. Hmmm, this is none too good."

"I've been ordered to hold this line for three days. Two more attacks like that and we'll be completely defenceless," Hawker said with his right hand over his mouth rubbing his stubble face. "Gawdfuckingdamnit."

"I reckon you have more coming?"

"Maybe, but before we run out? That's the 64 million dollar question, isn't it? Maillet won't commit to when the next shipment of ammo will arrive. They have to hold back some for the other defensive positions." Hawker paused for a second, then said, "Last night was a probe. They want us to use up our ammo."

"I can make a call and see if we can procure more." Ted pulled out a satellite phone from one of his ammo pouches, and moved away poking the keyboard. A few seconds later he said to Hawker, "It works, it's dialing..."

Hawker could see Ted was talking with someone in a not so friendly conversation. A few choice swear words were clear, while his free hand was waving in the air. Finally, he hung up and came back over to Hawker.

"Gawdammed cakeheads, bunch of desk jockeys. More ammo is on the way, a day or two at most. The problem is the manufacturers can't produce ammo as fast as we're using it up. Seems there are some lively battles in the Sierras, and like."

"Is this a one time offer, or can we expect a regular supply?"

"Well, my friend, that C3I couldn't guarantee. They did say they're trying to ramp up production. Catch-23. I'll believe it when I see it."

"Well, we'll have a tough time tonight trying to hold them off, and conserve ammo."

"We could try something we did in New Jersey. We had problems with suicide bombers running into camp at night. We just didn't have the manpower to guard the whole perimeter. So what we did was put logs, two foot high in a grid twenty foot deep. That was how we slowed them down. An idea from one of my staff sergeants. He read about it. Used in the civil war, I think it was. Don't reckon. But it did work. Slowed the fuckers enough to take them out before they could do some real damage.

"I suggest we make a maze of logs, wall to wall across the valley on the west side of the river. Then we let them get real close."

"Do we have time, though? To set all that up, I mean," Hawker said.

"Then we should start now, all available hands on deck. Get as much done as quickly as possible."

"In broad daylight."

"I reckon we got no choice."

Hawker ordered the construction to start, using all available men and vehicles. The tanks were used to mow trees down from the valley behind them. They had to cut some trees to fill in the need. The line was set up at one hundred meters from the river, meaning a two hundred meter firing range, a little close for Hawker's comfort.

By late afternoon, the work was progressing nicely. Hawker suspected they were being watched by the Chinese down the far end of the valley. He got a sinking feeling their log maze wasn't going to work.

Hawker toured the front lines chatting with troops trying to keep spirits up, not mentioning the ammo problem to anyone. He ran into Ray. "Glad to see you decided to stay."

"Did I have a choice with all the guilt you poured on me?"

"Nice to know I'm still intimidating. Your wife, she got out ok?"

"Yep, thanks, she's in Revelstoke waiting for me."

"You'll see her soon enough I suspect. Did you get any hits last night?"

"Well, I tell yeah, night shooting, even with flares, is damn difficult. I've never shot in the dark before. The movement of the flares made it difficult for me to tell a figure worth a bullet or just a tree's shadow dancing with the moving lights. I didn't feel it worth the chance taking shots I wasn't sure of.

"So, in short, I have no idea. I fired off a few rounds, but it was real confusing being at night. So I gave up wasting ammo."

"Good call. We need to save our ammo, that's for sure."

"Do you think they'll try again tonight?"

"Fucked if I know. I expect it though, so you need to stay on the line, all of you do. I'll make sure food is brought up."

"Great, it is getting close to dinner, and I'm quite hungry after moving all those logs."

The next assault started just after midnight. Hawker ordered a stand down until the Chinese were at the log maze. That meant they could not use their artillery, but they could still use mortars and their tanks on any vehicles.

When the advancement got to the one thousand meter line, the tanks opened fire on the vehicles, easily picking them off one at a time.

Hawker watched as the enemy got closer, and closer. He was getting nervous. If the log maze didn't work they were in serious trouble. It was a sea of green moving figures in his night vision goggles.

Then he noticed the images stumbling, and falling. They were at the logs. It was working. Hawker ordered open fire.

Tracers filled the night like millions of fireflies. Flares erupted like shooting stars parting the darkness. Mortars rained down on the advancing enemy beyond the logs.

Even the tanks got into the act firing antipersonnel canister shot. Its effect was devastating to the enemy. Every shot of the ejected tungsten balls took out scores. To increase the effectiveness and killing ability, the tanks were firing at the ground just in front of the advancing enemy. This turned the conical shape of the discharged shot into a thin wide fan as the metallic spheres bounced off the ground. Another trick from the U.S. Civil War.

Hawker ordered a cease-fire. He wanted to evaluate the effectiveness of their fortification, and keep the ammo usage down. A few shots were required to take out the odd moving body attempting to retreat.

By 2:00 a.m. it was all over.

Ted came up to Hawker. "Well, congrats are in order for my Staff Sergeant. His idea works."

"Oh, yeah. That it did. But how much ammo did we use. I'll know that soon enough. One more attack and we're done, log maze or not."

"Yeah, but I reckon they don't know that."

"I sure hope you're right."

Hawker got a few hours of sleep before daybreak, woken up by Williams handing him the report.

They were down to twenty percent small arms ammo, no more flares, but still half their mortar rounds left. And no word on more ammo. Not only that, they were almost out of food.

"Before you go ballistic, sir, I have radioed the FOB. The General promises he will get us more ammo and food before day's end."

Ted joined Hawker for breakfast, along with a few other officers, mostly American. Williams showed up interrupting their conversation. "Sir, I have good news. Really good news. Five thousand more shooters arrived in Revelstoke over night. Most of them are civilian volunteers. We got about twenty percent of them, they're just arriving now. Food has arrived too. Some ammo has also arrived and is being disseminated now. And, we have a request from the new volunteers."

"Thank God for the ammo. What's the request?" Hawker said.

"Well sir, the new cavy volunteers want to write home. We don't have a post office set up. Could I start one? We'll be getting mail in soon too."

"Least of my worries, Sergeant. Don't use any of our people for that. There must be someone in Revelstoke from Canada Post who can. How much ammo arrived?"

"Not enough to get us back to one hundred percent in small arms, but the Americans are full with their battery and mortar rounds."

"Well that is good news," Ted said joyfully.

"Except the weather is going to get worse. A big storm is moving in, should be here before nightfall." Williams said.

"Wonderful, wet and cold. Just what we need. Thank you Sergeant," Hawker said.

"Oh, and Sergeant. Get me some gawdamned razors!" Hawker ordered scratching his face with his fingers.

"Right, sir, soon as I find some," he said, but continued in a low voice, "Like the war hinges on him being shaven."

"I heard that," Hawker barked.

Hawker spent the rest of the day trying to get some sleep. But the intense thunder and rain made it difficult, especially since his tent was leaking on him. So he gave up and toured the front line. Talk was of the weather, lots of grumpy complaints, what the night would bring, and so on. Hawker did his best to keep spirits up. The first two victories certainly made that task easy.

There was no attack that night, in fact, not for the next several nights. Hawker was getting worried something wasn't right. They got the time they needed, and then some as he got word on the back defences. That work had slowed down, taking much longer than anticipated. He wasn't sure why a simple defence was taking so long.

Hawker met one of the scout teams out on the road that had come back from the mountain trails. Every three days a horse team would head deep into the mountains to supply and switch out the scouts. Teams of five men were on each of the two peaks on the north and south side of Sicamous. They were reporting on Chinese activities.

It was a very dangerous job, but there was no shortage of volunteers when Hawker asked. Two farm owners from the valley supplied the horses and guided the men through the long intertwining trails through the mountains.

"Any news?" Hawker asked the lead horseman.

"We haven't heard from any of the scouts in a few days 'cause we have been dodging Chinese," the man said. "They know we're there because of our radio transmissions, but not where. We have to move around a lot to elude them. That makes it difficult for us to see what they're up to. We almost got caught once. They fired on us. But we managed to get into a gully and away from them. I'm not sure how much longer we're going to be of value."

"Is that both sides?"

"Yes, sir. We lost contact with the north side yesterday. I don't think they've been caught. Just ex communicado for a while."

"Their replacements are scheduled to head out tomorrow. I'll send them in now. From now on, no more radio communications unless you guys see something important. Daily reports puts you at too much risk of being caught. Get some food and rest your animals."

A week went by with no activity from the Chinese. This allowed for more ammo to arrive, and to complete the back defensive positions. The longer they could keep the Chinese at bay, the better. Every day counted.

Hawker met the north scout team in the mess tent. They were fresh from the mountains.

"Sir, we couldn't radio, we've been on the run. The Chinese have brought in some heavy artillery. They placed them on the west peak, on the other side of town. They'll have a straight line of fire right on you here."

He hadn't even finished his report when explosions started in the distance. Hawker raced to the log road with Ted driving the Humvee. Artillery rounds were landing in the farm field, and getting closer to their lines.

Hawker called over the leftenant in charge of their battery. "If we can locate them can you hit them from here?"

"We should sir, just get us the exact coordinates."

Hawker called on the radio to get connected with the remaining scout team on the south side. Rounds from the Chinese were within their lines, so Hawker had to order a retreat. Ted raced back down the mountain in the Humvee. Artillery rounds had started well within their lines.

Hawker finally got in contact with the south scouts. "Can you pinpoint their exact location, over?"

"We think so, sir, we can see the smoke from their guns, just we cannot see the guns. Get some rounds down range and we'll give feedback, over."

Hawker ordered his M177s to open fire. Back and forth the scouts issued corrections, while the shelling on the defensive line intensified.

Scouts radioed they were on target, so the order was given to fire as fast as they could. Ted's battery followed along. It wasn't long before explosions were creeping up the mountain towards Hawker and his guns. It was a race as to who would hit home first.

The ground shook under Hawker's feet as shells landed within their own artillery emplacement. One took out a gun, throwing it into the air, careening into the trees down the slope in front.

Williams arrived in a vehicle, grabbed Hawker off the ground and stuffed him in the back seat. Hawker couldn't hear anything Williams said to him because of the high-pitched ringing in his hears. They headed back down the mountain. Hawker watched through the back window as more of their guns were taken out.

The shelling lasted for two hours. When it was over Hawker toured the damage. The carnage was horrendous.

Only one leopard tank survived by getting well behind the line. Hawker looked around the open field where the American artillery was looking for Ted. All the artillery pieces were nothing but twisted burning hulks. No one was alive. He noticed a helmet with a scorched head still in it. The front of the helmet had a full-bird Colonel emblem on it. Teddy Bear was dead.

"Gawd fucking dammit," Hawker snarled to himself slowly. "I'm going to miss his southern charm."

Hawker went over to the river bridge to observe the damage. The log maze was mostly obliterated. Only the road bridge remained intact, obviously deliberately avoided.

"Look's like they were targeting their artillery on the maze," Williams said coming up behind Hawker.

"What?"

"Their artillery was precision shooting, sir."

"I was thinking that myself. I suspect they have scouts in the mountains, watching us right now."

"Should I send in a team to take them out?"

"What's the point now, damage has been done. No. In fact, call our last scouts in. Any idea how many dead, Sergeant?"

"Well, that's the good news. Kinda. Relatively speaking, sir."

"Spit it out, Sergeant."

"Only about two hundred and fifty, times two wounded. Mostly the artillery crews here and up there.

"Blow the bridge, we're going to pull back to WC One."

In the early dawn the entire force from Perry River walked eastward to the next defensive line, called Wall of China One. Hawker was the last to leave.

He took one more tour of the carnage. He climbed the small ridge up to Beardale Miniatureland Castle campgrounds. All the buildings were destroyed and burning. Toy model trains were strewn all around. He picked up a plastic locomotive, and remembered Hewettson's words to him: Destruction.

With the complete quiet, except the waking birds singing, Hawker stood, as if in some other universe. None of it seemed real. Heavy equipment lay like Tinker Toys scattered on a living room floor, some twisted and contorted, scorched with fire.

Body parts littered the field where the American artillery was positioned. Heads there, arms and legs over there. Ripped torsos with intestines thrown like yards of rope.

He stood by a small stack of logs. He felt light-headed. His stomach lurched up. He puked his breakfast, some of it going into his nose.

He stumbled a bit and dropped his butt onto a log. He tried to hurl, but only yellow fluid dripped out of his mouth. His body was shaking. He couldn't hold the emotions back, though he tried to control it. The last time he felt anywhere near like this was when his mother died unexpectedly twenty some years ago at a young age.

The urge to sob uncontrollably over took him. "No!" he screamed.

He stood up. Held his breath with his eyes closed. He paused for a moment clearing his mind. Then looked back towards the enemy lines with anger in his face. "Fuck you. I'll avenge this. That's a promise."

He walked east.

CHAPTER 14

The Walls of China

Colonel Gary Hawker came around the ninety-degree turn south in the valley to see a sight before him like nothing he had seen in his entire military career. Every tree, every bush, every building, was removed throughout the area. It was like an enormous football field. He passed large rocks with various colours marking the distance as he walked the two kilometers of open killing zone to the wall in the distance.

But what astonished Hawker the most was the wall. He stood not one hundred meters from it and marvelled. It was at least twelve feet high of logs, laid with their cut ends facing the killing zone. The logs were intertwined with barbed wire making it a single knitted mass for five hundred meters from side to side across the valley.

Crews were hanging from ropes along the face of the wall attaching razor wire. This made the face of the wall an array of points and knives. Impossible to climb.

The wall even went over the river, water gushing from between the logs making a small waterfall. The logs also went over the railway line, which was just south of the highway; the double tracks had been removed the full length of the valley.

But the wall was not yet completely across the Trans-Canada Highway. The road rose from the flat valley floor then curved a bit to get over a natural slump of the mountain. The log wall followed the slump up to the road. There was a narrow opening to form an archway. The arch was held up by rails from the train tracks.

A man on the road under the arch yelled at Hawker waving his hand to get a move on, they had to close the arch up, he said.

Hawker got wet from a small curtain of water coming down from the arch as he entered into the back of the defenses.

Behind the wall a tank had chains running to the rails, which pulled as soon as Hawker was clear. The roof of the arch collapsed into the opening. Crews immediately got to work filling in the void with more logs hoisted in place by vehicles with clawed arms.

From behind, Hawker could see that the wall had two tiers. The base tier was twenty feet thick, the length of the logs. The top of that tier was a shooting platform. The next tier, six feet thick, was a shooting wall, capped with sandbags.

Ramps along the back of the wall allowed access to the upper level. Hawker went up one to get a view.

The top platform had planks laid across the logs to make a floor. The shooting wall, made from shorter length logs, was four to five feet high. Gaps in the sandbags allowed for shooting.

A thousand soldiers and civilian shooters lined every foot of the platform. Behind them was crate after crate of supplies. "So that's where Ted's ammo went," he said aloud. There were even some of their light artillery and mortars interspersed along the whole length of the wall.

A dozen tanks were also lined up against the wall, their barrels sticking through small openings.

The CNR line south of the road was three tracks. Railway crews were busy adding new switches joining the tracks together into a small yard. Two trains were there unloading equipment and supplies.

Hawker was intrigued by the four tank cars, obviously loaded with juice, as a leopard tank was being refuelled directly from one.

In the distance up the road, Hawker could see artillery, lines of guns all pointing down range.

This was no temporary defense; this was a major effort to repel a prolonged attack. The goal was to keep the enemy in the mountains as long as possible. This wall had the potential to keep the Chinese from advancing any further, Hawker thought.

The Eagle River had backed up behind the partial dam and was filling the lower part of the valley forming a small, but deep lake.

A number of pumps were along the bank, including some fire trucks. Long lines of hose rose up to the platform tier. Water was flowing through the logs keeping everything wet.

Hawker took some comfort that his defence at Perry River made this position possible. He regained some confidence they really could hold the entire Chinese army at bay.

Hawker looked down the open valley; a thought immediately came to his mind. Helms Deep from *Lord of the Rings*. He envisioned the horde that will soon come. It would be like the Uruk-hai. *But would our fate be the same as Aragorn's victory*, he thought to himself. In their dark hour would they be rescued by a white wizard.

Night was falling. It even began to rain.

"Get a grip," he said to himself. "There will be no rescue."

Two officers came over to Hawker, one was a U.S. Major. "You like my wall?" the Canadian officer said.

"Outstanding. You built this?"

"Not by myself, of course. All these men here built it, but it's my creation. Ain't she a beauty?"

"That it is. You're confident this'll hold them off?"

"It's all about buying time. Holding them in the mountains as long as possible. You're Gary Hawker, right? I'm Lieutenant Colonel Russell Bartek of the Second Combat Engineers. It's a pleasure to finally meet you, sir. I've heard all about your battles. Well done, my good man."

"Thanks."

The other officer put out his hand, "I'm Major Mitch Mitchell, U.S. Army, and two-I-C to Colonel Sparks."

"Good evening, Major. But I guess regrettably you are now FIC."

"Yeah, I guess so. Ted was a good man. He'll be greatly missed."

"No southern accent, where are you from?"

"North Dakota. I was with Ted for four years."

"I look forward to working with you, Major. Now, Russ, I have to ask, what's with the hoses and water?"

"Ah. That's to stop any fires. The pumps are pouring water over all the logs along the whole length to keep it wet. Wet wood won't burn."

Nodding, Hawker said, "Makes sense."

"Come, you must be hungry and tired, I have a tent and a plate of food waiting for you."

"Can I make a suggestion?"

"Of course."

"The Chinese have scouts in the mountains. Send in hunter teams. Take them out."

"Good idea, yeah. Right. Never thought about that. I'll get on it right away. Oh, are you going to take charge? I'm an engineer not a tactician, that's your expertise."

"Yes, in the morning, I'm tired."

"Good, because in the morning I have to build four more of these walls. I won't see you again unless you have to retreat. Good luck."

Early next morning, at sunrise, Hawker was up on the wall. The valley was thick with fog from the night's rain. The sun behind him warmed his back. He called Sergeant Williams to come up.

"Sir, here are the stats," Williams said handing Hawker a sheet of paper.

Hawker passed it back saying, "Read it, Sergeant." He turned to look back down the valley.

"Well, the short version is we have ten thousand boots, six thousand shooters, mix of civvy, and regular mils, half of those U.S. The bad news is we have only one and a half million rounds of ammo."

"What? That's not even four hundred rounds per," Hawker said turning to look at Williams.

"That's affirm, sir."

"Shit, we can fire that off in one day. And re-supply is when?"

"They are doing their best, sir."

"You defending their excuses, Sergeant?"

"No sir, just being realistic."

Hawker knew he had no choice; he just looked across the valley.

"Sergeant, I fear the lack of ammo is the least of our problems. I'm not one to put meaning to dreams, but I had one doozy last night. It woke me up. I dreamt this wall was under attack from Orcs."

Williams looked at him sideways.

"Yes, Orcs, Sergeant. They were lobbing firebombs from catapults onto the wall. It was burning from end to end. Even behind the wall was all on fire. "

He turned back to face Williams. "I've changed my mind. This is not a safe place to be. Drive me to the next fortification, I want to take a look at it."

Wall of China Two was five kilometers east of the first wall. Much of it was already done. Hawker met up with Colonel Bartek.

"Good morning, Gary, have a good sleep?"

"No." Hawker told him of the dream.

"Come on, Gary, it was just a dream. Doesn't mean anything."

"Maybe, but my view of your great wall has changed. Look, there's no way they'll commit troops across a two kilometer long, five hundred meter wide, clear killing zone. They just won't do it. What they'll do is pound the wall with artillery until they breach it."

"That could take days, though, maybe a week," Bartek said.

"Or less, but not with my men and supplies behind it. This is a much better location."

"Definitely the narrowest, not even two hundred meters wide. And over there the Chinese will have a bottle neck only eighty meters wide at the bend you just came through."

"It's not just that. You're behind a kink in the valley. The longest distance is what, three hundred meters?"

"Around there."

"That's way to close for artillery. The mountain would protect this location from shelling. Plus I can see behind us it's long and open. We can put our artillery back there, say a kilometer or more, and pound them as they come around the corner."

"I see. Right. Makes sense to me," Bartek admitted.

"So divert all your efforts to this location. I want the wall higher, much higher. Make it twenty feet. I'll call everyone from the first wall. Get the trains back behind this one, and our equipment. We'll leave a skeleton crew to man the first wall. Make them think we're still there. Where's your radio?"

Hawker ordered that they pull everyone and everything back during the night. Leave behind some thousand men to hold the first wall.

After he was done, he turned back to Bartek, "I also want you to lay a maze of logs, in a grid fashion from this wall out two hundred meters."

"I heard about that. It worked well I hear. Consider it done."

Hawker was back on Wall of China One managing the retreating effort they could do during the day. This included moving the train cars out of the area. He recognized the engineer. It was Kappy.

Hawker went up to him. "Hey Kappy, you're still working on this?"

"Hi, Colonel, yep doing my part. You guys need the supplies, and I bring it to you."

"I'm sure you're doing the best you can, considering. But I have to ask. Where is the diesel fuel coming from?"

"I brought those tank cars down from the refinery in Edmonton two days ago. The oil sands is in full production. The grade is not that great, however. This old girl doesn't like it much. I also heard fuel will be coming from out east."

"Well, we definitely need it. You better get this train out of here."

"See yea soon, eh?"

Hawker watched as the train revved up, sending streams of black smoke into the air. "See what I mean," Kappy said from the open cab window. The locomotive finally shuttered forward and the train got on its way.

Hawker milled about directing some of the retreat when he heard a sound he couldn't believe. The whomp whomp of a helicopter.

Someone on the wall yelled down that a civilian chopper was coming straight at them down the valley from the west.

It flew very low over top, circled around, and then passed overhead westward.

Major Mitchell came over to Hawker. "It's a news chopper," he said.

"No it's not. It's them." Hawker ran over to the closest Abrams tank. A Lieutenant was in the turret.

"Can you shoot that thing down with your fifty?" Hawker yelled at him over the noise.

"Maybe, better chance with a canister if all twelve of us shoot at it."

"Do it."

The lieutenant radioed to the other tanks. They backed up from the wall about one hundred meters. Someone on the wall yelled the chopper was coming back. The bird was high enough for the tanks to see it coming;

they adjusted their turrets and barrels. Just as the chopper was about two hundred meters from the wall the tanks fired all at once like a dozen gigantic shotguns.

The chopper immediately started to dart up, down, left then right, with a small trail of smoke. It flipped onto its back and crashed into the lake created by the log dam with a huge splash of flames, smoke and steam.

Crews went over to make sure no one survived. But the growing lake was too deep to walk across, and the chopper sank out of sight leaving the inverted tail sticking up.

"They won't do that again," the tank lieutenant said.

"Maybe not. But you can be sure he radioed in what we're doing," Hawker said. Turning back to Mitchell. "Get a message to our scouts. I want to know exactly what they're up to, if they've started to repair the bridge, and when they move their artillery into position."

"Copy that, sir."

Hawker wasn't going to wait. Soon as it was dark, he moved almost everyone back. He used a simple method so people would know if they were going or staying. Instead of asking for volunteers, if the person's birthday was on a Monday they stay behind. This left about a thousand men to hold off any first attack and make it appear the wall was fully armed.

A week had passed; Wall of China Two was completed. The wall filled the valley from side to side. At the highest, over the river, it was some thirty feet tall. Then it rose up the sides becoming twenty feet over the highway and railway bed. Ramps on both sides provided access to the top.

The top was covered with rough-cut planks. But the shooting wall was completely different. Instead of a single wall with sandbags, it was three shelves, only three feet high each, one over top of the other.

"What's with this shooting platform," Hawker said to Mitchell who was up there supervising last minute preparations.

"Oh, your Bartek is one smart cookie. He realized that this canyon being so narrow, that if you placed people shoulder to shoulder, the most number of shooters you can squeeze would be three hundred. A third of the thousand on the other wall. So he made these shooting shelves so three shooters can occupy the same location. They'll have to shoot prone, but we'll get a thousand barrels pointing down range."

"Outstanding. Where's Bartek?"

"He's back working on WC Three. He said it's another very narrow part of the valley. So it should be identical to this wall.

The message Hawker was dreading from the scouts came in. The bridge over the Perry River had been repaired and the Chinese were moving their heavy artillery into position.

The Chinese waited until dark to start the barrage. Hawker ordered a complete withdrawal back to WC Two. Then he watched from a safe distance as the bombardment destroyed the wooden wall of WC One. Most of the rounds were phosphorus at first, attempting to burn the wall. But after about three hours of that bombardment, and the wall not catching much on fire, they switched to high explosive.

Five hours they sent round after round. In the morning's first light, they stopped. The valley was full of fog and smoke. Hawker couldn't see any of the wall through the thick white. It also meant the Chinese couldn't see either.

It wasn't until after ten in the morning, when the sun was hot enough to evaporate the fog that Hawker could see what was left of the wall. The concentration of the damage was around the road and railway line. The wall was fully intact at the river, but beyond that it was a thorough wreck.

Bartek was beside himself as he looked through binoculars at his destroyed creation. "That was three weeks of work, destroyed in just a few hours."

Hawker thought the man was going to cry. "See, I knew this was going to happen. This is where the real battle will take place," Hawker said.

"When do you think," Bartek moaned wiping one of his eyes.

"Tonight."

"Tonight? Shit."

"Yeah. They'll think they have the initiative now, they won't waste it."

"Well I better get out of here to get back to WC Three. Get it done fast just in case they destroy this wall like that one."

"No, not this wall. This one they can't shell. They'll have to walk right up and ring the doorbell."

Mitchell came up to Hawker. "I have some stats. So you know where we stand."

"Yeah, fire away."

"We have ten thousand people, six thousand are shooters. Two thirds of them are in the mountains. Four thousand are my men, the rest yours. Of the three thousand of your shooters, two thousand of them are civvies. Well-armed civvies I will add. I've never seen such dedication."

"They're a great group of people. How's the ammo."

"Just a little over five million rounds. The last boxcar load arrived about an hour ago."

"Less than a thousand rounds per shooter."

"Yeah, not so good is it."

"Better than five hundred each. But a thousand, they could fire that off in a couple days. Can we expect more?"

"That's what I've been told. In a few days."

"Shit. This could all be over before then."

"Yea, everyone will have to conserve. Oh, I almost forgot. We have some mines. Not a lot, but enough to mine the first one hundred meters from the wall. I have men installing them now."

"That should help. Anything else, what about artillery and mortar rounds? Especially flares?"

"We should have enough flares to last a week. At least with this narrow valley we won't need to light as much up."

"That's affirm."

"Food is another problem. Thirty thousand meals a day. We have about two thousand civvies cooking back about a kilometer. They run the food up by trucks. The problem is we're eating faster than they can get food to us. Plus before long you're going to start to see dysentery."

"Why's that?" Hawker asked.

"Because everyone's eating with their dirty bare hands. No utensils, none. Dirty hands shoving food in their mouths is a feast for the bacteria to thrive in.

"Oh, there's more. It gets better. We have four times as many people delivering food and supplies into the mountains than we have shooters up there. I've had to move some off the line to do the re-supplying. You have crews out there that take three or four days to get supplies to."

"What's the problem," Hawker inquired.

"The terrain is brutal, even for the few horses, which we have nowhere near enough. So most of the supplies have to move on foot."

"I saw some all terrain vehicles," Hawker noted.

"Sure, if we had a hundred more. And fuel for them. Most of the fuel we get is diesel, we lack gasoline big time. This operation is getting too big, logistically."

"Catch 22. We need a big force to hold the Chinese off, but we can't supply the force we need. Wonderful," Hawker complained. "Does HQ understand our problem?"

"I make sure they're aware every day. And there's more. Bedding is a real problem, we've had to make camp further back were the valley is wider. We'll need to keep the road clear to move supplies, however.

"Lastly, I have made a plan for shifts. Shooters can't spend more than a few hours in the shooting shelves. Besides, we don't want them falling asleep. So they rotate out every three hours with twelve hours off each.

"Also, because of the terrain we can only have four tanks, two on the road, and two on the railway line, aiming down range. That's about it."

"I'd like to say good job, for what you can do, major. But we need to get the logistics solved."

"Copy that."

The first of the fighting started in the forests of the mountains just down the west of Wall of China Two during the night. Hawker had sent an additional thousand reinforcements up on either side of the valley.

It was working; the sound of gunfire was well west of their position. It lasted sporadically until daybreak, stopping only when the sun appeared from behind the mountains.

Well into the next night Hawker was woken up to new gunfire in the mountains. Seemed the Chinese were trying to outflank their position. It was what he would try to do. So he committed another thousand soldiers, almost all of them American, to reinforce that line, on both sides of the valley.

That left only three thousand to rotate shifts on the wall.

The mountains were very rugged, so Hawker figured the Chinese were having a hard time. By morning there was only the occasional sound of shooting. The rest of the day was quiet.

Just before dusk, scouts reported that a long line of Chinese had made it through WC One, and were spreading out across the valley, heading right for them. When asked, the scouts reported that Chinese artillery was being towed at the end of the column.

The south end of the wall had the longest view through the valley, about five hundred meters, until the bend took it out of sight. Scouts radioed in when the first of the Chinese wave came into view. Then they just stopped.

The next morning, Mitchell requested Hawker meet him on the top of the wall.

Two tall poles had been erected, with rope to the top. One soldier pulled out a Canadian flag, tied it to the rope, and pulled the icon to the top of the pole. The soldier started to sing *O'Canada*. Soon every voice on the wall was singing. A tear formed in Hawker's eye as he saluted the flag.

"'Stand on guard for thee.' has real meaning today," Hawker said aloud with pride.

Once they were done, a U.S. soldier raised the American flag on the other pole. Every American soldier sung their national anthem while saluting.

"This should show those mother fuckers who they're dealing with," Mitchell said.

This gave Hawker an idea. He called for Sergeant Williams.

"You wanted to see me sir," Williams said when he arrived at the top of the wall.

"Yes. I want you to send someone to Revelstoke and get every sound system you can find. Every bar, every school. Get it all here. And as many CDs as you can find. I want the speakers hung from the wall facing the enemy. I want music playing all day, as loud as possible."

"Roger that, sir."

The following day was the start. The Chinese stated to shell their position. The rounds first fell well back into the south side of the mountains. It slowly crept towards the line. Hawker was getting nervous. Was his assumption of the safety of the wall wrong?

Then the shelling stopped behind them. Hawker could hear explosions on the far side of the dogleg of the valley. He was right. Artillery can't land on them. He gave a huge sigh of relief. That meant the Chinese would have to get face to face.

Mitchell came up to Hawker. "Look, over there to the south, way up in the sky. A small plane."

Indeed, a small single-engine Cessna was flying in their direction, but well high.

"Checking the effectiveness of their artillery."

"Too damn high to shoot at," Mitchell said.

The plane circled overhead a number of loops, then disappeared west.

Nothing happened for two more days. But on the third day, Hawker was summoned to the wall. Mitchell greeted him.

"Look," Mitchell said handing Hawker binoculars.

"What am I looking for?"

"Your log maze."

"Fuck me. Gawddammit."

During the night, Chinese had removed some one hundred meters of the log maze.

"Tell me why no one saw that happen," Hawker demanded.

"In the dark. We couldn't see. We couldn't hear because of the music."

"Get some gawddamned night vision set up with our snipers. Turn off the music when it's dusk."

"Already ordered."

That night, Hawker was on the wall with Ray.

"Those night vision goggles working?" Hawker asked.

"It should work. I've never done something like this."

"I'm confident you'll be able to do this. It's only three hundred meters. Piece of cake for you, right?"

"In daylight, sure. Night, I'm not so sure."

Hawker watched through the night vision scope as green figures could be seen crawling towards the maze. One by one, snipers took out the images. Hawker personally spotted for Ray, and counted his kills.

After an hour it stopped. No more moving figures could be seen. As the hours passed the green images of the dead faded into the background.

"Good job, pass it along, Ray. Get off the wall, get some chow and some sleep. You'll likely have to do this again tonight."

"How many did I get?"

"Twenty-three."

Ray counted his ammo. "I've only sixty-three rounds left."

"I'll see if I can get more for you. If not, can you use another sniper rifle?"

"If you can get me a Remington 700, that will be seven six two, common ammo."

"See what I can come up with."

A team of U.S. and Canadian military snipers arrived the next morning. The Canadian Leftenant Doug Swanell, the highest-ranking soldier, announced their arrival to Hawker at the mess tent.

"Leftenant, we have some thirty civilian sharp shooters on the south side of the wall. Go join them," Hawker said making a sour look on his face. "Fucking powdered eggs. Like eating sawdust." He pushed his half eaten plate away from him, brushing off the egg from his hands onto his coat.

"You can send the civvies home, sir. Now we're here you don't need them."

"We need every shooter on deck."

"With respect, sir, they're just paper shooters."

"What's your problem, Leftenant?" Hawker snapped back. "They're mighty fine shots."

"I'm sure they do fine sir, against unmoving paper targets. But we're the pros when it comes to real combat."

Hawker got up and faced the leftenant almost nose to nose. "They're just as much professionals as you are, Leftenant. They saved our butts several times. Now I'm responsible to hold this line, and I need every shooter on that line. Understand?"

The Leftenant stood at attention. "Fully, sir."

"Relax. Just get your men fed, and up on the line before noon."

"Yes, sir."

In each of the following three nights the Chinese tried over and over to send men to remove the log maze. With the increase in snipers, the Chinese received the same results.

The fourth night, the Chinese tried to lob mortars onto the wall and maze. But to do so required the hostiles to be in the open at five hundred meters. Easy shooting for the snipers.

It got to the point where other soldiers were asking if they could give it a try. Hawker allowed it. The more they could practice the better it would be for conserving ammo. The day of the major push on their position was only a matter of time.

What did happen first were more attacks in the mountains. But they didn't last long and reports from the lines said they were slaughtering the enemy. The terrain was just too unforgiving.

Hawker and Mitchell went together for the morning flag raising. The anthem singing was blasted over the speakers hanging from the wall. Crews in the mountains said the sound was reverberating down the valley. The Chinese were getting the message loud and clear.

But this morning was different. This time music was coming up the canyon from the Chinese, trying to counter theirs.

"They're going to attack today, in broad daylight I'll bet," Hawker said to Mitchell. "Get every shooter and gopher up here."

"Copy that. Before I go, you really should give a speech to boost the men's morale."

"A speech?"

"Yep, Ted used to give good speeches before every fight."

"I'm not a speech person."

"Well, you should say something, especially if this is *the* battle."

Williams got Hawker a megaphone.

"Ok, everyone listen up," he said from the top of the wall. "I'm not into speeches. So this will be short and to the point. Make every shot count. Take your time and don't rush. Send these fuckers all to hell."

Cheers and yeahs filled the valley.

Hawker went down to the road and into a tent at the base of the wall. "Randy, right," he said to the young man sitting at a desk with electronics equipment.

"Yep, that's me, Randy the DJ. What can I play for you, Colonel?"

"I want you to play rock-n-roll when the shooting starts. Something with a good beat. Something that will inspire our men. Understand."

"Sure, you mean like the Stones, Boston, Rush, and some Eagles, eh?"

"As long as it is loud and fast. Good battle music."

The Orc horde started the march to the wall just after 9:00 a.m. They filled the valley as they came around the bend.

Hawker signaled to start the music. The DJ picked Wagoner's *Ride of the Valkyries*.

"Oh, absolutely perfect," Hawker said. On the megaphone he yelled, "At the two hundred meter line. Fire when ready!"

The gunfire was deafening. Mitchell came over to Hawker, got close to his ear and said, "Isn't that from *Apocalypse Now?*"

Hawker nodded. "The chopper attack scene."

"Right, with DeNiro making that famous quote, 'I love the smell of napalm in the morning.'"

"Duvall."

"What?" Mitchell yelled. The noise made it difficult to hear each other, they both had to speak in elevated voices.

"It wasn't Robert DeNiro, it was Robert Duvall," Hawker had to repeat over the barrage.

"Right, I always get the two mixed up."

"Excuse me, Mitch, I need to coordinate the snipers. Can you keep an eye on the line? Also, keep an eye on the sky for that plane?"

"Copy that."

* * *

Ray and his new friend George were on the wall chatting together when a Canadian forces Leftenant, along with a couple dozen other soldiers, came up the ramp to them.

"I've been ordered to join up with civilian sharp shooters, do you know where I can find them?" the officer said.

"That would be us. Hi, I'm Ray, and this is George."

"That's nice. I've been ordered by the CO to integrate my men with yours. I suggest you guys just stay out of our way. Get whatever we need when we call."

"Gary told me we were to work with you guys," Ray said.

"If you want to shoot, that's your business. Maybe you'll hit something. But us professionals will do the heavy lifting."

"I didn't catch your name," Ray said.

"Leftenant Doug Swanell." He didn't shake their hands.

"Well, Doug..."

"Leftenant," he said sternly.

"OK, well, Leftenant, I don't want to get into a pissing match, but can I ask how many you have personally sniped?" Ray said.

"Seventeen over three years while in Afghanistan."

George put his hand up to his mouth snickering.

"What's the joke?" Doug inquired.

"Well," George continued, "Ray here got thirty-three in one day at Vedder."

"Thirty-four, actually," Ray corrected.

"Fuck off, no way," Doug objected.

"That's right, laddy muck," George said, "thirty-four." George showed both hands up with all fingers, closed his hand then showed his fingers twice more, then showed four fingers. He then pointed to Ray nodding.

"You have thirty-four confirmed kills by sniping," Doug retorted not believing.

"Actually, no, more than that. Thirty-four was just one battle. Before that Gary, Colonel Hawker, got me to take out a tank commander who was shelling us. That was my first kill."

"These are all confirmed kills. You have witnesses." Doug's voice was unconvinced.

"No, not all are confirmed. Most are," Ray said.

"Confirmed is all that counts. I have many more, maybe twice as many, unconfirmed. You hit a guy, he crawls off and dies. That's not confirmed."

"I was under the impression that what counts is killing as many of the enemy as possible, regardless of confirmation," George said.

Doug just looked at him, then turned to Ray. "Ok, hot-shot, how far, my longest was twelve hundred meters."

"You got me beat there, I have to admit. The first shot was eight hundred, give or take."

"Eight hundred, no way," Doug said.

"Actually, I won Canadian long range championship, five years ago now I guess it was, at one thousand yards. All ten shots were bulls on figure eleven targets."

"That is good shooting," Doug admitted. "So you said that was one battle, how many have you killed to date? Unconfirmed kills." Doug looked at George.

"Not, sure, but more than sixty so far, several at distances of more than eight hundred meters," Ray said.

A big surprise came over Doug's face. "Well, I have to see this to believe it."

"Oh, believe it, laddy muck," George said. "I've no where near as many as Ray here, but even my score is better than yours. Twenty-nine so far. I plan to double that soon enough."

"None of our shooters here have scores below twenty. Several guys are over forty," Ray added.

"Well, I must confess, I did not expect this. That's one helluva score by any measure," Doug said.

"That's right, laddy," George said.

"Stop calling me laddy."

"Well, you're the same age as my son," George laughed.

"I'm not your son, so knock it off. None of you have a problem killing?"

"It was hard at first, especially that first shot against the tank commander. But after that it was simple enough. No different than paper targets as far as I'm concerned," Ray said.

"I need to see this first hand. So you, Ray, will be my personal spotter and I will be yours, how's that?"

"He's no Bonnie, Ray," George whispered into Ray's ear.

"No, but he'll have to do," Ray said chuckling.

"Who's Bonnie?"

"Ray's wife. She's been spotting for him for years..."

"More than twenty actually," Ray added.

"Why, then, is she not here, may I ask," Doug said.

"I don't want her near this, she's safe in Revelstoke. She had a hard time of it at Vedder."

"Understandable. Ok, men," Doug ordered, "Intersperse with these civvies. You are going to get an education for sure."

Doug picked a spot, opened his rifle case and got his weapon set up.

"That's the Timberwolf," Ray said.

"Yep, I've been using this girl for ten years now."

"Lupo ammo right?"

"Yep, five hundred rounds in the case."

"Well, this is my lucky day. My savage fires the same round. I've only got twenty-nine shots left."

"Hmm, between the two of us we'll go through five hundred pretty quick. When the gopher shows up I'll make sure we get some more. Let's get set up."

Ray and Doug picked a second level shelf over the road. Their rifles were set through a narrow slit in the sand bags. It was cramped, barely five feet wide; the two of them were shoulder to shoulder.

They could hear someone on a megaphone, but couldn't make out what was said. It was a short message, followed by cheering.

Both Ray and Doug were looking through their scopes when the view was filled with moving green figures coming out from the bend in the valley. Battle music filled the ravine.

"Jesus mother of God, no wonder you guys have a huge score," Doug exclaimed. "This is one helluva TRE. I never saw anything like this in Afghanistan. Hell, no point in spotting for each other, let's just shoot. We can hardly miss, especially at this short range."

"Maybe you'll catch up to me," Ray said smiling.

Not long after they were shooting, someone tapped Ray on back of the leg. He crawled out of the shelf. It was Hawker.

"Ray, pass this around. I want you guys to hold off."

"Why, we're getting good shots."

"Because they're too easy. I don't trust the Chinese, they wouldn't be sending so many into our line of fire..."

Hawker was overpowered by a blast from the leopard tank directly below them on the road.

The two of them held their ears, and then Hawker continued. "They won't be sending so many against us if they weren't up to something. I want you guys to scan the entire field for anything unusual."

Ray passed the message down the line.

Doug crawled out of his shelf. "Sir, you need to see this." Hawker crawled in beside the leftenant and looked through Ray's riflescope.

"What am I looking for?"

"Follow the road to the side of the canyon. About four hundred meters out."

"Fuck me," Hawker muttered looking through the scope. "They're setting up their own log wall."

"That's what it looks like to me, sir."

"A barrier. To block our view. Wonderful."

"They could launch mortars, cannons, even a tank behind that," Doug said.

"Yep. Leftenant, concentrate all your effort on taking those crews out."

"Roger that, sir."

Ray crawled back into place.

"Now we're going to find out what you are really made of," Doug said. "You spot for me, for the first five kills, then we'll switch. Does that sound fair?"

"Let's get at it."

Ray watched at twenty-four power at a half dozen Chinese moving logs and setting them in position. "Can you see those guys just to the right of the road, near that big rock."

"Yep. What's the distance and wind?"

"Wind is coming up the valley. The distance is—" Ray adjusted his scope's zoom so that a figure occupied two marks on his mil-dot reticle. Then looked at the zoom setting. "—five hundred and fifty meters."

Doug adjusted his scope. Then sighted. He said, "Sending." The Timberwolf fired. Ray watched as one figure dropped, a spray of red followed him down.

Doug said, "Sending." Another shot, and another body dropped. Ray watched as the rest of the crew hid behind the log. However, Ray could see part of a body protruding from one side of another log when he zoomed to twenty-four.

"I see a foot, just on the right, my right, of the logs."

"I can't see anything, what the fuck power are you using?"

"Twenty-four."

"Jesus, must be nice. I'm at sixteen."

"K, just a second." Ray re-adjusted his scope to sixteen power. "OK, one and a quarter mil-dots from the left edge of the road, that should be a body."

"Sending." The Timberwolf fired.

"Nothing, I saw the splash in front."

"Corporal," Doug said to the soldier on his immediate left. "Take that sucker out with your AS 50."

"I got him, sir," the Corporal said.

A load pop sent a fifty-calibre round down range.

The log jumped with a large ejection of dust. Ray thought he could see a red spray behind. "You went through that log?" he asked.

"Pine? Sure, that's nothing for a 50," Doug said.

Ray was about to start his turn at shooting, while Doug looked for targets. The sand bag right in front of them erupted sending dirt and dust through the firing slit. Then another shot hit nearby, ripping open another bag. Sand started to pour into their shelf.

"Some fucking sniper has us marked," Doug said. "I'd bet he's in the trees on the side somewhere. You look on the left bank, I'll check the right."

Shots continued to hit around them, making it difficult for the two of them to look for the shooter. Their fellow snipers were also getting specific shots at them. They had more than a few snipers hunting them.

"This isn't going to work," Doug said. "I'll be right back."

Doug left. He came back a few minutes later crawling back beside Ray. "Wait for it."

"Wait for what?"

"You'll see." Soon as he said that the artillery started to fall on the enemy. The shooting against them stopped. The steel rain fell for an hour, and then stopped.

For the next hour, Ray and Doug picked off targets. Then someone came down the line yelling, "Cease fire. Cease fire!"

"Who the fuck would order a cease fire?" Doug complained. "Bloody, hell." He got out of his shelf. "Wait here men, I'm going to find out what the fuck's going on."

* * *

Hawker went down to the tank that made him deaf while he was talking with Ray. He climbed up to the turret where the tank commander was sighting. "You see those fuckers moving logs around, four hundred meters."

"I see them now," the commander said.

"Snipers will be taking them out, but when you get a chance take those walls out."

"Copy that."

Hawker surveyed the top of the platform. Bullets snapped and whizzed over his head. One man right in front of him got out of his shelf and said, "The guy beside me just got a bullet through his head. Fucking lucky shot."

Two corpsmen came over and removed the body. Indeed, regardless of the thick sand bags, and logs, the sheer volume of rounds coming at them guaranteed a few would make it through the shooting slits. Hawker passed a few people who had been hit, few serious though.

He came across one Canadian soldier and a U.S. soldier working on a C7, they were taking it apart.

"What seems to be the problem here?" Hawker demanded. "I've seen too many weapon problems."

"He slammed on the forward assist and broke a pin. The weapon is combat ineffective," the U.S. soldier said.

Mitchell came over.

"Major, any dysfunctional weapons, I don't care why, take them off the line," Hawker ordered.

"Copy that, sir."

As Hawker made his way across the wall, shooters on the shelves were throwing empty magazines behind them, which he had to dance around so as to not step on them.

Someone was picking them up, and then handing them off to several "beebee stackers" opening boxes of ammo and loading the magazines. Once loaded, someone else would take them to the shooters on the shelves.

Hawker counted six people supporting two maybe three shooters. He got a sinking feeling. Plus he realized the loaders couldn't keep up with the shooters. He witnessed a number of occasions when the shooters would yell at the gophers when they were not getting reloaded magazines to them fast enough.

It got really heated between three shooters and gophers when a box, which full contained a thousand rounds of 5.56 ammo, was emptied in a few minutes and they had to wait for another crate to be delivered and opened.

One shooter came out of his shelf right beside Hawker, not realizing who he was, and started yelling, "What the fuck is the hold up here? We're out of ammo. Don't just stand around with your thumb up your ass, get loading some mags old man." The soldier returned to the shelf after a young woman handed him a loaded mag. She smiled at Hawker and shrugged.

Hawker sat beside her, grabbed a handful of cartridges, and started to hand load magazines.

After about an hour, Hawker realized something. He watched as the woman handed a mag to a shooter. He wanted to see how long it took the soldier to fire off those twenty rounds.

The mag flew back at his feet, followed by a cry, "Another mag!"

Hawker looked at his watch. Almost a minute. That sinking feeling intensified as he said aloud, "twenty rounds per minute, per person. Times a thousand shooters, that's twenty thousand rounds per minute, times sixty minutes. That's one hundred and twenty thousand... No, one hundred and twenty thousand in six minutes. Ten times that is..." he paused. "Cease fire! Cease fire! Everyone cease fire," Hawker screamed as he moved along the line.

One soldier on the bottom tier obviously didn't hear, and continued to fire as Hawker walked past. Hawker kicked him hard on the bottom of the boot, and said, "Stop shooting now!"

Major Mitchell came up, "What's up, Colonel?"

"If we keep this up we'll be completely exhausted of ammo before noon."

"Exhausted? My god," Mitchell said.

"Get all the officers here now, Mitch," Hawker ordered.

Mitchell turned and went up the line shouting cease-fire.

Leftenant Swanell came up to Hawker. "Who ordered the cease fire? We have a ton of targets."

"I did. We're running out of ammo." Hawker paused. "Leftenant, what's your kill ratio?"

"I'd guess one in seven."

"Right, more like one in ten if you're lucky. Don't bullshit me, Leftenant." Hawker paused some more. "Ok, Leftenant, keep your men shooting. We'll use you to keep their heads down. Go."

"Roger that, sir," Doug said as he left.

Mitchell got the other officers rallied around Hawker. "Ok, here's what we're going to do," Hawker explained. "Look, there's no way there are enough targets to shoot at. These guys are just blasting away wasting ammo. We're going to fire by volley on command from now on. One tier at a time."

The group looked confused.

"It's simple," Hawker continued. "Start with the bottom tier, they fire only at what they can hit. Each man must mark a target."

"We have quite a few who have only iron sites, sir," one officer interrupted. "It's too far for them to pick targets."

"Then take everyone who doesn't have zoomable optics off the line. They can load mags. As I was saying, each man on the bottom tier will mark a target, then fire only on command.

"Once they fire ten rounds, they leave. The second tier will then fire their twenty rounds. Take everyone off the top tier. When the bottom tier leaves to load their mags, the top tier takes their place. Does everyone understand?"

Hawker looked around. They all nodded. One officer said, "We fire in volleys. Like they did two hundred years ago."

"That's correct, Captain. It's the only way we can conserve ammo and make it last. Get to it gentlemen, we need the first tier firing ASAP."

The officers got the relays ready. Hawker got on the megaphone. "Mark your targets! On my command, bottom tier only." He waited a few moments, and then said, "Fire!"

A volley of guns shot in unison. Hawker waited for one minute, then said. "Think of this as an agony snap. Bottom tier only fire!" Another volley of fire in unison.

Williams came up to Hawker and said, "Try this whistle, they'll hear it better."

Hawker changed his call, "Shoot on the whistle!" Eight more times Hawker blew the whistle, followed by a volley of fire. He then commanded the bottom tier to exit, and started the barrage with the middle tier. While the middle tier fired, those who were on the top shelf filled in the vacant spots on the bottom shelf.

This went on until mid day. The volley of fire started to peter out when Hawker ordered the fire. Eventually, when he blew the whistle no one fired. It stopped. The only sound was the Rolling Stones: *You can't always get what you want*. Mitchell came up to Hawker. They both looked out across the field. There was no movement. No shooting from the Chinese line.

Hawker got a better look with his binoculars. Bodies littered from the curve in the canyon up to the log maze. On the south side of the killing zone some bodies were draped around the log maze up to the one hundred meter line.

The only movement west was that same Cessna circling high above.

"Mitch, get me a count of our ammo. My guess is quarter mill was shot."

"Fuck me. That's less than a few days left then."

"Four days, maybe three at best if they do this at night. You better get on the radio."

The following nights the Chinese tested the wall, each time they failed. Hawker continued to rely only on volley fire. Only once when the Chinese decided to test the slow rate of fire, and charged en masse, did Hawker allow two tiers to fire at will, along with a barrage of artillery fire, until the advance was stopped.

The Chinese tried to flank through the mountains several times, but the terrain and the defenses proved impenetrable. All the while the stock of ammo dropped precipitously.

One afternoon, while Hawker was getting some lunch, he got a call to get to the command tent ASAP.

"WC Two here," Hawker said into the radio.

"Gary, this is Maillet. T'ere won't be an ammo shipment for at least a week. What's your situation?"

"One more night of this and we're done. They'll be knocking at our door."

"I suggest you move back to T'ree Gorges Lake, now."

"Com'on, General. Don't they understand we can hold the enemy here indefinitely? If we can just get the ammo."

"Gary, t'ey understand. T'word is manufacturing can't keep up."

"Gawdfuckingdamnit." Hawker threw down the mic. "Sergeant Williams!"

"Yes, sir."

"Bug out, now."

"Sir," the Corporal on the radio said. "The General wants to talk with you."

"Yes, sir," Hawker said into the mic.

"Gary. Get your butt 'ere ASAP. Leave t'major in command of t'retreat."

"What? No, sir. I'm needed here."

"Sorry, Gary, but th's is an order. I've put t'is off too long as it is. Just get 'ere t'is afternoon."

"Gawdfuckingdamnit," Hawker said handing the mic back to the corporal.

Hawker walked into Maillet's office, which was in the police station in Revelstoke. He interrupted a conversation between Maillet and Bartek.

"... So am I to understand that we're abandoning all the walls?" Bartek moaned.

"T'at is correct, we're 'olding the line 'ere at t'river. Look, we're almost out of ammo and food. We can't supply our force so deep in the mountains. So take your crew to Roger Pass and prepare for a defensive position. You'll meet up wit' a Colonel Scoff, he's a U.S. marine engineer. He'll show you what needs to be done. Dismissed."

Bartek brushed past Hawker saying, "I see you are being reassigned too."

"You wanted to see me, General."

"Oh, excellent. Yes. Gary. Glad you made it back safely. I was supposed to do t'is weeks ago, but you were doing such a great job." Maillet sighed. "I 'ave new orders for you. You are to make your way to Fort McMurray on the first train out of 'ere in t'morning. "

"What? What for? Is this because I disobeyed your order at Sicamous? Or because I lost the line at Perry Lake?"

"Oh, no. No, not at all. You did what you t'ought 'ad to be done. No, t'is comes from t' top. You were requested. T'e powers t'at be want you to organize t'defenses at t' oil sands. T'is is a big job. Big responsibility. T'ere's nothing up t'ere. You'll have to start from scratch."

"They must think we won't win in the mountains then."

"I wouldn't go t'at far. I'd consider t'is a last stand, just in case. "

"Oh, a last stand all right. They must know something we don't. Gawddamnit, I was hoping to command the defenses here. Guess that will be you."

"Oh, no. Not me. I'm going wit' you as far as Calgary. I've been called to a meeting. A U.S. Colonel is coming to take charge of t'defenses here. I did 'ave 'is name 'ere somewhere. Where's 'is name, I wrote it down 'ere somewhere." Maillet shuffled papers on the desk. "Doesn't matter we'll be gone before 'e arrive. So pack your bag. You won't even 'ave time to say goodbye to your men."

"Can I choose some to take with me?"

"I don't see why not, go ahead. But not Williams, I need him 'ere to run logistics."

"That's who I wanted to take."

"I'd rather you didn't. 'e'll be needed to get t'new commander up to speed, and keep some consistency wit' t'men."

"Fine. I'll see you on the train later then." Hawker left the room.

Maillet and Hawker got into the cab of the locomotive. Kappy was the engineer. They were about to leave when Williams came running up calling them. "General! General, you can't leave!"

Maillet opened the window of the cab. "What is it Sergeant?"

"That American Colonel has been held back. We just got word."

"For 'ow long?"

"At least a week sir."

"A week?!"

"Sorry sir, you're going to have to stay until he gets here."

"Ok, ok, damn it." Maillet turned to Hawker. "Sorry, Gary, you're on your own. Good luck wit' t'defenses. I'm sure you will do a good job. I'll see you up in Fort McMurray when I get finish here. Check up on your work."

Maillet got out of the cab, frustrated at all the delays and all the setbacks. Now he would have to command a defense without Hawker, who was far more a natural than he was.

* * *

Maillet came into the headquarters before sunrise. He started his log for the day, but couldn't remember what the date was. He was having a brain fart. "Can someone tell me t'date," he yelled out of his office.

"It's July third, sir," a man's voice replied. "The year is 2016," came a female voice.

"Smart ass. I know what year it is," Maillet muttered.

Laughing started in the main room full of people.

"Comedian, all of t'em," Maillet said in a low voice.

Maillet got up and looked at the tactical map, which showed the locations of all defensive positions and the location of the advancing Chinese army.

The Chinese had made it to Three Gorges Lake, and were poised to enter the valley west of Revelstoke. Coloured pushpins on the map indicated their own emplacements. A line across the entrance to the valley on the west side of the bridges into Revelstoke indicated the front line.

"Sergeant Williams, can you come in 'ere please. What's t'is 'X' on t'road here?" Maillet said when Williams showed up.

"That's the road block, sir. Rocks, but mostly timber laid on the road. It was placed there during the night," Williams said.

"Who is t'is?" Maillet said pointing to a yellow pushpin near the X.

"Hmm, just a second sir..." Looking at the list, flipping pages, Williams stopped and said, "Sergeants Hoag and Koenig, U.S. Army. They're snipers with two civvies, like the other sniper teams."

"Are we in contact wit' t'em?"

"I can, sir, one moment." Williams and Maillet went into the communications room.

"Sierra Ten, come in, over," the Corporal on the radio set said. But there was no reply. "Sierra Ten, wake up, answer the goddamned radio, over," she said again.

"Sierra Ten, Sergeant Koenig here, over."

"General Maillet wants to speak with you, over."

Maillet picked up the mic. "Sergeant t'Chinese are coming up t'road. T'ey will stop in front of you. I want you to tell me when t'ey get t'ere, over."

"Roger that," Koenig replied.

A few minutes later, Maillet said on the radio, " Sierra Ten, I want you to prepare to take out any choice target."

"Roger that," he said again.

Someone else in the field got on the radio sending a message to Koenig.

"There's one vehicle coming up the road, four soldiers in it, over."

"Roger that."

Maillet got on the radio, "Sierra Ten, do not shoot at target. Repeat, do not shoot. We want more of t'em to show up first."

"Roger that," Koenig said.

"This is Sierra Eleven, come in Mother Goose, over."

"Go Sierra Eleven, over," Maillet said.

"Tango in civilian truck stopped right at Barricade. Four tangos, over."

There was a pause on the radio.

"Vehicle turned around and headed back, over."

Another long pause. "Sierra Nine to Mother Goose, Tangos en masse heading up highway, over."

A few minutes later, Sierra Eleven came on the radio. "Tangos now at barricade. The front vehicle is a white stretched limo. Several Tangos getting out. One appears to be a senior officer, over."

"That must be the officer Hawker talked with. Too bad the colonel isn't here to see this," Williams said to Maillet.

"Sierra Ten t'is is Mother Goose, are you t'ere, over"

"We're here..." Koenig replied.

"Sierra Ten, do you see t'at officer, over?"

"Roger that, we have a clear view of that target."

"You may take out target when you're ready, over."

"Wilco," Koenig replied.

"Why bother to shoot him. Just bring the canyon down on them?" Williams asked.

"Payback, Sergeant, payback."

A few tense seconds went by. Mallet was getting impatient. "Well, well?"

"Sierra Eleven to Mother Goose, Tango is no more. Good shooting Sierra Ten, over."

"Blow t'road," Maillet ordered. "Bring t'mountain down on t'em."

"Mother Goose to Blast One. Blow, blow, blow, over," the Corporal said into the radio.

From their location in Revelstoke, several kilometers away, they could hear the rumble.

Another radio operator piped up in glee, "Sir, great news. The Apaches and Warthogs arrived at Golden. They can be ready to strike first thing in the morning, soon as fuel arrives."

"Get t'em airborne, Sergeant."

"Roger that, sir. Boy will the Chinese get a big surprise!"

CHAPTER **15**

The Agony

Rita Harrington worked in the long-term care facilities on West First Street in Revelstoke.

She was writing her morning patient log when a fully armed soldier came to the front desk. "Can I help you?" she asked.

"I sure hope so. We need more nurses. We've lots of wounded at the hospital. We need everyone who can be spared."

"I'm the only nurse here. I can't leave."

"Not to be insulting, ma'am, but you look like you have been a nurse a long time."

"Twenty-two years."

"Good, then you'll do nicely."

"I'm a geriatric nurse. I haven't worked in a hospital in fifteen years."

"You know how to fix a wound? You must have sores and such here."

"I guess, if I have to. But bed sores are nowhere near the same as battle wounds."

"Can you please come and help. We have a lot of young men, and some women, who need your help."

"Tracy, can you come over here please," Rita yelled.

Tracy arrived at the desk.

"You'll have to be in charge for a while. I'm just going over to the hospital. See if I can be of any help. You should be all right here? Maybe while I'm out I can get a spot for our residents on the next train."

"Yeah, go," Tracy said.

"Is she a nurse?" the soldier asked.

"No, a PSW. She's trained only in day-to-day care. She's not trained to work with critically injured. Let's go."

Queen Victoria Hospital in Revelstoke was a small local health facility located in the south end of town. It only had ten beds, though it did have one operating room for emergencies and forty-six long-term care beds that were fully occupied. The residents were moved to nearby homes, freeing up beds for the wounded.

The battle in Eagle Pass was producing a lot of casualties, far more than the hospital could handle.

The Canadian medical corps had set up an array of tents in the parking lot, the lawn and adjacent properties including the park across the road. The school nearby, on Park Road, was used to house recovery of the less serious cases, while the serious cases were sent by train to Calgary after stabilization or quick 'meat ball' surgery.

The hospital parking lot was a sea of people, most of them with some kind of serious wound. The soldier took Rita to the front desk of the emergency ward. They had to navigate a large crowd of people. "Doc, hey doc!" the soldier yelled across the counter. A female doctor came out of a room; the front of her scrubs was heavily blotched with blood, some dripping down onto the floor.

"I found another nurse, the only one at that nursing home."

"Can you triage?" the doctor asked.

"I haven't done it, but I'll give it a try," Rita said nervously.

"Take her out front, soldier."

"Yes, ma'am."

They waded back through the mass of humanity, many of them crying, injured, and wounded, out the door into the parking lot. The soldier stopped and looked around. "I have no idea where to send you, ma'am."

"I can see them over there doing evaluations, and more vehicles are showing up. Thank you."

"You won't thank me by the end of the day, ma'am."

Rita slowly tiptoed around the occupied stretchers to where vehicles were arriving. Three jet aircraft, A10 Warthogs, screeched loudly low overhead going west, out to the valley beyond Revelstoke. The sound was deafening, and she couldn't hear someone yelling at her. She looked to her left. Someone was calling to her and gesturing for her to come over.

The young man had his hands covering the stub end of a soldier's right shoulder. The severed arm was lying on the soldier's chest. "You a nurse?" the young man sobbed.

"Yes."

"Please help him. I don't know what to do."

"He needs to get into surgery right away."

A man in scrubs working on a patient a few people over said, "Surgery's full."

"Here, let me try to stop the bleeding then," Rita said.

"You a nurse," the man in scrubs asked tersely.

"Yes."

"Then triage. Don't give aid."

Rita looked at the man, confused.

"Look, what's the first thing you need to do."

"Stop the bleeding," Rita said.

"Jesus Christ, woman. Is the patient even alive? Check vitals."

It never even occurred to Rita to check that. The depth of her feeling of helplessness was just like her first day as a nurse: all confused, at a loss of what to do. She took a pulse from the neck, nothing. She then opened the man's eyes. They were fixed and dilated.

"I'm sorry," she sighed to the young man. "He's dead."

The young man pulled his hands off the gaping torn end of the arm. Tears welled in his eyes; he wanted to use his hands to clear the tears, but they were soaked in congealing blood. "He was my friend. He wasn't even a real soldier, we just hung out together. We thought it was our duty to help stop the Chinese. Now Dan is dead. He was only twenty-two."

Rita handed him some cloth that was nearby on the ground so he could clean his hands off.

"Hey you, are you a nurse?" someone yelled at her a few feet away. "Get over here, I need your help."

Rita helped the young man to his feet.

"Hey, please, can you get over here, now," the man bellowed.

"Ok, ok, just hold on a second." She looked into the eyes of the young man. "Get out of here. Don't be dead like your friend." She left the young man and headed over to the doctor who called her.

"A train will be arriving from the front in a few minutes," the doctor said. "You'll come with me to triage. In the meantime, go over to that bus and pick the patients you think are savable."

"I'm, I'm..."

"Look, you need to get a grip. Just let your training work for you."

"But I've never worked in emerg."

"Welcome to your new job. Do you have any lipstick on you?"

"Lipstick? Yes, I think so, let me check. Oh, no I don't have my bag with me."

"Then use this magic marker," he handed her a black permanent marker. "Do you remember the letter system?" the doctor said. "A through D?"

Rita nodded.

"On their foreheads then. Anyone who doesn't have a letter on their forehead, triage them and assign a letter."

Rita walked around the people in the parking lot, many of them moaning, some calling for help. Each one had letters on their foreheads, mostly B, for 'they can wait'. A few with Cs were being moved to another area; a place to die away from the rest. The As were passing her carried on stretchers towards surgery tents as she made her way to the bus that had just arrived.

The mobile wounded got off the bus first, some helped by other wounded. She checked each one over. At first she wondered what to assign. She remembered that even though they are walking, their wounds could be bad and they might go into shock.

Those with bandaged arms and legs, who talked back when asked about their condition she assumed could be assigned a B, which she wrote on their foreheads.

One man looked pale and ashen as he tried to get down the steps. She touched his forehead, it was cool. He was unable to answer questions, and seemed weak and disoriented. He had no visible injury, but there was a bit of blood inside his ears when she looked. She wrote an A on his forehead and called for someone to take him into the hospital.

"This isn't too bad. I can do this," she said confidently.

After the last walking wounded disembarked, a soldier came to the door from inside the bus. "I'm a corpsman. The really bad ones, the ones on stretchers are in the back here, and I'll need your help with them."

She walked into the bus towards the back. The seats were removed from the last half of the bus. Both sides had stretchers suspended on chains from the ceiling. Stacked three high, two wide. Two columns on both sides of the isle, twenty-four in all.

"Two are dead for sure," the corpsman said with no emotion. "This one, and the one down at the back. I'll go get some help with the stretchers if you can triage the rest."

The corpsman slid past her practically pushing her body into the chain of stretchers. The one in the top tier moaned as his moved from side to side. She checked him over. He had several bullet wounds in the belly. Her first instinct was to label him an A. But would he survive into surgery?

The corpsman returned with six men. "Miss," the corpsman said. "You should triage them before they leave the bus. It's faster."

She wrote an A on the top patient. Then she went over to the one in the opposite row as two men unhooked the patient she marked and carried him off.

This one had a head wound. He was breathing, with a good heartbeat, but no response to stimulation. She could only check his right eye as the other was under the bandage, which covered the left half of his head. It was fixed and dilated.

She pulled back some of the bandage to see the wound. She could not see much; too much blood had mixed into the bandage that she was afraid to look further. So she felt the side of the head where the bandage was. She could not tell, but it appeared the skull was intact. So what to assign him? She wanted to assign him an A. But she remembered that surgery was full, thus the wait was going to be long. She realized she was playing god. She did not like it one bit.

His breathing changed to very rapid, then dropped to normal. That happened a number of times within a few moments. She changed her mind and reluctantly assigned him a C. She looked into the man's face after she wrote the letter. He was younger than her two sons, she thought. She wondered about the reaction of his mother.

"Move on, ma'am," the corpsman said. She moved to the next one middle row on the opposite side.

This one had a chest wound. She pulled open the tactical gear, then the clothing. She saw breasts. It was a woman. Rita pulled back the small bandage. The bullet had entered just under the right nipple; a large haematoma was forming under the skin. Rita looked at the girl's face. It was dirty, and her hair was cut short. Her breathing was slow and shallow. Rita took the heart rate from the wrist. It was weak and thready. "I wish I could take blood pressure."

"Sorry, ma'am," the corpsman said. "I should have given you mine, here. And my stethoscope, here. The bullet went right through that one. She had the only IV I had left before we got here."

She took a reading of the blood pressure. The best she could guess was that it was forty over nothing.

"I think her liver has been shot," she said to the corpsman.

"That's what I figured. Then she's done," he said.

"No." Rita cleaned the dirt off the forehead and wrote a double A. "This poor girl is the same age as my daughters; I won't be cavalier about life."

After an hour that seemed to take forever, Rita emerged from the bus. She sat on the last step in the doorway. Her hands were trembling. She was mentally exhausted from having to make life and death decisions. Of the twenty-four she triaged she wrote two Ds, three Cs and nineteen As. She figured once in surgery the doctors would re-evaluate anyway.

The doctor who told her to triage the bus came over.

"You took too long," he complained.

"What?"

"I said you took way too long. Fifteen minutes tops for each bus. You need to speed up."

"I'm doing the best I can."

"Goddammit, not good enough. People are dying. You're taking too long." He moved on.

Tears welled in Rita's eyes. She lowered her head into her knees.

The corpsman came up. "Sorry, ma'am, but I need to drive the bus up to the railway station. The train's arriving. It'll be full of wounded."

"Better I go with you then."

"No, ma'am. Best you stay here and triage as I bring them in. It will just be chaos there."

She nodded her head and got up.

With a few minutes to herself, she went into the hospital to get something to drink. She wasn't hungry, though she thought she should be, it was well into the afternoon. She went into the women's washroom to relieve herself and wash a bit.

She found the doctor that she first met, cleaning herself and putting on new scrubs.

"Hi, doc. Can I ask you about a patient?"

"I've seen so many today, I'm not likely to remember, but make it quick."

"It was a young woman with a GSW under the right breast. I put a double A on her forehead."

"Didn't treat that. Look for Dr. Clarke. He's the military surgeon working on chest wounds," she said as she rushed out the door.

Rita asked around for the doctor. One of the hospital staff said to check the roof; he often went up there to get away.

Sure enough, she found the doctor puffing on a cigarette on the roof.

"Hardly healthy doc."

"I actually quit years ago. But today, what does it matter. I found these on a patient; he won't be needing them anymore. Want one?"

"No thanks, doc. I want to ask you about a patient you may have operated on. A young female..."

"With a GSW in the right chest. I just finished operating on her. Was that you who put the double A on her forehead?"

"Yes."

"You shouldn't have done that. We aren't supposed to prefer one patient over another based on gender. You did that because she was female, didn't you."

"Maybe just a little. But I really thought if someone could get to her quickly, her life could be saved."

"Well, your gamble worked. They got your message and brought her in before several others."

"Is she going to be ok?"

"Maybe. The bullet just nicked the lung and the top of the liver, passing by a rib on the way out. I had to remove about a quarter of her liver. But she should recover. You do realize two young men died waiting for me to finish her surgery. Her moving up the line killed two men."

Rita played god again, her heart sank, a lump filled her throat. "But if she waited she would have died right?"

"Who knows. Maybe, maybe not. It's all rolling the dice here." He took a long drag on the cigarette, blowing the smoke high into the air. He coughed a bit and spat out the sputum.

"Is she awake? I'd like to see her," Rita said.

"She should be, but I have no idea where they took her. One of the tents on the lawn I suppose." He dropped the butt on the ground and put it out with his boot. "But you should wait. Give her some time to recuperate. You probably won't have time anyway; that train has arrived. We'll be swamped again soon. Again. Excuse me."

They walked to the door, which took them back to the real world.

Indeed, the bus showed up fully loaded, several nurses and military medics did the triage. Rita did that for three hours. And that wasn't the main group of injured. The decision was made to send the not so wounded to Cochrane by train. So Rita had to deal with the worst cases as they arrived.

Same routine as the first time, she evaluated the mobile wounded as they exited. Every one was given a B. One woman, near the middle of the pack, had nasty injuries on her right head around the ear.

"What happened to you?" Rita asked.

"An RPG exploded against a tree right beside me. I got hit with splinters. Glad I had my helmet on, it took most of the brunt. The corpsman got most of the wood out, but he said there's more in there."

"Yes, I can see them. Your ear is quite cut up, just a few bits of skin holding it on. You've cuts all over the right side of your head. You're damn lucky nothing hit your jugular."

"Well, doc, just sew me up so I can get back on the line."

"I'm no doctor, you'll have to wait in line with the rest of the walking wounded." Rita scribbled a big B on the girl's forehead knowing it would be hours before someone treated her.

Once the last one was out, Rita dreaded going to the back of the bus. It took all her muster to make her feet move. The same corpsman from the morning was working on a patient on a stretcher. The man's face was mostly missing, save for his right forehead and the right part of his jaw. His right eye was hanging where the mouth should have been.

"He's still alive and breathing. I got a trach into him. He's even awake, a bit. Can you help this guy here," the corpsman said pointing to another patient at the top of the opposite tiers.

The man's trousers were soaked in blood around the waist. He was unconscious. Rita cut off the trousers to have a look. She stood back in horror. "Oh my God…" she choked with her hand over her mouth.

"What is it?" the corpsman said.

Rita had to swallow and get her breath. "Look" Her voice quivered, the other hand pointing.

"I can't, I have to get this patient going. Just evaluate and get him off."

Rita broke out in a cold sweat, she felt nauseated. "His penis… It's… It's severed. One of his testicles. Its…, they're inside. Inside his underwear." She had to sit down as she was getting light headed.

"Roger, that's the one. It looks like splinters of bone lacerated his genitals. It's a real mess. Is his femoral artery severed?"

Rita reluctantly got the courage to get up and look. "I can't see. There's too much blood."

"There's a canteen of water on my belt, pour it over the wound and see. If it is severed then he's a C."

Rita did that, pouring the water over the wound. "I still can't see."

"Stick your finger in and feel for it, for God's sakes."

"What?"

"Get out of the way, I'll do it." The corpsman stuck his hand inside the left thigh, blood welled. The man moaned. "It feels intact. I can see where the bullet entered through the back of the left thigh. It must have hit the pelvic bone. Give him an A."

The man woke up, moaning more. His eyes opened. Rita quickly put the blood pressure gauge around his arm and took a pulse and pressure.

"Oh, you're going to be fine, your pulse is fine," she unconvincingly lied.

"Am I hit? I can't feel anything," he said in a croaky voice.

"It's not bad, they'll patch you up in no time."

The man lifted his head and looked between his legs. He screamed. "They shot my dick off!" He went on wailing that he wasn't a man anymore. He would never again make love to a woman, he cried.

Rita stuck her head in front of his to obscure his view. "You are going to be fine. One testicle looks in place, and I'm sure the doctors will be able to sew your penis back on."

The corpsman gave her a funny look like he knew she was lying. Rita wrote the A on his forehead.

Two men came into the bus. "Take this guy first." She looked at the corpsman. "Right!"

"You're the boss."

Tracy from the nursing home caught up to Rita sitting on the curb with her head down almost between her knees.

"I need to see you, now," Tracy demanded.

"What is it?" Rita lifted her head; her eyes were full of tears. Her red stained hands still shaking.

"They have emptied our residents, all of them. They moved them to homes nearby. They moved a bunch of wounded in and demanded we help patch them up. I'm not trained to do that, nor is anyone else. You've got to do something."

"Tracy, see that bus over there. Come with me and triage those patients. Some are missing arms. Some are missing both legs. Some have their guts ripped open. Some have their genitals sliced off. Some are crying for us to help them. The last one I just did I had to put a C on what was left of his head. Half his brain was lying on the stretcher exposed.

"Then when you are exhausted making life and death decisions, go behind the hospital where the priests have been giving last rights all day. Then over to the park across the road there where they're digging a mass grave. So, please, do what you can for our brave men. Do your part."

Tracy looked around at the stretchers heading to the building. "Ok, I'll go back. But I'll also have to check in on our residents. Maybe when these people all leave we can get them back into their rooms. You know they don't like disruption of their routine."

It was getting dark when Rita arrived at the back of the school where the not so wounded were. She was asked to check in on them once the triage had completed.

The not so wounded were mostly lying on the lawn or on the parking lot curbs. Rita went up to the closest to her. The man was in civilian clothing, but had military combat gear beside him on the grass. A woman was sitting beside him holding his left hand.

"You finally going to check us over and treat our wounds?" the man said.

"Yes, best I can."

"About fucking time," someone yelled.

"Hey, pipe down, they've been patching up guys hurt a lot more than you," the man said. Turning back around he said to Rita, "Just we've been waiting for almost eight hours, some more."

"That's terrible. I'm sorry you had to wait so long," Rita said. She looked around at the two hundred or more men scattered on the lawn. "What are we looking at here?"

"Mostly minor stuff, and a few broken bones. I've done something to my knee, hurts like hell and I can hardly walk on it."

"Oh, then don't get up. Who's the worst?"

"Those dozen there under the tree. They have bullet wounds, but mostly through and through flesh wounds. We've been trying to bandage them up best we could. There's one guy who has a bullet in his ass. That's him lying on his stomach."

It was very early in the dawn when Rita finished stitching up the open wounds. She then got to the broken arms, legs, a crushed hand and one with a shattered collarbone. Lastly, she got to the first man she talked with.

"What's your name?" Rita asked.

"Ray, and this is my wife, Bonnie."

Rita smiled at Bonnie. "Ok, Ray, let's see your knee."

She cut off the pant leg above the knee. As she lifted his left leg, he winced in pain.

"Breathe," Rita said.

"What?"

"You're holding your breath when you're in pain. You should breathe deeply. Just like they tell us when we're giving birth."

"It's my knee, not a newborn. Ouch, dammit, what are you doing?" Ray winced while Rita was pressing around the knee.

"I think you tore a ligament, maybe chipped some cartilage, ripped the meninges, or all of the above. It looks swollen. You can't walk on it?"

"No, I collapsed when I tried. It must have happened last night. We were running hard to get away from the Chinese. They were overrunning our position, and I was out of ammo. Ran as fast as I could, but the young guys, the Canadian Forces sniper team I was with, were a lot faster than me. Damn they are good shots."

"Better than you, Ray, I find that hard to believe," another man said.

"Oh, yeah, most definitely better than me."

"At least you got out," Rita said. "And you..." Rita looked at Bonnie, "you were there too?"

"No, I was here in town waiting for him. Gave me a huge worry waiting for him."

"Don't doubt it. But rather old for this silliness aren't you, Ray?" Rita said.

"Fifty-nine."

"Fifty-nine?! What the hell are you doing in a war at fifty-nine?"

"I thought I could do this. Kinda forgot I wasn't twenty any more. Not that I'm out of shape. I've been doing military style shooting events for years."

"Just not in a real war," Rita said sarcastically.

"Yeah, right. Just not in a real war."

"Well you're done. That's going to take a long time to heal. Months, maybe more. I've seen injuries like this with the elderly that never heal."

"Hey, I'm not elderly."

"Damn close to it, Ray," Rita retorted.

One of Ray's friends came over, he was about the same age. Rita had stitched a bullet graze on his left abdomen a few hours previous. "Can you not wrap up his knee so we can get back into the fight?"

"What's it with you? Your friend has a bum knee, and a few inches more and you would be dead. Haven't you had enough?"

"It not about having enough," Ray said. "It's about duty."

"Well, your duty now is to your knee. Duty won't do you or any one any good if you are permanently crippled or worse, dead. You will all be on the next train if I get my way."

Sergeant Williams showed up while they were talking, with half a dozen others, all carrying wooden crates or steel ammo boxes.

"Ok. Everyone listen up. Here is your ammo. Bomb up your mags, and report to the bridge. We have some breakfast ready for you."

Rita walked over to Williams. "These men are all wounded, and you want them to fight?"

"Orders, ma'am."

"Damn your orders, they are too sick to fight. That man over there can't even walk."

"He can shoot. We can put them all on the beach in the defensive position."

"Well, I won't let them."

One of the men got up, hobbled over to a steel ammo box, opened it and started to reload his mags. Several others opened other boxes. Some of the immobile civilian soldiers asked for boxes to be brought to them.

"I think you have their answer, ma'am. Oh, and Ray, sorry no Lupo, but I got you guys with the CZs some seven six two by thirty-nine. If you need a ride to the front, a Hummer will be by in about ten minutes. Good day ma'am," Williams said tipping his hat at Rita and walking off.

Before Rita could get some sleep—she was practically falling down with fatigue—she had to find out about the woman who was shot, and the poor lad who had the severed genitals. She wanted to see them both before they were shipped to Calgary.

She found the woman in one of the rooms of the hospital's long-term care ward. The woman was on an IV and an oxygen bottle. The double A was still on her forehead. She was awake.

"Hi," Rita said. "How are you feeling?"

In a groggy voice the woman said, "Like I was hit by a Mac truck. And

I'm thirsty."

Rita got her a damp cloth and told her to suck on it. "Thank you," she said. Rita looked at her chart. "You're Lynda Swift."

She nodded. "I'm a Vancouver cop." She paused a bit, "I was a cop."

"Well, you will be fine. I talked to the doctor who operated on you. But I have to apologize. It was me who wrote those letters on your forehead."

"What letters?"

Realizing Lynda likely hadn't seen herself in a mirror yet, Rita said, "Never mind, you'll find out soon enough. Well, I just wanted to check up on you. They're going to ship you to Calgary later today."

"There was another cop with me, my partner. John Revoy. He was beside me when he got shot, looked like in the eye. Then I got hit. Did he make it?"

Rita thought it was the young man beside her in the bus, but she decided to lie. "I'm not sure. I'm sure someone will be able to find out for you. It's been a pleasure to meet you. But I've been on my feet for more than forty-eight hours."

"Oh, my. Then you need more rest than I do. Thank you for saving my life."

Rita held her hand and smiled.

Out in the hall, Rita searched for a nurse. She found one in a room tending a patient.

"Can I help you?" she said.

"Yes, I'm looking for a patient who had his genitals severed. Do you know where he is?"

"Yes, he's down the hall. We had to sedate him."

"How is he?"

"He has nothing there. It was damaged too much. They may have to take his leg too. The bullet went right though the hip joint. It took the whole top of the femur..."

Rita just turned and walked out of the room with her head down.

* * *

Rita had finished tending to one of their residents in a house near the nursing home, and was heading to another house. She had spent the last five days hopping from house to house with Tracy tending their needs. She was walking along the main road, Victoria Street, which paralleled the railway line. She watched, with a number of people, as the last train, loaded with wounded and soldiers, was preparing to leave. People were running about in chaos.

The bridges over the river into town blew in a loud explosion, with secondary explosions following. Windows near Rita shook, some came off and smashed on the ground. She felt the concussion in her, with her ears popping. A large black and dark grey cloud rose in the west blocking the view of the valley beyond.

Four A10 Warthogs emerged through the dust cloud low over the town heading east. The unmistakable high-pitched whine of the engines in full throttle cancelled out the noise of vehicles on the road passing her. Rita put her fingers in her ears.

Then another one emerged trailing out of the canyon. It had an engine on fire; a long black tail of smoke followed it. The plane was so low Rita could see the pilot. It disappeared into the next valley, the smoke hung over the town drifting slowly to the south.

A soldier ran up along the train yelling, "Get moving, get this train out of here now!! They've come through the pass and are just on the other side of the river. Move it, move it!!" as he climbed into the cab of the locomotive. Thick black smoke poured out from the top as the engine revved up.

As the consist passed Rita saw Ray and Bonnie sitting amongst stretchers of wounded in an open boxcar door. Ray waved at her. Rita smiled with a contented sigh of relief.

Small explosions and shooting could be heard in the distance to the west. The crowd dissipated, few saying anything. The plume of smoke from the bridges had passed between the mountains following the lake south.

Rita looked around, found Tracy and told her they should return to the nursing home and finish getting all the residents back into their rooms.

Three quiet days passed and Rita was doing her rounds of the wounded in the tents in the hospital parking lot. The sound of vehicles could be heard in the west coming through the valley towards the narrows of the lake where the bridges once stood.

Gunfire erupted. Rita and a number of civilian and military personnel walked the short distance along Cashato Drive where it curved along a cliff forty meters above the swamp and lake below. It was called the Cashato Bench. A number of homes hugged the edge. A large crowd was in the back yards.

They had a spectacular view of the far bank of the lake, and overlooking the city to the north. On the west bank of the river they could see the Chinese gathering along the shore. Hundreds of them got into small kayak-like boats and paddled across the lake. They were towing lines of cable behind them. They reached the city side of the shore and secured the lines.

One by one, small air inflated paddleboats, carrying six Chinese soldiers each, pulled themselves along the cable to the eastern shore. The line of boats was non-stop. Rita figured thousands of them were crossing the lake.

"We all better go back to the hospital," someone said.

Rita didn't. She kept going, back into the city as she figured the fighting would be where her manor was. She ran or walked as fast as she could. By the time she got onto the main road, shooting was to the east of town, around the railway yard.

Chinese soldiers were everywhere, moving along the road in that direction. They paid her no notice.

When she got to the manor, Tracy was in a real state. She was all over Rita for leaving her alone as the Chinese arrived.

"Did they come in?" Rita said.

"No, but they will. They'll rape us, you know. I should have left when I had the chance. It's your fault I stayed."

"They won't do anything to us. Be reasonable," Rita bellowed.

Rita checked all the rooms, their residents were safe. By that time, all the shooting had stopped.

That night, Rita didn't go home, nor did she venture out of the manor the rest of the day. She spent the night in a vacant room.

The next morning, Tracy was on her case again. This time it was food.

"We only have enough for three days. And the chef isn't here. No one's here. It's just the two of us. It's just you and me to cook for thirty-five people, serve them, clean them..."

"It should be thirty-six including the two of us." Rita interrupted wanting the complaining to stop.

"Old man Winters died during the night."

"That's a real shame, he was a nice old soul. We'll, I'm sure whoever is now in charge will get us some food."

Rita went outside to see what was going on, and to see if she could muster the courage to walk to the hospital. She went to Victoria Street and looked around. No one could be seen anywhere. Then a couple of Chinese soldiers came by on bicycles. They stopped in front of her and aimed their rifles into her face.

"You go inside. Curfew!" one of them yelled a couple of times. Guess that answers that question, she thought. She went back to the manor followed by the soldiers, right up to the door. "You stay," one said.

Volley of gunshots could be heard not far away. Rita went to the door, looked around, and opened it. No one was in sight, but after a few moments, another volley of fire. This went on for most of the afternoon.

On the third day of the occupation, Rita had to do something, they were out of food. She ventured out the door. This time, the main road wasn't empty. It was line after line of Chinese soldiers marching east. Some were stationed along the road.

Again, one of them, a young female, pointed her rifle at Rita and told her to "go inside. Curfew." Seemed that is the only English they were taught to say, Rita thought. Rita tried to mimic eating, but the soldier kept the same routine. Finally a female officer came over hearing the noise.

In broken English she said, "There curfew. You must go back home."

"I'm in the manor, we have old people. We have run out of food."

"You show me," the officer said.

The three of them went to the manor. The officer toured the facilities while the soldier guarded the front door. Many of the residents who were lucid were frightened; asking Rita and Tracy what was going on.

Finally, the officer returned to the lobby. "You should have evacuated. You not supposed to be here. We not feed you," and she left.

Every day Rita took the risk and went out searching homes for food. Sometimes she would get lucky, mostly she would not. Medical supplies had also long been exhausted. Residents started to die off. At least the Chinese allowed Rita and Tracy to remove the bodies for burial. Burial was done by captured civilians or the few wounded Canadian soldiers who remained behind. Rita recognized one of them. She took that bullet out of his behind, which seemed so long ago to Rita.

Week two arrived and the Chinese had a solution to the starving residents. An officer, who spoke no English, arrived. One room at a time he fired his pistol into the head of each resident as armed soldiers guarded Rita and Tracy.

Tracy was beside herself sobbing. Rita was relieved their residents weren't suffering any longer. She figured they had done this at the hospital too. At least Lynda got out before this, she thought. Many more seriously wounded did not, including the soldier who lost his genitals. He was likely shot, she figured. That was a relief in her mind.

Rita went home, not her actual home as that was well up the valley, but someone's house not far away, guarded all the way by a soldier.

* * *

August was hot. With no power, Rita was sweating buckets confined in her home. There was no let-up of the curfew. The only outing allowed was the daily trek to the community center where she, and everyone else, lined up for their ration of food. In order to get that food, they were forced to listen to propaganda. A female Chinese soldier was on the PA system telling everyone how it will get better. How the Chinese will make for a better life. How capitalism brought them so much misery. Every day it was the same thing. She stopped hearing that background noise.

One day sometime in September, Rita wasn't sure what day it was, while she was in the food line, someone started to talk. That was a big no, no. Signs all over in big letters had QUIET! or NO TALKING! People had been executed on the spot for speaking to anyone else in the line. But an older man just ahead of Rita looked around first to see if the coast was clear. He whispered, "I heard we have them halted in the mountains. They can't move forward." He stopped when a soldier walked past the line. The man continued. "There was a big battle yesterday..." He buttoned up again.

The next day at the line-up, Rita was accosted by two soldiers pointing their bayonets at her, and gestured for her to follow them. One grabbed her by the arm and towed her along. They navigated her through the mass of wounded, all of them Chinese, in the high school parking lot.

She recognized a number of people working on the wounded. The female doctor, the male doctor who worked on Lynda, and the crabby doctor who scolded her for taking too long. He came over to her.

"About time you got here. We're swamped. Think you can handle superficial wounds." It wasn't a question; it was a clear demand with a sarcastic tone.

"I can try," she said back firmly.

"Then start over there by that truck, there's an officer with a small wound."

The bayonets escorted her to a stretcher. She was thrown down beside a wounded Chinese officer. The officer had his top clothes off. There was a gaping wound on his side under the left armpit covered in dark congealed blood.

She lifted his arm as he cried out in pain. She could see a shard of metal inside the wound.

"You fix! You fix!" the bayonet-wielding soldier said, pushing the blade close to her face. The wounded officer said something in a harsh tone to the soldier who backed off.

"Don't mind him," the officer said in non-accented English. "Just do what you can, please."

"I'll need to probe a bit. It's going to hurt."

"Just do it."

Rita tried to get her fingers around the metal to grab it, opening the wound in the process. The officer cried out in pain.

"Breathe," she said.

"What?"

"Why is it you men have to hold your breath when you're in pain. Just breathe deeply."

"It hurts when I breathe too much. Just pull it out."

Getting a grip, she tried to pull the shard out, but it would not move.

Fresh blood started to ooze from the wound obscuring her view.

She looked around. "I'll need some water to clean it out, and some gauze."

The officer spoke to the soldier, who left. "While we wait," the officer said to Rita, "what is your name?"

She told him.

"I am Captain Qigang Xinming Xiaofeng. I'd shake your hand but any movement is killing me."

"And you expect me to spell that name on my chart for you?"

"Ha, ah, oh, ouch, damn, don't make me laugh, it hurts."

"Are you hurt anywhere else?"

"I do not think so, a couple scrapes maybe. Nothing serious. Is this serious?"

"I can't tell, it's not deep, but if I can't stop the bleeding and if you get an infection, you'll be in trouble."

The soldier returned with a canteen of water, and some sheets that had been ripped into gauze. Rita poured the water onto the wound, and wiped it clean of blood with the cloth. She probed the wound with her fingers. The officer winced in pain.

"That hurts, can you get it?"

"It looks like it has wrapped itself around one of your ribs. I'll need some forceps."

The officer talked to the soldier, who then left.

"Are you married?" the officer said.

"What business is it of yours?"

"I am just wondering why you are here and didn't evacuate with the others."

"If you must know, my husband died a few years ago. He was diabetic and couldn't get his insulin."

"I am so sorry to hear that. Do you have a family?" the officer asked politely.

"I have four grown children and eight grandchildren."

"Eight grandchildren," the officer sighed, laying his head back and looking to the sky. "That is wonderful." The officer winced in pain. "Where are they now?"

"Calgary, and places east. I sent them away when you…" She paused looking for a polite word, "…*people* arrived."

"I am glad they are safe. But you stayed. Why?"

"For my patients. We were hoping to get them evacuated, but the military wouldn't give us a place on the train."

"But *you* didn't evacuate, you stayed behind, and now I have you tending to me," he said looking at Rita.

Rita didn't say anything, just held some gauze against the wound.

"It must be nice to have a big family," the officer said looking back at the sky. "We have one daughter and I just found out I now have a grandson. What is it like to have a big family?" The officer looked at Rita.

"Wonderful," Rita said with pride.

"I bet it is. Gathering for feasts," the officer said in a low voice, gazing skyward again. "Lots of children running around, getting into things they should not. I can only imagine how that must be. My daughter and her family live with us. They cannot afford to get their own apartment. Our apartment is only thirty square meters. You people have such big homes here."

"I did. I will never see my house again," Rita complained.

The soldier arrived with some tools.

"Pliers and cutters?" Rita said in disgust. "You're not a car I'm working on, Captain. Don't you have your own medics with supplies?"

"I am not sure, most are at the front I guess." The officer said something to the soldier. The soldier replied.

"That is all he could find. It will have to do," the officer said.

Rita grabbed the needle nose pliers out of the soldier's hand. She cleaned off the blood, which had refilled the wound. Grabbing the shard carefully with the tip of the pliers she tried to pry it off the rib. The officer screamed out in pain, moving his body quickly away from the offending instrument. Rita stopped.

"This is ridiculous. You need a local."

"That is not going to happen," the officer moaned recuperating from the pain. "Just do it."

"You're moving around too much, your men are going to have to hold you down."

The officer barked to the soldiers. They put their guns down, and held the officer, one at the shoulders, one at the feet.

"Here we go," Rita said. She tried again to grab the shard with the pliers, and pulled hard, but it would not budge. The officer's face was deep red, sweat beaded on his forehead. He finally let go and screamed.

"We need to give you a break," Rita sighed.

Calming back down, the officer tried to take his mind off the situation. "My wife was once pregnant with our second, but they forced her to get an abortion. I was away on officer training. You know of our one child policy in China?"

"You want me to feel sorry for you? Sorry, I can't."

Rita tried again with the pliers, making the officer scream out in pain.

"This isn't going to work. I'm going to have to cut the metal."

"Do it," the officer winced.

Rita grabbed the side-cutters, cleaned them off with some water, and started to make small cuts in the metal. Each nick sent the officer shrieking in pain. The thicker parts required Rita to use both hands and squeeze hard. Finally the shard was cut in two. The officer relaxed a bit. Using the pliers, Rita slowly rotated each fragment of the shard off the rib.

"Got them," she said showing the officer the two pieces of twisted metal. "But you're bleeding again."

She washed the wound with the last of the water, pulled out small remnants of his uniform that were wrapped around the rib and stuffed gauze into the hole. "Near as I can tell your rib is shattered in three places. You'll need surgery to fix that. I'll have to close the wound in the meantime. But I need to disinfect it. Is there any alcohol around?"

The officer gave an order to one of the soldiers, who searched through the officer's backpack.

"We are not a bad people, Rita," the officer said apologetically. "We are just desperate."

"And we're not? The whole world is desperate, Captain. It's been the rationale for all wars. At least you're going home now. But not me, right? I'm never going to see my family again, am I?"

"I have some influence, my father is a General here. I'll talk to him, see if I can get you across the lines."

The soldier found it; a small flask of Canadian Club whiskey. Rita opened the bottle, and was about to pour some of the content on the wound, but the officer gestured for him to have a swallow. He took a deep chug of the booze and handed the bottle back to Rita. She poured a large amount of it into the wound. The officer screeched out in pain and passed out.

Rita sewed the wound shut with needle and thread. When she was done, the officer regained consciousness.

"You're all done. That's the best I can do for you."

The soldiers got on either end of the stretcher and lifted the officer up. He reached out with his hand and grabbed Rita by the arm. "I can't thank you enough. You are a good person, Rita. I wish you well and you return to your family." They carried him off.

Rita stood there looking around at all the carnage. Her gaze fixated on the bodies covered over with blankets; some were children's blankets with cartoon characters on them. Tears welled in her eyes. She dropped to her knees and cried.

CHAPTER **16**

Calgary

Ray McGillis limped out of the Peter Lougheed Medical Center in Calgary, meeting Bonnie at the main entrance. She helped him along under his left arm. It was an hour walk, at his reduced speed, to the house they occupied just east on 60th Street.

The early October climate was sunny, but cold, it dipped below freezing the night before. The previous night's light snow had started to melt in the morning light.

"When we get home you've got to rest that knee," Bonnie said. "It hasn't improved in the three months we've been seeing the doctor. It's not going to get better unless you get off your feet, especially since we're moving to Edmonton next week."

"Yeah, yeah. I know. Would be nice if we could get a cab in this town... How long was the line-up?"

"Three damn hours. Another riot broke out. All I got was two days of food."

"Anyone hurt this time?"

"Just some shoving, not like the last time when they started shooting at each other."

"You did take the 85 with you, didn't you?" Ray said.

"No, I left the pistol at home, I didn't want it confiscated. I mean, there was a cop there today, he was taking any guns off people who showed up."

"Don't let that detour you, please take the gun next time. Those idiots though. Don't they realize they need cops at food distribution centers every time? So what did you end up getting?"

"Same as last time, you know. A loaf of bread, some cabbage, a pound of ground beef, though half of it is fat, a couple potatoes and some carrots. Oh, and some powdered milk this time. No tea still, I really miss my tea."

"More stew, wonderful," Ray said sarcastically.

"Damn bland without spices, not even any garlic. What did you do while I was gone? Visit some friends again?"

"I did. Not many left in the hospital. They've shipped out more east to make room for new cases coming from the front. Dave was still there, he's mending, but he said he'll never walk again. He ships out tomorrow. Oh, and remember that cop we saw in the train in Revelstoke? We met her in Sicamous."

"The one shot in the chest?" Bonnie said.

"That's her. I saw her in the hallway. We talked a bit. I didn't know, but she was at Vedder when we were there, guarding the escape train."

"She told us that at dinner. Remember, when she asked about my rifle?"

"She did? Oh, I don't recall."

"She's ok then?"

"Yep, she ships out tomorrow too."

"So, what did the doctor say about your knee?"

"She was too busy, I saw a physio. She showed me some exercises, but warned my knee will likely never heal. So I guess I'll be gimpy for the rest of my life."

"That's fine by me if it keeps you off the front."

They turned on the street to the home they had occupied. At the far end a number of people were in the middle of the road walking towards them. It looked like some scuffle was taking place. The yelling became louder as the group got closer. Bonnie took no heed, Ray watched them.

"I was thinking, while waiting in line, I want to leave. I mean, I've had enough of this. The rioting, the lack of food, the threat the Chinese will break through the mountains. I want to get out of here. As far east as we can get before winter," Bonnie demanded.

"What? No. I start that chief chemist position the fifteenth. We leave next week. It's a good job; we'll be on site. There'll be food, shelter and safety at the munitions factory." Ray didn't look at Bonnie, he continued to eye the group. It was clear two girls were being forcefully pulled along the street by five young men.

"I don't care. I want to get out of here. We can find work on a farm, or something," Bonnie continued.

"Work on a farm. A chemical engineer. Me with a bum knee. Hell, you sold clothing. You don't know anything about farming either."

"You can do something. I don't want to be here."

They reached the front of their home's drive, with the approaching group less than two hundred meters away. It was clear the young women were being corralled against their will.

"Bonnie," Ray said. "Get the 858, it's just inside the door."

"Don't get involved Ray. Leave it be."

"Just do it, please. And get the 85 for yourself."

Bonnie returned to the street with Ray's CZ 858, and handed him a mag. Ray rotated the loaded mag into the receiver, cocked the carbine, and limped into the middle of the street blocking the group's exit. He put the CZ up aiming, left hand gripping the magazine tight, both elbows tucked into his chest, just like he had practiced all those years doing close quarters competition-shooting events. The barrel pointed at who appeared to be the leader. They stopped about ten meters in front of Ray.

"What the fuck do you want old man? Get out of the fucking way," the leader said.

"Help us please, they're gonna kill us," one of the girls yelped.

The leader slapped her across the face. "Shut the fuck up, Lizard Butt." Both of the girls looked like they had been roughed up quite a bit.

Ray's heart was racing, his palms started to get tacky. This wasn't like sniping; he'd gotten used to that. This was close and personal. He took a deep breath and let it out slowly. "Let the girls go," he said calmly.

The leader laughed. "You don't have the fuckin' guts. I'd bet you haven't fuckin' popped anyone, you old fart."

From the corner of his left eye Ray noticed one of the men was slowly inching to flank him. Ray whipped the barrel around, took a shot, and snapped the sight back on the leader before the body hit the ground. The only sound was the ping of the casing as it danced along the pavement.

"I was on the front asshole. He just put my kills to over one hundred. Care to be one more?"

The leader started to move his right hand to his belt.

"Don't do it. I'll drop you and your friends before you can blink. Come and get behind me ladies."

They tried to get free, but the two men holding the girls wouldn't let go. Ray fired a shot into the right eye of the man beside the leader showering one of the teenagers with blood and bits of brain as the side of his head opened up. Both girls screamed.

The leader paused holding on to one of the girls' arm.

"Chill out, jefe. She's not worth it, man," one of the men said.

With a wincing look of anger, staring down a muzzle brake, he let the girl go.

Once the two young women were behind Ray, he said, "Now all of you put your weapons on the ground. Slowly!"

Very gradually the three men put their handguns on the asphalt. "Check it out. You're dead meat. Be real," the leader said.

"You three come anywhere near my property and I'll drop all of you. Now turn and walk back up the street. "

They didn't move.

Ray fired a shot over their heads. "Do it now!"

They turned and walked away. The leader gave Ray the finger as he backed up, then turned.

The four of them walked slowly into the house. Leaving behind two bodies with large pools of blood forming around them.

"This is exactly why I want to get out of here. You could have been killed, Ray," Bonnie nagged going through the door.

"Assholes, big men only when they have the power. Turn the tables on them and they run shitless."

"One day someone won't back down, and you'll be dead. Come on girls, let's clean you up."

After Bonnie and the two girls came down from getting fixed up upstairs, Ray had cooked some dinner, thin stew and milk made from the powder. The two girls thanked them both.

"What was it between you and those guys?" Ray inquired.

"They wanted us to toss up. With so many soldiers in town, they figured they could make a killing." Rose said.

"We aren't their only girls," Trisha added.

"Toss up?" Ray asked.

"Sex for money," Rose said.

"Hookers?" Bonnie said. "You both don't look fifteen."

"I'm thirteen, Trisha is fourteen."

"We were trying to run away, but they caught us," Trisha said.

"Where's your parents?" Bonnie asked.

At the same time they both said, "Dead." They refused to elaborate, tears forming in their eyes.

"They'll come back, with more of their friends. They'll kill all of us. I seen 'em do it," Rose said, her voice quivering.

"We need to get out of here then," Bonnie demanded.

"Not until next week," Ray said.

"No now," Bonnie ordered.

"We don't know when the next bus or train will be, maybe days."

"There's a bus to Edmonton leaving at one, that's where we were heading," Rose eagerly suggested.

"That's just under two hours, and we'll be on that bus, right Ray?"

Ray thought for a second, and then caved in. "Ok, ok. Pack up what we need."

The four of them made it to the bus stop just as the vehicle was arriving, loaded their little bit of luggage, and boarded.

Just over two hours into the drive a police roadblock stopped the bus. An RCMP officer came up the front stairs by the driver.

"Sorry folks, we have a situation up the road. You'll have to stay here. It may be a long wait."

"It's been a long drive, can some people get out and stretch their legs?" the bus driver asked.

"Sure," the cop said. Then turned to the passengers, and said, "Stay near the bus, don't wander off." He disappeared down the steps.

Ray and Bonnie were the last to get off. Ray looked past the two patrol cars that were blocking their route to where a few cops were standing at the crest in the road before it dropped into a shallow valley. He limped over to the cop who got on the bus.

"What's up?" Ray said.

"Nasty. Four or five Muslims killed at least one maybe two of our officers. They have automatic weapons. We're waiting for a sniper team from Calgary."

"When do you expect them?"

"Not for hours."

"Hours?" Ray thought, wondering if he should offer help. "I'm a sniper, was a sniper, on the front lines."

The cop's eyes lit up. "You have your weapon here?"

"On the bus."

"Get it."

Ray got the bus driver to open the cargo hold.

"Ray, why must you always be the hero?" Bonnie complained.

"I can't help myself. Look, I'm not even sure I can help. Won't hurt to see."

The cop escorted Ray past the roadblock.

"I'm Bob, what's your name?"

"Ray, so what's the story here?"

"We're not sure. The Edmonton officers were chasing them and called for our aid. We all met here at the same time. The Edmonton cop crashed into the perp's SUV. They have, like, a hundred automatic weapons. They started to fire on us."

Ray looked at him sideways. "A hundred?"

"Well, maybe not a hundred, but a shit load of them. All we have are these Glocks with one mag each. You must have been in the war, with that limp. Got shot?"

Ray gave a brief summary. Bob laughed. "Out of the war because you tripped. That's funny, dude. I wanted to fight, but I was ordered to stay a cop. Maybe the war will come to me."

"Careful what you wish for. How long have you been on the force, son?"

"Almost two years."

"Piss and vinegar."

"Piss and what? Vinegar?"

"Look it up. How do you know they're Muslim?"

"They were screaming about Allah and death to infidels. Alla-ack-bar, or something like that."

"Any idea what they were up to?"

"Nope, only the two cops chasing them know that."

Ray and Bob arrived at the three officers on the road crest. The valley dipped down to a junction where two cars, one an Edmonton police cruiser, the other a deep blue SUV, were kitty cornered across the intersection. At the far end across the valley up the road was another cop car, keeping its distance. The crossroad rose to the right and left, disappearing behind trees. A small creek went under a bridge just past the intersection.

"Who are you?" the RCMP Sergeant asked.

"He's our sniper," Bob said.

"No he's not, he's a civilian. Go back to your bus."

"Sarge, it's going to be hours for our guys to get here. Those cops down there need our help, now."

The sergeant looked Ray over. "Can you see what we're dealing with that thing? It's too far to make out what's going on."

"Sure." Ray carefully got on the pavement, pain shooting through his knee up to his hip. He found it difficult to get comfortable on the hard surface, his elbows disliking the pressure as he peered through the scope. "I see one body beside the SUV. It's a cop."

"There's a female officer there somewhere," the sergeant said.

"I see her, she's sitting on the ground leaning against her car, opposite side of the SUV."

"Is she dead?"

"No, she's moving."

"Likely wounded. Do you see the perps?"

Two men from behind the SUV stood up and started to fire their AK47s at vehicles on the road to the left. One then turned towards Ray's group and fired. Those standing ducked.

"He can't hit us," Ray said.

"They could get lucky," the Sergeant argued.

Ray looked up to the sergeant. "No, his rounds aren't snapping over our heads. The drop is way too much for that ammo, several feet in just a few hundred meters. He's not even close to us. At six hundred meters we're out of range."

"Can you hit them that far?" Bob said.

"Oh, yeah, easy."

"You are not to shoot. We wait for our own sharp shooters," the Sergeant ordered.

Ray watched as the one who fired at them moved away from the SUV towards the cop car. Ray cocked the Savage. The man rounded to where the female cop was sitting. He yelled towards Ray's position, firing his rifle into the air. He then started to point the gun at the cop. Ray could see the officer cover her head with her hands. Ray fired. The man dropped to the pavement.

"Holy fuck that was loud, damn cannon," Bob screeched covering his ears.

"What the hell! I told you not to shoot," the Sergeant yelled at the same time.

"He was going to shoot the officer," Ray said still looking through the scope, cocking the Savage. The casing pinged a number of times along the asphalt stopping at the sergeant's boot.

"I'll have you charged with murder, now stand down, and move away from that weapon," he ordered.

Another man moved quickly from the SUV towards the cop car.

"Shoot him!" Bob screamed.

"Stand down, now!" the Sergeant demanded.

The figure got to the second mill-dot to the left of the crosshairs, Ray fired. The man dropped just behind the cop car.

"Fuck me, you got him on the move! Strike back, shooting man," Bob roared.

"That's it, give me that damn weapon!" the Sergeant bellowed.

"John," Bob said standing in the way of the Sergeant and grabbing his arm. "Let him finish this, please."

The Sergeant pulled back, just as Ray fired again.

"Get one?" Bob said turning.

"Yep, he poked his head above the hood of the vehicle. So there should be only one left, right?"

"Maybe two," the Sergeant said.

The fourth man threw his AK47 from behind the SUV, and stepped out with his hands in the air. Ray zoomed to twenty-four power, put the crosshair in the middle of the man's head.

"Shoot that fucker!" Bob bellowed out.

"Mister sniper," the Sergeant said. "You shoot a surrendering man and I will arrest you for first degree murder."

"Fuck that," Bob retorted, "he's a cop killer. Shoot him!"

Ray dropped his head over the rifle butt for a few moments.

"Why are you waiting? Shoot him!" Bob begged.

Ray opened the breach, ejecting the live round. Leaving the bolt open, he got up wincing with pain in his knee. Leaving the rifle on the bipod, Ray said, "Bob, your Sergeant is correct. It's murder. I've come to the realization that, for too long, I have gotten a rush out of killing. I can't do this any more if I want to hang on to any humanity I have left." He limped up to Bob nose to nose. Poking him in the chest with his index finger Ray continued, "You want him dead? *You* shoot him."

Ray hobbled away leaving the Savage on the ground.

Bonnie hugged him hard when he got back to the bus. Holding on to her, he asked the bus driver, "Do you stop at the railway station in Edmonton?"

"Yes, it will be around 10 p.m., provided we get out of here soon."

Ray looked at Bonnie, "We're going to Nova Scotia. Is that east enough for you?"

"Of course it is," she hugged hard and kissed him.

* * *

General Ross Hughes arrived at the Marriott Hotel in Calgary just in time to make the meeting. This was an essential meeting to attend. All the high level commanders and politicians were there.

He entered the Trader Grill Room on the top floor. It was full of people, almost all of them in military uniforms, dominated by Americans with very high ranks. He found General Maillet talking with a U.S. three-star General by the floor to ceiling window, which had a spectacular view of the city, and the westward mountains beyond.

"Ross," Maillet gestured. "Come over 'ere."

They shook hands. "General, t'is is retired General Ross Hughes, he's been commanding our effort in Edmonton. Ross, t'is is Major General Sam Walsh."

"T'e General is in charge of 'is troops in all of Canada," Maillet said.

"He's taking over your charge, George?" Hughes asked.

"Yes, I'll be overseeing effort in Fort McMurray."

"Is that going to be a problem, General?" Walsh said. "You're not being replaced, if that's your worry."

"Oh, God, no. I was hoping you would. I'm supposed to be bloody retired. I've been at this for six months now, and with winter approaching I wasn't looking forward to spending my time fighting this war any longer than I have to."

"We all have to sacrifice..." Walsh was interrupted with a call to order.

Everyone shuffled to find a seat. Eighteen people filled the table, and ten others, aides to the officers, took chairs behind. The man at the head of the table was five-star General of the Army Brad Southwick. He was a very tall African American, his short black hair showing some grey. He sported a small greying moustache on a face that could have landed him a Vulcan role.

The only non-officer at the table, who sat beside the general, was an Air Force Technical Sergeant. She was typing on a laptop. There were also a number of civilians at the table.

"Welcome all," Southwick said in a deep bass voice with a touch of southern accent. "Before we start, I've some news." He read from a number of slips of paper in his hands. "Help is on the way. Ships from Norway, Jamaica, Europe, and even South Africa are coming to help us. They won't land for a few weeks yet, so we may not see them until the spring."

He swapped out that slip of paper for another. Southwick sighed. "A number of ships have left Israel with refugees. No one knows where they're going, likely North America. It says here some of those refugee ships have been sunk. Egypt, Syria, Iran and the Palestinians have succeeded in defeating the Israeli army. Apparently widespread genocide is happening. God help us, and the people of Israel."

He read from another slip. "India has entered the war. Seems they're not happy with the Chinese moving millions of troops across Afghanistan into Turkmenistan, where the oil fields are."

Another piece of paper, "The Taliban is now a nuclear power. Their control over Afghanistan has spread into Pakistan."

There were more notes, but he put the papers aside, then folded his hands together on the table and sighed.

"I always knew given the right circumstances humanity would resort to their barbaric state. So much for John Lennon's 'brotherhood of man' dream."

He shook his head, looking down. Then rose up to glance at the room and took a deep breath. "Enough of the rest of the world. Let's focus on our problem. Let the record show the date and time, it's October 11, 2016. It's 10:00 a.m."

Reading from a sheet handed to him by the technical sergeant, he rhymed off the names of the people around the table, who said "here" at each one. There was a wide array; the new Minister of War, the Minister of Defence, the Minister of Energy and the Minister of Agriculture, all from the Canadian Government, were seated together on Southwick's left.

Because of the coalition between the Conservatives and Liberals in the Canadian Federal Government, the Minister of Agriculture was a Liberal, so was the Minister of Defence, the other two Ministers were from the Conservatives.

At the end of the table, to the left of the Canadians, were Hughes and Maillet, with the Chief of the Defence Staff between them. Sitting opposite the government ministers was Walsh, and two admirals. The U.S. Secretary of Defence was directly to Southwick's right. Another civilian, sitting between the Secretary of Defence and an admiral, was from the CIA.

Southwick stopped the roll call there and said, "And who are you? I don't see you on my list."

"I'm not here, General," CIA said with a countertenor voice that still had a touch of cracking. He was a short balding man with beady little wide spaced eyes behind small rimless glasses, the arms of which pressed into the sides of his round unshaven face. He stood out from the formally dressed officers and politicians with his plain shirt, no tie and blue jeans.

"I can see you're not here, and I suppose you also don't have a name."

"Not one you'll know, General."

"So how about I call you CIA, that's where you're from aren't you?"

"Call me what you want, General. I'm just not here to observe."

"I'll bet you are." Southwick continued with the roll call.

"Good, we're all here," Southwick said. "I hope everyone had a good trip, and a good sleep. The agenda is simple. Gather information, isolate the problems, and solve those problems. And problems we have. Thus this is going to be a long meeting. Lunch has been arranged, and if need be the good folks who run this fine hotel will serve us dinner. I expect we may be here for bed time snacks."

The group chuckled. The Canadian female politician sarcastically said, "Wonderful."

"So the first order of business is to get the latest from our defensive efforts. General Maillet, the floor is yours."

"T'ank you, sir." Maillet got up and pointed to a map on the wall behind him. "Our defensive position in Rogers Pass 'as been very effective. The Chinese 'ave t'rown a lot at us since July, but t'ey have not penetrated our line. T'ey have repeatedly tested us, but we've inflicted casualties t'ey simply cannot sustain. T'ey even tried to burn us out wit' forest fire, but t'is has been t'wettest summer in decade, so it 'asn't worked. It actually backfired on t'em. T'ey had to retreat 'ere when the fire blew back at t'em. As long as t'supplies keep coming, and we get more air strike, I'm confident we can keep t'em in t'mountains t'rough t'winter."

"And further north," Southwick said.

"T'at would be General Hughes, sir."

Hughes got up and pointed to the map. "I can report the same thing. We have them stopped dead in their tracks. Right here at Moose Lake. Further north up here we also have them stopped. It's the only other pass through the Rockies, and damn close to the oil sands. The air strike on this bridge in July ended it for them. They have spent the summer trying to build a new bridge, but our Canadian Rangers have been very effective snipers, using 1942 Lee Enfields I will add. I'm also confident, as long as we continue to get supplies, we can hold them off through the winter. If the weather this year is as bad as the last few, which forecasters claim it will be, the enemy will have a hard time of it. It will claim many."

"Will that river freeze?" Southwick inquired.

"Yes, sir, it has in the past. Long range forecast says it will be another deep cold winter."

"So the Chinese will simply walk across."

"Yes, sir. If they can get through the deep snow. Once over the river they'll have to make it through the pass. In winter that's near impossible."

"But they could cross the river, then wait for spring to make it through the pass. From there they have a straight line to the oil sands."

"Yes, sir. They would."

"And no way of stopping them."

"That's why we're here, General. Give us the resources, and we should be able to stop them like we have elsewhere. Lots of them will perish over the winter. So far into the mountains supply logistics will be a nightmare. Hell, it is for us and it isn't even winter yet."

"Thank you, General, now what of the efforts at Fort McMurray?"

"Sir," Hughes interjected, "before you go to Colonel Hawker, I have something else to report."

"Go ahead, General."

"A group of our Rangers from Baffin Island radioed in some disturbing news you may not be aware of. The Inuit up there reported that Russian soldiers parachuted in over the summer. They have set up stations all over our islands in the Arctic."

The CIA man nodded.

"You know about this?" Southwick asked CIA.

"Not specifically, but we suspected this would happen." CIA replied.

"Nice enough you let us know about this. Care to be more specific?"

"As much as I can tell you."

"There's no privileged information here," Southwick said sternly.

"Oh, no General, that's not the issue. It's just the limitations of what we do know for sure and what we can guess at. We know for sure the Russians are not in this fight. We know they made a pact with the Chinese to stay out. And I think General Hughes' report explains why. They obviously took advantage of the focus on the Chinese invasion to invade Canada's north. It's not like we can do anything about it."

"For the resources," Southwick said.

"That's what this war is all about, jockeying for resources," CIA acknowledged.

"Great, Chinese steal our west coast, Russians steal our Arctic, and Americans steal the rest. We won't have a Canada left when this is all over," Leanne Loklear, Minster of Agriculture, complained.

"We're not here to steal anything, ma'am," Southwick said. "We're here to prevent your country from being taken over. That's what neighbours do. General Hughes, is there any indication that the Russians are being aggressive towards the indigenous people there?"

"No, sir. In fact, the opposite. According to the report I got, the Russians were being friendly with the Inuit."

"Well, as Minister Loklear said, Canada is shrinking and there is nothing we can do about the Russians." Southwick sighed. "Alright, Sergeant, put Colonel Hawker on the line."

"He's ready, sir," the Technical Sergeant said.

"Put him on speaker."

The phone clicked a couple times, then, "Colonel Hawker here."

"Colonel, this is General of the Army Brad Southwick. Can you fill us in on your progress?"

"Yes sir. It's going slow, too slow. We need more bodies, double at least. Company men are clearing a perimeter with their equipment, but it's been getting harder. We had a major snow fall last night; it's melting a bit. So it's getting tough. The oil sands is still producing, we should be able to keep up to two hundred thousand barrels per day."

"That's a small cry from what they can produce, what's the problem?" Southwick said.

"As with anything, people, sir. More than half their workforce is preparing defensive positions, and many others are preparing for evacuation when, or if, that comes."

"Will you be done for the spring?"

"I hope so, sir."

"Hope? I don't work on hope, Colonel. I want to know, can you get the job done?"

"Send me more boots and I can. It's all about people, General."

"Do we have any more bodies we can send there?" Southwick asked the room. "Hughes? Maillet?"

"You take men from our position and you'll weaken us," Hughes said. "We need to keep the Chinese in the mountains for the winter. We let them through, it won't matter how many people we send to Hawker."

"One of you Canadian politicians should have bodies we can use, surely."

"I had a meeting yesterday with the leader of the Canadian Chinese community, he was complaining that they are not being allowed to help at all," Loklear said.

"I'm not surprised by that, Minister."

"Well, it's unfair, General. He assured me his people left China decades ago to get away from Communism. They came to Canada for a better life. He was clear to me that they don't want to return to China-like conditions."

"And you trust them?"

"I think we can."

"Colonel Hawker, are you comfortable with that?" Southwick said to the phone.

"Bodies are bodies."

"Ok, Miss Loklear, contact your friend."

"Excellent, he's staying at the hotel. When we break for lunch I'll tell him."

"How many, a few thousand? That's no where near enough," Hawker said.

"Minister Loklear," Southwick queried, "do we have more bodies anywhere? Now the season's over, how about farm help?"

"I'm not so sure. They didn't have enough people themselves to harvest. So not a good year for crops. That early September frost killed off a lot.

Crop production is less than a tenth of what we should have produced. Fuel was a big problem. Many farmers told me that they had most of their crops still in the field when the first snow fell a month ago. So, they didn't have enough bodies either. I mean, I'm not sure we can count on too many from there."

"Get who you can, put out a radio call for help if need be," Southwick said.

"Not a good idea, General," Hughes objected.

"What? Why not?"

"I would not announce to the world we need help setting up defences up there. We need to be low keyed."

Several in the room agreed.

"So be it, Colonel," Southwick recanted. "We'll do what we can for you, Colonel Hawker. By the way, how's my rabbits doing?"

"Rabbits are all in their hutches. Feeding lines were tested and all works fine." Hawker said.

"And no one knows about my rabbits but you, right?"

"Roger that."

"Ok, Colonel, keep up the good work."

"Rabbits?" Richard Grayford, Minister of War, asked confused.

The CIA man shook his head at Southwick.

"They're going to find out, they should be told." Southwick said.

CIA shook his head more. "General, I highly recommend you do not."

"Ok, what's going on here? What are you people up to?" Grayford demanded.

"It's need to know. And you don't need to know." CIA retorted.

The room was shocked on the Canadian side.

Grayford pointed his right index finger at CIA. "Is this how you plan to operate in our country? Secrecy?"

Southwick didn't say anything for a few seconds.

"Don't do it, General," CIA warned.

"Piss off," Southwick barked. He faced the Canadians and folded his hands together on the table. "We planted twenty-four nuclear warheads around the oil sands project—" CIA sat back in his chair and threw his hands up. "—They're there just in case the Chinese take it over. If we can't use it, they don't get it. Understand, it's crucial no one knows about this."

"You did what..." "Oh my god, how dare you..." "Who gave you the authority..." came from the Canadian ministers.

"Wait until I tell the Prime Minister about this," Loklear threatened.

"He already knows," CIA said.

"No way...". "He would never approve this..." "If he knew he would have told me..." the ministers said.

"He knows, I told him," Southwick said sitting back in his chair.

"When was that? Certainly not before you put nuclear weapons on our soil," Grayford argued.

"It was after," Southwick said. "I had to wait until your government shuffling settled down. Besides, I didn't trust the pinko NDP. They wouldn't have kept it quiet. Once you had a new government, your PM agreed it was our best option."

"I don't believe he would ever agree to this," Grayford countered.

"Believe what you want. Doesn't change the fact we have done this," CIA said.

"For someone who's not here, you certainly are making your presence known," Grayford hissed.

Loklear pressed her index finger into the tabletop. "I demand you take them out, right now!"

"They won't be coming out," CIA countered.

"Colonel Hawker, you knew about this and did nothing to stop it?" Loklear demanded.

"I found out when I got here. They were already being installed. I was in no authority to undo it."

"I'm personally giving you that authority right now. Tell the Americans to remove the bombs. Do it now. That's an order," Loklear shouted.

"You don't give orders here, " Southwick warned, his finger pressed into the table. "I'm Supreme Commander for the continent, the nukes stay."

"This is outrageous. I won't stand by while we give up our sovereignty to you," Loklear cried.

CIA pointed his index finger at Loklear, his little eyes disappeared behind the squinting. "But you did to the Chinese for years."

"What do you mean?" Loklear said.

"You allowed the Chinese to buy up companies in the oil sands," CIA stated. "We objected to that, but you allowed a Communist country to take control of your energy resources. You made trade deals with Chi..."

"We had to, your economy was falling apart," Loklear interrupted.

"Our economy would have improved if we did more trade, especially oil, from Canada," CIA said angrily. He threw his hands in the air. "Instead, your government went on the road to abandon us, your closest friend and ally. So we had to continue to rely on conflict oil. It was disgraceful."

"It was your President who killed the Keystone pipeline..." Loklear argued.

"And so you went ahead with the Northern Gateway," CIA interrupted.

"That's enough," Southwick stopped them. "Mistakes were made on both sides. Throwing accusations around the room isn't going to solve our problem. How to keep the Chinese from taking most of our countries is our problem." He turned to Loklear. "You're aware they want more than just your oil. Now you have the Russians taking your Arctic. The nukes stay. So let's focus on the job at hand."

Loklear leaned back in the chair crossing her arms. "Children squabbling in a sand box."

"I beg your pardon," Southwick said.

"You heard me. I said you're a child. *'I can't have my toy, so I'll wreck it so no one can have it',*" she quipped in a child like voice.

Veins expanded on the sides of Southwick's temples. His eyes squinted. "With all due respect, Minister, this is no sandbox. This is deadly serious. If the Chinese get control of the oil patch, they will gain super power status, and regulate North America as their servants."

"You don't know that," Loklear snarled.

"Actually, we do," CIA said. "Go look at Africa. China bought up millions of acres in Africa just to grow food for the Chinese. All the while Africans starve. China's imperial exploitations around the world has been going on for decades."

"Seems that's falling apart too," Southwick added. "I read a report on my way here that a coup in Kenya has overthrown the government. So I suspect that could end the Chinese supply of food from there."

"And increase the Chinese need for our land," CIA included.

"Any more surprises, General?" Loklear leaned forward in her chair. "Are you war mongers planning to bring any more nukes into our country?"

"That's not necessary," Grayford interrupted. "We're not seeking war, war has sought us. I don't like this any more than you do. The Americans could have at least asked us first. But with Liberals like you, I suspect you would have said no without any explanation."

"Of course, you Conservatives would have said yes without question," Loklear wailed. "Obviously your leader did just that."

"Bickering amongst ourselves is taking our focus from the threat at hand," Southwick ordered. "Can we please focus on our problem instead of making new problems? The nukes stay, move on."

"I will ask again, General. Any more nukes?" Loklear demanded.

"No," Southwick said.

The tone needed to change. "If I may, General," Maillet said. "Gary, I'm planning to leave 'ere in t'e morning, is t'ere anything I can bring you?"

"A Timmy's double-double would be nice."

They all chuckled in the room, except Loklear.

"Ok, Gary, I'll do my best."

The technical sergeant hung up the phone.

"So, Miss Loklear, your food report wasn't very encouraging. Are we going to have enough to feed our troops over the winter?" Southwick asked.

She didn't answer, still fuming.

"General," CIA interjected. "U.S. crop production is no better than the Canadians. The loss of our refineries, well, a lot of farms just couldn't cope. We've had a complete collapse of farm production."

"So we can expect a lot of starvation this winter," Southwick sighed.

"Worse than last winter I'm afraid. Mostly in the cities."

"Great. Nothing we can do about that. What about cattle?"

The Minister of Defence lightly elbowed Loklear.

"The beef herd in Alberta is strong," Loklear mumbled coming out of her pout.

"Enough to feed our troops and civilians over the winter?" Southwick said.

"For Canada maybe, but not the whole west coast," Loklear warned.

"We should have enough livestock for our troops in the states," CIA acknowledged.

"But, General," Loklear continued, "understand we would completely decimate the beef industry. If we eat every cow, pig and chicken, we won't have any to breed for next year. It's been bad enough over the last few winters, especially last year, when just about every wild animal who could be hunted was hunted. I'm not sure the deer or moose populations will ever recover. Now we're going to consume all our livestock? We don't want to go the road the North Koreans did."

"We have to eat. People first. Get it done Minister. Next on my list is energy. Please update us on Canadian oil and fuel production, Minister of Energy, Don Ferguson."

"As everyone is aware, we lost several key oil refineries in New Brunswick, Montreal and Newfoundland," Ferguson said. "Levelled by low yield nukes. Plus west of Toronto. The Prince George refinery was destroyed by our retreating troops to prevent the Chinese getting it. Our plant in Burnaby is intact but in Chinese hands, though the pipeline from here to there has been shut down. So that leaves Sarnia, in Ontario, and the plants in Edmonton. Total output reached one hundred thousand barrels per day. Nowhere near enough. Half of that is being allocated for the war effort.

"As my colleague said, much of that didn't get to farms who badly needed it," Ferguson said.

"How about jet fuel, we desperately need that," Southwick said

"Production is increasing, but slowly. Almost all of the output from south Manitoba, from the Bakken, is being shipped by rail to Sarnia for processing into jet fuel, then sent here by rail."

"Sounds like a long roundabout Canada tour. Is there any way we can shorten this?" Southwick said. "Don't you people have a refinery in

Regina, isn't that in Saskatoon?"

"Saskatchewan, yes, we do, or we did. It's been out of service since last winter. They had a major fire, which destroyed much of the plant. It's being rebuilt. I was told they'll have it up and running by the spring."

"Sabotage?"

"No, General, malfunction because of the winter."

"Always something. Why can't the oil from the Bakken go to Edmonton for processing?"

"Can't. Those refineries are going flat out. In fact, output from the oil sands is backing up because plants in Edmonton can't process it fast enough. So, sending them more oil won't make them process more."

"What's our fuel situation in the states, Admiral?" Southwick said.

"Our output is very low," Admiral Sara Morgan replied. "The coup in Saudi Arabia killed off that supply. Argentina has cut us off. Mexico's export is nonexistent because of civil unrest there. Hurricane Zoë in August shut down a number of rigs in the Gulf of Mexico, one of the platform rigs is still on fire..."

"We have reason to believe that platform was struck by a submarine attack. The fire started after the hurricane hit," CIA interjected.

"They're going after our oil rigs?" Southwick said.

"You expect they wouldn't? Out there, in the wide open with no defence? I'm surprised only one so far was taken out. *So far.*"

"Be that as it may, we have no way to shut the oil off, nor put the fire out," Morgan said. "It's an ecological disaster."

"That was category five wasn't it?" Southwick said.

"The hurricane? Yes, the worst since Katrina eleven years ago. It was the third destructive hurricane this year. Of course, then there were the nuke attacks against our refineries." Morgan turned to look at the CIA. "And since this is the first time I've been able to talk with someone from the CIA. How *did* our refineries get wiped out? I'm sure people here would like to know how that happened."

"That was Homeland Security's jurisdiction," CIA retorted, looking down at the table.

"Well, CIA, they're not here are they?" Morgan argued. "But you are.

And you're supposed to be the *intelligence* agency. And you don't know?" She greatly and sarcastically emphasized the word 'intelligence'.

"We know."

Morgan folded her hands together and leaned towards CIA with a stern look.

"Then enlighten us. Please. I really want to know how nukes landed on American soil."

CIA looked at Southwick, who put both hands up and said, "Go ahead."

CIA took his glasses off, cleaned them with one of the napkins on the table, and put them back on, adjusting their arms to fit into the grooves in his temples. He then sighed. "We thought it was missiles. But that wasn't possible. We would have detected them, but they were low yield. So we suspected they arrived at each site by truck. We got a break. In the early spring, a large group of Americans crossed the border at Detroit into Canada looking for food. Fights broke out between the American and Canadian civilians. A truck got caught up in the combat just outside Sarnia in Ontario. Once officials got control of the situation the vehicle was found by police. It had one of the nukes."

"And how did these weapons get onto American soil?" Morgan demanded. "How was it that you people didn't find out before they sent us back into the Stone Age?"

CIA turned to look at Morgan. "Well, Admiral, as you know, with the collapse of the economy virtually no one was guarding our border. They could have just driven right in without anyone finding out." He threw his hand in the air. Erecting a finger one at a time he continued. "They could have come through ports, driven across from Mexico, or all of those."

"That didn't answer my question. I said, how come you people at the CIA didn't know what was going on? It was your job to know."

"Admiral," CIA said, the cracking in his voice increased, "we suffered the same collapse your people did..."

"So which refineries are still operating?" Southwick interrupted before another blame game erupted.

"Contrary to rumours, not all our refineries got nuked." CIA said, his voice returning to normal. "We simply have too many. They did solve one of our major problems. A nuke was set off in New Jersey taking out the refinery there, but it also took out the uprising of Muslims. Most of the nukes hit east Texas and south Louisiana, the bulk of our production. Refineries in California and the refinery in Washington State are now in Chinese hands. That's where they're getting their fuel from, but the output is low, not enough to supply their needs. This is why we don't see their aircraft. They don't have the fuel to run them."

"We do, though." Southwick said.

"Well, not really," Morgan replied. "It's not enough to give us prolonged air superiority. We're down to less than fifteen percent capacity. It should improve next year. A new refinery is being built in North Dakota to process the Bakken. But as you may be aware, that is a very low yield field. I have the output here somewhere. Give me a second." She shuffled papers. "Yes, here it is, current output is two hundred thousand barrels per day, a third of their height five years ago. And that low rate won't change. That's about it. Details are in this report." Morgan passed the bounded papers to Southwick.

"We thank you." Looking back to the Minister of Energy, Southwick said, "Minister, what is the status of natural gas production."

"No improvement is expected," Ferguson said. "Shale gas production continues to decline, rapidly. Conventional gas production also continues its accelerated decline."

"What's the problem?"

"The Energy Trap."

"The what?" Southwick said squinting his eyes.

"The Energy Trap." Sounding authoritative, Ferguson said, "When the overall energy available is in decline, there is less available energy to get the energy we need, especially when people are demanding more energy. The decline in oil, and the high demand for it, there is not enough fuel for natural gas drilling rigs. See, the problem is, as one analyst told me, shale gas operations suffer from the Red Queen Principle..."

"Excuse me, the what?" Southwick interrupted sounding confused.

"It's called the Red Queen Principle. It comes from *Alice in Wonderland*, or so I was told. It has something to do with running as fast as you can just to stay in place."

"I don't get it, what does that mean. In English please."

"Well, um, General, it's detailed."

"In a nutshell, Minister. Explain like you would to a child. Just like it was explained to you, I'm sure."

"Oh, um, well, yes." Ferguson appeared uncomfortable at the quip. He cleared his throat. "They have to add drilling rigs at an accelerated rate just to keep natural gas flows constant. That's because flow rates drop quickly after a well is sunk. But few, if any, new wells are getting drilled. So the rate of flow from existing wells is dropping. Precipitously I'm afraid. It basically comes down to there aren't enough rigs drilling for gas. And we have to divert lots of natural gas for the oil sands production. Plus fuel needed to move the fracking sand by rail. It's the energy trap again."

"So what you are saying is another winter of no heat," Southwick sighed.

"I'm afraid so, General. Several key factors of our complex system are failing all at the same time. A perfect storm, if you will."

"The Red Queen, the Energy Trap, perfect storm, working against us, hmm." Southwick frowned in agreement. "Not the only trap we find ourselves in. That brings us to Admiral Kraft, you have some updates on our military capacity?"

"Yes, sir. The high yield nuclear strike in Hawaii, we think from a submarine, took out our entire fleet there. Norfolk Naval Base was also hit in the same way as our refineries. At least that's what we suspect. We lost every ship there."

"How was it that so many of your ships were in port?" Grayford asked.

"Budget cuts."

"Same as us," Grayford agreed.

"It gets worse, I'm afraid," Kraft continued. "Another strike against our naval oil field wiped out our fuel supply for the navy. This has left what ships we have left stuck in ports with no country that will take U.S. dollars. And we have no way of getting gold physically shipped to pay for the oil.

"That was the bad news. But the good news is we have three nuclear subs still operational. Some of our subs have taken out ships bound for our coast, including all three Chinese aircraft carriers. Two we took out heading here, the other we took out while it was in port. That sub was sunk right after. In fact, we have lost about half our subs at sea to anti sub measures. Half of what's left remains in ports because we don't have enough crews to man them.

"I have a report here." Kraft passed it to Southwick. "We're having a problem getting food for those subs too. They can't go on missions for months on end without food. So we have only three subs at sea at the moment.

"Now that said, taking out their ships has had a noticeable reduction in Chinese abilities. This may be why we're seeing success in the mountains. We're seeing the same thing in the U.S.; their efforts have been stalled in the Sierras. I'm beginning to see the tide turning in our favour."

"I'll believe that when I see it," CIA muttered.

"And winter up here should be a big help," Southwick said ignoring the comment.

"Provided we can keep them in the mountains," Hughes said. "To do that we need more supplies. Specifically ammo."

"Yes, and that is why we have Mister Torres representing ammunition manufacturers here to tell us what they're up to. But first I have some questions for the admiral." Southwick said.

"Go ahead, General, unlike our CIA friend here I have nothing to hide," Kraft answered.

"What's the status of our aircraft carriers?"

"We have three operational. Well, sort of. The *Roosevelt*, the *Truman*, and the *Stennis*. We can put them to sea, but with no support ships they would be vulnerable. Besides they don't have any aviation fuel for their air wing. So we've hidden them."

"Hidden them? Hard to imagine you can hide an aircraft carrier in the U.S.," Southwick said.

"They're not in the U.S., General. They're in Antarctica. Those three subs are guarding them at the moment. We did have one in Australia, but when they surrendered to the Chinese, we moved it. The Chinese did capture one in port in San Diego, the *Carl Vinson*. That's the one that mutinied. Returned to port when the crew demanded. The Chinese have not been able to get it to sea. I hope the crew is responsible for that."

"What of the *George Washington* carrier strike group?" Southwick said.

"Sunk while engaging the Chinese fleet in the South China Sea."

"All of them?"

"All of them," Kraft said in a low voice, his head down.

"Sounds to me that our naval capability is nonexistent to impotent." Southwick bemoaned.

The Admiral didn't say anything; he just raised his right hand while shaking his head.

"Right... now, my next question, Admiral. Why didn't we get our missiles off and blast China into the ground?" Southwick demanded to know.

"Besides the manpower problem?"

"Yes, I've been told by the Joint Chiefs that we had a coordinated, widespread cyber attack. Have you made any progress in fixing that problem?"

"Right, that problem. Well, General, its not just software that was compromised, but also electronics; the hardware components. We did evaluations and testing and we discovered many of the components were made in China, of course like everything else. And assembled in plants in Canada, I will add. We suspect those components contained back door triggers or smart electronic bombs, for lack of a better term. The fact they failed all at the same time is no co-incidence. As for fixing them, not without making all new components. With Silicon Valley now in Chinese hands, that's not going to happen any time soon.

"On top of that, we know the Chinese hacked into a number of strategic satellites. Hell, they've doing cyber espionage on us for decades, likely to build up to this day. Now, those they couldn't take control over were destroyed by baseball-sized charges fired from their anti satellites. We have virtually no satellite communications, no GPS. No weather satellites. Hell, without satellites we can't even fly any drones."

"So we're impotent, everywhere," Southwick sighed.

"Being so dependent on electronics, I'm afraid so, General." Kraft shuffled uncomfortably in his chair.

"Clusterfuck. Do we have anything that works for us?" Southwick pleaded.

The room was quiet.

"Ok, Mister Torres, do *you* have any good news for us?" Southwick said.

"Thank you, General," Torres started. "I can tell y'all that we're making progress. Y'all know, it was difficult at first. But now we're mining homes for the copper to make bullets and casings. Chemical production for propellants is improving. For example, over the summer we built a new small arms factory in Edmonton because of the proximity to the oil. It should be on line mid month.

"Certainly over the last month your men in the field have been using less ammo. That's great, it allowed us to catch up. So I see no problem keeping up with demand in the future."

"Home Land Security liberated their two billion round stockpile," CIA added. "Some of that has been diverted here, that's what saved our asses. But there won't be any more from them."

"I thought they had five billion?" Southwick asked sounding confused.

"They did. The other three billion was fired off over the past few years dealing with small civil conflicts, quelling riots and gangs in cities. Plus, a lot of it was stolen by cops to defend their own families."

Southwick sighed and shook his head.

"Well, that ammo was just enough to give us a foot hold," Torres said. "Y'all know, we should be able to produce a billion rounds a year by next spring."

"One billion a year you say," Southwick said.

"Yes, General..."

Southwick put his right index finger in the air while he wrote with his left hand. "How many shooters do we have along the whole coast?"

"Four hundred thousand," Admiral Kraft said.

"That's soldiers or shooters?" Southwick said.

"That's shooters, sir."

Southwick wrote some more. "Hmm." He stopped writing. "Four hundred thousand into one billion is three thousand rounds per person per year. That sounds way too low. One of you is wrong somewhere."

The Admiral and Torres looked over their notes.

"Look, this isn't rocket science, people," Southwick explained. "In

Afghanistan we fired off five million rounds *a month*. That was a far smaller conflict that we have at hand right now. So, assume a single soldier can fire off thousands of rounds in a month. We need a hundred billion bullets made a month, not a billion. Sorry, not a month, a hundred billion a year, right?"

"Oh, yes, my mistake," Torres said sounding confused. He dropped some of his papers on the floor. Picking them up he said, "This number, I mean, must be in thousands. So yes, a hundred billion rounds a month, I mean, a year."

"Bullshit," CIA retorted.

"I beg your pardon," Torres said.

"Elaborate," Southwick demanded.

CIA flipped to a sheet in his notepad. "Ammo production right now in the U.S. and Canada hit one point four billion so far this year," CIA lectured. "All of it fired off. Almost half that came from the Lake City Army Ammunition Plant. And that's them full flat out. I find it very hard to believe you can up that by ten times."

"So how much ammo do we need?" Southwick asked.

CIA scribbled on his notepad. "Well, sir, if we say three hundred rounds a day per person, assume half the people in the field shoot that, that's sixty million a day. Assume we get into shooting matches ten days per month, is six hundred million rounds per month." He scribbled more. "That's seven point two billion per year. Give or take. A hundred billion per year? Never. But a billion a month is nowhere near enough. We still have civil unrest, which the cops and the National Guard still need to defend themselves against. Assuming they consume a third of the ammo produced, the rest going to the western theatre, we'll need more than a billion a month. I'd be safe if we assume fifteen billion per year. More than ten times current production. Impossible in my opinion."

"Mother of God." Southwick moaned.

"That's not the only problem," CIA continued with his right index figure in the air. "You get that many soldiers firing off that much ammo that fast, and you'll burn out every barrel on the line in a couple months. This is all theoretical, of course."

"You think this fight will go on for a year?" Southwick sighed.

"Who knows? No one does," CIA said. "Not much shooting is likely to happen over the winter. So any production now until the spring can be stockpiled. But yes, over all we should have at least fifteen billion rounds for next year. Impossible in my opinion, General."

"This is why we've run out a number of times?" Kraft questioned.

"Makes sense if we only produced a billion this year." CIA agreed. "We need ten times current production. Not going to happen."

"So you're saying we have lost this war?" Southwick said pointing his pen at CIA.

"No. I'm not saying that. I'm saying we don't have enough production for a prolonged shooting war, and we likely never will."

"Your numbers are speculative, right?" Admiral Kraft argued.

"To some degree, yes. However, as an example, we fired off some two hundred and fifty thousand rounds for every Iraqi insurgent we killed. Mini-guns are great, until you run out of ammo because of them. Now, if we use that number as a guide, how many Chinese are there? Some estimates are a million of them so far? Assume a quarter of them are on the front lines. Do the math."

Southwick was silent for a few moments. Then let out his breath slow and long with a small nod and his eyes closed. "So we do the best we can. Mister Torres, you're representing all ammo manufacturers, can you produce a billion rounds per month?"

"Y'all know, as others here have said," Torres answered. "If we have the people and resources, I'd say yes."

CIA snickered.

"But I have to ask," Torres continued. "How is the government going to pay for all this ammo?"

"We're under attack and you have to ask about your profit?" Southwick retorted.

"Y'all know, our employees have to eat, General."

"And they're getting food rationing, like everyone else, are they not?"

Torres didn't look too happy.

"The U.S. economy is in the toilet, the government is completely broke. We have nearly fifty percent unemployment. Those young enough have joined the fight just so they and their families can be fed. Everyone has lost their fortunes. Get over it. And get that production up," Southwick ordered.

"Yes, General." Torres said sheepishly.

Almost imperceptibly, CIA growled, "We wouldn't be in this mess if the government didn't print worthless funny money."

"The Minister is right, for someone not here, you certainly have a lot to say," Southwick bellowed. "Yes, we fucked up. Yes, we borrowed too much. Yes, billions of dollars of wealth was being sucked out of the U.S. every day. Yes, we were more occupied killing zombies and space invaders on TV, than real threats because it was not politically correct to deal with those threats. Yes, we're here now because of all that and more. But maybe you at the Central *Intelligence* Agency can give us a solution?" Southwick stared intently at CIA.

CIA was silent, looking down at his pen rolling in his fingers.

"That's what I thought. Mister Secretary, do you have anything to contribute, you've been quiet the whole time," Southwick said to the Secretary of Defence.

"I have nothing to add. I'm just going to take all this back to the Joint Chiefs."

Southwick looked at Loklear, her head was down almost on the table, her hands clasped around the back of her head. "Minister, is there a problem?"

She didn't move. Minister of Defence, Jeff Harris, sitting beside her said, "Leanne, are you all right?"

She lifted her head slowly. "I can't take this. All this talk of billions of bullets, killing hundreds of thousands of people. Nukes vaporizing millions, destroy the environment. We should just surrender." She was almost in tears.

"We are not going to surrender," CIA bellowed pounding his fist into the table making the glasses of water around him shake.

Loklear shot up to her feet. She was beet red. "You are hateful barbarians, all of you..." She threw her papers across the room, spilling her glass of water over the table. "You're playing God. Pawns on a chessboard. You should all die!"

Her aide tried to control her, but she threw the woman's hands away,

"Don't touch me," she screamed, her head up high looking down.

"Keep your grubby paws off me. Don't come near me. Any of you! We wanted to get off oil years ago. I wanted us to go green. But noooo, we were stopped at every step."

She looked around the room, pointing at each person in turn. "You stopped us, and now look where we are. Millions will die now. You're all to blame." She started to stumble over her words. "Tens of thousands of people's blood is on your hands! Not mine. I won't have any part. None!"

"Sit down," Grayford ordered. "You're not making any sense."

Guilt filled her posture. She dropped her head. "The exponential growth culture we developed is the problem, plain and simple. Population growth, economic growth *cannot* be sustained on a planet with finite resources. We consume everything. And when it's all gone, we consume each other." Her voice cracked. Her lower lip trembled. "Humans are a scourge. Earth would be better if we all just died."

"Leanne, please sit and calm down," Harris consoled with his hand out to her.

"Calm down? Calm down?" Her face turned deep red again. "How about you calm down! Calm down, stupid thing to say. All of you are stupid. Stupid immoral pathetic excuses for humans! Barbarians! All of you!"

"Please, Minister," her aide said. "Please, let's go to the lady's room."

"Leave me alone. Stay away," her voice shrieked. "You don't order me. No one orders me!"

"Take her out of the room, now," Southwick demanded to Harris.

"Come on, Leanne," Harris said as he gently grabbed her left arm.

Tears dripped down her face, her makeup racooned. "What? Where?"

"Let's go outside for some air. Come on, please."

"I have to leave. Yes, I need to get out of here," she cried.

Loklear left the room, talking incoherently, with Harris and her aide helping her.

"We obviously need to take a break. Fifteen minutes," Southwick ordered, got up and left the room.

The rest of the civilians went for a bathroom break. Hughes walked over to the table at the window and poured himself a glass of water. Maillet joined him. "Wow, total meltdown, eh. I 'ope she's all right."

"Anyone would snap under this pressure. I wish this was a Canadian Club," Hughes sighed.

"I could use a belt myself," Maillet agreed.

They didn't say anything for a few moments.

"Looks like the Yanks have taken total control of this, eh?" Hughes said.

"You're surprised by t'at?"

"No, I guess I shouldn't be. I'm sure the CDS isn't happy with it. He didn't say a word."

"I 'ad a meeting with 'im yesterday, t'ey're actually relieved. Grayford said he was 'appy the U.S. is taking the responsibility off his 'ands. T'new government is still trying to get control of t'city."

"Yeah, what happened there? One day the Liberals and NDP ruled with a Liberal PM, the next day we had a Liberal-Conservative government with a Conservative PM. How did that come about?"

"Sneaky if you ask me. T'Conservatives got t'Speaker of t'ouse to rule on occupied riding. Since those MPs in BC were NDP, t'ey couldn't represent t'eir constituents any more. So t'Speaker ruled t'ey couldn't be in power any more as t'eir seat count was too low. From what I 'eard it was quite t'uproar. T'en t'Liberal PM quit in protest. More likely from t'pressure of t'war."

Hughes shook his head. "So the NDP is officially out of government. Good, about time. Well, the Conservatives should be better, should be," Hughes moaned taking another sip of his water.

They stood silent for a few moments.

"Your family still on base?" Maillet said.

"For the time being. They're packing up to head east. I don't want them anywhere near this mess."

"Good, good. T'at's good."

They stood silent looking out at the mountains.

"Hey, isn't this supposed to be an election year in the U.S.?" Hughes said.

"Next mont'. But Sout'wick said Congress is meeting to extend the President's mandate, considering most Americans won't be able to vote anyway. Wit' t'chaos and all, t'ere is no way any candidate could campaign."

"Clusterfuck indeed."

Maillet poured himself a glass, and drank it all at once. They both looked out the window towards the mountains. Their white peaks contrasted with the clear sky. Not one cloud disrupted the bright blue.

"I had a couple young boys stationed at the base come to me asking if they could help," Hughes said breaking the silence. "They weren't more than fourteen. They said they had been playing Call of Duty, and wanted to fight the Chinese. They thought they were trained," Hughes chuckled. "I had to remind them that in a real war, once you're killed you don't respawn somewhere else. I told them to go home. What a fantasy world we have created."

"Sad part is, t'ey may end up fighting, and dying."

They stood not speaking for a few moments.

"Do you t'ink we can 'old them off until t'spring?" Maillet said.

"I don't know. The big question is, if we do keep them in a stalemate, what will their next move be."

The sky filled with a blinding white flash.

CHAPTER 17

Betrayal

Erik Stein walked into his Mineral Ore Deposits course classroom to give the last lecture of the semester before the Christmas break. The class wasn't even half full, but typical over the past four years since the economic collapse. He was just getting into the lecture when UBC's new President, Senior Colonel Zhuge Wěi Míng, came in and sat beside a student. The student seemed to know the colonel. Erik gave him a glance, while the Colonel stared at Erik throughout the whole lecture.

With only a few minutes remaining Erik asked the class, "So who can tell me the geological setting of betafite and where it's been found?" A few hands went up, but Erik ignored them.

"General, why don't you give it a try," Erik said with his eyes looking over his glasses, one eyebrow raised.

The Colonel was quiet, just stared.

"Come now, General, it hasn't been that long since you took geology, has it?"

A vindictive look came over the colonel's face. Then the student beside the Colonel piped up and said, "In Bancroft, Ontario. The uranium ore is formed in Carbonatite deposited from migrating fluids at depths of twenty-five kilometers."

Erik's gaze moved over to the student. "You are correct, and what's that process called?"

The student couldn't answer. "Metasomatism," Erik said. "OK, people, that's it for us. Just a reminder, your papers are due next week on my desk. Check for the exam date, and I'll see you all there. Have a good Christmas."

The class got up and left, some came to the front and dropped off their papers. Three students handed memory sticks to Erik, their papers in electronic format. Erik opened his laptop and copied the files off each stick. One student, the last of the three, said, "Make sure you get *all* the files in the folder called Cassiterite."

"I see them. Transferred," Erik said not looking at the student until he handed the memory stick back. As the student grabbed the stick, Erik held on to it tight preventing the young man from taking it. "You've done a good job, Luke," Erik said releasing the stick. The student smiled then left the room.

The Colonel exchanged a few quiet words with the student beside him. He left leaving the Colonel and Erik alone in the room.

Erik gathered his books, and stuffed the papers from the students into his brief case, closing it. He sat at the edge of the desk, took his glasses off, and asked, "What do you want, General?"

"How did you know I studied geology, Herr Stein?" the Colonel said.

"I looked you up. You took your undergrad right here at UBC, you specialized in geology."

"That was a long time ago. I didn't know about that question. What was that mineral, professor?"

"Betafite. A uranium ore."

"Betafite, yes."

"Of course, you wouldn't know about it. The mystery of its origin was solved by an amateur geologist in 1988. Long after you graduated from here. So you couldn't know, I was playing with you, General."

"Of course, you were. But interesting you checked up on me, Herr Stein."

"I'm sure you of me."

"Indeed, of course I did."

"So what do you want, General? You've managed to stay out of my way for months. Why the visit now, did you solve that murder?"

"Your city's police are still looking after that. It's been a bit of time, Herr Stein, so I wanted to see if you are as good a professor as my grandson says you are."

"I figured that was your grandson. So if you have nothing more, you'll have to excuse me, I have work to do." Erik started to get up. The Colonel stood as well blocking Erik's exit.

"I want to give you the heads up, Herr Stein. There are some changes going to happen over the winter."

"Like what, you going to finally feed our people? Surrender? Or just leave?"

"Yes, that reminds me. Here is your food credit voucher." The Colonel walked over and handed him a yellow card. "I made sure you got a Class B food allotment. And this is your new travel card for next year. It will allow you to come and go to the university during daytime only. And your new identity card."

"How nice of you to give me special treatment," Erik said sarcastically. "Why would you personally deliver them and not one of your minions?"

"I want to make sure my professors, my good professors, are happy."

"Yeah, right. You're just checking up on me."

"No, it's not as clandestine as that. You will be teaching a new batch of students over the winter. Plus you can't do your Arctic research any more. So you will be rewarded with an increase in your food ration."

This stunned Erik. In the past seven months of the occupation, food for the oppressed was lowered even more than it was during Black Winter. It was barely survivable calories. Rumors were circulating that BC's Chinese inhabitants were getting more as the occupiers tried to repatriate Canadian Chinese. Rumors were also circulating that more food was provided to those who played the occupier's game. To Erik, and many others by this time, those people were collaborators.

Erik was, at first, insulted by the offer, but then he thought about it. He could share his extra food with some of his friends that he knew were suffering. It would be illegal, of course, as others who shared were cut off from their extra portion.

"I think you're bribing me to co-operate, General."

"No, please, professor, this is our appreciation of the important work you do in teaching our future leaders."

"Right," Erik said sarcastically. "So the battle isn't going as planned is it, General. I've seen more soldiers coming off ships. I'd hazard to bet you were expecting to get to the oil sands by now. But you haven't have you, General. I've heard rumors that we have stopped you in the mountains."

The Colonel was silent for a few moments.

"Yeah, that's what I thought. Our boys are giving you a bigger scrap than you figured. Looks good on you." Erik walked past the Colonel to leave the room.

"We are through the mountains, and into the plains of Alberta."

Erik stopped, as this was news to him. "That's not what I've heard. We have your men stone cold in the mountains."

"Then you heard wrong. We got through once the bombs were dropped on your command and control. Nuclear bombs."

Erik's eyes opened wide.

"That's right, professor. Yes, it is true your people had us stopped. We were almost beyond the mountains. That all changed when two nuclear bombs were dropped on Calgary, and another on Cold Lake, where your Air Force base was located. Once your command and control was eliminated, your people didn't have the will, or the resources, to fight. They either left or surrendered."

"You're a liar. You're not so cold as to exterminate millions of people."

"Believe me, professor, this wasn't my call. I had no part in this genocide."

Erik turned to leave.

"Professor, please." Erik stopped at the door and turned to listen. "We are not treating your people with disrespect." The Colonel paused. "I am not treating your people with disrespect. We are a communist nation; we are going to bring communist values to the people of British Columbia, hopefully to the rest of North America. You will be far better off."

"General, if I had a sense of humor, I would think you're trying to be funny." Erik closed the door staying in the room. "China isn't a communist country, you haven't been for decades. China is a fascist country. Now that you've vaporized millions of people, you're on par with former dictators of history." Erik poked his finger into the Colonel's chest.

"Fascist? No, we are not fascist, how can you possibly say that, Herr Stein?"

"Well, General, if we had the internet up and running I would take you to Wiki, but since we don't I highly suggest you get an old fashioned dictionary out and look up the definition of fascism."

"Since I don't have one handy, Herr Stein, how about you tell me what you think we are."

"And I thought you were smart, General, you don't even know what fascism means. Yes you do, you're just testing me, as usual. But I'll play your game. China used to be a communist country, until you allowed for private ownership and private enterprise, but not the democracy that should go with it. A lot of privileged people at the top got very rich off of Walmart, right, General? Soon as that happened you were no longer a communist country, but a fascist country. To top it off, you have adopted one of fascism's main ingredients: violence, with mass extermination and world domination desires. You make me sick!" Erik left the room.

Back at Erik's lab, he had only just got the papers out of his brief case when the colonel walked in. "What the fuck do you want, General? Why are you hounding me?"

The Colonel sat in the same chair as before. "I want to ask you some questions."

Erik looked past the Colonel, including getting up and looking out into the hallway.

"What are you looking for, Herr Stein?"

"Your sidekick, you know, the one you always bring armed with an Ak47?"

"No, this is just the two of us. A friendly visit between science comrades."

"Look, General, I have papers to mark, what do you want?"

"I want you to tell me if you are part of any underground. We have been getting reports of sabotage, and some people going missing, some of our friends..."

"You mean collaborators."

"Herr Stein, please. We are all friends here."

"Fuck you, General. You are no friend of mine. And no, I'm not part of any 'underground'." Erik made air quotes with his fingers. "And if I were, you would never know, and I know that you would know that I was part of such underground, so I could be and tell you I'm not and you would think I'm not, because why would I if you are watching me so much? But since you are watching me, then I can be part of an underground, even though you know I am and pretending I'm not."

The Colonel looked stunned.

"Yeah, that's what I thought. Now, please, General, I need to get to work."

The Colonel got up and started to go out, but turned and looked back at Erik as if he was going to say something, but just left the lab.

A few hours later, Carl came into Erik's office.

"I heard the Colonel came to visit you."

Erik nodded.

"Bloody hell. He thinks you're running some resistance movement. He's interrogated me at least a dozen times, not just about you, but others in the department they're watching. You aren't part of any resistance are you?"

One of the biggest concerns of Erik's family during the rise of Nazism was well meaning friends who had made deals with the occupiers. Fear being the motivator. Erik was now living in an era of continuous fear.

That fear brought out the worst in people, ordinary people. Betrayal was rampant, and no one could trust anyone in Germany. Say one wrong thing to someone you thought you could trust, and you wound up in front of a firing squad.

"No, I'm not involved," Erik said standing up. This was, of course, more to protect his friend, the less Carl knew the safer he would be.

"I guess I have no choice but to believe you. You did hear about Suzan?"

"No, but I haven't seen her for a few days, what's happened?" Erik sat at the end of his desk.

"She had been visited by some people, interrogators actually. They're... they were trying to get her to repatriate to communism, or Chinese or something. She refused. I was forced to be in one of the meetings. She told them to fuck off several times. One of them, a woman in a military uniform, slapped Suzan across the face. That's when they threw me out of the room. That's the last I saw her. That was three days ago."

Erik turned back to sitting at his desk, dropping his head into his hands.

"I'm sure she is alright, just taking a few days off," Carl sighed.

Erik looked back at Carl knowing he was lying.

"Anyway, look at this." Carl, wanting to change the subject, brought out his meal ticket. "I finally got my orange card. So we, Wendy and I, would like to have you over for Christmas dinner."

Erik pulled his card out of his pocket and showed it to Carl.

"How the hell did you get a yellow card? That's one below white, the highest you can get. The last one you had was red, just one above black, which is starvation. How did you rate this?"

"The General just gave it to me. For doing such a good job."

"Good job? Good job? What the fuck? How the hell do you rate a card better than mine?"

"This has nothing to do with doing a good job, it's a bribe. This is his way of knowing what..." Erik stopped.

"Knowing what?"

"Never mind. Yes, I'll be there for dinner, and with this card, I'll be buying."

After Carl left, Erik opened a file he got from the student's sim-card. Erik was shocked, and a sense of outrage filled his body. Suzan's body was found on the beach near the airport. She had been shot in the back of the head.

Erik opened Word, wrote a short message, saved it on a memory-card, pulled it out, got up and left his lab.

Over the following week coming to Christmas Erik was visited by a few students over non-science matters, some he knew, some he didn't, asking him if he knew how to fight back against their occupiers. Some told him of horrible stories of Chinese brutality, but worse, the lack of food. Erik made no attempt to take the bait, as he figured the colonel was fishing with these students. Until he got a visit in his lab one day from former student Karen Levenson. They hugged, and greeted each other, then got down to business.

"Karen, you were working on kimberlites up in Nunavut, what brings you here?"

"I had to come home. Demand for diamonds had been dropping since the economic crash anyway. But, I tell yeah, this last winter was brutal on the equipment. It was the coldest ever recorded up there. They even had to ship the aboriginals out, many were found frozen to death. I've been back since February. I stayed to take care of my parents. Which is why I'm here to see you." Tears welled up in Karen's eyes. "My parents are starving." She broke down crying. Erik hugged her.

After a few moments Erik asked, "What color is their food card?"

"Black. All old people get black."

"What's yours?"

"I was just upgraded to red, because I got a job teaching at a school." Karen showed it to Erik.

"You haven't signed it yet."

Karen shook her head.

"Well, neither have I." Erik pulled out his yellow card, grabbed Karen's red card, and put the yellow one in her hand.

She looked up into his eyes. "You don't need to do this, I'll figure something out."

Erik held the hand tight around the card.

Karen smiled. "I can't thank you enough. How can we fuck these people up?"

Erik knew what she was asking. Was she a plant? Not likely. Erik met her parents, salt of the earth people. Karen got her PhD under Erik. They even co-authored a paper during that time. He knew her politics. Her Jewish parents were descendents of Holocaust survivors. Erik took the chance.

"We've already started, months ago," he whispered. Erik indeed had already approached a few people he knew he could trust. They had been secretly meeting in the drill core storage building when they could. A communication system was set up in the building where certain rock cores were positioned and angled that would mean when the next meeting would be. The next one was the following day. Erik invited Karen to join.

They met in the core building just after 4:00 p.m. Erik took a tray of cores, as if returning them to the library. He knew he was being watched. Meetings were quick, no more than five minutes. Messages were transferred with memory sticks. The sticks would be left in strategic locations based on a code dependant on the day of the week.

Karen went with Erik to the building. Only one other person was there.

"Hi Chuck," Erik said.

"Good afternoon, Professor. I put the cores where you wanted."

"Excellent, thanks."

Erik got the rolling stepladder and placed it along a tall wall of shelved rock cores. He climbed half way up, and placed his samples in a shelf. He moved a length of core on another tray out of the way and picked up a memory stick, placing it in his pocket. Then descended.

"Let's go, we can read this at my place."

Karen didn't have a bike, so Erik walked beside her with his in tow. Soldiers and local police guarded all the entrances to the university village. One of the officers stopped them, as if he had been waiting for Erik, and demanded to search.

"Open your pockets," the officer ordered, "and place everything in this tray."

Erik placed some loose change, his keys, and the memory stick into the tray held by the cop. The officer picked it up. A soldier came over, picked up the stick and said, "What's this?"

"Mostly my mineral data I have to analyze, and some of my student's papers which they submit electronically. So unless you want those students to fail, please don't destroy it."

The officer nodded at the soldier as he put it back.

Erik picked up his property and passed through the gate saying, "Have a good evening, gentlemen."

Back at Erik's home, after they had a bit of cheese, some pork and a tin of pears, it was a merger dinner, Erik fired up his laptop. He inserted the memory stick and read the message.

"So how does this work, Erik?" Karen asked.

"I issue instructions, place them on the stick, which is hidden in the library as you saw. Someone else looks at the core in one of the rows, if it's a specific rock type, the person knows there's a message. They get the stick, then copy the message onto other sticks, which are then disseminated around the city."

"How do you know it's not getting intercepted?"

"In a way we don't. We're a very small group at the campus who know each other. Citywide we don't know who's who. We have to keep it as small as possible. Once the messages get to small groups outside campus, then those groups have to figure out on their own what to do. At the moment all we're doing this early is gathering data; how many troops are arriving, who is collaborating. Shift schedules. Stuff like that. I have another laptop at the library I keep this all on. It's well hidden. It used to be the library's database computer, but no need for that since new cores aren't coming in and few people are borrowing samples. Once I get this message, I'll transfer the file to that machine tomorrow. Let's see what it says.

"Not much. Looks like four more ships unloaded equipment, heavy machinery. Another unloaded oil and diesel fuel. Hmmm, heavy equipment. They already cleared the bridges, I wonder what this is all for? Oh, look at this. Bridge sections were unloaded off another ship last night. That's it. Damn, nothing about the nukes. Nothing about how far the Chinese have advanced. I wondered if the general was lying about the nukes."

"Nukes, what nukes?"

"The General said they dropped nukes on Calgary in October. If it happened I would have thought we would be seeing it in these messages by now. But our coverage is scant."

"Can you get this information out?"

"Someone tried with short wave. They found him within an hour and shut him down. No one has seen him since. So we have no way of getting any of this east. Not yet anyway."

"Can you do anything?"

"If we had explosives, maybe. Right now nothing. Well, not really nothing. The most important aspect we have to follow is collaborators. The Chinese can't do much without them. Most of the problem with these collaborators is they are being used to flush us out. We have had to dispose of some of them."

"Kill them?" Karen said surprised.

"Yes. Otherwise we'll be killed if we're found out. We're seriously looking at dispatching the Chief of Police."

"What? How?"

"We haven't figured that out yet. Look this is all too depressing; let's change the subject. Tell me about your time searching for diamonds."

They talked until it was past curfew, so Erik made up the sofa bed for Karen.

They were woken by a rapid knock at the door. Erik answered it, Karen behind him.

"Professor Stein?"

"Yes."

"Schist."

"Now?"

"Right now, professor."

"Alright, let me get dressed. I have to go. Something's happened," Erik said to Karen.

"Can you trust him?"

"He gave the code word, schist. Means I need to go right now."

"I'll come."

"No, it's too dangerous."

"I want to come."

Erik reluctantly agreed.

The man took them stealthily to the beach area south of the airport. They had to move quickly from shadow to shadow. The night was cold, their breath vaporizing into a mist. Snow had started to fall, though the ground already had patches of the white water from the day's precipitation.

A number of people were gathered down by the shore. A man was on his knees, hands tied behind his back. Someone came up to Erik as soon as he arrived.

"We have the Chief of Police. We know he was personally responsible for a number of executions. We have a photo of him doing one last night. We think he killed one of your colleagues. We lured him with a false tip, and brought him here. I wanted to kill him, but some said not to, it would just bring the Chinese down harder on us. I had no choice but to get you here to make a decision."

"Outstanding, good job." Erik looked around.

Four people showed up behind Erik. They illuminated flashlights on everyone.

"Hands up! All of you!" a familiar voice said.

Karen left Erik's side and walked over to the Colonel. "What took you so long? Did you hear everything?" she said.

Erik was beside himself. One soldier beside the Colonel aimed his bayoneted rifle at Erik.

"Well, Herr Stein, so I was right after all. You are the leader of the underground."

Erik didn't say anything, just darts towards Karen. Then he said, "What the fuck is the matter with you people. It's like a bad cliché in the movies. Someone always has to betray their friends to the enemy."

"I have to save my parents. The Colonel has agreed to move them to better quarters and better food if I..."

"If you what?" Erik said fuming.

Karen didn't say anything.

"Well, Herr Stein, my patience has been rewarded. Didn't you wonder why I didn't have you executed? All this time I've put up with your arrogance. I could have had you killed at any time. But I figured you, or someone like you, would be involved in the underground. From the first day I met you, I figured you would be a bad apple. So who is smarter than whom now, Herr Stein?"

The Colonel had moved closer and closer to Erik as he spoke, until he was nose to nose on the last sentence. He pushed Erik with both hands forcefully, sending Erik into the arms of one of the underground men.

Erik regained his balance. "Strike three, you're out," Erik said calmly.

The three armed guards dropped to the ground, one moaning. All had arrows through their backs. Four men emerged from the darkness behind the colonel, one pointing a crossbow at him.

Karen moved back to Erik. "Wow, I can't believe this worked!"

The Colonel's eyes were wide open as she stood beside Erik.

"Oh, come on, General," Karen laughed. "Did you honestly think I would betray a long time friend? You know nothing of loyalty. I played you like the proverbial fiddle, and you fell for every word. We knew you bugged Erik's house."

"And my lab," Erik added.

"You will die for this, including your parents," the colonel snarled gritting his teeth.

"I think not," Erik said. He turned to the man who caught him.

"Everything ready, I presume?"

"As planned professor. We got your guns. Which reminds me." The man pulled a pistol out of his pack. It was in a Ziploc bag. "Here's your handgun. Right where you said it was."

"Thanks," Erik said putting it in his pants' waistband.

Erik walked up to the Colonel, nose to nose. "Too bad you never read the book *Every Man Dies Alone*. You would have gotten enlightened. You people are so predictable. I could write a computer model of your behavior. I planned this for months, even got Karen to agree with your betrayal of me. So who is smarter now, eh?" Erik poked the Colonel in the chest with his finger.

Erik turned to the crossbow man. "Do it quick."

"After we get you out of here."

Erik went over to Karen. "If I could give you an Academy Award I would. Wonderful performance."

"Oh, my god, when you first contacted me, I never thought your plan would work."

"I had to do something about the police chief. I know he killed Suzan, and many others. God damn fucker!" Erik went over to the chief and kicked him in the stomach. He collapsed into the snowy ground coughing through his gag.

"We need to get you out of here, Erik. I guess I will never see you again." Karen hugged Erik hard.

"You be safe," he said to her, his voice cracking.

"I have my own way out. My parents will be fine now with your yellow card. Nice bonus."

"Come, professor, the boat's here," the underground man said grabbing his arm.

Erik got in a small inflatable dingy with two men in it. They rowed away from shore. Erik looked back as the man with the crossbow fired a bolt into the colonel's head, and another bowman fired an arrow into the police chief. The large flakes of snow eventually obscured his view.

They rowed across the Straight of Georgia into an inlet on Gabriola Island. A fishing boat was hidden in the inlet. Erik got on board, thanked the two rowers, who disappeared into the falling snow.

The boat was very old, with a wooden hull and deck. It had a front cabin and a covered area at the stern. A tall mast stood in the middle of the deck, with two large booms disappearing into the night on either side. The smell of fish was pungent.

"Welcome aboard, perfessor, I'm Bill, and we'll leave it t'ar, no last names, eh?" a short stalky man, with a long beard, said. Erik couldn't make out too much of the man in the dark, save his thigh high boots and yellow rubber overcoat. "Not to worry ol' man," Bill said, "yar not t' only refugee we've rescue, eh?"

Three other men were crew. They escorted Erik into the bowls of the boat.

"Sorry, ol' man, we're gonna 'ave to put yeas under t' boards. It's a tad wet 'n noisy in t'ar. But you'll be safe when we get barded by the navy. Herrs a bag of food. But don't piss down t'ar, t' goddamed commie will smell it, even above t' fish. T'ats how old Brad got caught, save his soul."

One of the men handed Erik a wet suit. "It gets cold in there, put this on."

Erik stripped, and put on the wet suit. The men took his clothes.

"What will you do with my clothes?"

"Burn 'em," Bill said.

One of the crew threw his handgun out a portal.

"Hey!" Erik objected.

"No guns, can't take the risk," the man said.

"There's a memory stick in the pocket. Very important I keep that," Erik said.

Bill rummaged through the pockets and found the stick. "I'll put it in a safe place."

Erik thanked them all, and crawled into the narrow cavity under the floor behind the engine. He was pinned between the two drive shafts with no ability to even turn over. He lay on his back. One of the men put a bag under his head. Then dropped a Ziploc bag of cookies on his chest.

"Just 'til we clear t' islands. Couple 'ours we'll let you out," Bill said as they screwed the floorboard over Erik's head.

It was the most uncomfortable experience of Erik's life. But it was his lifesaver. He had lots of time to think between revs of the diesel engine. The shafts spun on either side of him. He had to wiggle a bit to one side as a shaft was rotating against his hip. Water filled the cavity about half way up his body. Every now and then a small pump started and the cold water dropped to below his butt, then the sea slowly started to rise again.

He lost all time. He was cold. He wondered when he would get a break. Then the engine cut out completely. Here was a chance to get some relief, he hoped. But the time went by with nothing. Then he heard footsteps, lots of them. Through the floorboards he heard talking that made the shivering worse. They were being searched.

"You're late, you were supposed to be at sea by now," an authoritative voice said.

"Damn engine trouble. We spent t' night try'n to fix it," Bill said. "You people want us to catch all we can, so t' sooner we set out t'ar t' more we catch, eh."

The heavy boots, definitely not fisherman's, walked onto the board where Erik entered his crypt. It creaked and groaned under the weight. "Your boat is falling apart," the voice said. "I'll be checking your catch when you get back."

"t'at won't be for 'r month, we're goin' way up t' coast, were t' fish 're."

The boots left. After a few moments the engine fired up and Erik's relief from the noise ended.

Erik thought it would never end. The engines were so loud he couldn't even think, combined with the fumes, the cold water, he felt sick. He also had to piss in the worst way. He figured he would relieve himself when the water level was high, so the pump would take his urine with the rest of the water.

The engine slowed, then stopped. The sea was rough, the water around him sloshed about. Someone was drilling the floor. Then bright light blinded him.

"Help him up," someone said. Two men pulled hard to get him out of the cramped space. Erik was so cold he couldn't help.

"Get him to the galley."

They tried to get him up the stairs, but with the boat tossing like a cork, they dropped him twice. Once they were on the deck, the engine started up again.

It was dark with thick cloud, the wind was blowing hard, freezing rain pelted Erik's face. Finally they got him into the galley. They got his wet suit off, while naked Erik felt even colder. They put him into a small shower like a puppet, no larger than the coffin he had come from. They turned on the hot water. Steam filled the chamber. Wonderfully refreshing. Erik's fingers could move. He could feel his toes sting.

They helped him into a jump suit that was toasty warm. He started to feel human again. The table, room for only four, very tightly, was set for him. Coffee, and hot stew was waiting. Erik wolfed it down, and babied the coffee with his hands unable to lose grip of the hot mug.

"How long was I down there?"

"Ten 'ours," Bill said. "T'ank t' lord for short days in winter. You wouldn't have lasted 'nother 'our. We're far 'nough from shore now you shouldn't need t' go back down t'ere."

"You mean if another boat comes?"

"Sometimes t'ey do t'is fur oot."

"Can't I just be one of the crew?"

"Nope. See t'at paper on t' wall t'ere? It has t' names of all t' crew, and yours ain't t'ere, ol' man."

"Was that the Chinese who came about before?"

"Nay. He ain't no Chinaman, he's t' 'arbour inspector. Rat he is."

"Fucking cocksucker more like it," the man to Erik's left grunted.

"He'll get 'is cumupance one dar," Bill said. "Fer now we can forget 'im."

"Where are you taking me?" Erik said.

"Alaska pan'andle," Bill said. "Once on shore y'll spend t' winter wit' t' abors."

Erik looked confused.

"Aboriginals. Natives," the left man said.

Erik nodded. "When do we get there?"

"Two days," the left man said.

"T'ree dars," Bill corrected.

"Then what for you guys?"

"We catch 'r fish, and 'ead 'ome. Commies expect us to return wit' 'r catch. But t'ey can't force 'ow long we'll be goon. You need yer sleep, up front in t' fox'ole. Bed is already fer yeah."

They took the boat into an inlet, lee side to the wind, with fewer waves to upset the night.

They arrived at the coast in three days, mid morning. Three canoes came to meet them. Erik thanked the crew. Bill handed him the memory stick. "Best luck, ol' man," he said shaking Erik's hand.

Erik turned to see the name of the boat, *Archean Era*. The boat was as old as its namesake, Erik thought.

Once on shore the men gave him a pair of snowshoes. It had been decades since he had worn such, so one of the men had to put them on his feet properly.

It was a long hard march in the snow, until dark, when they got to the village along a small stream. Erik's legs were killing him, still sore from the cramped crypt, aggravated by miles of bowlegged walk in snowshoes.

He was greeted with high curiosity. A young man, missing most of his teeth, met him. He had long black hair covering part of a long thin face protruding from a fur hood. "I'm Bluebear. Russ Bluebear. Come with me. Don't mind the onlookers, it's not like you're the first one through here."

Russ took Erik to a small shack, for lack of a better word. It was blistered chipboard walls, stained with years of water. The roof had a blue tarp draped over it to stop the rain and snow from coming in. Snow had fallen off the roof to make a three foot high berm around the building. Smoke came out of a makeshift chimney. The grey wisps hung in the trees.

Inside was one room. It had a sofa with years of wear. A wood stove was in the corner near the door. A counter was at the far end with a sink, but no running water. A bed was opposite the sofa. Over the bed was a large flat screen TV. Shelves of DVD disks filled the wall around the TV.

"This is your house for the winter," Russ said

House? Erik thought. But decided not to comment on the hospitalities. "I don't understand."

"We can't move you in the winter, too much snow and too cold. You'll spend the winter here, with us. Our guest and tell us your stories."

"There's no washroom."

Russ moved his hands towards the woods.

"Ah, I see. And a shower or bath?"

"That building there," Russ said pointing to the right.

"And food?"

"That building there to the left. We eat together. It's dark, best you sleep. There's bread on the table, butter, some powdered milk and water in that jug. There's enough wood to last the night but you'll have to feed it every two hours or you'll freeze. It's expected to go down to minus thirty tonight, wind is picking up. Big snow tomorrow." Russ left the room, if you can call it that.

A kerosene lamp gave some light, but the musty smell was overpowering, worse than the fish stench on the boat. Patches of black mould adorned the corners. Some of it had been spray painted over to mask it. The drywall was heavily stained with water, chunks of it were missing in several places exposing the insulation, it too dotted with black mould.

There were electric lights on the ceiling, but when Erik tried the switch nothing happened. He figured no fuel for the generator. So much for TV then, he thought.

He was wishing he was at his fishing cabin, somewhere to the east of him in the mountains. It was far more comfortable, and safe to be in than this shack. But he had to make it home for four months.

CHAPTER **18**

The Final Battle

General Gary Hawker was sitting at his desk in the command trailer at the oil sands north of Fort McMurray. He was writing his daily report when he stopped and closed the laptop. What's the point, he thought as he looked up at the map. Red arrows circled the oil sands. They were surrounded by the Chinese. Estimated enemy troop size was between one hundred and two hundred thousand compared to their twenty-four thousand shooters. The Chinese had already attempted one assault, but were held back when an air strike carpet-bombed the front lines. Hawker was informed there would be no more of those, the war effort didn't have the fuel, a situation which got worse because of Black Winter II.

Then there was the unauthorized attack against the Chinese southern arm by a civilian promoted to captain. It was successful; opening up the road and railway line so more supplies could arrive. That in turn precipitated the nuclear bomb hitting south of Edmonton, or so the High Command said.

They were completely cut off after that attack. There would be no more supplies, no more people coming.

The shortage of supplies was apparent over the winter. He had become much thinner. His face was shadowed with several days of uncomfortable, itching, unshaven stubble. Somehow razors weren't considered essential requirements. He did manage to get someone to cut his hair recently, so at least he felt a little more human.

But it was the constant bouts of acid reflux burning his throat, which annoyed and concerned him. An infliction that hounded him since he took command of this defence nine months previous.

Something also new in his life was depression. The long winter brought with it too much time to think. He did a lot of that, especially on Christmas day, which he spent alone, and hungry.

He thought about his wife, and his children, often. He thought that he would never live to see his grandchildren once they were born. He thought that his wife would never know what would happen to him.

"Happen to me." That thought rarely left his mind.

He wondered how she was getting along without him. She was a stern woman, quite capable of doing the right thing, one of the great qualities that attracted Hawker to her those many decades ago. He missed her rational arguments with him. He missed the fun times. He missed the great sex they had as young adults; on beaches, in forests, even once in a canoe while on a trip in Algonquin Park in Ontario.

His mind drifted to the best of them all. He was stationed at Base Borden, and while on leave, they canoed up the York River near Bancroft in Ontario. There was a quaint waterfall far into the forest, with a small secluded beach at the bottom. It was late September, but the sun was warm. They spent the afternoon naked; swimming, and making love four times until the sun set. His biggest satisfaction was bringing his wife to orgasm. He smiled at that thought. First time he smiled, he figured, since the war began.

But most of all, he missed her company. He had no one to confide in since the war began.

His last words to her, "I'll be home in a couple days," haunted him, badgered him, like being smothered in his own excrement.

His thoughts of her were shoved aside as he looked up above the door to the trailer. Every day that little grey metal box, with the red button inside, waited for Hawker.

The box appeared to have a constant Cheshire Cat grin, with the antenna on the side giving him the finger. It taunted him relentlessly.

He placed the nuclear trigger up there not only to keep it safe, but also to be in his face to remind himself what he would ultimately have to do.

It was a no win situation. He hated no wins. He didn't believe in no win scenarios. But there he was in the ultimate no win.

Every day the thought of that act, mixed with the reflection of his wife, occupied most of his mind. She would approve, of course, that was the type of woman she was.

The front lines had been quiet, something that made Hawker extremely nervous. The wait was torturous. He had just gotten off the radio with NORAD, to ask about the twenty-four nukes that the U.S. planted as a last resort. He was told to hold off detonation as long as possible. Apparently the U.S. government was trying to negotiate a cease-fire, and a Chinese pull back.

Hawker didn't believe in miracles.

A knock at the door of his trailer interrupted his thoughts.

"Come in."

A female Corporal entered carrying a tray of food and a cup of steaming hot chocolate. "Your dinner, sir," she said.

"Just put it on the table, I'll get to it in a bit."

"Sir, you have to eat. It's chicken, potatoes, beans, a roll. I'll be back in thirty to make sure you've finished your chow."

"You remind me of a Sergeant I once knew. Seems a lifetime ago."

"Things aren't going well, are they, sir."

Hawker paused, not saying anything.

"They're going to attack soon aren't they, sir."

Hawker looked up at the Corporal. Under her cap, with her brown hair, cut very short, was a pretty young woman with blue eyes. His son's fiancé came to his mind.

"Can you get out of here? Back to Edmonton?" Hawker asked.

"Maybe, if I wanted to. But I want to stay and see this through."

"Admirable, but foolish," he snarled. "When did you eat last yourself, you look too scrawny for my liking." A quip he realized made no sense in light of the last task he must do.

"Soon as I leave here, sir."

"Where's the rest of my staff?"

"Chow, sir."

"Soon as they're done get them here, ASAP."

"Roger that, sir." She left.

Hawker sat at the table in front of his food. He moved the grub around with his plastic fork. It wasn't appetizing. His intuition told him their time on earth was coming to a close.

"Fuck it, what's the point," he hissed throwing the fork across the room. He did pick up the hot chocolate and sipped on it.

The three trailer staff showed up just after it got dark. One of the officers, a woman, said, "General, you didn't eat your chow."

"Not hungry."

Hawker got up and left to take a walk and get some fresh air.

The night was clear and crisp. He walked past the mess tent. There was much talk, punctuated with laughter and jocularity. He couldn't understand how people could be so cheerful. *They were at the meeting when the nukes were announced weren't they?* he thought.

He toured the medic tent. Casualties were light. Most of the serious wounded had been moved south thanks to the unauthorized attack against the southern Chinese arm. Hawker snickered at the irony. A civilian officer who took matters into his own hands, against orders, saved hundreds of lives of critically wounded. Those wounded would heal and continue their lives. All because of the act of one person.

At the back of the medic tent was a large stack of body bags, waiting to be filled. *Irrelevant*, Hawker thought.

Behind the stack of bags was a huge bonfire. A young boy, barely teenage, was throwing uniforms and other clothing into the flames. Most were soaked in blood. The pile was so high to burn, Hawker figured, the poor guy would be at it all night.

Hawker then passed by the shower tent. He was thinking of getting cleaned up, except the line was too long. He was offered to butt in, but declined thanking them. "What's the point in getting clean anyway," he muttered to himself.

He avoided the morgue. Behind those tents was the burial site. Long deep trenches had been freshly excavated, also waiting to be filled. *Irrelevant*, Hawker thought again.

It was just after midnight when the distant sound of pops started. Hawker was at the edge of tent city looking out to the lines a mile away. He could see flares erupt in the sky and gently float down. The pops got more frequent.

Hawker took the M4 off his shoulder, opened the breach to make sure a round was in the chamber. He took it off safe, and attached his bayonet to the barrel.

People started to pass him going to the front, most running, others carrying supplies too heavy for them to run.

Hawker grabbed a black Lieutenant from Jamaica. "I want you to go back to the tents, get everyone, cooks, grave diggers, suppliers, everyone. Get them all armed, and as much ammo as you can find. I want a line formed along here."

"Yes, sir."

Hawker stopped any soldiers who were not sending supplies to form a line, and to pass the order down that line.

It wasn't long before faint dark images, silhouetted by the dancing flares and flashes behind them, moved quickly towards the line.

"Our men. Do not fire!" Hawker yelled a few times.

Didn't matter, some on the line opened up anyway. Hawker had to run along the perimeter yelling, "Cease fire!"

Those that made it to the line screamed that the Chinese had over-run their position. Hawker managed to convince some to stay and join the defence, but most wouldn't and just ran off. *Idiots. There's nowhere they can go to get away from death,* Hawker thought.

One who arrived out of breath, a young man in a Norwegian uniform, and a bullet wound on his arm, said, "How will we know if it's Chinese or our own men?"

"When they start shooting at us," Hawker said.

The Norwegian found a spot nearby to anchor himself, and pointed his weapon down range.

A few stragglers made it to the new front, out of breath, some wounded. Then no more.

The line was a mix of anyone who could hold a weapon. Some lay in the dirt. Some kneeling behind barrels or boxes. Some behind vehicles. The line wasn't anything formal at all. Hawker knew this would not hold the enemy back. But he wasn't going to give up so easily. He felt a new wave flush through his body. A new confidence. He was pissed, mad as hell that the Chinese were going to force his doom.

Throughout the whole war, from Vedder, to Merritt, to Eagle Pass, and the Walls of China, he hadn't fired a single shot in anger. Tonight that would change.

He was behind a small stack of firewood, his M4 aiming down range. Flares opened the darkness. There they were. Hawker yelled to wait. The enemy got closer, but did not shoot. "Wait!" he hollered again. With the flares swaying in the sky like ballet dancers it was difficult to judge the distance in the dark.

"Ok, let 'em have it!" Hawker fired. At first he fired one shot at a time, picking targets. But soon there were too many, so he flipped the "fun switch" to full auto, and opened up with short bursts. With so many advancing targets, spray and pray was getting answered. It didn't take long for the carbine to eat through the ten magazines on his chest.

Snaps and whizzes from enemy bullets filled the voids between their own barrage. People around Hawker started to fall, some screaming, some had their lives end instantly.

The Jamaican officer came up behind Hawker. "Sir, General, you must get out of here. You have to get back to the trailer!" he yelled trying to be heard. Hawker turned to answer him, but he lay dead. Hawker thought for a second, and realized he had to leave. He didn't want to, but he knew he had to.

He ran back through tent city. As he neared the south end where the trailer was, he could see his own people running away from the line intermixed with Chinese soldiers screaming and shooting. He watched as three Chinese soldiers came across a doctor coming out of the medic tent. They bayoneted him to death, laughed, then moved on.

Hawker was getting worried he wouldn't make it. He figured he would have to stealthily move from tent to tent. He pulled out his Beretta, and racked it. Then removed his webbing gear, taking the two magazines for the pistol out first, and put them in his left leg pocket. He removed his helmet.

He dodged and weaved his way from tent to tent. Many times the Chinese ran right past him in the dark. Bodies littered the ground impeding his path. Some were still alive crying for him to help them. He had to stay focused. They were all going to die, be evaporated anyway, if he achieved his objective.

He made it to a tent opposite the trailer, but Chinese soldiers were running between him and his fate. His thought was that the enemy had no idea what was in that trailer.

Once the last of them passed into the darkness, he made a dash to the door. He opened it when a sharp pain penetrated his back. He fell at the entrance. Bullets riddled the trailer. Hawker watched as his staff fell, blood splattering.

He crawled to the female Lieutenant closest to him. She was still alive.

"I'm sorry, sir," is all she could say, several times over and over until she spoke no more.

Hawker could feel his own life leaving him. He turned towards the door, but he could not get up. His legs wouldn't obey orders. He tried several times to figure a way to get at the box above the door. He then realized he had made a colossal mistake putting it up high, out of reach. "Gawdfuckingdamnit," he snarled. "I should have hidden it on the floor."

His pain was joined with the sinking feeling his misjudgement may have cost them the oil sands, may have allowed the Chinese to win the war. One mistake, from one person.

He lay down unable to move, his life was draining as fast as the blood leaving him. He was exhausted, thirsty, and cold. He began to shiver uncontrollably.

But the grey box beckoned him, like a cheap whore. He had to give it one more try. Any movement, even a little, sent pain rushing through to his head. Though no pain below his waist. He lay back down, the room going darker and spinning.

Someone came into the trailer. He wondered who it was. He wondered if he could tell this person to push the button. The voice was familiar. He tried to put the voice to a face. He knew this person, he thought, but had to confirm who. He opened his eyes as much as he could. Through the dark he could see who it was. It was Ben Robson.

Hawker was relieved. He knew Ben would do the right thing. He tried to talk but the words wouldn't come out. He was thinking what to say, but his mouth wouldn't speak.

Then another person fell into the trailer. "Glad to see you're still alive, boss!" he said laughing. "Damned confuckulated now, eh!"

Hawker couldn't understand how someone could be so cheery.

Another person entered the trailer.

"So this is all of us that's left?" the second voice said.

Hawker knew that voice too. But only vaguely. He tried to see who it was, but couldn't, it was too dark.

Shots then filled the room, throwing papers into the air. Streams of light came through the new holes in the walls.

"Damn, where is it? Smitty look around for it." Robson said.

Hawker wanted to speak, he knew what Ben was looking for, but he couldn't get the words to come out. With all his effort he forced his right hand to point above the door. He breathed in as much as his lungs could hold.

One last attempt he said, "Do it!"

CHAPTER 19

Escape from B.C.

April couldn't come quickly enough. The air was warming; the snow was melting, early for a change. Birds were chirping, chipmunks scurried around the village. Then it dawned on Erik Stein: no dogs. He hadn't even thought about that all winter, keeping to himself since the snow was relentless. When he asked Russ, the answer was fingers to the mouth chewing.

The day came on the first of May. Russ and four others took Erik into the mountains.

They walked for days, carrying heavy packs of food, and one sleeping bag each. North for the most part. The men hunted on the way, mostly rabbits, but some grouse and wild turkey. The men were good hunters, long experienced. By the thirteenth day they came to a great lake.

"Atlin Lake," Russ said. "This is as far I... we go."

The other men looked around, then in the distance one waved.

"That's your canoe. Go north and you'll hit the highway into Whitehorse. There you'll meet those who'll get you east. Lots of people like you will be there."

They waited four days with Erik, caught fish, snared rabbits, and one deer, which they took down with one shot of their rifle. With the canoe loaded, they shook hands. The men disappeared quietly into the bush leaving Erik to himself and the silence, except the light breeze making fine ripples on the lake.

The view was spectacular. Mount Adams was to his left, westward. Llewellyn glacier stretched right down to the water. Bluish-white capped peaks melted into the clear sky.

Erik spent five to six hours per day going up the water, stopping each night on the banks, but still no highway.

After thirteen days, the food all consumed, and Erik exhausted, he came to the top end of the lake. He had canoed almost seventy miles. A hand painted sign said "THIS WAY" with an arrow north. He followed the path and emerged from the bush at a dirt road. Another hand painted sign said, "Alaska Highway" with an arrow pointing to his left, north.

That night, with a fire going and his stomach empty, he heard footsteps crunching the gravel. A man emerged into the light.

"I assume you're going to Whitehorse?" he said still standing.

Erik stood. "Yes."

"Out of food I'll bet"

"Very much so."

The man handed him a length of dried meat. Erik devoured it.

"Caribou."

The man laid out a blanket, stomped out the fire and said, "We leave at first light."

"Why did you put the fire out?" Erik complained.

"I could see you for miles. Trust me, you don't want that out here."

Following the narrow road, they walked for a full day in a valley before arriving at another lake. They stopped for the night at the lakeside Little Atlin Lodge. They were the only ones there.

The next morning Erik gazed at the sight. The lake was like glass. Small insects danced on the surface. The distant hills across the water reflected off the surface. Little whips of cloud were mirrored on both sides of the horizon. If it wasn't for the circumstances, Erik thought a couple weeks fishing there would have made a great vacation. A fish jumped in the distance.

They arrived at the highway that mid-afternoon. Another person was there with a horse and cart. The man who brought Erik grabbed a new full backpack then disappeared back into the trail.

For four days they traveled the highway towards Whitehorse. The black flies were horrendous. Erik had to cover every inch of his body in the hot sun.

Whitehorse was void of internal combustion engine vehicles. Lots of horses filled the streets; most pulling carts, but others had riders. Everyone was carrying a gun. It looked like the typical old western movie with a modern backdrop. Erik and his escort arrived at the Westmark Klondike Inn. It's where all escapees, as people like Erik were called there, stayed before moving on. His escort told him the police chief would visit him in the morning.

Indeed he did, very early the knock came to the door. Erik opened it.

"Good morning, Mister Stein, is it?"

"Erik, yes, come in."

"I won't stay long, we're meeting three other escapees like you for breakfast to get you up to speed. I'm Paul Rutherford."

They went into the restaurant where three other people, one woman and two men were seated. Paul introduced them to Erik. "This is Mark Kirkland, Greg Collins, and Rita Harrington. They all came in the last few days. Group, this is Erik Stein."

Erik shook their hands and sat at the table. Paul called a waitress over. "Ham and eggs all around. Tea too," he said. Seating himself he said to the group, "So you can see things are pretty normal here. Hell, we have no fuel, so everything's done by horse. But you can see no Commies. They won't come up this far. So I'll lay out the plan, then I have to go.

"In two days we'll start to move you east through the Northwest Territories, then to Inuit, then to Churchill, Manitoba. From there you'll be on your own."

"Just the four of us?" Erik asked.

"Yes, more is too much food to carry, we have to have a driver. Three isn't worth it. Five more people are expected tomorrow, or sometime this week. So I have to move you out soon. I'll be back in the morning to send you off. Have a good meal, and enjoy our fair city."

It was quite the feast, a breakfast like before the economic collapse, all locally made or grown.

Each one in turn gave their story.

Mark started. "I'm from the states. It's a long story, but the short of it is I was involved in sabotage in California. It's taken me a year to get here through the mountains. Almost got caught several times. If it wasn't for the kind heart of a lot of people, a lot of you fine Canadians, some who I never met, I'd be dead."

"I'm from the Rocky Mountain Rangers at Prince George," Gregg said. "The Chinese spent the summer rebuilding the oil refinery there, until we destroyed it two months ago. I've been hunted ever since. Again, like Mark here, for the grace of God, and of good people who risked their lives to get me here."

Rita had her turn.

"I was a nurse in Revelstoke. I was behind the lines. Last October I had to help a Chinese Captain with a chunk of shrapnel in his side. He was so grateful for me helping him that he promised he would get me across the lines so I could get back with my family. I didn't think it would ever happen. Several days passed so I figured the promise was hollow. But then he showed up. He said his father, a commanding general, wouldn't agree to let me through, so this captain took it upon himself to take me north. At great risk. He wasn't supposed to. He took me past Prince George, and drove as far north as he dared. Then dropped me off at some lake. He told me to wait there and just left me.

"Then the next day two native men arrive by horse and cart, and brought me here."

"I don't get it, how did he know where to drop you?" Erik asked.

"Oh, that's the interesting part. The captain said they know all about this place. About people coming here from the south. They call it the Whitehorse Underground Railway. He said they know all about it, but there's nothing they can do to stop it."

"So any idea what's going on?" Erik inquired.

"With the war?" Rita said.

"Yes."

"As far as I know, the captain wouldn't say much about that, is they have gotten to the oil sands and had it surrounded. That's all I know."

No one else knew any more.

"What about Calgary," Erik said. "Was it nuked?"

"Yes, or so the people here said," Mark sighed.

Erik shook his head. "Those fucking bastards."

The next day they were loaded into a carriage with two horses. The men sat in the backbench, with Rita beside the driver. Paul was there late to send them off. "You'll go east for the summer. By September you should be in Churchill. Good luck all of you."

Erik pulled out his memory stick. "Can you get this to the authorities? It has sensitive information about the Chinese?"

"No. I have no way of getting it anywhere. Best you take it yourself."

They arrived in Churchill Manitoba just before Labor Day. The group was horrified to find out that nuclear warheads had been dropped on the oil sands project and in the passes of the Rockies. It happened early spring, when they were making their way across the Northwest Territories and had no way of getting any news of any kind. It essentially ended the war.

The four of them took the train to Winnipeg. The two men said their goodbyes and parted going in opposite directions looking for family, and work.

Erik and Rita were alone on the platform.

"So you're heading out to find your family," Erik said sadly looking at the pavement, shuffling his feet.

"That's the plan." She looked at him with a small smile.

Erik looked up at her. "But how will you know which way to go?"

"I was thinking of starting with my sister in Sudbury. Her husband works in the mines there. I'm hoping my children and grandchildren went there. She's the only other family they have."

"You should write first before going all that way," Erik suggested.

"No, there's nothing keeping me here. Is there?"

Erik looked into her eyes. "I'd like it if you stayed with me a bit more."

"Oh, haven't you had enough of me by now," she said laughing. "I mean, you saw me almost naked while I was bathing in a creek. And we were crammed in a tent all summer. Suffered together with shit food. Had sore asses together from that horrible cart ride for four months. So you claim to not have had enough?"

"It was quite the adventure," Erik chuckled.

Rita smiled. "Yes, it was quite the adventure wasn't it?"

There was some awkward silence.

"Well," Erik paused for the right words, clumsily continuing. "I'm... I'm going down to the oil field south of here. I should be able to get a job." He paused a bit more getting the courage. He felt like he did when he was first dating in high school, a very self-conscious time for Erik. He got the courage. "You can stay with me and write your letters from there."

"Why Erik. Is that a proposal?" Rita said gleefully.

"Well, yes, I guess it is."

A big smile came over Rita. "When do we leave and where are we going?"

Erik's courage returned full force, the young boy evaporated. "Pierson, Manitoba, as far south and as close to the Bakken oil field as we can get. I'm going to find out how to get there."

Erik pulled the memory stick from his pocket. "This is now a year out of date. The war is finally over. So I guess there's no point in giving this to anyone." He dropped it into the waste bin by the wall.

The next morning they hopped into a CPR train heading west. The crew said they could stop at Pierson.

He asked in town where one could stay. They were told the community centre was a makeshift motel, of sorts. At the centre, the woman at the desk asked, "Is that one cubical or two?"

Erik looked confused.

"We don't have any rooms, honey. Just cubicles." She looked at Rita beside Erik. "May I suggest you two go over to the hardware store. They have apartments overtop. You can stay there until you get better accommodations."

The next morning Erik woke with Rita beside him. She was still sleeping. He kissed her bare shoulder, and pulled the blanket over it. He went into the bathroom to shower. Rita was awake when he got out.

"You're up early," she said yawning.

"Bus leaves in a few minutes to the oil field. I'll likely be all day."

"I'll be here for a repeat of last night." She purred like a kitten.

Erik smiled, went over and kissed her good-bye. It was like the past year was thirty with Rita. It was a natural fit for the both of them, rare when someone is over sixty.

The bus arrived at the main gate of the oil field, and Erik was directed to the project office. An old fellow with a long greying beard, and long hair tied in a ponytail at the back, was the project manager. His bulking body filled the space behind his desk. He did not get up.

"What can I do fer ya old fella?" he said in a deep voice more fitting to be on radio than behind a desk at an oil field.

"I'm a geologist and looking for work."

"A rockhound, eh. Let me see." He looked through some papers in a binder. "Where did you learn geology?" he said not looking up.

"I was professor of sedimentary geology and mineralogy at UBC."

The man stopped looking and turned to Erik. "Can you interpret siltstone shale markers from drill cores?"

"Yes, I worked on that type of rock in the Arctic."

"The Arctic yeah say, eh? Hmm." He rubbed his beard. "Do you have any money?"

"No, broke."

"We don't use money, it's worthless to us. You get paid in food vouchers. Here's some to get you through the week. You're hired. You can start in the morning. Be here by seven a.m."

CHAPTER **20**

The Decent Thing

Jason Gagnon arrived at the gates of the Bakken oil field complex in a bus with the next daytime shift. He was looking for employment. He was directed to the foreman's office. An old fellow with a long greying beard, and long hair tied in a ponytail at the back was the project manager. His bulking body filled the space behind his desk. He did not get up.

"What can I do fer ya young fella?" he said in a deep voice more fitting to be on radio than behind a desk at an oil field.

"I'm looking for work," Jason said.

"You an a mill'n otha's," he laughed. "Sorry to in form ya, but you're a tad late my lad. I've had many like yas all summer. I've nothin' fer ya."

"Dam, I really need the work, my wife and son are depending on me. I'm sorry to have bothered you then, good day." Jason started to walk to the door.

He was just about to pass through the opening when the old guy said, "Wait, my friend. How old is ya son?"

"He was born in June. In Calgary."

"So ya came from the battle? Take a seat and tell me what's going on. We get scant news here."

Jason came back in and sat down. He then explained how he and Kelly escaped from Vancouver. How he got work in Calgary for the summer organizing food shipments to the front. When asked why he left Calgary, he said, "Kelly was getting nervous about being so close to the fighting, with a newborn and all. When we left the Chinese had taken over Revelstoke and making their way through the Rockies. So she demanded we head east and look for somewhere out of the line of fire. We've been on the move since the first of September. Almost three weeks now."

"Can ya farm?"

360

"No"

"But you know about food by the sounds of it."

"Yes, my father-in-law managed a grocery store before he died four years ago. I used to work at his store and after he died they made me the manager. Then I worked for the government dispatching food shipments arriving at the port in Vancouver before the Chinese arrived, uninvited."

"Well, ya may be of 'elp anywho. Farmers we're short of fer sure. Go see my sister in the hardware store in town, her hubby's a farmer. He's hav'n a 'ard of it finding competent workers. Ya maybe what he's lookn' fer."

"Wow, thanks a bunch. I really appreciate it."

Jason managed to get a ride back on the bus with the exiting shift workers. The local Home Depot wasn't hard to find, and got to meet the old guy's sister, Sue Barnes. She definitely was the old guy's sister, even with the long ponytail, but minus the beard, and a lot thinner.

"Paul sent you?" she said. "I always knew he had a big heart in that big belly of his."

Jason explained his story again.

"Well, my hubby will be here soon for supplies. You can ask him then, in about an hour or two. I can't guarantee he'll have a job for you or not. But can't hurt to ask. He'll interrogate you. He's had so many city folk claim they can do the work only to bum out in less than a week. Not too many can handle fourteen hour days."

Jason spent the hour with Kelly and little Tom at an apartment above the hardware store. They had little money for food, so lunch was sparse. Two apples and a bit of raw milk Sue gave him.

Jason came down late in the afternoon to find a two-horse cart sitting outside the store, with an older fellow and a younger man loading sacks off the cart into the store. Sue introduced him to John, her husband.

John indeed did interrogate Jason, for an hour in a small room at the back of the store.

"Where's your family staying now?" John said at the end of the interview.

"Upstairs."

"Oh, that flea bag, rat infested pigsty. That won't do with a young'n.

Look, there's an abandoned house next to my property. They all died last winter. Some of those doomer folks from the city, Brandon I think. They bought the property five years ago to wait for the end of the world to come. They put up a wind turbine, but it blew down last winter. They even have solar panels on the roof, but the winter has so much snow they didn't produce any power most of the time. But they simply didn't understand farming, and starved, or froze to death, one of the two. They kept to themselves, rarely talked with anyone. Sue talked to the woman a couple times, but very aloof. Very sad, they had two children. We didn't know they were dead until the spring.

"So, if you're inclined and not superstitious you can move in there. The home is complete with all the furnishings, dishes, and such."

"How far is it from here?"

"Two and a half hours by horse and cart. I'll take you there if you want to leave now."

"Does this mean you'll give me a job?"

John thought for a second. "Well I was only helping you find shelter for the winter. But what I can do is trade you work for food to get you through the winter. God help us if we have another bad one, it's already getting cold outside. Below zero 'gain tonight. But let's not get too pessimistic, shall we? What comes is what comes. Let's get your family as I have to head back before it gets dark."

The house was a mess. The former family didn't maintain the property, it was grossly overgrown. At least with fall in full swing, the weeds were dying off. But the house itself, a Victorian style brick sided, needed not only paint, but also replacement of much of the wood. The shingles definitely needed replacement as many were missing, replaced with tar slapped on in a sloppy fashion. The rest of the shingles were well curled. Jason wondered how he would replace them, especially before winter.

The problem was the solar panels covered the whole roof on the south and west sides. They would all have to be removed just to replace the shingles. "What a stupid idea," he said aloud.

The home was two stories. A large kitchen occupied the full back of the home, with a living room on one side, and a dining room on the other at the front. The upstairs had three bedrooms and the only bathroom.

Jason was carrying little Tom around on his back looking at the property. There was a large garden plot, at least an acre if not more, but well overgrown with weeds. An adjacent field, also about an acre, had a large number of fruit trees. With the leaves dropped Jason couldn't figure out what they were. Most were still young, likely not planted too many years ago.

Beside the barn was the wind turbine, down and twisted, weeds growing through the structure. The turbine itself was small, maybe five foot in diameter, hardly large enough to power much, Jason thought.

A greenhouse was attached to the back of the house. It was dome shaped like a half a gigantic soccer ball stuck in the ground. It was thirty feet in diameter, and some fourteen feet tall at the apex. The panels weren't glass, but clear triangle polycarbonate sheets with cells of three layers. The frame was two-by-fours held together with aluminum joiner plates and bolts. Jason looked at the small brass plate at the door.

"Growing Spaces," it said, with the year 2014. Jason was quite impressed with it. They could grow food all year with this, he thought at first, until he got inside.

Kelly held her hand over her mouth as she viewed the mess in the kitchen. Pots and dishes, sitting in the sink all summer, stunk submerged in black water. A dead rat lay drowned, bloated and floating on top, maggots crawling on the exposed side. Other movements caught her eye scurrying along the floor.

The floors were all well-worn pine boards, the knots of which protruded above the worn lengths making the floor uncomfortable to walk on.

There was a nice pine table and chair set in the dining room, all neatly arranged. The living room had one well-worn sofa, which Kelly figured had families of mice in it.

Upstairs, a shiver ran down Kelly's back when she entered the bedrooms and realized a family had all died in each of the beds.

"This will not do," she said and headed back outside to find Jason. But Jason was in the greenhouse.

He met Kelly in the kitchen on his way to find her, as she was looking for him.

"You need to see this," he gestured.

They went into the greenhouse. Planting beds stood about two feet above the dirt floor, with a maze of walkways, nearly three feet wide. Dead plants filled the beds, some dangling from wire mesh up to six feet tall.

"Look at this. Tomatoes over there, cauliflower here. And over here peppers. All dead. I figured they froze over the winter. I don't see any heating anywhere. There's a tank on the north wall, but it's empty, probably water was in it. I'll bet they tried to use it as a solar sink. No way a building like this would be able to make it through a winter night without freezing. Bet you that's what happened to them. They expected this to feed themselves through the winter. If they had a day or two with no sun, no way it would even heat on those days. A mistake that killed them."

"So how's it going to benefit us?" Kelly asked sceptically.

"I saw an old wood stove in the barn. I'll put that in here for heat. No matter how much they tried, we cannot live any kind of modern civilization without wood or fossil fuels. Damn alternative energy sources. Cost these people their lives."

They went back into the kitchen.

"Quite the mess," Jason said. "But this should do us fine."

"This will not do. We need to get back to town for the night," she said rather firmly trying not to gag. She explained what she saw.

"It's too far to walk. We'll have to spend the night here."

"You better go look around before you make that choice. It's disgusting."

After a review of the inside by Jason, he decided they would sleep in the dining room.

"With the rats?" Kelly retorted. "Not on your life. I'm going next door to plead with John to spend the night there. You can stay here if you want."

Jason agreed.

John was in the barn working with the cattle when they showed up. Two Jugs, those Pug and Jack Russell terrier mix, greeted them jumping high in the air, their coiled tails fanning

"How's the house? Do you for the winter will it?" John said cleaning his hands with a rag.

"Not at all. It's more rat infested than the apartment I'm afraid," Jason said.

"Disgusting," Kelly gagged.

"You don't say. I haven't been there since the spring. I guess the rats moved in since. Well, my two jugs will take care of them PDQ. I'll take them over there tomorrow. You can stay in the loft over that barn over there until we get them cleared out."

"I have a question about the heating system," Jason said. "I saw the furnace, but I don't understand how it works."

"Oh, that's a ground source heat pump," John replied. "My cousin puts them in. Lots of farms heat their homes with those."

"Those take heat out of the ground right?"

"Correct, pipes in the ground circulate a fluid, picking up heat from the ground. It's the most efficient method to heat a home. Our house has one, put it in, oh, going on ten years ago now."

"But it needs power to work, right?"

"Yeah, that's right. Well, we just need to get power working again for that place."

"Question, then. Can I put one in the greenhouse?"

"I don't see why not. I can talk to my cousin. I'm sure we can get one installed. That is a neat greenhouse."

The loft was set up as a small apartment, one bedroom, and a small kitchen. They would have to use the outhouse however.

The next morning, after John inspected the house next door, he suggested Jason and Kelly stay in the loft for the winter, it would be warm enough with the wood stove. Then during the winter Jason could work on cleaning up the house between chores at the farm. Kelly helped John's wife, Sue, with making bread, which they sold in town.

The Bakken oil field was a magnet for everyone moving east getting away from the fighting; thousands of people every day, even during the winter, would trek through town. John's farm was well off the main road, so no one would come by his place. It was very quiet, especially in winter.

The oil field was crucial in supplying fuel for the fight. It was shipped by rail to the few refineries still operating, specifically in Edmonton since the oil sands had shut down for the winter. That left little petroleum for local requirements, including farms.

That meant farming returned to the days of manual and beast of burden for energy. That meant long hours for Jason on the farm. It also meant low yields. John often complained that his oat and wheat crop was less than a quarter during the boom times. No fuel or chemicals to prepare the land, sow the seeds and harvest the crop quickly. It was all done by hand and horse cart, just like the 1800s.

Worst of all, John would always complain, was the short growing season over the last few years due to the deep winters. "Where the fuck was that global warming we were promised," he said on more than one occasion.

John's farm also contained about two hundred cattle, fifty of which were dairy. A small number John was hoping would increase in the spring with new calves, he explained during Thanksgiving dinner when all his local relatives came over.

"If all goes well, and I don't lose too many milkers over the winter, we should almost double our stock. Chuck next door said he'll trade me for some pigs in the spring. We could do with some pork of our own. This ham came from his farm. I traded him a beef cow for three pigs. That should do us for the winter, even with our new guest," he said looking at Jason and Kelly.

"Any news from the front?" John's brother-in law, Paul, from the oil field asked looking at Jason.

"Paul you know we get scant second hand news, and often weeks or months old," John said.

"Well, I do have somethin' very big," Paul continued. "I heard from the railroad boys that those fuckn' commies dropped nukes on Calgary. It's gone. Just recently, they said."

Everyone stopped eating like pressing the pause button on a DVD player.

Paul added, "Yea, they took out our command centre, now the commies can, and will, just walk right through." He waved his right hand, with fork and a chunk of ham, through the air.

Jason had a big lump in his throat. His last letter from his brother Tom came from Calgary three weeks ago. Tom was working for the military effort loading supplies into railcars for the front, transferred there from Revelstoke just before that city was evacuated.

Kelly looked at Jason knowing what was on his mind. She leaned over to him and whispered, "Maybe he got your invitation to join us in time."

"So there's nothn' stoppn' 'em now," Paul added stuffing the ham into his bearded mouth.

"Winter," John muttered in a low voice. "We can only hope God gives us a brutal winter again."

"John, don't you say that," Sue said sternly. "Lots of our friends died last winter because it was brutal. You want more of that? We're a long way from the front."

"A long way now," Paul bellowed. "But that won't last. They also want the oil we produce right here."

"And our food, though they may not be aware how bad the growing season has become in recent years," John said.

"Well now you've totally wrecked Thanksgiving. I think we need to pray to God," Sue complained lowering her head and reciting the Lord's Prayer a second time, the first being before they started eating. She ended with, "God help us deal a blow to the invading heathens without more of our own lives lost."

"Amen," went around the table.

Indeed the winter was brutal again. The Bakken oil field had to be shut down due to the bitter cold and the load of snow they got dumped with. Black Winter II was a repeat of the previous winter.

Jason, his family and his hosts survived to spring, though they had to shoot almost half of their livestock because of the cold. They even had to run fires in the barns to keep them somewhat warm. It was a blow; it meant not as many cattle in the spring to rebuild their numbers. It meant the following year would be lower resources to sell. Jason was told in March that he could not be kept on the farm come the spring, and they should be prepared to start a family farm in the abandoned home next door.

Luckily, they got lots of help from John's family making the house liveable. They burned all the beds and beddings. Steel roofing from an old barn fallen down was carefully removed and put on Jason's home. John's cousin put in the ground source heat pump for the greenhouse.

But what sank Jason's heart every day was the lack of any news of his brother. He had given up thinking he survived the nuclear attack of Calgary. News from the front wasn't good. The little bits that finally started to flow from the west were grim. The Chinese were advancing eastward and appeared unstoppable.

Every time Jason went into town, on a horse John had lent them for the summer, he went to the post office for news. No letters from his brother, not unexpected, but also he would meet other townsfolk who did get the dregs of mail that managed to show up months late. That's when the rumors would circulate.

The Chinese were in Edmonton. The Chinese were close to Edmonton. They had occupied the oil sands. They were being held at bay at the oil sands. The contradictions were rampant and no one knew what to believe.

In late May, on one of his visits, he went into the post office where a ragged man, long dirty hair hanging off his ripped and dirty military clothes, was facing away talking to the postmaster. An M14, with nine rings made from thin strips of very aged masking tape on the barrel, was slung over his shoulder. The postmaster behind the desk said, "That's him right there."

The man turned to face Jason. Under the long beard and dirty face was Tom. Jason hardly recognized him, but grabbed and gave him a huge hug.

The first words out of Tom's mouth was, "Can I get something to eat, bro?" He hadn't eaten in days, he said. Jason took him to the restaurant across the road.

A young pretty brunette, around Tom's age, showing a bit of cleavage with the top button of her uniform undone, served them at the table. "What can I get for you boys?" she said.

"Nothing for me, but my brother here will have the most expensive thing on the menu."

"That will be a t-bone, sautéed with onions, with eggs and mashed spuds," she said.

"Make that steak well done," Jason said. "And he'll wash it down with a beer, one of those local brands." He turned to Tom and in a low voice said, "Not as good as a Labatt's, but it's suds."

She looked at Tom, he just nodded. Tom's eyes followed the girl as she went back into the kitchen.

Jason had to know how he escaped the nuke attack.

"I saw it," Tom said. "I just got your letter and left the city not hours before the attack. I was in a convoy of trucks heading east. We saw the flashes, almost blinded us. Thank God we were facing away. Three separate blasts. The last blast knocked over all the trucks like Lego blocks. I thought we were dead for sure. Some did die when their vehicles overturned. Luckily I was in the cab of a big rig. We watched as the mushroom clouds rose over our heads.

"From that point on I was on foot. Not one person came out of Calgary that I'm aware of."

"So we lost the war. I guess it is only a matter of time before they arrive here," Jason sighed.

"Maybe not," Tom said. "I spent the winter in Regina..."

"You spent the winter in Regina and didn't write?" Jason interrupted.

"We'll, I wanted to, but there was a complete blackout in the area, nothing was allowed to leave the city. No mail, no news, nothin'.

"The new command centre was set up just south of there, well away from the city. But we heard news every now and then as military people came into the city. I was a waiter at a restaurant, and got to listen in on the chatter.

"Seems they had the Chinese stopped during the winter. There was no movement at the front until the spring. I left as soon as I could to get here, so I don't know what's happened since. But I did hear that the winter was very hard, on both sides. Edmonton was still in our hands last I heard.

"So being so important a place I guess they wanted to keep their location secret."

"So some good maybe," Jason said.

"We can hope."

The waitress came to the table with Tom's food. As she bent over to put the plate down, Tom got a good look down her top at her grapefruit sized breasts as if beckoning to him. She noticed and smiled saying, "Enjoy your meal now," as she left.

Tom devoured the food in nothing flat. Once done Jason said, "We need to get you home, get you cleaned up and meet your name sake."

Jason stood and picked up the M14. "Hey, this isn't mine. Mine had a synthetic stock, this one's walnut."

Getting up, Tom said, "Yeah, sorry bro. I met a U.S. Lieutenant who had this..."

* * *

Tom watched as a number of U.S. soldiers climbed up into the boxcar, finding whatever space they could to sit. The officer, a Lieutenant, dropped his keister beside Tom pushing him, Simon and Trevor into the wall.

"Hi boys, we meet again. We're squeezed in like sardines," the officer said.

The train lurched out of the Sicamous yard, throwing anyone standing into the laps of those sitting, to much groaning and swearing.

"You guys were at chow earlier, weren't you," the Lieutenant said to Tom.

Tom nodded. "You're Shooter."

"That's right. Very nice, this Canada of yours," Shooter said. "One day I'll come here for a vacation." He smiled to the young men.

After a few moments, when the train was weaving through Eagle Pass, Shooter said, "You boys leaving the fight?"

"In a way. We're not good at doing war, I'm afraid," Tom said.

"We're goin' to Revelstoke. Helping with logistics," Simon added.

Shooter nodded, "Important work someone has to do. Good for you."

"Where're you going Lieutenant?" Trevor asked.

"We're all going home. Our work here is done. We're hoping to get a train in Calgary back to the States. With all our boys coming up we should be able to hitch a ride home," he said.

"How come you've got two M14s," Tom inquired. "Kinda heavy to have two of them, isn't it? I had my brother's, but when they figured I wasn't going to fight they took it."

"This one is mine..." he pulled his scoped M21 forward. "...but this one I got off a dead hero. He killed nine of the enemy in the battle at Vedder, hence the rings he put on the barrel. I found this beside his burnt and mutilated body in Merritt. The Chinese ambushed them as they drove into town. But we got revenge. Come to think of it, I never knew his name. That's unfortunate."

Shooter thought for a moment. Then handed the banded M14 to Tom. "Here it's yours."

"Why me?" Tom said.

"I shouldn't take it to the states. It needs to stay at home and safe. Keep it as a reminder of the fallen. Of the sacrifice your people have made for freedom," Shooter said.

* * *

"...I guess he's back in the states now," Tom finished.

"Wow, interesting story," Jason said.

"He told me about the battle at Vedder, his time in Afghanistan. Glad it was him and not me, man. I'm not cut out for that shit."

As they walked out, Jason could not hold back. He turned and hugged his brother hard, "I'm so glad you're alive. Hey everyone, this is my little brother! He made it back from the fighting, alive!"

Everyone clapped, and those in the room who knew Jason congratulated him, including the waitress. She winked at Tom.

The late September day was cool; winter was coming early, again. Jason, Kelly, little Tom on her back, and Tom, along with Tom's pregnant wife Sandie, the waitress, were in the field picking vegetables. They spent the summer fixing the house, and nursing the garden. There was enough to get them through the winter, the rest Jason figured he could sell.

Their greenhouse was working with the new heating system, but Jason wasn't counting those winter vegetables until they actually produced.

Kelly poked Jason in the back with her rake. "Jason, men coming on the road."

Jason looked up and slowly moved toward the cart where his AR15 was hanging. Five men came up to the fence along the road to the family's plot. They were armed, shotguns mostly, but two had bolt action hunting rifles.

"Do you have some food we can have?" one said.

"No, I'm sorry, we don't have enough for ourselves," Jason answered.

There was a long tense pause. The two men at the fence were looking Jason's family over. The silence broke when the same man said, "You have plenty. You can share with us." The tone was not a plea, it was a firm threat.

"I have my own family to feed, sorry. Please move on," Jason said nervously.

Kelly had little Tom tight in her arms, facing away from the men.

A few more tense moments passed. Jason eyed the men, looked down at his AR formulating how to get it quickly. Or should he go for his pistol? No, that wouldn't work. He would have to rack the gun first. The AR was his quickest option, on safe, with a round in the pipe.

Tom looked at Jason. Jason made an eye gesture towards the M14 lying on the ground beside Tom. Tom's eyes widened, then slowly looked towards the men at the fence.

The man with the shotgun raised it pointing at Tom who was closest. Jason picked up the AR15 and fired two rounds, double tapped, into that man. It was the first time he had had to discharge his rifle at anyone. It was the second time he even pointed a gun at anyone, the first time being back in Kamloops a year and a half earlier.

One of the men with a hunting rifle fired off a round at Jason, the bullet from which snapped loudly in his right ear. Jason got two rounds off into him.

The other three ran down the road in the direction they came. Jason ran to the fence, with Tom right behind him picking up his M14. They both hopped the fence and knelt in the centre of the dirt road. The three men were running away from them. Tom looked at his brother for some sign.

"We have no choice. If we let them live they'll come back. Most likely when we're sleeping, and slit our throats," Jason pleaded.

Jason turned on the optic to his rifle, then slowly raised his carbine to his cheek. Carefully he placed the red dot onto the back of one of the running men and fired a single shot. The man fell face down into the dirt. Tom brought his rifle up and aimed. But he was shaking too much making the barrel move all over.

Jason fired his second, then third shot into the backs of the other two. They both dropped, skidding a bit, then lay motionless on the road in a cloud of dust.

The first man Jason shot was crawling towards the ditch. Jason walked up to him, kicked the shotgun out of the way and pointed his pistol at the wounded man's head. "Is there any more of you?" Jason demanded.

The man rolled over, the exit wound in his mid stomach was bleeding profusely. "We only wanted food," the man said with earth puffing out of his mouth as he spoke. "We didn't mean any harm."

"Your friend aimed a gun at my brother. I wasn't going to take any chances."

"Oh, my, I'm dead aren't I? You funkn' killed me. After all I've been through to die like this. It's not fair."

"I'm sorry," Tom said. "Is there anything we can do for him?"

"No. He'll bleed out."

"Fuck, man, we need to help him," Tom pleaded.

"We can't. We barely have enough food for the winter as it is. What we have left I was going to sell for kerosene, which we need for the winter. We can't do anything for him."

The man groaned in pain holding his stomach. His breathing was labored. The bloodstain on his clothing expanded. Then he groaned no more. Jason and Tom didn't even notice for a few moments.

"So now what do we do?" Tom sighed. "We can't leave the bodies lying here, man."

"Yeah, it will be a magnet for coyotes and wolves. Go over to Barnes' farm. Borrow a horse and cart. We'll take the bodies over to the old grave site."

"Bloody hell, man, now we have to spend hours burying these poor guys."

Tom walked away, leaving Jason to look down at what he'd done. It started to sink in that he may have made a mistake, which cost the lives of five people. He broke out into a cold sweat. He wanted to hurl.

He got back to the fence line where Kelly and Sandie were kneeling over one of the bodies. "He's still alive, barely," Kelly said. "What do we do?"

"You too?"

"Too what?"

"Tom said the same thing."

"Well, what do you expect? You fired first before we could even negotiate."

"He aimed a gun at Tom, I had to react."

"Such a shame. Such a waste of life. They were just hungry. We could have given them something," Kelly retorted.

"If we run out by next March you wouldn't say that."

"Have we lost all our humanity?"

"Humanity is a luxury we no longer have."

"If it wasn't for little Tom, I wouldn't want to live like this," Kelly snarled.

"People lived like this for thousands of years. The only difference is we came from a modern society. This is the new normal, back to the old normal." Jason sighed.

"He's dead," Sandie said checking his pulse. A tear ran down her left cheek.

A small number of people from around the local farms came to help bury the bodies. Seemed the five men had tried a number of places to get food and work. Rumors were abundant that small family farms were being raided, everyone killed, by armed gangs. Trust to strangers was totally lacking. Thus, no one would offer the five men anything, chasing them off at gunpoint, a number in the burial detail recalled.

Two weeks after that event, Jason and Kelly were cleaning up the last of the potatoes when Kelly poked Jason with her rake. Jason looked up to see a lone person coming down the road. This one was in military uniform, though well worn. He was Chinese.

"Kelly, get on the ground."

"Don't shoot him, Jason!"

Jason hopped the fence and held is carbine pointing at the soldier just fifty meters away. The man stopped. He had a rifle in his hand, but made no move. Then he slowly let the firearm drop to the ground, kicking it away from him, and put his arms into the air.

Jason moved in closer to get a better look. The man was young, maybe mid twenties, but scrawny, with sunken eyes, and sunken cheeks. His clothes were torn, his boots were held together with silver duct tape, all worn and tattered. He didn't move.

Jason came up to within talking range. "Do you speak English?" Jason ordered, rifle pointing at the man.

The soldier shook his head.

Kelly came over beside Jason. "Kell, go back with little Tom."

"He's sleeping. Look at this poor guy. He must have been wandering all summer. How could he have survived for so long on his own?"

"Best he could. Who knows how many people he's had to kill to stay alive."

"You don't know that. He may have survived because of people's good will. He doesn't look scary, he looks scared."

Kelly pulled an apple out of her pocket. The soldier saw it and jerked forward a bit. Jason brought the rifle up to his face aiming at the man's head. The soldier stopped.

Kelly moved closer and held out the apple to the soldier. He did not move but eyed Jason. Jason lowered his rifle completely down, muzzle away from his target. Slowly the soldier reached for the apple. Grasping it he shoved it into his face and devoured all of it in seconds. He even took the tiny bits that were on his face out of his dirty hands with his tongue. He then brought both his hands together in front and bowed to Kelly.

"See, he's harmless," Kelly said grabbing the man by his left arm and took him towards the house.

Jason picked up the battered SKS rifle the soldier threw down. It was empty with a bent barrel. The breach block wouldn't even move back it was so seized. Jason threw it into the ditch.

Back at the porch of the house, Kelly gave the soldier some carrots and beans, which he devoured just as quickly as the apple. Jason sat across from him, he pulled his handgun from its leg holster, racked it, put it on safe, and placed it on the picnic bench, barrel facing the man. The soldier barely took note.

Jason pointed to him and held his nose. "You stink," he said. The soldier stopped eating, a frown came over his face and he nodded.

While the soldier ate, little Tom cried a bit in his basket. Kelly picked him up. The soldier looked at the child and smiled. He made a gesture with his hands as if he was holding a baby. He pointed to little Tom, then pointed at himself.

"He has his own child. Back in China I'll bet," Kelly said. "He must miss them very much."

Jason's bother Tom returned coming onto the porch after his day helping on the Barnes' farm. "Holy shit! He's the enemy!"

"Not any more," Kelly said. "He's a starving person in need. Nothing more."

"What are we going to do with him?" Tom asked.

"I suspect once he's filled himself, he'll just move on," Jason said hoping.

"He won't make it through the winter," Kelly interjected quickly.

Jason wasn't sure what to make of the situation. He'd had enough of the massacre. He'd had enough of the stupid useless killing. Ending those five men's lives had a profound impact on Jason. It knotted his guts ever since. He figured the only way the old normal would become the new normal is if they sat back and let it happen. He wanted desperately to become human again. To do that would mean to do the human thing, not the old human, but civilized human, even if it meant one act at time.

Jason picked up the pistol and put it in his holster.

"What's your name?" he said to the soldier.

"Jason, he can't speak English," Kelly said.

Jason pointed to himself "Jason." Then he pointed to Kelly, "Kelly." Then he pointed to Tom and said, "Tom." Then pointed to the soldier.

The soldier looked at the three of them and repeated their names as he pointed to each person. He then pointed to himself and said, "George."

Tom laughed. "Yeah, right, and I'm Jesus Christ. That's not his name."

"It's probably something too difficult for us," Kelly said. "You George?" she said pointing to him.

"Me, George," he answered back.

"Some of them do have English names," Jason said. "The guy at our distribution centre was a Chinese immigrant; he had a Western first name."

George pointed to the field where a couple of cows were grazing. "Me…" then he made a gesture as if he was milking a cow.

"Farmer?" Kelly said. "You're a farmer?"

George pointed to Kelly nodding his head and said, "Farmer."

"So he's a farmer back home. We could certainly use some experienced help here," Kelly said.

"No way," Jason replied.

"Jason, this poor fellow is thousands of miles from his own family. He'll never see them again. We can at least do the decent thing and help him out of his miserable life," Kelly argued.

"Old man Barnes could use more help, especially if this guy is experienced," Tom added.

"I guess after all the slaughter it is the decent thing we can do," Jason capitulated.

George looked them all over after the last bit of carrot disappeared, and smiled.

www.ingramcontent.com/pod-product-compliance
Lightning Source LLC
Chambersburg PA
CBHW050029030726
47506CB00001B/179